PRAISE FOR *THE HUNT FOR BIGFOOT*
Book One in the Human Origins Series

Another good addition to the cryptofiction library...For those that want to complete their Bigfoot fiction library, pick this book up.

Loren Coleman, author of
Bigfoot! The True Story of Apes in America

The characters were well done and I found myself wanting to learn more about them. The action is well thought out and written with real dialog...I might add that having passed through Yoho National Park many times I was impressed with the accuracy of the descriptions [in this book]...So, did I enjoy this book? Do I recommend it? Yes to both.

Dan Fabian, Bard's Ink

A lively, exciting and gripping piece of fiction...If you are even remotely interested in cryptozoology, ancient cosmic visitors, the legends of Atlantis, human evolution and more, then grab a copy of [this book] as soon as possible.

Nick Redfern, *Phenomena* Magazine

An exciting, well researched rollercoaster ride of a novel...[I] enjoyed every last page.

Paul Vella, Center for Fortean Zoology

I encourage everyone who enjoys mysteries to read this book. You can also astound your friends by the knowledge you acquired concerning human evolution or the lack thereof.

Andrew Grgurich, *Marquette (Mich.) Mining Journal*

A good read for an evening-campfire setting gathered around in front of pitched tents near a lake.

Independent Publishing Review

PRAISE FOR *LORD OF THE DEAD*
Book Two in the Human Origins Series

Shiel uses her extensive knowledge of archaeology, anthropology, and Bigfoot to write a very rich story....I would highly recommend this book.

Paige Lovitt, Reader Views

Incredible high adventure...The pace is frenetic and the story lends plausibility to an number of evolution theories. We rated this book a solid four hearts.

Bob Spear, Heartland Reviews

[This book] immerses the reader in the strange and murky worlds of human origins, archaeological secrecy, and ancient cultures. With believable characters, a fast-paced plot, and a fantastic premise at its heart, Shiel's book is one not to be missed by anyone with an interest in the mysteries of this world and beyond.

Nick Redfern, author of *Body Snatchers in the Desert*

You end up just going along for the ride...This is a great adventure story.

Andrew Grgurich, *Marquette (Mich.) Mining Journal*

RELIC
OF THE
ANCIENT
ONES

Other Books by Lisa A. Shiel

Fiction

From Jacobsville Books

Faces of Bigfoot: Short Stories about the Unexpected Results
When Human Meets Sasquatch

The Human Origins Series

The Hunt for Bigfoot (Book One)
Lord of the Dead (Book Two)
Bigfoot Beginnings: Short Stories about Close Encounters of
the Sasquatch Kind (Backstories, Vol. 1)

Nonfiction

From Jacobsville Books

Creature of Controversy (Forbidden Bigfoot, Part One)
Top Secret Sasquatch (Forbidden Bigfoot, Part Two)
The Evolution Conspiracy
Backyard Bigfoot

From The History Press

Forgotten Tales of Michigan's Upper Peninsula

From Trails Books

Strange Michigan (with Linda S. Godfrey)

Relic of the Ancient Ones

Book Three in the Human Origins Series

Lisa A. Shiel

Jacobsville Books

Lake Linden, Michigan
Toll-Free: 1-866-341-3705

ISBN: 978-1-934631-14-0 (pbk.)
ISBN: 978-1-934631-13-3 (e-book: EPUB)
LCCN: 2012935836

Manufactured in the United States.

Jacobsville Books
www.JacobsvilleBooks.com
1-866-341-3705

Publisher's Cataloging-in-Publication Data

Shiel, Lisa A.
    Relic of the ancient ones / Lisa A. Shiel.
      p. cm.
    ISBN-13: 978-0-9746553-0-7 (pbk.)
    ISBN-10: 0-9746553-0-9 (e-book: EPUB)
    1. Alternative histories—Fiction. 2. Michigan—Fiction. 3. Unidentified flying objects—Fiction. 4. Grand Canyon (Ariz.)—Fiction. I. Shiel, Kerrie, ill. II. Title. III. Series: Human origins series.
PS3619.H53 R45 2012
813'.6—dc22

                                                2012935836

PROLOGUE

THUNDER RUMBLED. RIDLEY SKIDDED TO A STOP AT THE INTERSECTION OF the two tunnels. His heart thudded as if it might burst out of his chest. His breath came in gasps. The air, moist and warm from the humidity of the storm, clung to his skin. Panting, he swiped the back of his hand across his brow. The sweat transferred to his hand and dribbled down his wrist under the sleeve of his shirt.

The light from his lantern petered out before reaching the end of either tunnel. At the end of the left-hand tunnel lay a simple rectangular hole carved out of the ceiling that functioned as the entrance to this underground labyrinth. In the other tunnel, directly ahead, he would find a dead end. Behind him awaited...the unknown.

Lightning flared.

Ridley squinted. The light admitted through the entrance dimmed little on its journey down the tunnel. The storm outside was biblical in proportion, yet he knew the tempest stemmed not from the heavenly father's will, but from something far less benevolent. Something evil.

Thunder exploded. The walls shook, raining bits of earth around him. The floor trembled so violently that he struggled to stay upright.

A voice chuckled. A feminine voice.

A shiver tickled the back of his neck, raising the hairs.

A figure slightly darker than the shadows approached from where the tunnel dead-ended in front of him. She strolled into the lantern light, a serene smile on her lips. There she halted, painted with golden light from his lantern, her hands dangling at her sides, head tilted to the left. She was beautiful, he must admit. Poison often dripped from the loveliest flowers.

She waggled a finger at him. "Naughty boy, trying to escape us."

The lantern light quivered. No breeze stirred the air. He glanced down at the lantern. His left hand, clamped around the lantern's handle, trembled. His own tremors bled into the lantern, wavering the flame. Fool. Coward. He chastised himself silently, though it would do no good. Each encounter with her affected him this way, disturbing him on a level deep within him and in a manner he could not explain.

His brother would not shudder in the face of a mere woman. Yet Broderick had never encountered a woman such as this one. A fallen angel. The handmaiden of evil.

Ridley tightened his right hand around the strap of his rucksack, slung over his shoulder. Nothing he'd found here, none of the artifacts stashed in his backpack, mattered without the single prize which he had sought for so long and for which he had forsaken his family. He prayed Fanny could forgive him. He prayed God could forgive him.

Whoomp.

He glanced at the entrance. The sound originated outside. Now, in the wake of the concussion, he perceived another sound. A whirring, distant at first, grew louder and nearer with each thump of his heart. The sound was unnatural, unearthly, and unlike anything he had heard before. *It's them.*

The woman chuckled again, her voice softer, more ominous.

"Please," Ridley said, "let me be. I will find it for you, given time—"

"This was your one last chance, love," she said in her melodic brogue, "and you frittered it away on a whim."

"Not a whim. Intuition."

"Nevertheless, you wasted your final chance—and I do mean *final.*"

Her tone hardened on the last word. She slipped a hand under her blouse. A soft pop followed, as of a snap being flicked open. She slid her hand out from under the garment. In her fingers, she clasped a long-bladed knife.

Ridley glanced at the entrance. The lightning had ceased. A hint of a breeze tickled his skin. Whatever object or thing made the whirring, it had stopped its approach. The sound roared above the mountain from a stationary position, the din drowning out even the sound of his heartbeat. Fear sliced through him. He felt his very soul rend. He could not flee via the hole through which he entered. The tunnels offered no alternate routes. Unless…

No, it was a desperate hope.

But he had no other.

The woman peeled back her lips in a menacing grin. Her body quivered with laughter muted by the whirring outside. She raised the knife in front of her, turning the blade so the light glinted off its metal. His chest tightened. His mouth went dry. He might fend off the woman, but then he would fall victim to whatever abomination lay in wait above the entrance to the tunnels. The invisible hand of Death reached out for him, and nothing in heaven or earth could save him. This was his fate, to die without completing his mission, without returning home.

He dropped his rucksack. He would never hold in his hand the relic he'd sought for all these years. He would never comprehend its mysteries.

The whirring silenced. A beam of light appeared over the entrance. The light, so pure in its whiteness, drew a cone of brilliance on the floor beneath the hole.

The back of his neck tingled. They had arrived.

"Poor darling," the woman said, her tone oddly cloying. "You know your time has come. Stop fighting. Let it be over and done with."

His brother's last words to him echoed in his ears. Broderick had said, "Your mission will be the death of you, dear brother." And he had been right.

A new sensation rippled through him, hot as the whitest flame. He clenched his fists until they ached. Yes, he may die this day. But the choice to die with cowardice or with honor lay in his hands alone.

Ridley said, "I may die today, but by God, I will fight you until my last breath of life is spent."

She shook her head.

He turned sideways to glance down the tunnel behind him. A desperate hope would suffice.

The woman said, "It didn't have to be this way. We were such good friends at the start."

He let out a harsh laugh. Friends? No man called her friend. No living thing on earth looked upon her as an ally.

Ridley spun on his heels and sprinted down the corridor away from her.

Her voice echoed behind him. "You only prolong the inevitable."

He saw the doorway up ahead on the right. He could make it.

Thwack. The knife lodged in the doorway as he veered right into the chamber.

Her footsteps clapped down the corridor.

He ran to the farthest corner. A metal ring protruded from the earthen floor.

Thwack.

Pain lanced through his back. He staggered two steps, stumbled, and smacked onto the floor face-first. His forehead struck the metal ring. Something warm trickled down his back from a spot between his shoulder blades. He bent his right arm around to feel the spot. His fingers grazed the hilt of her knife, protruding from his back. The pain cut through him once more, stronger, hotter. He winced, gasped, dropped his arm. His ears rang. His vision swam to and fro. No, no, no, not yet.

A shadow fell over him.

He reached his left hand into his trouser pocket, closing his fingers around the bronze key. So long as the key remained with him, his enemies lacked the knowledge to locate the relic themselves.

She knelt beside him, stroking his hair. "It hurts, doesn't it?"

He tried to speak. The words emerged as a croak.

She yanked the knife from his back. Agony coursed through him. He clenched his teeth, and more pain webbed out from his jaw.

He forced out one sentence, his voice a rough whisper. "You shall—never—find—it now."

"Yes, we shall." The woman caressed his cheek with back of her hand. "We have your brother."

A shiver rattled his entire body, triggering a cascade of pain that made him wince and gasp. He knew what her words meant. Dear lord, if they had Broderick, then all was lost. They would triumph.

She rolled him over onto his back. Strangely, the pain had vanished. He felt cold and numb, somehow detached from his body. Blackness encroached on the edges of his vision. *Oh Fanny...*

He knew it would end this way. Like a sixth sense, some part of him felt it creeping up on him from the moment he agreed to aid the fallen angel and her masters. He sensed his own death.

She stabbed the knife into his heart.

His eyes drifted shut as he sank into oblivion.

1

The shores of Lake Superior
Shadow Bay, Michigan
Sunday, May 15

A WOLF HOWLED. THE CRY PIERCED THE NIGHT FROM SOMEWHERE IN THE forest behind her. Erin Turner sat still and silent as the howl faded. In front of her, the surface of Lake Superior looked as black as oil in the moonless night. Wavelets, invisible in the dark, lapped over the sandstone slabs that underlay the water, disappearing under a layer of sand at the water's edge.

Erin leaned back against the cliff. The beach had changed since November, the last time she'd visited it. The sandstone cliffs eroded a little more in the interim, though they stood three feet tall as before, undulating along the shoreline like echoes of the waves that carved them. In November, the sandstone slabs had lain bare. A thin ribbon of sand rimmed the cliffs back then. Tonight sand sheathed the beach between the water's edge and the cliffs.

The wolf howled again.

A breeze tickled her, raising goosebumps on her arms and the back of her neck. She flipped the hood of her sweatshirt over her head. Above her, the forest extended right up to the edge of the cliffs. To her right, about thirty feet away, a fir tree had fallen over onto the sand. One of the autumn windstorms must've knocked down the tree and driven the sand onto the beach.

Erin gazed at the sky. Millions upon millions of stars glittered in the rest of the sky, more stars than she'd ever seen until she moved here, to the edge of the earth. Sometimes she felt as if she lived at the cusp of the abyss where early mariners would scrawl on their maps "there be monsters here." She had yet to meet any monsters in the Upper Peninsula of Michigan—unless human resources managers counted. In a job interview, she sometimes felt like a peasant girl held captive by evil nobles who tortured her with psychological assessments, rather than the rack. Unfortunately, no knight ever came to rescue her from the vocational inquisition.

Her stomach tightened. She had a job interview tomorrow.

The sky. She focused on the stars and the void between them. Nothing matched the northern sky, especially at night. No light pollution tainted the view. No air pollution either. What had the ancient people who lived here 7,000 years ago thought of the sky? How many stars had they counted? Had they recognized constellations of their own design? In that distant eon, millennia before the first recognized explorers from Europe set foot on the American continent, an enigmatic people had mined an estimated half a million tons of copper from this part of Michigan's Upper Peninsula, a region called the Keweenaw Peninsula.

She picked up the bag of chocolate-covered peanuts that lay on the ground beside her. Her hand bumped her digital camera. She grabbed several of the candies out of the bag and popped them into her mouth.

In the sky, to her right, a light flashed.

Erin blinked. An airplane? One of those things eyes do when they're tired?

The light flashed again. Larger. Closer. A perfect white sphere the size of an aspirin held at arm's length. The orb pulsed three times, then stayed lit. The miniature moon shone brighter and whiter than the real thing would have.

A star-sized light dropped out of the bottom of the faux moon. A second light emerged after it, followed by a third, a fourth, a fifth. A total of eight smaller orbs dropped out of the mother orb. They encircled their parent, spinning around her like lights on a turbocharged ferris wheel.

The babies spun away from their mother one by one. The small lights lined up in a chevron formation above the mother ship.

Erin reached for her digital camera. Did the lights signify vessels, or some kind of free-floating energy? She sensed the lights had mass. They were vessels. Ships. Craft. And on what precisely did she base that belief? She had no evidence to support her intuition. Yet she *knew*.

The lights fell out of formation. In groups of two, they merged with the mother light. Reunited, the craft pulsed twice. It glided northward, toward Erin and the forest behind her. The light enlarged as it drew closer, until it glowed the size of a baseball held at arm's length. As the UFO passed overhead, Erin tilted her head backward to watch.

A shiver raced up her spine.

The light winked out.

Erin looked down at her lap. She still cupped the camera in her hands. Shoulders slumped, she stared at the camera. She'd intended to do something with it…

She yawned. Her eyelids seemed to flutter shut on their own. Get up, she ought to get up off her duff. She willed her legs to move. Nothing. Her arms. Nothing. She opened her eyes, inhaling deeply. The fog enveloping her brain thinned a little. She'd meant to take a picture. Duh, that's why she brought the blasted camera. Why did she hesitate?

Because something clouded her mind in the instant she spotted the UFO.

Snap out of it, she commanded herself. The fog thinned a bit more. What in tarnation was the matter with her?

In one motion, she slung the camera strap over her shoulder and jumped to her feet. Down the beach she tromped, to the sandy slope that accessed the beach from the road, up and over the slope to the Ford Explorer parked along the right side of the two-track. As she climbed into the Explorer, the wind kicked up from a whisper to gusts that lashed her hair into her face. Depositing the camera on the passenger seat, she shut the door.

The gusts outside segued into a gale. The trees swayed. Sand blasted off the beach, scouring the rear window. She started the engine, switched on the headlights, glanced at the clock above the radio. It read 10:30. She'd spent less than half an hour at the beach.

The candy. She'd left it on the beach. Oh well, maybe seagulls liked chocolate.

She strapped on her seatbelt, released the parking brake, shifted into drive, and eased the Explorer onto the two-track. In the beam of the headlights, saplings dipped down across the road, their tops nearly touching the ground. She needed to get off this road before a tree toppled onto her car. She veered around one sapling. Another dove down toward the car. Its branches scraped across the driver's window.

The Explorer jounced over a pothole. Her teeth clacked together. Ouch.

A light glanced in the trees to her right.

No, not in the trees. *Through* the trees. A beam of light above the forest shined down into the trees, its glow spreading out through the forest. She couldn't distinguish the light's source.

Hands tight on the steering wheel, she guided the Explorer along the rutted path. The light tracked through the trees, keeping pace with her. Static electricity prickled the hairs on her head and the back of her neck. Up ahead, the main road intersected with the beach road. She braked hard.

The beam of light vanished.

The Explorer rocked to a halt. The seatbelt dug into her bosom. Her heart thudded. The blood roared behind her eardrums. Static electricity tingled over her skin.

Erin leaned forward to glance left and right down the main road. No traffic. She looked across the intersection, to where the road dead-ended at an old farm. There hovered three lights, each as wide as her car. The lights levitated behind the farmhouse, about fifty feet off the ground.

Her hands trembled. What had she gotten herself into? She gripped the wheel tighter. Follow a UFO to the beach, at night, alone. The idea sounded reasonable half an hour ago, when she'd first noticed a white light shooting back and forth across the sky in the distance. From her bedroom window, the light seemed quite close, so she jumped into the Explorer and took off in the direction where she saw the light. No thinking. She just did it. The moment she turned onto the beach road, the light had vanished. Twenty-odd minutes later, it reappeared.

Now she was alone. In the middle of nowhere. Nothing around but a vacant farmhouse and three gigantic balls of glowing white...whatever the hell they were. Brilliant plan.

The orbs burned brighter than the lights of a football field. Behind the glare, she could make out nothing.

She gaped at the orbs.

The lights contracted into pinpoints, then disappeared. She blinked.

Trees. The farmhouse. Above that, stars and a wisp of a cloud. Nothing else.

She glanced out the rear-view mirror. Darkness.

A chill washed over her. She cranked up the heater and drove home.

A WET CLOTH RUBBED AGAINST HER FACE. ERIN OPENED HER EYES. THEY FELT hot and gritty. She blinked a few times to clear the blurriness, squeezing her eyelids to encourage tears.

Amber eyes stared directly into hers. The dog licked her nose.

"Freya," she mumbled, "cut it out."

The black mutt licked her on the mouth. The dog's tongue felt like a wet washcloth.

"Bluck," she sputtered.

Pushing Freya away, she sat up in bed. The clock on her bedside table said 10:15. She had slept for nearly eleven hours, and she could've slept longer.

Freya wagged her tail. Erin patted the dog's head. The canine sashayed out of the bedroom into the hall.

Erin yawned. Her head felt heavy, her body stiff. Her head usually felt like this the morning after taking a full dose of antihistamines, but she took none last night. She stretched and yawned again. Joints cracked, muscles protested. She must've slept in a bad position after collapsing in an exhausted heap on the bed last night. The lethargy that overtook her last night lingered this morning. What happened to her?

Orbs. Three of them. Enormous. Dazzlingly bright.

She shivered.

Jumping off the bed, she walked over to shut the bedroom door. Another yawn escaped her. She inhaled deeply and shook herself in hopes of shedding the lethargy. No such luck. She dressed and did yoga, which helped a little. By the time she sat down in front of her computer at the desk in the corner, three feet from the foot of the bed, her head felt lighter—in a good way. She checked her e-mail.

Five new messages popped up, two of them obviously spam, which she deleted. The third message asked her to moderate a comment submitted to her blog. She opened the message and skimmed the first line of the comment, which said, "You are a total freaking idiot." Nice. She deleted the comment. The fourth message came from Harry, the one-named man she'd been trading e-mails with for several months. He refused to tell her his full name. Although she usually ignored messages from anonymous people, something about this guy intrigued her. He liked to discuss ridiculed subjects, such as aliens visiting Earth in the remote past and advanced human civilizations that mysteriously vanished. He was one of five people who subscribed to her blog, and he'd left comments there several times. He was her biggest fan.

Today Harry's message consisted of two lines: "I have sent you a package which you should receive in a few days. I may be out of contact for the unforeseeable future."

A package?

A box wrapped in brown paper that exploded in her face. Or released poison gas upon opening.

Oh please. No one would waste a perfectly good bomb on her. Harry talked before about sending her an early Christmas present. She told him not to bother. Apparently, he ignored it.

The last message in her inbox sported the subject line "Invitation to Apply." Sounded like spam, but what the heck. She opened the message.

```
Dear Ms. Turner,

SNW Enterprises is pleased to invite you to apply for the
position of Librarian Archivist. We reviewed your resume on
the FindALibJob site and were impressed with your background.
The Librarian Archivist position requires an MLS, cataloging
experience, and a keen interest in history. After browsing
your blog, we feel you would be the perfect candidate for
this position. To apply, simply respond to this message.

Sincerely,
Anna T. Newman
Recruitment Director
SNW Enterprises
```

She'd never seen a library job with such a short list of requirements. Only an MLS—a master's degree in library science—plus an unspecified amount of experience. And she couldn't believe looking at her blog would encourage anyone to offer her a job. Of course, no one had offered her a job yet. Ms. Newman simply invited her to apply. Maybe they needed to gather more resumes before hiring the company president's nephew, to make it look like they performed a fair search. Memories of rejection letters flashed in her mind. *We have decided to continue the search. We chose a more qualified candidate. While your resume impressed us, we decided not to fill the position.* All code for "go away, loser."

What had she written on her blog lately? She opened the site in her web browser.

A banner across the top of the home page declared, "The Maat Files: Exposing the True History of Our World." The background image showed the constellation Orion, with its belt of three stars.

Three lights. Huge. Her skin tingling.

She blinked. Scrolling down the blog page, she skimmed the post titles: Mysterious Mounds of the Americas, Are the Tiny Skeletons of Flores Aliens, The Ice Age Conspiracy. Hmm. Whichever of those garnered her an "invitation to apply" for a job, she wouldn't question the offer. As Ms. Newman instructed, she replied to message.

The clock on her computer read 11:45. Time to get ready for her one o'clock interview.

Law Offices of Ronald De Luca
Shadow Bay

A RE YOU?" RONALD DE LUCA ASKED.

Erin snapped back to reality. While her eyes had been staring at the man across the desk from her, she hadn't seen him. Or listened to him. Loose papers, manila folders, and unopened mail lay in stacks on the desk. Ronald De Luca sat with his hands clasped over a yellow legal pad. On the wall behind him, a plaque displayed a shark-toothed fish, probably a pike.

"Miss Turner, are you all right?"

"What?" She met De Luca's gaze. "Yes, I'm fine, sorry."

"I asked if you're comfortable using spreadsheet software."

"Oh, um, yes. I can use just about any kind of software, and what I don't know I can learn."

He squinted at her from behind his glasses. The light from his desk lamp reflected on the lenses, creating a false haze. He sighed.

Oh no. She knew the sound, and the look. The interview was over. Sure, they might go on chatting for awhile, but she had lost the job.

De Luca said, "The receptionist position is demanding, and requires both focus and attention to detail."

She nodded. All words had vacated her brain. What could she say anyway, after displaying the exact opposite of focus and attention during the interview?

Twenty minutes later, after regaling her with the story of how the pike on his wall came to hang there, De Luca rose and offered his hand to her. She pushed up out of her chair and shook his hand.

He said, "Thanks for coming in. We'll let you know."

The wooden door creaked as she opened it to exit De Luca's office, trudging out and through the reception area to the front door. Once outside, she paused. Her car, where was her car?

Parked right where she left it, half a block to the left. She should check her post office box first, though. She turned right and walked three blocks to the Shadow Bay post office, a small brick building with an even smaller parking lot. Inside, she headed straight to her box and unlocked it. A single item awaited her—a package, wrapped in brown paper, slightly larger than a hardcover book. She pulled out the package. In lieu of a return address, someone had scrawled the name "Harry."

Already? She got his e-mail this morning. Maybe he forgot to contact her until today, after mailing the package last week. Maybe she forgot to check her e-mail for several days. Jeez, she couldn't remember if she checked her e-mail yesterday, or the day before, or the day before that. The fuzz on her brain muddled everything. One thing and one thing alone remained clear in her mind.

The lights. Bright and white and huge.

She growled at herself. Maybe she hadn't really seen those lights after all, maybe she imagined the whole thing. No. She remembered.

Locking her box, she stuffed Harry's package in her purse. The walk back to her car got the blood flowing and washed some of the fuzz out of her mind. As she settled in behind the steering wheel, she fished out Harry's package and unwrapped it. He'd used enough tape to hermetically seal a mummy. The brown paper concealed a white cardboard box fastened with more tape. After prying the tape off the box, she dumped out its contents.

A hardback book, cloth covered.

The cover was nicked and smudged, the title barely legible. *A Spiritualist History of Ancient Egypt* by Gilbert Covington. Never heard of him. Spiritualists believed in communication with the dead, séances and the like. She flipped through the book's yellowed pages. The text itself contained no drawings, although someone scratched notes and symbols in the margins on select pages. The notations looked recent, not yellowed or faded like the rest of the book, and they appeared to have been written in two different hands. She flipped back to the title page. There she found a note addressed to her scribbled in a tight cursive hand. "Erin," the note began, "I offer my life's work for your perusal. Do with it as you see fit. Best wishes, Harry."

Doodles in the margins of an ancient book constituted his life's work? How sad. She'd gotten the impression he was a professor of some kind, though he never confirmed her suspicion. He rarely said much of anything about himself. Now she'd inherited his life's work in the form of screwy scribbles. Well, what did she expect from an anonymous guy she met over the Internet. He could be a twelve-year-old, or a senile octogenarian, or a total psychopath. Then again, maybe he was just lonely.

She dropped the book on the passenger seat and headed home.

3

The Turner Home

As ERIN PULLED THE EXPLORER INTO THE DRIVEWAY, SHE SPOTTED HER mother on the front steps of the house. The front door was open behind her. Freya poked around in the grass inside the fenced yard, her nose to the ground. A breeze ruffled Mom's short gray hair.

The manufactured home featured pale gray siding with blue shutters, and a metal railing for the steps. The entryway was recessed with a gable above. The sloped roof, with gables at either end, helped the mobile home look less like a trailer. Three windows on the front of the home looked into the master bedroom on the right side, the living room in the center, and another bedroom on the left end. A five-acre field stretched out behind the house, while the woods came within a hundred feet of the house on either side. The fifty-foot gravel driveway led to a dirt road that ran north-south. The nearest neighbor was three miles away to the south, but Lake Superior lay a mere half mile to the east, on the other side of the road. On a windy day Erin could hear the waves crashing against the cliffs that lined the shore. Sometimes she swore she could even smell the lake.

Climbing out of the car, Erin gazed at the woods. Aspens, birches, and maples predominated. Evergreens filled in the gaps. The tallest trees, mainly pines, towered eighty feet above the house.

A chill shimmied up her neck, triggered by the sensation of being watched. She glanced at the road. No one there. She looked back at the house. Her mother smiled and waved.

A breeze probably triggered the chill. A wind off Lake Superior was often nippy.

Erin unlatched the gate, walked through, and latched it behind her. Freya dashed up to her, leaping up to plant her paws on Erin's tummy. Erin patted the dog's head and scratched behind her ears. Satisfied, Freya returned to her lawn inspection.

As Erin reached the front steps, her mother said, "A woman called for you earlier. Wouldn't say much, something about setting up a meeting. She said you'd know what it was about."

"Did she give a name?"

"Anna something. It started with an N."

Anna Newman called her. Setting up a meeting must refer to a job interview. Weird. Why wouldn't the woman say she wanted to set up a job interview? Who knew, maybe Ms. Newman was paranoid about privacy and didn't want to get in trouble for leaving a message with someone else. The whole thing, starting with the way Anna Newman contacted her in the first place, smelled funny. Still, someone racking up her eighth month of unemployment lacked the luxury of passing up even the screwiest interview.

"It's about a job I applied for," Erin said.

"Ohhh."

Her mother's voice had a cheery lilt. After filing 127 applications, enduring nine interviews, and burning 118 rejection letters, Erin knew her voice no longer took on an optimistic tone when she discussed job prospects. She appreciated her mother's enthusiasm but—

"Your friend Chloe called too." Mom looked at the package in Erin's hand. "What's that?"

"Nothing. An old book somebody sent me."

"One of your Internet buddies?"

"Yep."

The only non-Internet friend she had was Chloe Pelletier, a girl Erin worked with at the Shadow Bay Public Library until the library closed due to budgetary problems eight months ago. Unlike Erin, Chloe lacked a master's degree, in library science or anything else. Chloe barely made it past high school graduation. Her boyfriend, Greg Virtanen, had a PhD in comparative literature, though he worked in the local feed store. When talking to Greg and Chloe and the people she'd met over the Internet, Erin felt like less of a failure, or at least less of a freak. Everybody she knew had trouble finding a decent job.

She had trouble making friends too. People either dismissed her as a loony librarian, too crazy to tolerate, or treated her like a free therapist minus the advice. The latter category liked to talk but not to listen, and they certainly didn't want her to offer possible solutions to their problems. Those folks were fair-weather faithful, glomming onto her when they needed to unload their troubles but disappearing at the first hint that Erin might need a real friend.

Sidling past her mother, Erin went into the house. The front door opened onto the living room, with the kitchen beyond it at the back of the house. To the right, the door to the master bedroom hung partway closed. She crossed the living room into the short hallway that led past the bathroom on the left, to her bedroom at the end. As she passed the open dining room on her right, next to the kitchen, she glanced through the doorway located at the rear of the dining room. The back room was intended as a third bedroom, though it actually served as a storage space.

Her father didn't seem to be in the house. He must've gone out to this workshop, a little metal shed behind the house. Her father built wood furniture to sell at local fairs. He couldn't have lived on that revenue alone, but it nicely supplemented his retirement income.

She continued into her bedroom, shutting the door behind her. Her mother had left a sticky note on her computer monitor, with details of the two calls for her. Sitting down at her desk, she set the package on the desktop, picked up the phone, and dialed the number Anna Newman had left. The woman picked up on the third ring. Erin introduced herself, then asked about the interview.

"Does tomorrow morning work for you?" Anna Newman said with a British accent. "Ten o'clock?"

"Sure. Do you want references?"

"We can discuss it tomorrow."

Ms. Newman excused herself and hung up. At least Erin had learned one thing about Ms. Newman. The woman wasn't a chatterbox.

Tomorrow. Ten o'clock. Ugh.

She withdrew the book Harry sent her from its packaging. She started to crumple the paper wrapping, then stopped. She smoothed out the paper and searched for the postmark. There. She tapped her finger on the postmark. The package was mailed in Kingsford, Michigan, on May 13. On Friday someone mailed the package from Kingsford, a town on the Michigan-Wisconsin border at the west end of the Upper Peninsula, about 150 miles from Shadow Bay. Harry told her he lived in Arizona. Either he first sent the package to someone else who mailed it for him from Kingsford, or the mysterious Harry had been in Kingsford three days ago. She remembered telling Harry she lived in Michigan, but she purposely withheld the exact location, not even telling him she lived in the Upper Peninsula. Had he gotten so close by accident?

She flipped open the book. Many of the notes and markings inside it seemed like a code of some sort. Skimming through the pages, she saw no obvious legend or key. This was a code, not a map. What did code-breakers use to decipher messages? She should've watched more spy movies.

Go for a walk. Get some fresh air. Then she'd feel better, more able to crack a code.

After changing into sweatpants and a T-shirt, and slipping on tennis shoes, she headed outside. Her mother was in the kitchen now, washing dishes. Outside, Freya—recognizing Erin's intention to go for a walk—scampered to the gate, whimpering and panting. Erin hesitated. Freya tended to pull at her leash. She hated to disappoint the dog, but after a long day she was too tired to wrestle with her.

Long day? Sleeping late followed by one job interview that lasted forty-five minutes. No, the day had not tired her. The night before had.

Three orbs. Glowing.

Don't think about it.

Freya went silent, her body stiffening, gaze locked on something past the gate. She growled softly.

Erin studied the road, the woods. Nothing popped out at her. She tilted her head to listen. Birds chirped. Deep in the forest, a woodpecker hammered away. She discerned no other sounds.

The dog whimpered, spun around, and ran under the front steps.

"Fine, be that way," Erin said. "I'll go by myself."

Five minutes later, she had walked out of sight of the house. The trees stretched up over her head, curving over the road. A strip of blue sky mirrored the path of the road below. A woodpecker's cry, reminiscent of the call of a jungle bird, echoed through the woods.

Crack.

She froze. Something snapped a twig. A bear?

Moving only her head, she glanced around. Animals could be hard to see, especially if they stood still. She panned her head left and right again, slower this time, then turned sideways to check behind. Trees, grass, gravel. Any wild animal could've caused the sound. She lived in the woods, for pete's sake.

Sighing, she started off again.

Crunch.

Goosebumps prickled her skin. *Get a grip.* She spun around.

Empty road. Shadowy woods.

The first pang of a headache pierced her brain. She shut her eyes, rubbed her temples. Maybe she ought to go home. If every little noise flipped her paranoid switch, a walk wouldn't clear her mind.

A weight slammed into her from behind. She tripped, tumbled to her knees, threw out her hands to stop the fall. Over her shoulder, her attacker panted. He swung a tanned arm around her neck into a headlock. She scratched at his face. He punched her in the side, under her ribs. Pain ricocheted through her. She cried out.

He slammed his fist sideways into her left arm. More pain. Her ears rang. Black mist encroached on her vision. Her body felt weak. She struggled to breathe. She thrust her right elbow backward but met air. Swinging her arm up over her shoulder, she grasped at his head. Her fingers clutched hair. She yanked.

He grunted. Wrapping his left arm around her waist, he hoisted her up and flung her to the side. She sailed through the air, inches off the ground. Her right hip struck the ground first. Gravity rolled her over and over, down the steep sides of the ditch alongside the road. By the time she rolled to a stop at the bottom of the ditch, she felt woozy.

Her attacker leaped into the ditch, straddling her. She tried to knee him in the groin but her leg flailed far from its target. He knelt over her and grasped her left arm. Her vision was blurry. His face, though close enough she could've touched it if she could've moved, looked like an out-of-focus photograph.

"Bastard," she mumbled.

Something pricked her arm. She wanted to look. Her head refused to turn.

His blurry shape receded from her. Crunch-crunch-crunch-crunch.

Her attacker had run away. The dizziness subsided, and she sat up. Her vision cleared as the weakness and lethargy lessened too.

A light flashed. She saw it out the corner of her left eye. When she looked left, though, she saw nothing. Every muscle in her body ached, and her left arm throbbed where the man first struck her with his fist, then stabbed something into her flesh. Or had it happened the other way around? Christ, the whole incident blurred into a chaos of images and sensations, none of them pleasant.

A moment later, she clambered out of the ditch and crawled onto the road. In either direction, emptiness greeted her.

Her attacker had vanished.

Eagle River

THE TWO-STORY LOG HOUSE NESTLED IN THE EMBRACE OF THE PINES, FIRS, and birches. The latter had yet to leaf out, and looked naked next to the evergreens. Alex MacKay sat at a cedar picnic table across from Ellen and Frank Whelan, the middle-aged owners of the log house, a few yards from their home. A blue file folder lay open on the table before them with photographs fanned out across it. The photos showed stone implements—hammerstones, chopping tools, arrowheads—used by the peoples who lived in this area in ancient times. Beginning about 8,000 years ago, those ancient humans mined copper in unknown, but apparently great, quantities. After nearly 7,000 years of mining, they stopped. Copper mining in the region wouldn't start up again for another 3,000 years, during the Industrial Revolution.

Alex learned all of this in the last few hours. Before the Whelans contacted him, he knew nothing whatsoever about Michigan's copper industry, ancient or modern. American archaeology wasn't his forte.

Frank Whelan rooted through the photos and plucked out one, handing it to Alex.

The photo showed a statue lying supine on a felt mat with a ruler aligned next to it, all of it inside a glass case. According to the ruler, the statue was 4.5 inches high. It looked to be carved from ivory, probably from a hippopotamus, like similar statues he'd seen. The figurine had two legs and two arms, and in that respect resembled a human being. In every other way the figurine resembled no human. Bug eyes. A wide, flat nose above a thin and narrow mouth. Hunched shoulders. Spindly arms. Sagging breasts. No visible hands. Stumpy feet. The almond-shaped head seemed too large for the body. Alex had studied figurines like this before, up close.

In Egypt.

The statue was a dead ringer for the predynastic figurines manufactured by the Badarian culture in Egypt, circa 4400 to 4000 BC. Although the stone implements documented in the other photos dated to the same general period, they hailed from a different continent. The Archaic Tradition of ancient Michigan had, mainstream archaeologists declared, never met ancient Egyptians of any period.

"Where did you say you got this?" Alex asked.

"A friend down by St. Ignace gave it to us," Frank said. "He found it when he dug a posthole for a new fence. The statue was buried six inches down, not ten feet from where he dug up a hammerstone the year before."

"And the statue was stolen last night?"

"Somebody took it while we were sleeping. We didn't hear a thing."

Ellen fidgeted. She opened her mouth as if to speak, then shut it.

Smirking, Frank nudged her in the ribs. "Tell him. That's why you called these people."

She made a face at him. To Alex, she said, "He doesn't believe me, but I know what I saw. I'd gone down to the kitchen for a snack around 10:30 last night when I saw a flash of light coming from the artifact room. I went to check it out, and that's when I saw the—the ball of light. It was hovering over the case where the statue had been. But the statue was gone."

"Then what happened?" Alex asked.

Ellen bit her lip. "The ball flew out the window, straight through the glass, without breaking it or so much as scratching it. A second later I heard a car engine down at the road."

Alex glanced over his shoulder at the two-lane paved highway a hundred feet away, at the end of the gravel drive. Trees blocked the road from sight, except when he looked straight down the driveway.

"The car drove away," Ellen said. "I couldn't see what it looked like. The ball of light had…disappeared."

Alex looked at Ellen. "Disappeared as in poof, or disappeared as in it went out of sight?"

Ellen shut her eyes for a second. When she opened them again, she shrugged. "The car distracted me, and when I looked back in the direction of the ball it was already gone."

Rolling his eyes at Alex, Frank shook his head.

Alex felt like smacking him. If the toad had seen half the things Alex witnessed, he wouldn't feel quite so cocksure about his view of reality.

"May I see the artifact room?" Alex asked.

Ellen nodded and instructed her husband to wait there. She led Alex up the porch steps, through the wood-and-glass front door toward the back of the house. A doorway on the right opened onto a kitchen bigger than his motel room. Ellen turned to a closed door on the left. Pulling keys from her pocket, she unlocked the door.

"Is the door always locked?" Alex asked.

"Uh-huh. Last night it was locked too. I saw the flash of light underneath it."

As she shoved the keys back in her pocket, she swung the door inward. The room inside was dim, with little light penetrating the trees outside the windows. Ellen stepped through the door and flipped a light switch. Warm light poured down from bulbs set into the ceiling, cascading over the display cases situated against the walls on three sides of the room. Some of the cases stretched from floor to ceiling, while others sat like fish tanks atop solid wood stands. The display case in question, the only one now empty, backed up to the far wall adjacent to a window.

Alex approached the display case. A slight indentation in the felt mat indicated where the statue had rested until last night. Both the glass and the stand looked unscathed. Gently, he placed a hand on either side of the glass enclosure and lifted.

An alarm squealed.

"Oh!" Ellen shouted.

She rushed to a keypad next to the doorway, above the light switch, where she punched in a code. The alarm kept squealing like a bad opera singer reaching for high notes. Ellen's lips moved in what must've been a silent curse. She punched in the code a second time.

The alarm silenced.

"Sorry," Ellen said.

"Was that alarm on last night?"

"It's on twenty-four hours a day."

"What about the windows? Any alarms there?"

She shook her head. "Frank wouldn't pay for that. He said wiring the cases was good enough. Besides, the windows are still locked from inside. I checked last night."

Hmm. Someone could enter the room without triggering the alarm, but if they tried to access the case, the alarm would liquefy their brains. He assumed a thief would've shattered the glass to grab the artifact and run. The evidence before him pointed to no thief, no human whatsoever, having set foot in the room during the robbery. The solitary thing known to have entered the room last night was a glowing orb.

The phenomenon of orbs was a controversial topic among UFO researchers, or ufologists. Those who preferred to dismiss the orbs pretended that the sole evidence for their existence came from digital photographs. Since the advent of digital photography, numerous photos had surfaced showing partially transparent orbs that were not visible at the time the photograph was taken. The anti-orb camp said these photos captured nothing more exotic than dust particles or insects. The majority of the orb photos probably did show dust or bugs, though some of the photos had been taken under circumstances which precluded those explanations.

The main problem with the debunkers' arguments, however, involved the evidence they ignored—eyewitness sightings of glowing orbs, of varying sizes and colors, witnessed with the naked eye. Anyone who wrote off all glowing orbs as dust or insects either failed to look at the eyewitness data in the first place, or chose to disregard it out of a personal prejudice against such sightings. Alex had examined the evidence. Ellen was not the first UFO witness he'd interviewed. She wasn't even the first person he'd spoken with whose artifacts had seemingly been stolen by a glowing orb. Some of the victims called the police, others didn't. The Whelans fell into the latter category. Frank said he "wouldn't call the police," though he refused to explain why. Maybe Frank bought some or all of the artifacts in his collection on the black market.

Alex visually surveyed the items in the display cases. The artifacts came from ancient cultures worldwide, including Egypt and China, as well as the Americas.

"Dr. MacKay?"

Hands still resting on the glass case, he glanced at Ellen.

She said, "Do you think…I mean is it likely…the light could come back?"

"Whatever it was, it got what it came here for. I doubt it'll be back."

"It came back once already."

"What? You saw the orb before?"

She nodded, biting her lower lip.

"When?" he asked.

"About a week ago. Frank didn't believe me, he still doesn't. That's why I called your group last night."

He had wondered about that. Her call to the toll-free sightings hotline had been logged at 10:48 PM. Ellen reported her sighting minutes after the encounter, but her husband still refused to call the cops the next day.

He took it back, Frank wasn't a toad. He was a weasel. A sneaky, smarmy, crooked—

"I saw the other orb," Ellen said, "around the same time of night. It was bobbing around in the yard, about six feet off the ground. Looked exactly like this one. The middle was bluish white and splotchy, with a bright white ring around it. I watched it for about a minute, even opened the living room window to see it better. Couple times I thought I could see the trees behind it, through the bluish middle part. Then it shot up into the air out of sight."

"Did you see or hear any vehicles?"

"No."

"How about voices? Or footsteps?"

"No."

She said nothing about feeling frightened during her sightings. Her actions, as she related them to him anyway, betrayed no fear. Now, as she recounted her experiences after the fact, she bit her lip intermittently, avoided direct eye contact, and kept her hands in her pants pockets.

"How did you feel during the sightings?" he asked. "Scared? Excited?"

"Neither. I felt…numb."

Alex looked down at the empty space that once held the predynastic figurine. Numb. He wished he could feel numb at this moment, as if what he'd seen and learned in his lifetime didn't confound him. It did. How did glowing orbs steal artifacts? How could glowing orbs exist at all? Why did certain artifacts attract the miniature UFOs? Questions came easily. Answers eluded him.

Yet he knew one thing for certain—the identity of the man driving the car last night, the man Ellen saw speed off down the highway in the orb's wake. His name was Rassul.

Alex thanked Ellen for her time, and for entrusting her sighting to him and his colleagues, and left the house. Without a word, he strode past Frank, who hunkered at the picnic table as before. Alex's car, a rented sedan, was parked in the driveway. He got in and pulled out onto the highway, heading south. A few minutes later, spotting a scenic turnout, he pulled over to check his e-mail on his cell phone. One message awaited him. It contained three words.

Find Erin Turner.

Shadow Bay

How tall was he?" the sheriff's deputy asked.

Erin stared at him. He held a little notebook and a pen, writing down everything as she told it to him. They stood on the road in the area where she'd been attacked.

"I don't know," she said. "Like I said, he was behind me."

"Eye color? Hair color?"

"I saw his arm, nothing else."

The deputy nodded as he jotted something down on his notebook. "A tan arm, you said, eh? Would that be a natural tan, or one of those spray-on jobs?"

A curt response popped to mind, but she swallowed it. A headache stabbed at the backs of her eyes. Her jaw ached. She tried to relax her jaw muscles, without success. Every time she moved, pains webbed outward from the spot in her side where her attacker had punched her. Must have a nice bruise forming there.

The deputy held his hand suspended over his notebook, ready to record her response. No smirk. No arching of the eyebrow. He seemed to actually want to know about the tan.

"I'm not sure," Erin said.

She had recounted her story twice already, once back at the house and again here at the scene. To her left, she could see the scuff marks where she fought with her attacker. Her gut twisted. A wave of dizziness hit her, and she shut her eyes for a few seconds until the feeling passed.

When she'd told her parents about the attack, they insisted she call the police. They couldn't overlook her state as she staggered into the house an hour ago—hair mussed and flecked with grass, clothes smudged with dirt, a scrape on her cheek, scratches on her arms. When the deputy suggested returning to the scene of the crime, her parents had wanted to come along. She insisted they stay home. Why, she wasn't sure. Being here, she felt...weird.

"I didn't see any tracks," the deputy said, "from a vehicle or from shoes. Some scrape marks where ya fought him off, that's all."

Fought him off? The statement made it sound as if she won the battle.

The deputy said, "Without a description, it'll be hard to catch the assailant."

"Yeah, I figured."

"Sure ya don't wanna see a doctor?"

She shook her head. The thought of a hospital made her headache worse.

A few minutes later, the deputy walked her back to the house. He had given her his card, in case she thought of anything else later. As he drove away in his cruiser, she shuffled up the steps and into the living room. Her parents sat on the sofa. Her mother clasped her hands on her lap, her gaze on the door before Erin had opened it. Her father pretended to read a newspaper, though his left foot tapped out a drumroll on the carpet.

Mom asked, "How you doing?"

"Okay," Erin said. She flopped into the easy chair kitty-corner to the sofa.

Dad peeked around his newspaper at her. "What did the officer say about catching the son of a—"

"It's unlikely, since I didn't see his face."

He squinted at her. "You should see a doctor."

"I wish everyone would quit telling me that. I do *not* need a doctor."

"Okay, okay."

Her mother said, "We just want to make sure you're all right."

Erin sighed, rubbing her temple. "I know, I'm sorry. I'll feel better after I take a shower, and get all this grime off me."

"Good idea."

With a groan, Erin pushed up out of the chair onto her feet and walked toward the bathroom. She felt a hundred years old. And filthy. Like a corpse buried in the dirt for a century. Her attacker probably intended for her to end up that way, facedown in a shallow grave.

No. She shut the bathroom door. If he'd intended to kill her, he would have. Nothing happened to deter him. No witnesses, no noises to suggest someone might be coming, no reason for him to have stopped. Yet he had.

In the shower, she let the hot water beat down on her aching body. The events of the past twenty-four hours made no sense. Did something connect them? Three things of note happened to her in the last twenty-four hours—her UFO sighting, the e-mail from Harry and the subsequent package in the mail, and a man assaulting her on the road. Maybe the man wanted the book Harry sent her. She carried nothing with her on the walk, no purse or fanny pack, so the man couldn't have thought she had the book with her. He made no demands during the attack.

Five minutes later, she stepped out of the shower. Although the water washed away the dirt, the other physical evidence lingered. She scrutinized herself in the mirror. The scrape on her cheek looked like a smear of red paint. Her eyes were bloodshot. Below her rib cage, on the left side, a purple bruise the size of a fist had formed. She turned her torso sideways for a better look at the bruise. A flash of red caught her eye. She looked at her upper arm. There, about six inches below her shoulder, a two-inch scratch drew a line out from a red puncture mark.

What on earth happened to her?

ERIN SHUT THE BEDROOM DOOR AND SAT DOWN AT THE DESK. SHOULDERS slumped, she eyed the sticky notes her mother had stuck on the computer monitor. She'd forgotten to call Chloe. Picking up the phone, she dialed her friend's number. After Chloe answered on the third ring, they exchanged the obligatory greetings.

Chloe said, "Where you been?"

"I know, I keep forgetting to call. I'm a horrible friend."

"Nah, you're okay. How 'bout lunch tomorrow?"

They agreed to meet at noon, at Oramo's Cafe. When she mentioned her morning interview, Chloe exclaimed, "Awesome!" Erin let that go, for the moment. Whether or not the interview might prove awesome remained a mystery, so she resisted complaining about it until afterward. As for the assault, that story could wait until tomorrow. She said goodbye to Chloe and hung up the phone.

Harry's book lay on the desk in front of her. Another mystery awaited her on those pages, in the notes and symbols scribbled in the margins. She wanted to crack the code. Right now, though, her eyes felt gritty and her head heavy. The book could wait until tomorrow.

Dragging herself over to the bed, she crawled under the sheets. Her eyelids wanted to shut. She let them. Her body went limp as she sank into sleep.

Lights. Pure white. A trio of orbs. She tried to run, but her legs refused to move. The lights, large as beach balls, swirled around her in a dervish dance. The lights warmed her face like a blush. She tried to move her arms. Her entire body was paralyzed. The lights swelled in size, now ten times larger than before.

Static electricity tingled her skin. Her heart raced. *Move*, she willed herself, *move*. An orb rushed at her head-on.

She woke up, heart pounding. Eyes shut, she still felt the heat on her face. Just a dream…

Rolling onto her back, she opened her eyes.

White light. She stared straight into the mottled bluish face of an orb.

Erin yelped. She flung herself sideways off the bed onto the floor. Pains stabbed her left side, spreading outward from the bruise. She gasped and shut her eyes. When she opened them again, the light was gone.

Panting, wincing from the pain, she lay motionless on the floor for a minute or two until the agony subsided. She pushed up into a sitting position. The room was dark, empty. Her hands trembled. She took one deep breath after another. When the shaking stopped, she rose and turned on the overhead light at the switch by the door. The full-length mirror on the back of the door reflected her image back at her. Her cheeks were red.

She tiptoed to the nearest window, which looked south toward the woods. The moonless night obscured the trees. Above, the stars glittered. Had her nightmare spilled over into her first waking moments? Or had it been real?

The flush on her face suggested the latter. An orb followed her home.

Her stomach tightened. She shut off the light and crawled back into bed.

Tuesday, May 17

Erin sat at her desk, hands poised over the computer keyboard. Because she'd fallen asleep last night before eight o'clock, she woke up at 5:30 this morning. She'd already gone for a walk with Freya, eaten breakfast, and written a new post for her blog. Her entire regimen took an hour and fifteen minutes. Now she had plenty of time leftover to ponder Harry's book.

The notes in the margin were written in two separate hands, one tight and crisp, the other loose and sloppy. The sloppy hand reminded her of her own writing, albeit worse. Which writing was Harry's? The sloppy one, she thought, because his e-mails had seemed disorganized, with words left out here and there and sudden changes in subject matter. In Harry's book, the neat writing focused on correcting errors and outmoded translations in the text, such as when the author referred to the pharaoh Ikhnaton. The neat writer had corrected the name to its modern form, Akhenaten. The sloppy writer—Harry, she would assume—seemed to write in some sort of code. Time to break it.

If she could.

Navigating her web browser to a search engine, she considered what phrase to try. Harry's notes looked like nonsense, groupings of random letters arranged as if they formed words. Where he had drawn symbols, below each he had scrawled an alphanumeric code that always began with the letter G. Where no symbols appeared, his notes included only alphabetic characters. In two places, however, he had written notes in plain English. Well, sort of. The first instance was the note on the title page addressed to her. The second instance appeared on the first page of the first chapter, above the chapter number. The note said, "To whom it may concern, may you Blaze a trail to enlightenment through *veritas*."

Veritas meant truth in Latin. Why use Latin instead of English? Maybe he was a snob who liked to flaunt his Latin fluency. He hadn't seemed like a snob in his e-mails. The note must mean something in relation to his encoded writings.

She typed "encoded messages" and pressed the search button. A list of results loaded onscreen. Most of the pages discussed how to encode e-mail messages and other online content. At the bottom of the list, she found a page called "Cryptography 101." She clicked the link. The page provided a brief description of cryptography. It was, quite simply, the science of encrypting information to deter spies. Methods of encryption were known as ciphers, with keys required to use the ciphers. She clicked a link to a history of cryptography. A table of contents appeared on the screen, with each topic in the contents linking to another page. She skimmed the pages for substitution ciphers, the Gronsfeld cipher, rail fence ciphers, and the Caesar cipher. All worked in similar ways, by replacing the message text with other letters or numbers derived via a set formula. One of the simplest, the Caesar cipher developed by the Roman emperor Julius Caesar, shifted each letter in a word to another letter. For instance, shifting each letter in the word DOG forward by two letters changed the word to FQI. Of course, the person receiving the message must know how many steps to shift each letter and in which direction to shift it. If Harry used a Caesar cipher, she had no clue how many steps to increment each letter or whether he had incremented them backwards or forwards in the alphabet.

She perused the page for the Vigenère cipher. Although invented by Giovan Battista Bellaso in 1553, later historians erroneously credited the cipher to a crony of France's King Henry III. The crony's name was Blaise de Vigenère.

Blaise. She flipped back to Harry's note about a trail to enlightenment. "May you Blaze a trail," it said. Why was the word blaze capitalized? Had he used a homophone for Vigenère's first name as a clue, indicating his use of a Vigenère cipher? If so, maybe the rest of the sentence contained the key. According to the website, a Vigenère cipher used a table in which the first row consisted of the entire alphabet and each subsequent row contained the alphabet shifted forward one letter. A single row at the top and a single column at the left served as controls for encoding and decoding letters.

```
    A B C D E F G H I J K L M N O P Q R S T U V W X Y Z

A   A B C D E F G H I J K L M N O P Q R S T U V W X Y Z
B   B C D E F G H I J K L M N O P Q R S T U V W X Y Z A
C   C D E F G H I J K L M N O P Q R S T U V W X Y Z A B
D   D E F G H I J K L M N O P Q R S T U V W X Y Z A B C
E   E F G H I J K L M N O P Q R S T U V W X Y Z A B C D
F   F G H I J K L M N O P Q R S T U V W X Y Z A B C D E
G   G H I J K L M N O P Q R S T U V W X Y Z A B C D E F
H   H I J K L M N O P Q R S T U V W X Y Z A B C D E F G
I   I J K L M N O P Q R S T U V W X Y Z A B C D E F G H
J   J K L M N O P Q R S T U V W X Y Z A B C D E F G H I
K   K L M N O P Q R S T U V W X Y Z A B C D E F G H I J
L   L M N O P Q R S T U V W X Y Z A B C D E F G H I J K
M   M N O P Q R S T U V W X Y Z A B C D E F G H I J K L
N   N O P Q R S T U V W X Y Z A B C D E F G H I J K L M
O   O P Q R S T U V W X Y Z A B C D E F G H I J K L M N
P   P Q R S T U V W X Y Z A B C D E F G H I J K L M N O
Q   Q R S T U V W X Y Z A B C D E F G H I J K L M N O P
R   R S T U V W X Y Z A B C D E F G H I J K L M N O P Q
S   S T U V W X Y Z A B C D E F G H I J K L M N O P Q R
T   T U V W X Y Z A B C D E F G H I J K L M N O P Q R S
U   U V W X Y Z A B C D E F G H I J K L M N O P Q R S T
V   V W X Y Z A B C D E F G H I J K L M N O P Q R S T U
W   W X Y Z A B C D E F G H I J K L M N O P Q R S T U V
X   X Y Z A B C D E F G H I J K L M N O P Q R S T U V W
Y   Y Z A B C D E F G H I J K L M N O P Q R S T U V W X
Z   Z A B C D E F G H I J K L M N O P Q R S T U V W X Y
```

The process was relatively simple. To encode a message, choose a keyword. Locate the first letter of the keyword in the control row of the table and trace down the column beneath it. Next, find the first letter of the message text in the control column and trace across the row beside it until it intersected the column already selected. Now the first letter was encoded. Repeat the process for all letters in the message text, repeating the keyword as many times as necessary. The word DOG encoded with the keyword SLOBBER became VZU, since S cross-referenced with D translated into V, and so on.

She printed out the Vigenère table from the website, then got out a pad of paper and a pencil. Harry said to blaze a trail to enlightenment through *veritas*. Should she use the Latin word, or its English translation? She'd try both. Choosing a short note scrawled at the top of the opening page of the first chapter, she tried decoding the first line of the message with *veritas* as the keyword. She found the first letter of the keyword in the control row and traced down the column until she reached the first letter in the encoded message. Following that row leftward to the control column gave her the decoded letter.

The first word-like grouping translated as BNQRSS. Okay, *veritas* didn't work. She repeated the process using "truth" as the keyword. The resulting word sent a tingle down her neck.

DANGER.

A lump lodged in her throat. She stared at the word.

Swallowing, she decrypted the rest of the message.

```
DANGER COMING
TRUST ALEX
HE WILL FIND YOU
```

Alex. She knew no one by that name, online or off. If Harry thought she'd trust a stranger based on the word of another stranger, he was mistaken. No, she took it back. He wasn't mistaken, he was stark-raving mad.

He will find you. Was it a threat or a promise? Was Alex the man who attacked her yesterday? Though Harry seemed nice, she knew him solely from e-mail contact.

Decode the rest of the messages. Then she might understand.

Right now, though, she needed to get ready for her interview at ten o'clock. Deciphering this much of Harry's code took two hours. Anna Newman had e-mailed her directions to the "private residence" where the interview would take place, and where the job would be if she got it. Subtracting the forty-five-minute drive to the interview location left her half an hour to dress and spiff herself up.

"Morning."

Her mother stood in the doorway to the bedroom, one hand resting on the jamb.

Erin said, "Morning."

Eyebrows scrunched, Mom raised a finger to point at Erin's face. "Your scratch. It's gone."

Erin touched her right cheek where the scrape had been. Smooth. She ran to the door, pulling it open enough to see herself in the full-length mirror on the back. Her face was clean. Turning sideways, she lifted the left side of her shirt. The bruise where her attacker slugged her had vanished. She pushed up the sleeve of her shirt. The puncture mark and its accompanying scratch were gone.

Mom peeked around the door at her. "You okay?"

"Um, yeah." She pushed the door all the way open. "Guess I'm a faster healer than I thought."

"Maybe you were abducted last night."

Abducted. The word struck her brain like a hot spear. She swallowed. Hard.

Forcing a smile and a laugh, she said, "That only happens to you."

"Don't be so sure," Mom said. Turning to leave the room, she added, "Maybe it runs in the family."

Erin watched her mother walk down the hallway into the living room. Abducted. The word refused to leave her mind. She knew her mother's story, but it had nothing to do with her. The orb that hovered over her bed last night did nothing to her other than elicit a flush in her cheeks. Or had it done more? How could she explain her sudden recovery from her injuries?

While she dressed for her interview, she tried not to think about it, any of it. She failed.

Half an hour later, she marched out of her bedroom and through the living room to the front door. Just as she grasped the door knob in her hand, her mother called to her from the kitchen.

"Wait!"

Erin pulled the door halfway open and waited. Her mother, one hand behind her back, trotted across the living room. She held out the hand she'd hidden behind her back. Her palm and fingers cradled a Taurus 9mm semiautomatic pistol, slim and lightweight, specially designed for concealed carry. Her parents preferred the big .357 Magnum revolver they kept in their bedroom. However, back when she worked at the library, they'd bought the 9mm for her to carry because she often worked evenings until after dark. Since she never got around to obtaining a concealed carry license, the gun slumbered in a kitchen drawer for the past year and a half.

Her mother shoved the gun into her hand. "Here."

"I don't have a license."

Mom folded Erin's fingers around the gun's grip. "Take it anyway."

Erin nodded. She slipped the gun into her purse and walked out the door.

Revenant Point

Erin TURNED INTO THE DRIVEWAY, EASING THE CAR TO A STOP IN FRONT OF A fifteen-foot-wide wrought-iron gate. A sign at the head of the gravel road had warned "PRIVATE ROAD NO TRESPASSING," and the road sign had identified the two-track as Revenant Point Road. Twin pillars composed of gray bricks bookended the gate, separating it from the wrought-iron fence that disappeared into the woods on either side. Across the top of the gate, the iron twisted into letters that spelled out the name Revenant House.

Revenant. The meaning of the word flitted about at the edges of her mind, a smidgen out of reach. She'd have to look it up later in the dictionary.

Erin looked around for a button to push, an intercom, or something that might grant her access. She saw a single device, a camera mounted on the left-hand pillar. She waved at the camera.

A mechanism grumbled. The halves of the gate split, creeping inward. She drove through the entrance. The gravel driveway wound through a forest dense with evergreens whose boughs cast a permanent twilight on the path below. Two minutes passed before she rounded a ninety-degree curve, and the trees parted to reveal a massive house.

The gothic architecture and rectangular outline reminded her of a medieval castle, though other details seemed more Victorian. The house stretched perhaps a hundred feet across and at least forty feet high, with two full stories and a third attic story. Twin turrets capped the house at either side of a trio of gables. Below the center table, and the second story windows, stood the front entrance—a double door with inset stained-glass windows. In total, the front of the house sported twelve windows including the three attic windows. The windows stuck out from either end of the facade. Constructed of gray bricks like the gate pillars, the house felt more like a cliff face than a home. Here and there red bricks, arranged in diamond shapes, broke up the monotony of the sandstone.

The driveway segued into a circular path in front of the house. The green center of the circle hosted a small fountain made of gray stone, complete with angels reaching their wings heavenward. Another vehicle, a black Lexus SUV, sat directly in front of the front entrance. She parked behind that vehicle, and climbed out of the Explorer.

The front door of the house swung open. A woman walked out across the porch, down the steps toward Erin. The corners of her mouth curved up slightly as the woman proffered a hand to Erin. She grasped the woman's pale, slender hand.

"I'm Newman," the woman said with an English accent. "And you're five minutes early, Miss Turner. Excellent. Punctuality is essential, but earliness is a virtue Mr. Wessick appreciates."

"Mr. Wessick?" Erin asked.

"My employer—and, perhaps, soon to be yours as well."

Erin said nothing. What could she say? *Oh, gee, I really really hope so too!* Ugh. She would say that if she wanted to sound like a hopeless dork. No other words came to her, so she kept her mouth shut.

Newman towered at least six inches taller than Erin, thanks in part to the four-inch heels she wore. Erin's flats boosted her height by a mere half inch. Newman wore her black hair slicked back in a bun, save for her bangs that curved over her forehead in a flawless wave. Her eye makeup was in earth tones, her lipstick a matte color a shade pinker than her skin. Her navy blue suit hugged her body, while the skirt ended six inches above her knees.

Erin glanced at her own clothes. Her apricot pantsuit had wrinkled a bit on the drive over and scuffs marred her off-white shoes. She'd corralled her long, tawny hair into a barrette. Her bangs spiraled into curlicues despite all efforts to tame them. She'd long since given up on the notion of having perfect bangs like Newman's. Instead, she let hers go wild and brushed them to the sides. Her blouse was a tad tight, a situation she remedied by draping a scarf around her neck and down the front of her blouse. If she got this job, she'd buy some new clothes that fit right.

Newman spun on her stilettos. "Let me give you the grand tour."

Erin scrambled up the steps after her. Pausing halfway across the porch, Newman spread her arms to gesture at the entire house.

"The manor was built in 1855," Newman said, "by Lord Colban, who emigrated from England to this region seeking a remote new home. He was also rather obsessed with the occult, and believed the large copper deposits in the Keweenaw Peninsula would produce mystical energy conducive to séances and other occult rituals."

Above the front door, a stone gargoyle bared its teeth at them. Its blank eyes seemed to follow Erin as she trailed Newman through the doorway. Once she'd shut the doors, Newman launched into a speech she must've given many times before. Over the next fifteen minutes, Erin learned more about this house than she knew about her own home. The manor—not a mere house, Newman admonished—sat on the fifty-acre Revenant Point, a sliver of privately-owned land sticking out from the northern edge of the Keweenaw Peninsula. After the current owner, Samuel Wessick, bought Revenant Point and its namesake manor twelve years ago, he immediately started a restoration project that lasted five years. Now the house existed in, as Newman put it, "virtually Victorian condition."

Discounting closets and bathrooms, the house featured twenty-one rooms, with eleven downstairs and ten upstairs. Downstairs the porch, vestibule, and passageways featured pine floors restored to better than their original condition, with a modern stain to enrich the natural color. Newman's heels ticked on the wood flooring as they crossed the vestibule, a small and rather pointless room inside the front door, and strolled into the main passageway. Straight ahead, a staircase hugged the walls on its way up to the second floor. On the right side, under the second floor landing, was the door to the cellar. Paintings by artists whose names Newman rattled off as if Erin should recognize them hung here and there on the gray walls.

Jeez, her entire house would fit in the space occupied by the manor's drawing room, library, and parlor.

All the interior doors stood closed. Not necessarily sinister. This was someone's house, after all, someone who might cherish his privacy. She wouldn't like strangers gawking at her possessions.

Because of the closed doors, the "grand tour" constituted wandering up and down the main passageway through the downstairs. Although it looked like one passageway to Erin, Newman referred to the portion extending rightward from the staircase as the east passage and the opposite end, which stretched leftward from staircase, as the west passage. A north passage split off from the west passage heading toward the kitchen and some other rooms. They did not take that passage. They did not go upstairs. They did not open any doors.

A feeling niggled at her, one she couldn't quite place. Maybe the cavernous house had gotten to her. Maybe the feeling stemmed from Newman's comment about the original owner's interested in the occult. Or maybe the Keweenaw's copper deposits really did possess mystical powers.

Nah.

The tour ended in front of the main staircase. Erin gazed at the paintings on the walls. Landscapes, mostly. One still life. No people in any of the paintings she could see from her vantage point.

No people.

Portraits might hide in the closed rooms. She shouldn't assume the manor's artwork contained no images of human beings—at least until she saw inside the rooms. If she saw inside them. If hired, would she be allowed inside those rooms?

Well, they'd have to let her into the library.

"Ms. Newman," Erin said, "I was wondering—"

"Just Newman, please."

Had Erin insulted her? The woman spoke with little inflection, and her expression offered no reassurances either.

Newman said, "Did you have a question?"

Erin felt her cheeks flush. "Um, yes. I wondered, um, about the closed doors. Is the librarian archivist restricted to the library?"

A hint of a smile tugged at Newman's lips. "No, of course not."

Erin's cheeks felt ablaze. She half turned to look at a painting behind her, hoping to keep Newman from noticing the radioactive glow of her cheeks. Either it worked or Newman was too polite to say anything.

"Now," Newman said, "into the library for the interview."

They moseyed down the east passage to the library door, on the south side of the corridor. As Newman opened the unlocked door, Erin glanced upward. Above the door, a wood carving inlaid in the wall depicted two human figures clad in Egyptian-like garb. Facing each other, they held their hands up with the palms out, as if praising the object between them—an orb with rays of light emanating from it. A glowing orb.

No. It was the sun, of course. The carving showed ancient Egyptians worshiping the sun.

Catching movement out the corner of her eye, she looked right toward the main staircase. A shadow darkened the pine floor, a shadow in the shape of a human torso.

A chill traced down her back.

"Please come in," Newman said.

Erin glanced into the library, where Newman waited beside a wooden desk.

The shadow. Erin swiveled her head in the direction of the staircase.

The silhouette was gone.

She walked through the doorway, under the Egyptian sun, into the library.

Revenant House
Wednesday, May 18

VOICES MURMURED INSIDE THE LIBRARY, BEHIND THE CLOSED DOOR. SAMUEL Wessick unlocked the door to the drawing room, opposite the library, and entered the room. He shut and locked the door behind himself, then flipped the light switch. Two floor lamps ignited, one situated beside the couch a dozen feet from the door, the other stationed between the windows on the back wall. Beyond the windows, green grass extended for fifty feet, where the earth plummeted into a vertical cliff. Past the cliff, blue sky.

Desheret lounged on the couch, staring out the windows. She twisted her torso to peer at him over the couch's back. The hair of her long black wig flounced when she turned her head toward him. She stretched her left arm across the couch's top. A smile widened her mouth and narrowed her eyes. Her eyes seemed to glitter.

"Darling," she said, her voice soft and husky. "I've missed you."

His pulse quickened. He clasped his hands behind his back and exhaled slowly. The feeling subsided.

She arched an eyebrow. "Didn't you miss me?"

"Contrary to your assumption, I can exist outside of your presence."

"You're in a mood today, Samuel. Did the librarian turn you down?"

"Newman is interviewing her as we speak. She will accept."

"Now who's guilty of assuming too much?"

"It's a fact, not a presumption."

"Of course, my love. You always get what you want."

Not always. If Erin Turner refused his offer of employment, all his plans would disintegrate. He would be forced to inform those he worked for of his failure. The last time someone failed them, their response was less than sympathetic. He clenched his jaw. He must not fail. He could not fail. By whatever means required, he must bring Erin Turner into the fold.

The phone rang.

Wessick marched to the table at the end of the couch. At the opposite end, Desheret swung her legs up onto the couch and stretched them out toward him. The slit of her long skirt fell open, revealing her creamy flesh up to mid-thigh. The child had no subtlety.

Child. She was thirty years his junior, yes, but hardly a child. In this era, she qualified both to vote and to drink. Still, on occasion she behaved like a child.

The phone rang again.

He snatched up the receiver. "Yes."

Rassul's voice rasped through the phone line. "I have the item."

Wessick said, "Bring it here."

"I am outside, however I do not think you want me to come inside."

"Use the back entrance. Newman has her in the library."

"Should I bring it to the drawing room?"

"Take it to the usual place. *Now.*"

Wessick smacked the receiver down into the cradle. Rassul could not have known Wessick's location in the house, unless Rassul hid somewhere behind the house in view of the drawing room windows. The man was spying on him. For the pleasure of it—the same reason Rassul assaulted Erin Turner. The violence was unnecessary, Wessick explicitly forbade Rassul from using such measures.

Desheret said, "What's the matter?"

Wessick hissed, "Rassul, the insolent brute—"

He stopped himself. The anger was boiling inside him. He must relax. Whatever Rassul had done, the situation could be remedied. Using men like Rassul brought risks, which Wessick chose to accept because of the man's other talents.

Relax. He closed his eyes, loosening his grip on the phone. He inhaled, held the breath a heartbeat, then let it out slowly. The tension seeped out of his muscles, borne on the breath he released. The boiling cooled, as if the heat leeched out with the breath too.

He crossed in front of the couch and settled onto it. The cushioning gave under his weight. He leaned his head against the couch's back.

These days Rassul wore dress clothes, which Wessick selected for him. A man clad in khaki pants and shirt with filthy work boots looked like a thug—or a digger. When he'd met Rassul in Egypt six years ago, the man had been a digger for hire who traveled from one excavation to the next, putting his shovel to work for whichever archaeologist paid him the most. Wessick offered Rassul more money than any archaeologist could afford, along with a chance to utilize his less desirable talents.

He needed Rassul to blend in, though. Six years of working on the man's style deficiencies garnered nothing but headaches. Wessick smoothed the front of his silk shirt. Once a digger, always a digger.

Desheret wiggled her bare feet. Her toes raked across his thigh. Giggling, she tossed her head back to fling her wig's tresses away from her face. A necklace with an Eye of Horus pendant draped down her chest. Both the chain and the pendant were fashioned from 24-carat gold. She took the chain between her thumb and forefinger. Twirling the pendant, she smiled at him without parting her lips.

He asked, "What progress have you made?"

"We haven't seen each other in days." Feigning a pout, she dropped the pendant. "And you haven't kissed me hello yet."

He shoved her feet off the couch. "Let's forego the games this morning, please."

Her smile flattened. She squinted at him. If she were twenty years older, lines of tension would've fanned out from her eyes. The smoothness of youth spared her from such ugliness. He, however, felt the wrinkles cinching tight around his eyes and across his forehead as he crinkled his brow at her.

She slid across the cushions toward him. Planting one hand on the couch's back and the other on the cushion next to his right knee, she leaned in close. The necklace swung away from her chest, grazing his arm. He studied the Eye of Horus, one of the most sacred symbols in ancient Egypt, a symbol of regeneration and wholeness. A single eye, with a curved line above it representing an eyebrow. A straight line projected down from the bottom of the eye, along with another curved line that ended in a curlicue.

"You know," Desheret said, "you may be an attractive and brilliant man, Samuel, but you have a lot to learn about manners."

"Whose etiquette would you have me follow, ours or theirs?"

"Mine." She crooked a finger at him. "Say hello to me properly."

He took her face in his hands and kissed her. "Hello."

Flashing her contained smile, she sat back against the couch beside him.

"How goes your project?" he asked.

"You know how it goes. Like squeezing water from granite. Time isn't on our side."

"Yes, quite literally. But soon the situation may change."

"If you say so. And what are you up to today?"

"Waiting, as usual."

"Then we have time to play."

She hopped to her feet and trotted over to the bookshelf in the corner. From under a stack of papers, she extricated a cardboard box. When she shook the box, game pieces rattled inside it.

"No," he said. "It's time for you to go home."

"Only if you go with me."

"I've just returned from there. You should make an appearance, or they'll wonder what's become of you."

A scowl twisted her face. She tossed the box back onto the shelf. The pieces inside clattered. She stomped to the couch, flopping onto it with a thud that reverberated through the floor. "I hate it there."

"It won't take long. You must go."

"I know." She hugged herself. "Everything feels wrong there."

Slouched beside him, head down, arms wrapped around herself, she looked smaller. Almost like a child. Almost innocent.

He knew better. She was no innocent. Yet he also knew she would sustain the petulance until he assuaged her fears.

Drawing her into his arms, he whispered, "It will be over soon."

She pulled away from him, hopped to her feet, and sashayed out of the room.

Desheret could be equally as insolent as Rassul. Though he had yet to witness her darkest side for himself, he sensed she could also prove as dangerous as Rassul.

At least the plan advanced on schedule. By Saturday, he would have Erin Turner within his grasp. Soon after, he would possess the power so many had sought yet none had found. The power would belong to him.

A light sparked outside the window. He looked up at the vista beyond the glass. An orb of glowing light hovered at his eye level inches from the window. The orb hung suspended there for a second before contracting into nothing, too quickly for the human eye to comprehend.

"I know," he said. "It belongs to you."

But not for long.

ERIN GLANCED OUT THE BAY WINDOW, WHICH OVERLOOKED THE CIRCULAR driveway. She'd thought, for a second, she saw a light outside. Nothing there. Her eyes, or maybe her nerves, played tricks on her.

Thump. The noise came from elsewhere in the house and sounded close.

"Probably the cat," Newman said.

"Does anyone live here?"

"Mr. Wessick visits on occasion, but his main residence is in New York. If you take the position, you will be the sole permanent resident."

"I'd have to live here?"

"Yes. Mr. Wessick decided someone should live here full-time, to discourage burglars. You wouldn't be responsible for any housekeeping or maintenance of the grounds. Only the library."

Living here. Newman's e-mail said nothing about the residency requirement of the job. The manor was huge, empty, and evoked the aura of a museum. The library, with its shelves eight levels tall and its domed ceiling at least fifteen feet above the floor, felt like a cathedral to books. The ceiling looked like a Roman dome, an effect Newman told her was achieved with wallpaper, the same method used in Victorian times. The walls were painted dark green. In remodeling the manor, Mr. Wessick chose to equip the library with far more shelves than a true Victorian library would've had. That's why Newman called the manor "virtually Victorian." An enormous rug covered most of the wood floor.

In front of the bay window stood a mahogany desk with cute little skinny feet and no ornamentation, unlike the bookshelves. Erin sat, as straight as possible, in a padded wooden chair in front of the desk. Behind the desk, Newman occupied a modern executive's chair upholstered in leather. Indirect sunlight glistened on her hair, and on the polished desk. Erin squinted in the glare.

Newman asked, "Would living here be a problem for you?"

"Uh, no." Erin shifted in the chair. "No problem at all."

"Do you have any other questions?"

"No, I don't think so."

Newman arched an eyebrow at her.

Erin cleared her throat. She hated this part of interviews. The interviewer expected the applicant to ask insightful questions, thereby proving she deserved the job. If knowing the right questions to ask demonstrated worthiness, then Erin was totally unworthy. Faced with the do-you-have-any-questions question, her mind blanked.

Newman said, "Wouldn't you like to know the salary?"

Erin's cheeks heated up anew. "Yes, right."

Grabbing a pen out of a desk organizer, Newman scribbled on a small notepad. She ripped off the sheet, leaned across the desk, and held the paper out to Erin. She took the paper. On it Newman had scribbled a dollar figure.

Erin swallowed a gasp. The figure was three times what she made at her last job.

"Is the figure acceptable?" Newman asked.

Erin forced her lips into a slight smile she hoped looked nonchalant. "Yes, it's fine."

After the usual spiel—we have other people to interview, we'll call you, thanks for coming—Newman led her out of the library into the passageway. Erin glanced up at the relief of Egyptians worshiping the sun. Those two figures were the only people visible in the manor's artwork, or rather, in the artwork visible from the public areas. Instead of worrying about the lack of human figures in the art, maybe she ought to consider why the lack of people bothered her. The manor's owner, Mr. Wessick, might simply prefer landscapes.

Nevertheless, her stomach tightened. The closed doors, the Egyptian relief, the ridiculously high salary…

Get a grip.

As they passed the main staircase, Erin asked, "Will there be a second interview? With Mr. Wessick, I mean."

"No." Newman spun left into the vestibule. "You will likely never meet Mr. Wessick. He is quite busy."

Outside on the porch, Newman bid her goodbye. Erin climbed into the Explorer and started down the driveway. Passing through the open gates, she noticed once again the wrought-iron letters spelling out the manor's name, Revenant House.

Revenant. It meant ghost. The word might have other meanings as well, ones she couldn't remember. "Ghost" fit the house and its creepy vibe—and its original owner, old what's-his-name, the occultist. What rituals did he and his cohorts conduct in the manor? What dark forces did they attempt to contact? What's-his-name might hang around the manor to this day, incorporeal, deceased yet unwilling to abandon his home. A resident spirit would explain the manor's name—unless Revenant House was its original name.

She eased the car out onto Revenant Point Road. A light flashed in the rear-view mirror. Slowing the car, she studied the mirror's image. The road dead-ended about a block past the gate. There, a dark blue sedan sat parked alongside the road. A figure, probably a man, swung the driver's door shut after himself. Sunlight glinted off the side window. The first flash must've occurred when he opened the door.

Was he following her?

She floored the accelerator. Gravel sprayed up around the Explorer. The car shot forward down the road. In the rearview mirror, the other car's image shrank into nothing.

The lump in her throat lingered.

A FEW MINUTES LATER, SHE STEERED THE CAR ONTO THE HIGHWAY. A MINUTE later a dark blue sedan showed up in her rearview mirror. A different car. She hoped.

The other driver flashed his headlights twice.

Erin decelerated, pulling over onto the shoulder to let the other car pass.

The other driver slowed too. He flashed his headlights again. Erin waved for him to pass. The other driver stopped his car in the middle of the road. Okay, if he wanted to play it that way…

Erin slammed her foot down on the accelerator. The car surged forward, pinning her to her seat. She swerved back onto the pavement and watched in the rearview mirror as the other car dwindled into a speck. Thank heavens. She let out the breath she'd held.

The blue sedan roared up behind her. The other driver honked his horn. He jabbed his finger up toward the sky.

Her heart thudded. She gripped the steering wheel so tightly her fingers ached. A squirrel dashed out into the road between the cars. The other driver braked. As the Explorer rushed ahead, Erin swerved around a curve. *Dear lord, please don't let the car roll.* Past the curve now, she kept the speedometer at eighty. The blue sedan didn't reappear.

Her hands trembled. Tears stung her eyes, blurred her vision.

Up ahead, a sign indicated a rest stop. She pulled into the semi-circular drive, stopping in front of the bathrooms, where a stand of trees concealed her from the road. The bathroom, she needed to use the bathroom. Instinctively, she grabbed her purse as she swung the door open and got out.

A car whizzed past on the highway. She heard it but didn't see it. The blue sedan, she hoped, heading in the wrong direction. Away from her.

She shuffled to the bathroom, ducked inside, and shut and locked the door behind her. The bathroom was more of an outhouse, with a stench emanating from the toilet despite the closed the lid. She breathed through her mouth. Forget this. She left the bathroom.

Next to the shed that housed the bathroom, a gravel trail led off into the woods. At the head of the trail a small wooden sign announced "waterfall" above an arrow pointing down the trail. She could just make out the sound of water gushing in the distance. A walk might clear her head, calm her nerves. She wandered down the trail. The gushing grew louder, turning into a dull roar. After a minute, maybe two, the trail swung right and the trees gave way to a clearing around a waterfall no more than fifteen feet high. The waterfall spilled into a pool thirty feet wide, which flowed into a stream. A wooden bridge let visitors ford the stream, crossing onto another trail on the opposite bank. No sound except the waterfall's broke the silence.

Erin took two steps onto the bridge. Looking down over the railing, she stared into the swirling waters where the waterfall's pool emptied into the stream. Reflections of the trees, the bridge, her face all shimmered and twirled in the eddies as if she peered through a portal into another reality where the laws of physics collapsed.

The waterfall rumbling. Her face warping. Water bubbles dancing around the image.

Orbs of light.

She jerked her head up and glanced around. No orbs. She hadn't actually seen any lights reflected in the water. Had she?

Crunch, crunch. Footsteps on the trail. Someone was coming.

The gun. In her purse. She ripped open the zipper, dove her hand inside, and yanked out the Taurus. Flicking off the safety, she chambered a round.

A figure exited the woods on the trail. The man stopped a few feet from the bridge. When he spotted the gun, he raised his hands palm out.

He said, "I'm not here to hurt you."

"What color is your car?"

He sighed. "Yes, I was the one following you."

The stranger looked a few years older than her, probably in his late thirties. His light brown hair was cut short, like her father wore his hair during his military days. The stranger stood six feet tall, with a physique beefy yet not overweight. He wore gray slacks, a powder-blue dress shirt, dark brown leather hiking boots, and a leather jacket the same color as his boots. He looked like a businessman on vacation rather than a stalker. He was... attractive. Sort of. If you liked maniacs.

She did *not*.

"Who the hell are you?" she asked.

He scrunched one side of his mouth. "Alex MacKay."

Trust Alex, Harry told her in his coded message. This Alex? No, some other Alex who chased her down the highway beeping and waving his arms. She had so many of them to choose from.

She said, "Why are you stalking me, Mr. MacKay?"

"Actually, it's doctor."

"Fine. Dr. MacKay—"

"Call me Alex."

She glared at him. "If you want to be called Alex, why did you correct me when I called you mister?"

"For accuracy."

Slowly, he lowered his hands.

She crinkled her eyebrows at him. He let his arms dangle at his sides, his lips no longer twisted. She glanced down at her right arm, in which she held the gun. Her arm hung down, the gun's barrel aimed at the ground. She didn't remember dropping her arm. Dammit.

She raised the gun.

Alex said, "I take it you haven't heard from Harry. He was supposed to prepare you."

"For what?"

"Me."

Harry might've meant his encoded note to prepare her. Then again, Alex might've written the note and mailed the book to her himself.

Alex took a step toward her. "I'm not stalking you."

Yeah, right. She waved the gun in the direction of the path behind him.

"Walk that way," she said.

He opened his mouth to argue. She shook her head.

Sighing, he turned and trudged back up the path. She followed ten feet behind him, close enough to keep an eye on him, far enough to duck out of the way if he lunged at her. She felt like one of those tough chick characters in the movies—not like a fraud pretending to be tough, but like a mortal possessed by the spirit of such a movie character. Odd.

Neither of them spoke on the way back to the parking lot. At the trailhead, Alex paused with his back to her. Over his shoulder, he said, "What now?"

"You get in your car and leave."

"I need to talk to you. It's vital."

"I'm sure." She walked around beside him, still ten feet away. "Get in your car. Drive away. Do not follow me."

"Don't you want to know *why* I was following you?"

"Not really."

He looked at her sideways. "You didn't see it, did you? The glowing orb above your car."

Her stomach flip-flopped. She swallowed the lump in her throat.

"That's why I was waving my arms like an idiot," he said.

"Why were you following me in the first place? I saw you outside the gates to Revenant House."

"I was following Harry's instructions."

She wavered her index finger over the trigger then pulled it away, resting it on the barrel. Could she shoot him? Could she shoot anyone? So far life hadn't forced her to make the decision. In a life-threatening situation, with adrenaline coursing through her, maybe the decision would prove easy. Right now she lacked sufficient motivation.

"Like I said," she told him, "get in your car and drive away. Do not follow me. Do not put some sneaky tracking device on me or my car so you can find me later. Understand?"

He nodded.

"Good."

Alex lifted his foot to take a step toward her and his car behind her. His gaze landed on the gun. He froze mid step. Scrunching his mouth again, he spun around to march past the front of the Explorer and down the other side to his car. She watched him open the driver's door, climb in, and shut the door. The sedan's engine rumbled to life. Alex steered his car around hers, out of the parking lot, and onto the highway. The engine noise faded into silence.

She got in the Explorer and left.

Oramo's Cafe
Shadow Bay

ERIN FOUND CHLOE SITTING IN A BOOTH BY THE FRONT WINDOWS. THE sunlight set fire to Chloe's red hair and, with her short haircut, she seemed to have a fiery halo around her face. At twenty-five, Chloe could've passed for fifteen. Her round face, coupled with the smoothness of her pale, freckled skin, lent her the complexion of a teenager. Chloe dressed like a teenager too—a black spaghetti string tank top, low-rise blue jeans, platform sandals, and three stud earrings in each ear. As Erin walked past Chloe to climb into the booth, she glimpsed the butterfly tattoo on the back of Chloe's right shoulder.

"Hey, girl," Chloe said. "How was the interview?"

Erin shrugged. She plunked down into the booth, onto the bench opposite Chloe.

"Aw, come on," Chloe said. "I'm sure they loved you."

"My resume stinks. I stink at interviews. My wardrobe stinks. What's not to love?"

Chloe leaned forward, sniffing. "I don't smell anything."

"Very funny. I'm not sure I'd want the job anyway. That place gives me the creeps."

"Tell me all about it while we eat. I ordered our usual."

A waitress approached with a tray bearing their usual order, turkey sandwiches with potato chips and root beer. When the waitress left, Erin recounted her morning between mouthfuls. Hearing herself tell the story, it sounded ridiculous. Creepy old mansion. Mysterious closed doors. A wealthy, enigmatic boss. No one would believe the story, except her parents and Chloe.

When she finished the story, Erin said, "They probably won't offer me the job."

"Of course they will. And you've *got* to take it. I'm dying to see the house."

Erin wolfed down the last few bites of her sandwich.

Chloe made a face.

"What?" Erin asked.

"Your negative energy is bumming me out."

"Gee, thanks."

"I didn't mean it in a bad way. Go to the beach or something and chill out, maybe it'll tone down your aura so you'll stop eating like a sumo wrestler."

Chloe's sandwich lay half eaten on her plate, beside a pile of chips that had diminished in size by perhaps a few chips. Erin's plate was empty, her glass one-third full.

"I was hungry," Erin said. "Being stalked will do that to you."

"Stalked?"

Erin related her encounter with Alex MacKay. She still couldn't believe her behavior. Looking back on the encounter, she also couldn't believe Alex MacKay gave up so easily when he insisted he must talk to her about something "vital." Maybe the gun scared him. He hadn't acted scared. Her tough chick impersonation apparently fooled no one but herself.

She omitted the part where Alex claimed a glowing orb tailed her. If she mentioned that, then she'd have to mention her sighting on the beach.

"Whoa," Chloe said, "would you really have wasted him?"

"I don't know."

Resting her elbows on the table, Chloe bent forward and grinned. "Was he cute?"

Erin fiddled with the salt shaker. She shrugged.

"He was cute, wasn't he?" Chloe giggled. "I wouldn't mind being stalked by a hunk."

"Stalking is not a prelude to dating."

"But he knows Harry, the old guy you met online."

"I have no idea how old Harry is. I know nothing about him. So why should I trust someone claiming to be his friend? And don't say because Alex is cute."

"Sooo," Chloe said, "you admit he's cute."

Erin gritted her teeth and hissed out a breath between them.

Chloe leaned back in her seat. "Did he say why he was following you?"

"Uh…no."

They talked for another fifteen minutes, about nothing in particular. Chloe paid for their meal, as usual—and Erin let her, as usual. Despite Chloe's lack of employment, and her live-in boyfriend's low-paying job, the girl never wanted for money. Her parents, who amassed a fortune by running a chain of office supply stores out west somewhere, provided a cash flow whenever necessary. Chloe rarely said much about her parents, and Erin didn't push the subject. Chloe's boyfriend Greg sometimes did push, though. Erin recalled several times, back when they both worked at the library, when Chloe showed up to work in a tizzy because Greg had been bugging her for details about her past and her parents. "The past is done," Chloe always said, and though Erin echoed the sentiment in general, she understood Greg's desire to learn more about the girl who shared his home and life. Greg and Chloe had a weird relationship, for sure.

Outside the restaurant, Erin and Chloe paused. Erin had parked to the left. To the right, five cars down, she spotted Chloe's cherry-red Volkswagen Beetle.

A man dressed in jeans and a gray T-shirt hunched beside the Beetle, his butt resting on the car. The man ran a hand through his golden-blonde hair.

"What's Greg doing here?" Erin asked.

Chloe glanced at her paramour. A scowl darkened her face for a heartbeat. As quickly as the scowl came, it vanished, replaced by a smile.

"My sweetie came to meet me," Chloe said. "He likes to surprise me."

Still slouched against the Beetle, hands jammed in his jeans pockets, Greg glowered at the sidewalk.

Chloe called his name. When he looked up, she grinned and waved at him. Greg's expression didn't change. He pushed away from the car, his gaze locked on Chloe.

Erin called, "Hi, Greg."

He said nothing. His gaze didn't waver from Chloe. His lips were flattened in a line, his forehead creased from the tension of his expression.

"Uh-oh," Chloe said, "bad day at work."

They said goodbye, and Chloe made Erin promise to call her if "the cutie-pie," by which she meant Alex MacKay, reappeared. Chloe sauntered toward Greg. She tried to hug him, but Greg twisted away from her.

Erin walked to the Explorer. Driving down the street past Chloe's Beetle, she glimpsed the couple standing on the sidewalk. Greg's eyes bulged as he gesticulated with both hands, stabbing his right index finger at Chloe's chest. His face turned red.

The driver in the car behind Erin honked his horn. Realizing she'd slowed to a near stop, she pressed down on the accelerator. She glanced at the right side mirror just in time to see Greg slam the Beetle's passenger door closed after Chloe. The little car rocked with the concussion.

Lover's tiff? Chloe mentioned a few times before that Greg disliked the money stream flowing from her well-off parents. After one of Chloe's remarks, Erin commented that a man who wouldn't marry his girlfriend had no business whining about where she got money. Chloe snapped back that she wouldn't marry him if he asked because "marriage is dressed-up slavery." The anger drained away in an instant, though, and Chloe's normal cheeriness flooded in behind it.

Erin never mentioned the M word again.

TWENTY MINUTES LATER, ERIN TURNED THE LAST CORNER BEFORE HOME. A couple minutes after that she drove out from under the canopy of the woods. Spotting the house on her right, she noticed a dark blue sedan in the driveway and a shape on the front steps. A person. After she pulled into the driveway and parked the Explorer beside the sedan, the figure on the steps resolved into a familiar countenance. Alex MacKay sat on the top step, with his feet perched on the lower step, petting Freya. The dog kept her back feet on the ground with her front feet on the step below where Alex sat. Wagging her tail, Freya licked Alex's hand.

Traitor.

Erin hooked the strap of her purse over her neck so that it hung diagonally across her torso. Climbing out of the car she marched through the gate and across the yard to the steps. Alex looked up at her.

"What the hell are you doing here?" she said. "I told you not to follow me or track me."

"I did neither."

A half-suppressed smile tugged at the corners of his mouth. He scratched behind Freya's ears with his right hand while his left rested on his thigh, fingers dangling.

She folded her arms across her chest. "I suppose you were driving around and just happened to find yourself here."

"No, I came here on purpose. But I neither followed you nor tracked you electronically."

"Then how exactly did you get here?"

"I drove."

She felt her face flush. She dropped her hands to her sides, fisting them. His restraint of the smile faltered a bit. She tapped out a drumroll on the cement walkway with the toe of her shoe.

He stopped smiling, suppressed or otherwise.

"Sorry," he said. "I didn't mean to upset you. Harry gave me your address. I printed out a map from the Internet and drove here this morning, then I followed you to Revenant House."

A lump materialized in her throat. She swallowed it. Alex followed her all the way from her house to Revenant Point without her noticing. Anyone could've followed her, at any time. How many others did she fail to catch tailing her?

A gust of wind rattled the gate. She glanced at it. "You invited yourself into the yard?"

Alex shook his head. "I honked the horn and your mother let me in."

Her parents met him? She felt the lump, cold and hard, re-forming in her throat.

Alex rose to his feet, stepping down onto the walkway. "Your parents interrogated me, politely. I assume I passed the test, since your father said I could wait out here for you."

"What did you tell them?"

He stared at her for a moment.

She stared back.

"Oh," he said, "you mean about us. I told them we met online when you applied to work as a volunteer at archaeology digs run by the foundation I work for."

Us. He used the word as if they were a team. As if she trusted him. She settled a hand on her purse, feeling her gun inside it.

"Who do you work for?" she asked.

"It's, um, complicated." He glanced over his shoulder at the house. "Maybe we should talk about this somewhere else. Could we go for a walk?"

She pushed past him and clomped up the steps to the front door. Opening the door a few inches, she shouted through the gap.

"I'm going for a walk with—" She hesitated. "Alex."

From deeper in the house her mother's voice echoed back. "Okay. Have fun."

She shut the door.

"All right," she said. "Let's take a stroll, Dr. Alex."

TEN MINUTES LATER THEY'D TRAVELED HALFWAY TO CANADA, OR AT LEAST that's how it felt. Alex peered through the forest on either side of the walking trail down which Erin led him. The trail, twice as wide as his feet, meandered through the woods behind the Turner house. Aspens, birches, and evergreens formed a canopy overhead. Deeper into the forest, shadows prevailed among the wild ferns, weeds, and moss that concealed the trees' roots. In the distance, a woodpecker hammered.

Erin took wide steps at a brisk pace. Alex followed her at a near trot to keep up. Either she had an urgent appointment in the primeval depths of the forest or she enjoyed testing his stamina. Though he hated exercise for exercise's sake, he got enough of a workout in the commission of his duties to think of himself as reasonably fit—or so he thought, until now. Erin outpaced him in spite of wearing a business suit and dress shoes, not exactly recommended attire for the woods. Her light brown hair flopped up and down with every step, like swells on a stormy sea. Each time the sunlight struck her hair, it ignited golden-red highlights. She fisted and unfisted her hands in rhythm with her footfalls. Though she exuded anger, directed at him, he couldn't stop himself from tracing her figure with his gaze. Her shape was the epitome of feminine, neither plump nor thin, rounded out by curves in all the right places.

A droplet of sweat trickled down his left temple.

He grasped Erin's forearm. She halted, half turning toward him. Her gray eyes glinted with pale blue highlights.

"You haven't spoken a word," he said, "since we left the house. How long do you intend for this forced march to go on?"

"Until I feel like speaking to you."

"I understand you're angry—"

"You've been stalking me."

"Point your gun at me if it makes you feel better."

She puckered her lips, glancing at his hand, which still grasped her arm.

He let go.

In retrospect, following her may have been a mistake. The cloak-and-dagger routine was new to him, so naturally he screwed it up, but the stakes were too high to handle things out in the open. The dearth of traffic on the highway simplified his task. He kept a good distance between Erin's car and his without losing track of her. Even when she rounded a curve, and he lost sight of her for a moment, he reacquired her with little trouble once he'd maneuvered around the curve. Parking outside Revenant House seemed like a good idea at the time. He'd thought he could see Erin coming down the driveway before she saw him, but the trees blocked his view, forcing him to get out of the car to watch for her. That was how she saw him. Some secret agent he made.

Now, as she unpuckered her lips, she met his gaze straight on.

He shifted his weight onto his left foot and the inside of his forearm brushed against the bulge concealed under his jacket, a Glock 9mm pistol berthed in a shoulder holster. The man who'd convinced him to buy the gun prided himself on his status as a mercenary. Alex liked the gun. He'd started to like the man who'd recommended it. But he would never get used to working on the boundary of illegality.

Or sometimes a hair over the border.

He was a mercenary. No use denying the truth.

His employers hadn't authorized this mission, mainly because he'd had no time to contact them for approval. On recruiting him into their organization last year, they told him he could act on his own discretion if circumstances required immediate action. He'd decided on his own to undertake this bit of espionage.

Ferreting out Oded Rassul and his master, discovering the man's objectives, might prove vital to the overall mission.

Where was Rassul now? The slimy worm slipped out of Alex's grasp, metaphorically speaking, twice. Russell would pop in, steal an artifact, and pop out again without leaving a trail. During the ten months he'd tracked Rassul, Alex realized the man worked toward a goal. With total focus, he strived to achieve his mission. Each city or town he visited played some role in the plan, yet Alex had yet to determine the nature of Rassul's task. He knew where Rassul went, what he stole, what establishments he burgled, but nothing more. Alex had a hunch, founded on no evidence, that Rassul's home base lay somewhere nearby on the Keweenaw Peninsula.

Alex yawned. Although he'd slept a little on the flight from Berlin to New York, sleep eluded him on the subsequent flights from New York to Philadelphia and Philadelphia to Detroit. The drive up from Detroit intensified the fatigue. The pit stop in Detroit left him no time for snoozing, since he'd spent all of two hours in the city.

"Am I boring you?" Erin asked.

Alex shook his head. "Jet lag."

He took a deep breath, rubbed his neck, and straightened his posture. Time to dive in.

"Your life may be in danger," he said. "Harry was supposed to explain all of this to you, but I guess I'll have to do."

Erin blinked. "My life may be in danger? You can't just blurt that out and move on to the next topic."

"Sorry."

"Why on earth would anyone want to kill me? I'm as unimportant as a person can get."

"You clearly have more value than you think. It probably has something to do with your blog."

"People leave rude comments on my blog, but I don't see how my rants about ancient history or the paranormal could incite anyone to come after me in person. Rude commenters never use their real names, which tells me they're cowards."

"Somebody else must've read your blog. Harry did."

She huffed out a breath. "I am sick and tired of hearing about this blasted Harry person. I have never met or spoken to him. Why should I trust you or believe anything you say when your only reference is a complete stranger?"

A new wave of weariness hit him. He scuffled to the nearest tree and leaned against it.

Erin eyed him, chewing the inside of her cheek.

"Oded Rassul is here," Alex said. "He's a nasty piece of work who's in the employ of someone even nastier. I don't know who yet. "

"Rassul sounds Arabic. Oded is Hebrew though, isn't it?"

"Yes. His mother was an Israeli archaeologist. His father was Egyptian, worked in the Cairo Museum for awhile."

"And your guy?"

"He's not my guy. Rassul was a digger, until six years ago."

"A digger."

"A manual laborer who helps out at archaeological excavations. Digs with a shovel, mostly, hence the term."

"I know what a digger is. What I don't understand is why one would want to kill me."

"As I said, he was a digger until six years ago. Then—poof!—he's gone."

"Poof?"

Alex averted his gaze to the forest. How clever of him to use a pansy word like poof when trying to impress a beautiful woman. Maybe he should write a letter instead of speaking to her. He usually did better with the written word.

He rather doubted she'd agree to wait while he composed a missive.

"Rassul went off the radar," Alex said. "He abandoned a job in the Valley of the Kings and nobody's heard from him since, not even his mother."

"What else do you know about him?"

"He's a thief and a murderer. That's all I need to know."

ERIN STUDIED ALEX. HE LEANED AGAINST THE TREE AS IF HE MIGHT FALL OVER without its support. If he passed out, she was not carrying him back to the house. He could lie in the woods until paramedics showed up to retrieve him.

What a horrible thing to think. Well, he was a stalker after all.

"What did he steal?" Erin asked.

"Artifacts." Alex pushed away from the tree. "I first caught up with the little worm in Tokyo, where he stole a Jomon figurine from a museum."

"You caught him stealing it?"

"No, I saw him casing the museum in the afternoon. The Jomon artifact vanished that night."

"Let me guess, it went poof."

Unlike a moment earlier when he'd used the word poof, he didn't blush. Instead he rolled his shoulders back, straightening his spine. He looked her square in the eyes.

He said, "Exactly."

"What?"

"A security guard was about fifty feet away from the doors to the Jomon Hall, where the figurine was kept. He saw a flash of light inside the hall. When he rushed in to investigate, nobody was there. But the artifact was gone."

"Poof."

"Precisely. And a dozen other artifacts have disappeared the same way, always when Rassul is town and always after he's paid a visit to the establishment earlier in the day."

"What other artifacts has he taken?"

"He's taken thirteen in total. Celtic, Egyptian, Olmec, prehistoric American. He's gone after figurines, amulets, scrolls, you name it. Some were stolen from museums but most were housed in private collections."

Jomon. Egyptian. Olmec. On her blog she'd contemplated the possibility of a connection between ancient cultures, especially those of Egypt and the Americas. The Jomon, a mysterious culture from Japan, dated back thousands of years—just like the ancient American cultures and Egypt. She recalled seeing photos online of Jomon statues that looked like bug-eyed aliens, similar to statues from predynastic Egypt.

She asked, "What do you think Rassul wants with me?"

"I wish I knew. On your blog, you talk about connections between ancient cultures. Rassul steals artifacts that have to do with those cultures."

"Lots of people blog about those topics."

"Harry investigated the connections firsthand, and he contacted you. Now he's dead."

"What? He's dead?"

"I assume he is. He never stays out of contact for more than a day, and I haven't heard from him since Thursday."

Harry, who studied the same connections she pondered, was missing and presumed dead. Like the artifacts, Harry had gone poof.

Her stomach flip-flopped.

"Wait a minute," she said. "Harry e-mailed me yesterday. He can't be dead."

"He sometimes uses an e-mail scheduling service to send messages while he's away from his computer. When I say he never stays out of contact long, I mean phone or in-person contact."

Harry mailed her the book on Friday. From Kingsford. Alex would surely want the information—and the book. Tell him. Don't tell him. Tell him. Don't tell him. The options ricocheted in her mind, loud as gunshots.

"Tell me," she said, "why are you interested in me?"

"I'm not. I want to stop Rassul, protecting you is a secondary objective."

A means to an end. That was how he saw her.

"Right," she said. "Well, at least tell me Harry's full name."

"Harriman is his last name. Harry's a nickname."

"What's his first name?"

Alex hesitated. "He'd kill me if I told you. He hates his first name."

Enough of this. Dr. Alex MacKay could search for his primary objective, whatever it was, without her cooperation. Not that he'd asked for it. Not that she'd help him if he did ask.

She marched past him down the trail, back the way they'd come.

"Where are you going?" he asked. "I need your help."

Erin froze. Her heart skipped a beat. Why, she couldn't imagine.

Make nice, urged that annoying little voice in her head. She told it to shut up.

Without turning around, she asked, "What kind of a doctor are you anyway?"

"I'm an archaeologist."

"A rude, presumptuous one."

"I know. I'm sorry."

Erin turned to face him. "You sure apologize a lot. For a rude person, I mean."

Alex shrugged one shoulder. "I say the wrong thing. Frequently. It's a character flaw."

His expression reminded her of the look Freya gave her after the dog flung both front paws onto her belly and accidentally knocked her flat on her butt. Ugh, she felt like a heel. The heel of a callused, filthy, repulsive foot.

"Just don't lick my face," she said.

"Pardon?"

"Never mind." She stuffed her hands in her pants pockets. "How about we start over?"

His expression brightened. "Okay. First we need to figure out why Rassul's interested in you."

A gust of wind rocked them both. The leaves of the quaking aspen trees sizzled, sounding like rain.

"I'm tired," she said. "Let's do that tomorrow."

From his pocket, he brought out a tiny notepad. He jotted something down on it. Ripping off the sheet, he strode toward her and handed her the paper.

"My cell phone number," he said.

She took the paper.

He looked past her shoulder. His body stiffened. He stopped blinking.

Twisting around, she glanced down the trail.

Six feet above the ground in the center of the trail, its outer ring burning white, floated an orb.

Erin shivered. Goosebumps prickled her arms as a memory unreeled in her mind. Waking in the night, an orb hovering over her face, its glow heating her cheeks. The next morning, her wounds gone.

Alex crossed his arm in front of her, settling his hand on her right forearm. Gently he pulled.

"Get behind me," he said. "Slowly."

She sidled past him. He situated himself between her and the orb fifteen feet away. She peeked around his shoulder. A chill kissed her cheek as her skin brushed against the leather of his jacket sleeve. She slipped the gun out of her purse, holding it with the barrel pointed at the ground, her index finger hovering over the trigger.

The glowing ball hung there. Its mottled interior sparkled.

The orb rushed toward them. It halted an arm's length from Alex.

He bent his right arm to cover her, with his hand touching her hip.

She whispered, "Maybe we should run."

"Might make it angry."

The orb shot straight up into the sky.

Erin tilted her head back. The orb was gone.

Alex dropped his shoulder and ducked his head to look down at her. His face was a little above hers, mere inches away. He stared into her eyes. The sun's rays accentuated the multiple shades of blue in his irises. His hand still rested on her hip, his fingertips exerting a delicate pressure. She shuddered, as she had on first seeing the orb, though this shudder felt different—warm, and not entirely unpleasant. She ought to move, but she couldn't.

In a soft voice Alex said, "Are you okay?"

Unable to speak, she nodded.

Alex withdrew his arm, stepped a couple feet away, and faced her.

The shudder subsided. She folded her arms over her chest, to see if she could. Her muscles obeyed. Perhaps her voice had returned too. One way to find out.

She cleared her throat. "You don't seem upset by what we just saw."

"No."

"Why not?"

"I've seen strange phenomena before."

Though the shiver had faded, the sensations accompanying it lingered. The desire to trust him. The urge to confide in him. The orb might've wielded some kind of mind control over her, an influence she couldn't detect that nonetheless provoked an involuntary response in her. Yeah, that must be it.

Coward.

She tucked the gun inside her waistband, flush against her back.

"I should leave," Alex said.

"No."

The word came out before she could stop it. The orb's aftereffects? She wished. All right. She would admit the truth, if only to herself. She wanted him to stay. He was, after all, the one person she could confide in without fretting over whether the news might induce panic. If she told her parents everything that happened, they'd worry about her. Chloe probably would too, or she might simply not believe any of it. Alex believed. His reaction to the orb, and his statement about seeing strange phenomena, demonstrated his belief. She could tell him. Everything.

She walked past Alex, gesturing for him to follow. "I want to show you something."

Two hours later they sat at her desk. Alex had brought a chair from the dining room which he plunked down next to her desk chair, where she sat with hands folded on her lap. He flipped through the book Harry sent her, *A Spiritualist History of Ancient Egypt.*

Her parents had waylaid them on their way into the house to invite Alex to stay for dinner. He'd helped her father barbecue hamburgers, bonded with Dad over bad jokes, offered to wash the dishes for her mother, and chatted with Mom about UFOs. After dinner Alex went out to his car to get his "attaché." She decided he meant a briefcase. He used words she'd never heard another human being use in conversation before. A couple minutes later he returned carrying a soft-sided leather briefcase with a top flap secured by a metal clasp. Who called a briefcase an attaché?

He was an archaeologist. Academics loved their big, fancy words.

Sighing, Alex slapped the book closed. He grumbled, "Cryptic old coot."

"I cracked his code, by the way."

Alex glanced at her sideways. "You did."

"Don't have to sound quite so surprised."

She snatched the book from him and fanned through the pages. The page edges were yellowed. A few were torn. A number of the pages bore the tell-tale crease mark on the upper right corner where someone marked the pages by folding over the corners. The crease marks testified to the defacement, though the pages lay flat now.

All the pages but one. The corner of page 298 preserved its fold.

She opened the book to that page. The corner was folded into a perfect little right triangle. Someone, presumably Harry, underlined in blue ink a line in the middle of a paragraph. The line read, "To date, no one has discovered the tomb of Ikhnaton." In the margins, the neat note-maker had corrected the spelling to Akhenaten. Gilbert Covington, the book's author, employed the Greek versions of ancient Egyptian names where possible, an old-fashioned style that few scholars clung to today. Covington also used an outdated transcription of Akhenaten's name, referring to him as Ikhnaton. Beneath the correction, the messy writer—Harry—had drawn a series of pictographs, four to five symbols on each line, a dozen lines of pictographs total. Some symbols she recognized as Egyptian hieroglyphs. Alternating lines consisted of hieroglyphs, with the remainder constituting a pictographic script unfamiliar to her. The unknown script reminded her of something, but she couldn't place what. Although she'd taught herself to read Egyptian hieroglyphs, her skills were far from expert. She could figure it out, though doing so would take time.

Gee, she could ask the archaeologist sitting right next to her.

She only had Alex's word he wasn't working with Rassul. Actually, he'd never really denied working with Rassul, or even mentioned disliking the man. But he called Rassul "the little worm."

Rassul stole artifacts from various cultures, according to Alex, including Egyptian and prehistoric American relics. The book Harry sent her dealt with Egyptian history, specifically the Amarna Period, a time of mystery and chaos modern historians understood far less than they liked to admit. Most of the "facts" about the period depended on huge assumptions, which in turn relied on minimal evidence from the archaeological record.

The Amarna Period acquired its name from the chief archaeological site where remnants of the time were discovered, a place located in the desert along the east bank of the Nile. Known today as Amarna, in ancient times the site was called Akhetaten. During the Amarna Period, a pharaoh named Akhenaten attempted to overthrow the theological system Egypt had lived by for thousands of years. He'd replaced the pantheon of gods and goddesses with a single god known as the Aten, a solar deity who manifested himself as the light of the sun, generally depicted as the sun's disk-shaped face with rays stretching down from it. Each ray ended in a small hand proffering an ankh, the symbol for life.

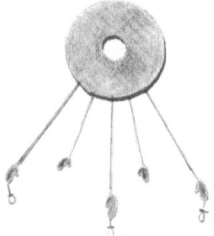

Akhenaten outlawed the old gods. He shut down the old temples and, most Egyptologists thought, persecuted anyone who evinced a devotion to the old gods. He'd abandoned the old capital city to found a new one in the middle of nowhere. He named the new capital Akhetaten, or Horizon of the Aten, though no one knew exactly why he chose the name. Some scholars believed he associated the mountains near the site with the horizon out of which Egyptian mythology said the Aten rose each morning.

For seventeen years, the pharaoh ruled from Akhetaten along with his chief wife Nefertiti, the beauty whose face was preserved in a famous bust now housed in a Berlin museum. Egyptologists assumed Akhenaten died after the seventeenth year. Though some Egyptologists claimed a mummy found in Tomb 55 in the Valley of the Kings belonged to Akhenaten, they lacked proof. The mummy had an elongated skull, a feature in line with depictions of Akhenaten. Yet depictions of other Amarna figures, such as the royal daughters, also showed elongated skulls. The mummy in Tomb 55 could've belonged to one of his relatives. After all, the experts could agree on neither the age nor the sex of the mummy.

The pharaoh's appearance had long baffled Egyptologists because of his elongated, effeminate figure with wide hips and apparent breasts. His face was long, narrow, and angular with lips as thick and wide as any supermodel's. His belly sported a paunch. His fingers and toes were elongated too. Egyptologists argued about whether he suffered from Marfan syndrome, a disease that caused a similar appearance, or if he simply wanted himself portrayed as bizarre to engender fear in his subjects. His children were depicted with elongated, egg-shaped heads too. Egyptologists claimed the elongation symbolized the "egg of creation." They had no proof for that theory either. Where Akhenaten was concerned, all theories rested on conjecture. The same went for most of ancient Egyptian history.

To her, Akhenaten looked like an alien. On her blog, she discussed all aspects of her theory. Which explained why nobody stopped to read it. They thought she was nuts. Maybe she was. But she doubted it.

Didn't crazy people think they were sane?

She tapped the hieroglyphs on the page. "Can you read these hieroglyphs?"

Alex ran his finger over the symbols. "Certainly."

Harry seemed to have situated the lines of hieroglyphs in between the lines of unknown pictographs on purpose, suggesting the paired lines contained parallel text. If she—okay, if *they* could decipher the hieroglyphs, they might also understand the pictographs.

Or Harry could be a nutcase who thought he was channeling Akhenaten's spirit.

Alex hissed out a breath. He slouched back in his chair and rubbed his eyes. "The hieroglyphs are nonsense."

Erin slid the book toward her and flipped through it. The neatly written notes differed from Harry's in more than their legibility. The neat handwriting, a tight cursive with nearly invisible loops on the F's and g's, lent those notes an air of masculine certainty.

She tilted the book toward Alex, tapping a finger on the neat writing. "Do you know who wrote in this book? I see two different kinds of handwriting."

"I wrote what you're pointing at. Harry wrote the notes you can barely read."

The masculine handwriting belonged to Alex. She studied him for a moment. Despite his slumped posture, and the fatigue evident in his expression, he looked neat rather than disheveled.

She said, "Tell me about Harry."

"He's a professor of English at St. Damasus College in Utah. Linguistics is his passion. That's how he got involved with studying ancient cultures."

"Hmm."

She returned her attention to the book. The text described how Amenhotep IV ascended to the Egypt's throne after his father, the pharaoh Amenhotep III, died. Five years later, Amenhotep IV changed his name to Akhenaten, signaling his conversion to a new faith system. Whereas previous pharaohs exalted the power of the Egyptian pantheon, with the god Amen-Ra as their patron saint, Akhenaten adopted the Aten, the sun disk, as his sole deity. Worship of other gods became verboten. Although the average Egyptian kept worshiping the entire array of gods in private, publicly everyone pretended to follow the pharaoh's lead.

Covington expounded on the dry details of pharaonic succession, as well as where and when important artifacts were discovered. The author composed his text with all the verve of a coroner documenting an autopsy.

"I'd like to know more about Harry," she said.

Alex sat forward. "Let me see the book again."

She passed it to him, and he opened the book to the folded-over page. He supported his head in his right hand, fingers shielding his eye, blocking his view of her.

Opening the web browser on her computer, Erin navigated to a search engine. She typed in "Harry Harriman" and hit enter. The search netted five results. One led to the web page of a grad student at Arizona State University who posted a paper he wrote. In the paper's bibliography, the student cited the article "Evidence for and Implications of Physical Mutations Present in the Royal Family of Amenhotep IV/Akhenaten," published in the *Journal for Near Eastern Studies* and written by "Harriman, M. J." An asterisk followed the name. She scrolled to the bottom of the page where a matching asterisk preceded a note: "My old professor Harry Harriman likes flirting with the lunatic fringe, but this article still contains good info."

Lunatic fringe? She liked Harry better already.

The next link in the search results list took her to an abstract of an article by Harry, this time for the *Journal of the Foundation for Amarna Research and Exploration*. She'd never heard of the foundation. The abstract described the article as dealing with "controversial new evidence for a connection between the Amarna court and the New World." Cool.

The last three results took her to pages that no longer existed.

She searched again, this time for "M. J. Harriman." Her search netted fifteen results. The first hit led her to an article describing how Harry had been denied tenure twice over the years, at other universities, because of his interest in the connections between ancient cultures worldwide. "Harriman firmly believed," the article said, "these diverse cultures, which accepted history says never met, converged somewhere in Central America in a sort of ancient United Nations summit. His colleagues scoff at the idea."

Duh, of course they'd scoff. Overturning an idea as deeply entrenched as the no-contact theory would take decades, if it ever happened. Each generation of academics clung to their theories like shamans guarding sacred amulets. To say "gee, we were wrong all these years" would mean *they were wrong*. No professor wanted to put himself in that position. After all, a PhD meant you knew everything.

She glanced at the PhD-holder sitting next to her. Alex remained engrossed in Harry's notes.

If the ancient Egyptians never traveled to the Americas, why did some of the Anasazi petrolgyphs look identical to Egyptian hieroglyphs?

Over the past two years, she'd accumulated a collection of photographs gleaned from the Internet that showed rock art credited to the Anasazi, the Fremont, and the Mogollon. All three cultures existed in the ancient Southwest but disappeared without a trace before the first Spaniard set foot on the continent. The photos in her collection represented two kinds of rock art—petroglyphs, images scraped onto the rock to expose the lighter stone under the dark exterior; and pictographs, images painted onto the rock. Every image she'd collected included a symbol similar or identical to Egyptian hieroglyphs. The remainder of the symbols in the photos resembled nothing she'd seen before.

She'd correlated the rock art symbols with their Egyptian counterparts, then tried translating the rock art based on the hieroglyphs. The resulting text made no sense. Either the rock artists used the hieroglyphs purely as decoration, or they adapted the hieroglyphs to their own language, rendering the Egyptian translations meaningless. To decipher the glyphs, she needed a Rosetta Stone—identical texts written in both languages, like the famed stone Napoleon's savants obtained in Egypt around the turn of the nineteenth century. The Rosetta Stone contained the same text written in Egyptian hieroglyphs, Demotic script, and Greek letters. The stone helped Jean-Francois Champollion crack the code of ancient Egyptian hieroglyphs.

Erin scrolled down the results list. The fourteenth stopped her. The link was to a news article with the headline "An Academic Mystery: The Disappearance of M. J. Harriman."

She glanced at Alex. He drummed his fingers against his temple, still shielded by his hand.

Clicking the link, she waited as the article loaded. Dated yesterday, the article appeared in a Utah newspaper. She skimmed the first paragraph.

```
Eight days ago, Dr. M. J. "Harry" Harriman stepped onto
a plane at the Salt Lake City airport, setting off on an
expedition to study Anasazi rock art in New Mexico as part
of his ancient linguistics project. He was never seen again.
```

The newspaper article described how Harry boarded the plane in Salt Lake City, headed for Albuquerque, where he should've met an unnamed friend for a research expedition not sanctioned by his employers at St. Damasus College. Harry and his friend planned on driving out to a remote Anasazi ruin discovered a couple months earlier. But Harry never met his friend. Though security cameras at the Salt Lake City airport recorded Harry boarding the plane there, cameras at the Albuquerque airport malfunctioned on that afternoon. Authorities couldn't check to see if Harry exited the plane. Another passenger, who sat near Harry during the flight, reported the professor had disembarked. No one knew where he went. M. J. Harriman vanished.

Would she?

Oh please. No one would bother bumping off a librarian from the north end of nowhere. Nobody read her blog, despite what Alex thought. Apparently her rants about the fallacies of conventional history, the dictatorial attitudes of academics, and the ignored evidence for connections between ancient cultures interested nobody other than herself. The traffic stats for her blog proved it. She didn't matter enough to warrant anyone spending the time and effort to make her disappear.

Harry flew to New Mexico to study rock art. Petroglyphs and pictographs. His note on page 298 paired lines of Egyptian hieroglyphs with lines of what looked like pictographs.

"Gimme the book," she said.

Alex lifted his head, furrowing his brow. The skin under his eyes was dark, his eyes bloodshot.

"Please," she said.

He slid the book toward her. She focused on the handwritten hieroglyphs and pictographs. Her vision was blurry. Her eyes felt gritty and hot, her neck ached, and mental molasses gummed up her brain. The first hieroglyph was… something.

Alex laid a hand on her shoulder. "You look exhausted. I know I am. Let's pick this up tomorrow."

"Good idea."

Alex stood and stretched.

Erin shut the book.

A COUPLE MINUTES LATER SHE STOOD OUTSIDE THE YARD GATE WATCHING Alex climb into his car. The sun had dipped below the tree line, though its afterglow lit the sky. Pink tendrils of clouds draped across the heavens, spreading out from the horizon behind the trees.

Alex started his car's engine. He rolled down the driver's window and said, "I should wait until you go inside."

"I can take care of myself, thank you very much."

He stared at her. She stared at him.

Finally he rolled up the window and backed out onto the road. After a pause he drove off down the road to the left, out of sight behind the cover of the trees.

To the right, among the trees perhaps fifty feet away, a light glinted.

A blasted orb. No, the glint had been too small and concentrated. The fading sunlight might've reflected off a shiny surface, like glass—but glass from what?

Somewhere within the trees, from the spot where the glint originated, a shadow moved.

Erin froze.

Her heart pounded. She backed up until her butt bumped the gate post.

A bird fluttered up out of the brush, soaring over her head past the house.

Had the bird somehow caused the flash of light? It seemed unlikely. She wanted to run inside the house, lock the door, and curl up in bed with her gun. If she told her parents that they might have a prowler, they'd rush outside, fully armed, to confront the trespasser. The man who attacked her yesterday might own a gun. He certainly had a nasty temperament. What if he brought friends this time? What if the orbs helped him? She couldn't risk it, though she didn't know what "it" was.

Grow a spine, for pity's sake. She could do this by herself.

She leaned back against the gate post. The gun pressed into her spine. She'd forgotten about it. The gun had been snug inside her waistband the whole time she and Alex pored over the book. Pulling out the gun, she flicked off the safety and chambered a round. An unused bullet popped out of the barrel. It plunked onto the ground in front of her feet. Now she knew for certain the gun was ready.

The gun raised in front of her, finger over but not touching the trigger, she skulked down the driveway.

At the road, she swerved right. A dozen yards from where she'd seen the glint, she stopped.

"I know you're there," she said. "Show yourself or I start shooting in your direction."

A figure stepped out of the trees. The man leaped over the ditch and halted in the road facing her, his feet spread apart, mouth set in a line. In his right hand he grasped a knife with a three-inch curved blade. He tilted his hand. Light glinted off the blade.

The man stared at her, eyes narrowed to slits, mouth open a bit.

His deep brown skin matched the color of the arms that seized her yesterday. His black hair was cut short. His eyes looked almost black. He wore green camouflage fatigues and matching boots.

The man strode toward her, stopping twenty feet away. He curled his lips in a sneer.

In a raspy baritone, he said, "Know that they are watching you. And I am watching you. If you cannot find what we seek, you will have no further use to us."

He spoke with a Middle Eastern accent. Egyptian? Alex said Rassul was half Egyptian. This must be the little worm himself.

"What do you seek?" she asked.

"That is what you must discover. You have the key now. If you stop wasting time flirting with MacKay like a whore, you can identify the relic and *find* it."

He twirled the knife like a gunslinger spinning his revolver.

She aimed the gun at his chest, approximately where his heart would be. "Tell me, Mr. Rassul, who do you work for?"

Tilting his head, he widened his eyes a sliver.

"Yes," she said, "I know who you are."

"Find the relic now. Before we lose patience with you."

He pulled an object from his pocket. It was the size of a remote starter for a car but its surface was shiny, smooth, and free of buttons. He pressed a corner of the object.

Behind him, a pinpoint of light appeared. The light expanded, at first inch by inch, then accelerating. Within a few seconds the light swelled into a disc of light eight feet in diameter. The disc flared bright white.

Erin squinted, throwing her right arm up to shield her eyes. No heat. No sound.

The brilliance dissipated into a dull glow. She lowered her hands. Her throat tightened, her stomach lurched, her thoughts twirled in nonsensical whirlwinds. What she saw couldn't be.

The disc had become a circle of light floating a foot above the road, in mid air. Through the circle's interior, she gazed out on a desert vista. She stepped sideways to peek around the circle. Beyond it, she saw the road and trees. But the desert vista inside the circle blocked her view of the road behind it. The circle served as a window within the world.

Her pulse thundered in her ears. It couldn't be. Yet it was.

Rassul turned and strode into the circle. The ring of light telescoped shut behind him, leaving nothing in its wake.

Erin blinked. Her vision darkened at the edges. *Breathe.* She sucked in a breath, letting it out gradually. The orbs could turn into...what? Portals into other dimensions, windows to distant lands, bridges to other times...

God almighty, what had she gotten mixed up in?

Rassul's words echoed in her brain.

Know that they are watching you.

She looked up at the sky. Someone with a hell of a lot of power expected her to find an unnamed thing and find it fast.

No problem.

6

Revenant House
Thursday, May 19

THE PHONE RANG. SAMUEL WESSICK GAZED OUT THE WINDOW AT THE LAKE for another moment, his back to the rest of the drawing room. As the phone rang a third time, he stepped away from the window to snatch the cordless handset from the phone on the table. He muttered, "Yes."

"She doesn't know," Rassul growled.

"To whom and to what are you referring?"

"The Turner woman. She doesn't know where the relic is, or what it is. I used the knife to scare her—"

"You what?" Wessick tightened his fist around the phone. "I specifically told you to *stay away* from Erin Turner."

"She is distracted. We need her on track."

Wessick clenched his teeth. He hissed, "I forbade you to threaten her."

He stopped to draw in a deep breath. The anger was boiling inside him. He must relax. Using men such as Rassul brought risks, great ones, about which he'd warned his employers. They paid no heed. Bloodshed meant nothing to them, except as a means to achieve their own ends. And so he found himself tethered to Rassul, his skin stained with the blood of those whom Rassul deemed of no further use.

Wessick gritted his teeth. *Relax.* He closed his eyes, loosened his grip on the phone, and willed his jaw muscles to soften. He exhaled slowly, inhaled again for a count of eight, held the breath for two heartbeats, then exhaled once more. The tension seeped out of his muscles, borne on the breath he released. The boiling cooled, as if the heat leeched out along with the breath.

Still grasping the phone, he crossed to the sofa and dropped onto it. The cushion indented under his weight. He leaned his head against the sofa's back.

"Now," he said into the phone, "tell me precisely what happened."

While Rassul recounted the incident with Erin Turner, Wessick gazed out the picture windows at the lake. Beyond the cliffs, sunlight poured down from a clear sky to glint off whitecaps on the lake. The wind buffeted the manor, scraping branches against the windows and rattling the glass.

Rassul, finished with his tale, said, "They wanted her frightened."

"Bringing Erin Turner into the fold requires subtlety. Flowers, not fire, attract the bees."

"Perhaps, but I don't answer to you. They have no quarrel with my tactics."

"I answer to them. They placed you in *my* employ, which means you *answer to me*."

Rustling at the other end of the line betrayed Rassul's fidgeting. Seagulls squawked in the background of the call. He envisioned Rassul seated sideways in his car, door open, legs angled to plant his feet on the ground outside the car.

Rassul said, "I will use whatever tactics I wish, to encourage the Turner woman to help us."

"By 'us' you had better mean me."

At the other end of the line, seagulls shrieked.

"Remember," Wessick said, his voice hard, "I have my own tactics for meting out punishment."

Silence for several seconds. Rassul cleared his throat. "She will not be harmed."

"Good. I have another task for you."

Wessick explained the task to Rassul and hung up the phone. He had reasserted control. For how long?

At least the other project was going according to his wishes. Desheret played a vital role, one she disliked but would maintain until he told her otherwise. This evening she should return from her journey home—with good news, he hoped. As for Erin Turner, his plans for her would progress into stage two later this morning. He would find the relic, in spite of Rassul's blunderings. Erin Turner would help him.

Whether she knew it or not.

He left the drawing room, locking the door behind him. The manor felt as silent and still as a tomb. He followed the east passage beyond the main staircase and vestibule into the west passage where it dead-ended at the dining room door. He turned right into the north passage. At the end of the passage, he crossed into the back stairwell and climbed its spiral steps up to the second floor. In the upper north passage, he stopped at the second door on the right. The door was shut. Unlocking the door, he swung it open, flipped a light switch to the left of the doorway, stepped into the room, and shut the door.

The original window had been bricked over long ago, so that this room more than any other in the manor evoked the ambience of an underground tomb sealed for millennia. The rest of the manor lacked central air or heat, receiving warmth from fireplaces and wood stoves placed strategically throughout the manor. In this room, however, he'd installed an environmental control system that maintained a temperature of seventy-two degrees Fahrenheit and a relative humidity of fifty percent. Preserving the items stored in the room demanded strict controls. His employers brooked no mistakes when it came to the collection entrusted to his care.

A long display table stretched across the twelve-foot length of the far wall. He approached the table. Clasping his hands behind his back, he surveyed the collection. Artifacts from the ancient civilizations of Asia and North Africa sat beside items fashioned by cultures both more mysterious and more ancient that once existed in the Americas, Europe, and the Mediterranean rim. Those ancient peoples unknowingly contributed to the collection Rassul had amassed for him, at the behest of his employers.

Wessick picked up a humanoid figurine from Japan. The clay statue, dated to approximately 3,000 years ago, possessed a narrow waist that blended into equally slender hips. Blocky shoulders tapered into a thick neck, topped by a vaguely triangular head inset with almond-shaped eyes. The mouth of the humanoid figure gaped wide—in surprise, he wondered, or in horror?

His employers provided him with a list of artifacts he must acquire, whatever the cost. Their reasons remained a mystery to him, though he harbored suspicions.

Erin Turner must uncover the reasons. Find the connections between the artifacts. Comprehend the grand scheme behind his employers' actions. She must solve the mysteries. He knew she could. She was the one they had waited for, as proved by the first test. After thousands of years and countless attempts, at last they'd found the *satseshat*, the link to complete the chain. He had found Erin.

She must find the relic. Soon.

The countdown had commenced.

The Turner Home

Eureka! erin threw her arms up in the air, dancing in her seat. she understood Harry's notation. Last night the hieroglyphs paired with pictographs looked like nonsense, though the pictographs seemed familiar. This morning she knew where she'd seen them before. The pictographs, some of them anyway, were among those in her collection of Internet photos showing rock art attributed to the Anasazi and related tribes, the ancient inhabitants of the American Southwest. The other pictographs must hail from the same region.

She scooped the last spoonful of cereal from the bowl on her desk. While she chewed, she browsed the pictograph images she'd accumulated. Harry's book lay on the desk in front of her, open to the page with his hieroglyph/pictograph notations. In the nine pairs of lines, she found a dozen pictographs matching the ones in her photos. Now she just needed Alex to help her translate the text.

Alex's face flashed in her mind. Those blue eyes. The perfectly proportioned features of his face. The serious, sincere expression. Did he have a sense of humor? She could explore the facets of his personality later. This morning she needed a different sort of knowledge.

She navigated to a search engine, typed in "Alex MacKay," and hit enter.

His name yielded hundreds of results, most leading to information about people who were not the Alex MacKay she'd become acquainted with—among them a gray-haired diplomat, a pimply teenager, two women, a heavily tattooed man, and a 103-year-old gentleman who recently died. Limiting the results to sites with ".edu" domains culled the list somewhat, yet still required her to skim dozens of results to ferret out links referring to the correct Alex MacKay.

Sixteen of the hits stemmed from multiple mentions of four journal articles he'd written, the most recent dating to six and a half years ago. Though the links took her to abstracts of the articles, rather than the full text, she gleaned enough from the abstracts to infer the gist of the articles. Alex had written mainstream articles supporting mainstream ideas about history, with a focus on Egypt's Eighteenth Dynasty. Did Nefertiti rule as Smenkhara after her husband, the pharaoh Akhenaten, died? Why did Akhenaten really choose a remote desert site as the location for his new capital city? How much of an influence did Queen Tiye have on her husband, Amenhotep III, Akhenaten's father? Interesting, but none of it explained his current interest in all things strange and nonmainstream. None of it explained his interest in her. His interest in her *interests*.

The fourth article in the list asked, "Where is Akhenaten's body?"

The phone on her desk warbled softly. Her mother would answer it in the living room, so she ignored it. The phone rang twice more and stopped.

She skimmed the abstract for the article about Akhenaten's body. Alex talked about the Tomb 55 mummy, apparently concluding that any identification of the mummy as Akhenaten remained speculative at best. The last line of the abstract asked, "Might his subjects have interred Akhenaten neither near Amarna nor in the Valley of the Kings, but at a location far from any sites currently known to historians and archaeologists?"

Someone rapped on the door.

Erin glanced up at the open doorway. Her mother held a cordless phone identical to the one on Erin's desk. Her mother said, "It's a woman for you. Says her name is Newman."

"Oh. It's about the job."

Erin grabbed the receiver from her desk and punched the talk button. She heard a beep as her mother disconnected the other phone. When she glanced at the doorway, her mother had already left.

Her stomach flip-flopped. She sucked in a breath, let it out, and raised the phone to her ear. "Hello."

"It's Newman. I'm calling to offer you the position of librarian archivist at Revenant House."

Erin couldn't speak. Couldn't think of words. She must've misheard Newman.

"Are you there?" Newman asked.

"Um, yes." Brilliant. She'd stun them with her eloquence. "I should tell you, I don't actually have a car. My last job, uh, frankly didn't pay enough to let me buy my own car. I have to borrow my parents' car. I can't exactly take it with me—"

"We can help you get a loan, with no down payment and reasonable interest. Mr. Wessick has contacts at several financial institutions. Would that help?"

"That would be...nice."

"Are you accepting the position then?"

"Yes, absolutely."

"Excellent. Can you start Monday morning, nine o'clock?"

What was today? Erin checked the date on her computer's clock. Thursday. She had the weekend to convince herself she didn't dream this conversation. She tried to sound confident as she said, "Monday sounds perfect."

"Wonderful. You can move in Sunday. If you arrive by noon, I'll stop in to give you the key."

Erin hesitated. She almost forgot about living at the manor. The creepy vibe exuded by the place would wear off after awhile, she hoped. Given how much they were paying her, however, she could put up with a slight case of the willies. She said, "I'll see you Sunday. And thank you so much for this opportunity."

"We're grateful to have you in the fold."

They said their goodbyes, and Erin hung up. What did Newman mean by "in the fold"? Nothing, it was a saying. She needed to quit seeing sinister plots in every turn of phrase.

Outside, Freya barked. After a minute, the dog fell silent.

She resumed her web search. Of the last eight hits, three led to a series of pages on a site dedicated to archaeological research in Egypt's Valley of the Kings, an ancient cemetery where pharaohs of the New Kingdom constructed their tombs. The links from her search led to pages discussing an American expedition that took place ten years ago. Staffed with archaeologists from various universities but funded by a private foundation called the Vidatha Society, the Sandstrom expedition—christened after the society's lead archaeologist, Angelika Sandstrom—sought evidence of a predynastic presence in the Valley of the Kings. Such evidence would've supported Sandstrom's theory that the pharaohs of the New Kingdom used the Valley as a cemetery because the region always served as one, even in the centuries before Egypt united under the first pharaoh. Conventional wisdom rejected any use of the Valley as a cemetery before the New Kingdom.

Halfway down the page, she found a photo of the expedition's members. They stood lined up in three rows, some wearing hats to shield their eyes, others squinting in the sunlight. In the second row, she spotted a familiar face. Well, sort of familiar. The young man, posed with hands on his hips, grinned at the camera. She checked the caption for the name of the fellow. Yep. The man with the giddy grin, who looked as happy as a kitten in a catnip patch, was Alex MacKay.

So he did know how to smile.

Returning to her search results, she learned the rest of the hits linked to pages where one academic or another chose to defame Alex MacKay.

...the worst kind of charlatan...

... ignorant, arrogant, and pathetically insane...

...promotes vulgar ideas solely for the purpose of gaining publicity...

...a peddler of pseudoscience who must have studied archaeology under Dr. Seuss...

In the final insult, an article quoted an anonymous professor who asked, "Does MacKay really have a PhD or are his credentials, like his evidence, pure fabrication?"

Sure, she'd Called Alex rude, but she simply could not identify with the comments from his peers. What did he do to provoke their wrath?

Then she saw it. The last hit.

Six and a half years ago, Alex wrote an article for the *Journal of the Foundation for Amarna Research and Exploration*. The article was called "Predynastic Burial Reveals Presence of ETs in Ancient Egypt." The journal's website reproduced the entire article. She printed out the text.

Footsteps shooshed down the hall toward her bedroom.

Erin looked up at the instant Alex marched across the threshold into the room. He shut the door. In his left hand, he gripped the handle of his leather satchel, the thing he called an attaché.

"Moving in?" Erin asked.

"What?"

She nodded at the bag. "You brought a suitcase."

He flattened his mouth into a line, something between a smirk and a grimace. The light from her desk lamp reflected in the blue of his eyes.

"It's not a suitcase," he said. "It's my attaché. I keep important papers in it."

She closed her web browser. The printer whirred, busy spewing out the pages of Alex's article.

Alex plunked his satchel on the floor beside the desk. He walked over to the wooden chair that sat by the window, grasped it in both hands, and carried it over to the foot of the bed near his satchel. She left the chair, a refugee from the dining room, in here because she knew Alex would come back today. He placed the chair beside hers, facing the desk. When he sat down, spine straight and hands resting on his thighs, his left elbow grazed her arm. She thought about slouching to the left, far enough that his arm couldn't touch hers, then dismissed the idea as ridiculous. Instead, Erin folded her legs under her to sit cross-legged in her chair. She clasped her hands on her lap.

She said, "Good morning to you too."

"Sorry." He fixed his gaze on the book. "Good morning."

"Okay," she said, "straight to work it is. I haven't decoded Harry's notes yet, so why don't you help me with that?"

He nodded.

The book lay on top of the printout of the Vigenère cipher table. She tugged the sheet out from under the book, flattened it out on the desk to the left of the book, and explained the Vigenère cipher. Together they decrypted Harry's notes scribbled throughout the book. She read off the encrypted letters one by one, then Alex decoded them using the table and the cipher key, the word "truth." He transcribed the decrypted text onto a notepad she'd given him. A couple hours later, they finished the task.

Alex slumped back in his chair. He tossed the pen onto the notepad and let out a long sigh.

"Garbage," he said. "Utter garbage."

Erin grabbed the notepad. Alex had filled five letter-size sheets of paper. As she flipped through the pages, random phrases popped out at her. Most were comments on the book's text. The rest were, as Alex observed, garbage. *Car needs new brakes*, read one note. *Call Joe to get borrowed books back*, said another. A stranger note spelled out *break my spine*. Sure, whatever. Maybe Harry got drunk one night while encrypting his messages.

"Why," she said, "would anyone encrypt trivial nonsense?"

Alex shrugged.

"That's the extent of your insight?" she asked.

He shrugged again, this time scrunching his mouth too.

She grumbled.

He arched an eyebrow at her.

"You know Harry," she said. "Why would he waste hours encrypting notes about his car and the books some guy borrowed from him?"

Alex opened his mouth.

She held up her hand. "Don't answer yet. *Think* about it."

He shut his eyes, rubbing them with the fingers of his right hand. After a moment, he looked at her.

"Harry was paranoid," Alex told her. "For good reason, it turns out. He also enjoyed a peculiar sense of humor. Sometimes he encrypted the notes he wrote on his students' papers, to see if they could figure out the cipher."

"Therefore…"

"He might've encrypted routine notes to fool spies, like Rassul. It would have the added benefit of giving him a good laugh at their expense."

"At our expense, you mean."

He leaned forward. With the thumb and forefinger of his right hand, he flipped through the book's pages. "What he actually wants us to see must be hidden in plain sight. It could be something that appears meaningless."

"Like the hieroglyph/pictograph thingy."

He smiled, barely, a ghost of the grin she'd seen in the old photo. "Thingy?"

She batted his hand away from the book. Flipping to page 298, she tapped her finger on the paired lines of hieroglyphs and pictographs.

Alex's smile morphed into a frown. "Those hieroglyphs are nonsense."

"Exactly."

He stared at her.

She tapped the page harder. "Something that looks meaningless, remember?"

"Those hieroglyphs don't *look* meaningless, they *are* meaningless. Total, complete gibberish."

He grabbed the notepad from her and found the page she'd written on yesterday when she attempted to translate the hieroglyphs. He ran his fingertips along the first line of symbols.

"What does this mean?" he asked. "I'll tell you. It says serpent, king, land, motion, face, for, seat, man. Incredibly meaningful, isn't it?"

"Each hieroglyph can represent more than one word or sound, right?"

"Yes, but no matter how you translate these, it makes no sense. Some of the symbols are determinatives, which aren't used by themselves."

"Because determinatives reinforce the meaning of the words they follow. Hieroglyphs can also be ideograms representing concepts, or phonograms standing for sounds."

He looked at her sideways, his jaw parted. "That's right. How did you—"

"I've been teaching myself ancient Egyptian."

"Not many people would bother learning a dead language."

"Guess I'm not like other people."

"I'm positive of that."

He smiled, a little more than before. Her heart thumped.

She focused on the notepad.

A determinative never appeared by itself, since its purpose was to reinforce the meanings of other words. Ideograms might go it alone, but phonograms always stuck together in word groups. The sun symbol as an ideogram might mean the sun or, as a phonogram, it could stand for *ra*, meaning the sun in the sky or the sun god Ra.

The determinative that looked like a pair of legs walking meant the word preceding it dealt with motion.

Both symbols could also have other meanings, and both appeared in Harry's notation.

"Let's try something different," she said. "Tell me every possible meaning of the hieroglyphs in this notation."

She pointed at the first symbol. Alex rattled off several meanings for the word. After jotting down what he'd said, she moved on to the next symbol, and the next, and the next. Half an hour later, they completed the job. Now they needed to weed out the possibilities to find meanings appropriate to the context, whatever the context was. First, they should puzzle out that mystery.

Rassul told her to find the relic. Maybe Harry wanted to find it too. His notation might tell them where or how to find the unknown item. Flimsy reasoning. Still, she had nothing else.

Alex shook his head. "No Egyptian would write this way. The grammar's terrible. This can't be Egyptian because—"

"Stop. What if the person who wrote this text wasn't Egyptian? What if he had only a basic understanding of the hieroglyphic language?"

"Even Egypt's enemies understood their language."

"Expand your mental horizon." She tapped the first line of pictographs. "These look like other rock art attributed to the Anasazi and Hohokam. Tribes who lived in North America during ancient times."

"Tribes unfamiliar with the Egyptian language."

She nodded.

A frown creased his face. He bent down to unzip his satchel. From its depths, he extracted a folded paper and proceeded to unfold it. A map. He offered it to her.

She took the map. "What's this?"

"I found it in Harry's apartment, tacked to the wall. It seemed important."

Erin unfolded the map. It spread out to three feet wide by two feet high. Printed in block letters, the words "United States of America" arched across the top of the map. With a red felt marker, someone had drawn a big circle around the intersection of the state lines for Colorado, Arizona, New Mexico, and Utah—the Four Corners region. The Anasazi, Hohokam, and related ancient tribes lived in the Four Corners and, although the territory inhabited by those groups extended beyond the Four Corners, the region housed the most famous of their monuments.

Alex turned toward her, leaning closer to trace the circle with his index finger. "Harry must've traveled to this area."

"Looks like."

"Harry disappeared ten days ago."

"When he flew to Albuquerque."

"Yes. How do you know?"

"Research." She canted her head toward him, smiling a little. "That's what librarians do."

He crinkled his brow.

She spun her chair around, swiveling it away from him. Since her desk stood a few feet from the foot of the bed, she could reach it if she rotated her chair. She laid out the map on the bed. "Where was Harry going?"

"He didn't tell anyone his final destination."

"Paranoid guy, huh?"

Grabbing the notepad, she thumbed through the decoded text of Harry's notes. One jumped out at her, virtually screaming for attention: *Break my spine.* Unlike the other notes, comprised of banal messages, this notation was singular. Why would Harry want his spine broken? She picked up the book and fanned through the pages, then shut it. Next, she turned the book in her hands to examine the cover. The title and author's name were embossed on both the cover and the spine. She ran her fingertip down the spine.

Break my spine.

She groaned, "Duh."

"What?" Alex asked.

She flipped the book upside down. The spine's bottom was sealed with cloth lining, which extended up inside the spine to seal the sewn-together pages. She righted the book. At the spine's top, the cloth lining had been cut with a sharp tool, and a clear substance filled the gap between the pages and the spine. She poked at the clear gunk with her fingernail. Someone sealed the gap with a hot glue gun.

Break my spine. Harry was a sneaky devil.

Prying at the glue with the nails of her thumb and index finger, she pulled it out a millimeter at a time until the glue plug popped out altogether. She raised the front and back covers parallel with the spine and tipped the book down. A black object the size of her fingernail tumbled out onto the desk. White lettering etched on the object spelled out the term "micro SD."

Alex snatched the object. "A memory card. Can your computer read it?"

"Yep."

From a drawer she retrieved an adapter, a black sleeve that the micro SD card slid into, making the tiny card big enough to fit in the slot built into the front of her computer. She slid the adapter into the slot. The file manager automatically opened onscreen, displaying the contents of the micro SD card. It contained a single image file and a text file. She opened the image.

A rocky cliff filled the photograph. The smooth face of the cliff featured petroglyphs, etched figures that gleamed white against the reddish background. On the left side of the image, a hand held up a ruler for scale. The petroglyphs formed a single register with nine lines. The entire inscription measured eighteen inches tall by ten inches wide.

She opened the book to page 298. The symbols Harry drew underneath the hieroglyphs matched the petroglyphs shown in the photo.

Alex leaned over to see the photo. His shoulder bumped hers. He mumbled, "Sorry."

"Sorry is your favorite word, isn't it?"

He pointed at the photo. "Those are the symbols in the book. But where is this?"

"The Four Corners?"

"An awfully wide search area."

"He must've left a clue to the exact location."

She opened the text file on the micro SD card. The file read, "A rancher contacted me about this and graciously allowed me onto his land to see it. I couldn't figure it out but I know you two can, because THEY know you can. Find the relic."

"Great," she grumbled. "What is this blasted relic?"

"The term relic," Alex said, "used to refer to bodily remains preserved and venerated as religious icons. These days a relic can be almost anything left behind after a culture dies or a settlement falls into ruin."

"Any moldy old thing. Perfect, that narrows it down."

Where would they find the relic? Both Rassul and Harry ordered her to find it. Neither man seemed to know what or where it was. Harry must've had an inkling. Why else did he go to the Four Corners?

The map. She spun her chair around. Leaning forward, she braced her elbows on her knees and scanned the map, then flipped it over to examine the backside. Harry made zero notations on the map, aside from the big red circle. She laid the map face up again. Vertical and horizontal lines drew a grid on the map. Numbers at the margins denoted each line of latitude and longitude.

Thump-thump.

Without raising her head, she glanced up at Alex. He'd hauled his chair closer to hers, his attention locked on the map. He bent over the arm of her chair, his head a finger's width from hers. His breath tickled her cheek.

She frowned at him. "Do you have no concept of personal space?"

He tipped his head toward her, zeroing his gaze in on hers, his nose grazing hers. Indirect sunlight sparkled off his blue eyes. He arched an eyebrow at her. The air felt laden with electricity that arced over her skin.

"I'd say I'm sorry," he whispered, "but it would only annoy you."

His voice was soft, almost seductive.

She scooted her chair sideways away from him. She focused on the image of the petroglyph panel on her computer screen. Harry's petroglyph/hieroglyph notation in the book included the first few lines of symbols from the petroglyph panel. Either he meant the notation in the book as a hint that they should treat the petroglyphs is hieroglyph equivalents, or he tried and failed to make sense of an Egyptian translation for the petroglyphs. Harry believed she and Alex could figure it out together. Maybe he was right. Yet the thought of working with Alex for an extended period of time made her...uncomfortable. Still, he knew Egyptian better than she did in the petroglyph panel seemed like the key. The key to what, she couldn't say. Drat, she needed Alex's help.

She felt him staring at her.

"Let's finish the translation," she said. "And drop the doom-and-gloom attitude. We can figure this out if we try. Together."

"Yes, ma'am."

Dear heaven, she hoped she was right. If the translation wasn't the key, or if they failed to understand the text, Rassul would come for her.

And this time, he'd do more than punch her.

ALEX RUBBED HIS EYES AS ERIN CLICKED ON THE DESK LAMP. TWILIGHT HAD taken over the room, seeping in from outside where the last fingers of daylight tickled the night sky. They'd fiddled with the translation of the petroglyph panel until it made a sort of sense, if one assumed the text's author knew nothing about ancient Egyptian grammar. He read over the translation, written below the hieroglyphs, which he'd copied onto paper. He'd separated the translations for the individual hieroglyphs with dashes. He glanced over the first line for the umpteenth time.

```
serpent - god/king - Two Lands - motion - upon - water -
[this] - place - sit/reside
```

It read like random words cobbled together by a lunatic. The final line made even less sense than all the others combined, because it contained numbers interspersed with two letters.

He sighed and mumbled, "It's still nonsen—"

Erin growled.

He arched his eyebrows. His mouth fell open involuntarily. She flashed him a closed-mouth smile. Either she felt compelled to rip him to shreds with her bare teeth, or he annoyed her. Again.

"Now you're a werewolf?" he said.

"Don't say the N word and I won't growl at you anymore. It's worse than the S word."

"I see." What word could he substitute for nonsense? "It's, um, incoherent."

"Maybe not."

Elsewhere in the house, a door banged shut. Outside the window, a cone of light sliced across the sky from ground level.

"What the blazes?" Alex said.

"Oh, that's Mom signaling the UFOs."

Did this family have no sense whatsoever? Signaling to UFOs, for crying out loud.

Alex leaped to his feet. Before Erin could say anything he bolted out the door, down the hallway, and into the living room. Footsteps slapping behind him let him know Erin was following. Shadows cloaked the empty living room. The door to the master bedroom, which also stood empty and dark, hung ajar. He heard muffled voices outside the front door. Flinging open the door and surging through it, he bounded down the steps into the front yard. Peripherally, he saw Erin trot out after him. She shut the door.

Her parents huddled in the driveway, their gazes fixed on the sky. Mrs. Turner held a pair of binoculars that she raised to her eyes occasionally. Pointing at the sky, she handed the binoculars to her husband. Once he'd taken them, she plucked a bulky, cylindrical object from the ground at her feet. The object sported a handle underneath, which Mrs. Turner grasped with both hands. The spotlight burst on, bright as car headlights. She aimed the spotlight at the sky.

Alex halted at the gate. Something wet brushed against his hand.

The dog, Freya, squatted alongside him with her ears erect. Alex patted the dog's head. Tail wagging, the dog licked his hand a second time. She made a noise that combined groaning and whining into a single exclamation. *Grrreeoo*, the dog said.

Erin walked up beside him. Ambient light transformed every object, whether tree or human or dog, into a specter of darkness. Mrs. Turner raked the spotlight across the sky from horizon to horizon. Finally, she directed the light straight up into the star-filled sky, switching the beam on and off in quick succession so it blinked as if spelling out Morse code.

The dog's collar click-click-clicked as she trotted around the yard.

"Are you people crazy?" Alex asked.

"No more than you," Erin said.

"Pardon?"

Erin chuckled. Though mere feet from him, the near darkness lent her the appearance of a murky apparition. He concentrated on the glob he presumed was her head.

Nodding at Mrs. Turner, he asked, "Why does she do it?"

"In the interest of intergalactic peace and understanding, naturally."

The spotlight blinked twice more. Its beam pierced the eastern sky.

Erin chuckled again. Though he assumed she was mocking him, the girlish lilt in her laughter gave him pause to reassess the situation. Considering how much ridicule she must've endured, due to her interest in the paranormal, would she stoop to mocking him?

No. She might growl, but she wouldn't ridicule him.

Then again, his judgment let him down before.

To the east, high in the sky, a light pulsed.

During the period when Harry vanished, the security cameras in the Albuquerque airport had gone haywire—nothing but snow on every camera in the concourse. Although both another passenger and a flight attendant certified Harry disembarked at Albuquerque, no trace of him turned up since the moment he stepped off the plane. The authorities found a witness who swore he'd seen Harry enter the men's restroom twenty minutes after his plane landed. The police refused to believe the witness, solely because of what the man claimed happened next. He said a flash of white light exploded inside the restroom. The witness rushed inside to see what happened, in case anyone needed help. The restroom was vacant.

Thanks to the malfunctioning cameras, the witness lacked corroboration for his story. The authorities assumed he was lying to get attention. Alex spoke to the man in person thirty-eight hours after Harry's disappearance. The story—and the witness—convinced him.

Erin asked, "What is it?"

He told her.

She was quiet for a moment, then she said, "Rassul stepped into a portal of some kind created by one of those glowing orbs. Think it's connected to the flashes of light?"

"Almost certainly."

"How?"

"Advanced technology or hocus-pocus. Take your pick."

He surveyed the sky. Countless stars populated the heavens, more than he had ever seen in his life. Yet more than red dwarfs and gas giants lurked in the depths of space. Hell, more lurked on this planet than anyone knew.

Some people knew. He knew. Erin knew. He wished she didn't, for her safety, because knowing brought enormous danger. Understanding, however, could bring a death sentence.

Memories assailed his mind's eye. Rocks plummeting. Blood. Screams. Silence inundating the crevasse. Then a single voice, weak and tremulous, begging "help us please God help us."

"I have to leave," he said.

Fumbling with the gate latch, he unhooked it with a clack and thrust the gate open. Erin urged him to "wait" but he ignored her one-word plea. He stormed through the gate to his car. The gate banged shut behind him, the latch chinking into place. Ripping the driver's door open, he hurled himself onto the seat. The sedan rocked. As he slammed the door shut, he noticed Erin's parents staring at him. He summoned a smile and waved. They reciprocated the gesture. He waved at Erin.

Hands resting on the gate, she scowled at him.

He rolled down the window called to her, "I'll be back tomorrow."

Her scowls softened a bit. He could hope for no better tonight, so he rolled up the window and backed the car out of the driveway, accelerating down the road.

An orb flitted out of the trees to his right. It zipped across the road in front of him, disappearing into the trees to the left. He slammed his foot on the brake. The car jerked to a stop.

No one would harm Erin. Not them, whatever they were. Not Rassul. Not the owner of Revenant House. No one. He would make certain of it, even if he died trying.

In the trees to his left, partly masked by leaves, a light shimmered.

Rolling down the window, he stuck his head out into the night and glared at the orb. "You won't win."

The light pulsated.

"Show yourselves, you malicious cowards."

The orb rocketed out of the woods straight toward him. He ducked backward. An inch from the window the orb executed a ninety-degree turn to shoot up into the sky.

Head tilted up, Alex leaned out the window. The orb was gone. They intended to frighten him with a demonstration of their power.

He shouted into the sky, "Is that the best you've got?"

A star flashed red.

Friday, May 20

ERIN HAD MULLED OVER THE LAST LINE OF ALEX'S TRANSLATION FOR AN HOUR, and she felt no closer to comprehend its mysteries. A series of numbers combined with two single letters, with no explanatory text, might refer to anything. Maybe the rest of the petroglyph panel contained the explanatory text, but the rest of the translation made no more sense than the numbers. Feeling like a masochist, she read the numbers again.

Thirty, six, seven, ten, N, one, hundred, twelve, seven, thirty, five, W.

Her gaze locked on the translation, she let her vision swim in and out of focus. If this method worked for magic eye paintings, why not for nonsense translation?

Oh no. Now she was using the N word. Next she'd start apologizing incessantly.

Wait. The letter N. She re-focused her vision. The letters N and W seemed to separate the numbers into two discrete groups. Numbers paired with letters. It meant something, but the realization dangled just out of her mental reach.

The map.

It lay on her desk, folded into a small rectangle. Snatching up the map, she flung it open to its full size and lifted it in front of her. Too close. She whirled her chair around.

"Ow!"

Erin jumped. Lowering the map, she peeked over its top edge at the source of the exclamation. Alex's expression displayed a mixture of irritation and bemusement.

"What?" she asked.

He rubbed the right side of his face. "You smacked me with the map."

"Oh." She wheeled her chair closer to the bed, flattening the map on the quilt. "I forgot you were there."

"What a compliment. Maybe I should strap a flashing red light to my head."

"Maybe," she said, not really listening to him anymore. The map siphoned her full attention. This map, like most, included a latitude-longitude grid overlaid on the main content. Both latitude and longitude could be divided infinitely by adding decimal places inserting more lines into the grid, thereby increasing the accuracy of the coordinates.

"You found something," Alex said.

"Mmm…possibly."

"What is it?" he asked.

She grabbed the notepad with the translation on it. The last line seemed like gibberish because it spelled out mostly numbers. *Thirty, six, seven, ten, N, one, hundred, twelve, seven, thirty, one half, five, W.* The letters N and W could signify north and west. If she assumed the "one half" fraction was connected to the preceding number, and if she rearranged the numbers a little, she ended up with 36, 7, 10, N, 112, 7, 30 1/2, W.

Latitude 36° 7' 10" north, longitude 112° 7' 30.5" west.

A location. On the map, she traced the lines for 36 degrees latitude and 112 degrees longitude to their intersection. The map lacked the minutes and seconds, so she estimated the location. The last line of the petroglyph panel encoded the coordinates for a location somewhere inside Grand Canyon National Park. To find the exact location, she needed a map of the park.

She spun her chair toward the desk. Her knees bumped into Alex's. He made his irritated-bemused face again.

"Sorry," she said, "but you're in my way."

He smirked at her. "Your apologizing needs some work."

Facing the desk, she grabbed the mouse and navigated to a search engine. Within a few minutes she'd found and downloaded a detailed map of Grand Canyon National Park, complete with latitude and longitude grid. With a map displayed on the computer screen, she hunted for the coordinates she gleaned from the petroglyph panel.

Alex leaned close to her, peeking over her right shoulder. "What did you find?"

The map showed Grand Canyon National Park, as well as neighboring areas outside the confines of the park. The Colorado River bisected the map. North of the river, ancient names dotted the landscape, marking geologic features—Hindu Amphitheater, Shiva Temple, Horus Temple, Cheops Pyramid. Historians claimed the explorers who named the geologic features chose ancient names, many of them Egyptian, because the newly founded discipline of archaeology made such names popular. In the nineteenth century, the Egyptianizing movement brought ancient style back into vogue, from stone sphinxes to the mummy unwrapping parties that no fashionable Victorian could miss.

A movie played in Erin's mind. Candlelight flickering as a Victorian gentleman uncoiled the linen wrappings from a musty corpse. Exactly how she wanted to spend a Saturday night—dancing with a lifeless, dried-out body. Of course, that would make a mummy a bit livelier than the men whose paths she'd crossed while working at the public library. They looked around her rather than at her. They studied their wallets, exchanged meaningful looks with the computer, or counted the loops in the carpeting. She might as well have been a robot. At least a mummy would have an excuse for ignoring her. His eyes had been removed in the embalming process.

She felt a gaze on her now, as Alex studied her out the corner of his eye. His breath tickled her cheek. Feeling a slight pressure on her right thigh, she glanced down to find his hand resting on her leg. Her mouth went dry. She could neither move nor tear her gaze away from his hand, and specifically his middle finger, which he'd begun tapping lightly on her thigh.

Alex had shifted his gaze to the computer screen. He seemed unaware of his hand's current location.

She grabbed the tip of his index finger, lifted his hand off her thigh, and shoved it away. "Back off, doctor."

She didn't move. She'd hoped formality might cow him, but she was wrong.

"You're in my personal bubble," she said.

"Sorry." He leaned back in his chair, retreating into his own bubble of personal space. The corners of his mouth twitched as if he were fighting off a smile. "You're sensitive about your territory. Duly noted."

"It's not my territory, it's my—" Drat, she could think of no way to end the sentence without sounding snippy. She gave up and turned to the computer screen. With the mouse she zoomed in and panned the Grand Canyon map until she found the precise coordinates from the petroglyph panel. They specified a locale in the vicinity of geologic formations known as the Isis Temple and the Cheops Pyramid.

Alex said, "You figured out something."

A statement rather than a question. He expected her to answer the question, though, as if he'd asked it. If she told him, and Rassul killed him because of the answer—if Rassul killed *anyone* because of it—how could she live with herself? Harry, Rassul, and Rassul's nameless puppet masters expected her to solve the mystery of the petroglyphs. What of her then?

He's a thief and a murderer. Alex's words, spoken just yesterday, whispered in her mind. He seemed to know Rassul. Why hadn't the thief and murderer bagged himself an archaeologist?

Her eyes burned. She'd forgotten to blink. Her gaze remained bound to Alex's, like he'd cast a spell on her that stripped her willpower. Baloney. She blinked. Looking at the map, she cleared her throat. Alex watched her, unmoving, for several seconds. Finally he looked at the map too.

"What did you find?" he asked.

She explained the coordinates to him, finishing by tapping her finger on the screen. "The coordinates lead here, but my theory has one flaw. How could ancient people have used the exact same coordinates we use today?"

The ancient Greeks measured latitude, using the equator as a starting point. Measuring longitude, however, proved more difficult without accurate clocks to measure time differences. Not until the sixteenth century did someone invent clocks accurate enough to enable the plotting of longitude. The location of the prime meridian, the starting point for longitude, varied from culture to culture until 1884, when Greenwich became the official prime meridian. Knowing all this, Erin wondered if her idea about the petroglyph panel was correct. The numbers looked like latitude-longitude coordinates. But interpreting them as such required using the modern latitude-longitude grid. How could ancient people living in the region now known as the Four Corners have known the right coordinates to use to allow people born hundreds or thousands of years later to find the intended spot?

The ancient people, whatever their identity, composed their message in Egyptian hieroglyphs. Ancient Egyptians were not supposed to have traveled to the New World. If she accepted one dogma-shredding idea, why not another?

She shared her concerns with Alex. When she finished talking, he said, "It's worth a shot."

"What do you mean?"

"If there's the slightest chance the petroglyph panel references a location, then we have to go there."

The cottony feeling in her mouth spread down into her throat. Her lips felt parched too. She licked her them. We. He wanted her to go with him on a quest to find a relic sought by murderers. She might cast her own life to the winds, but what if the bad guys found her parents? They might be in danger even if she stayed home and hid under her bed. If she told them nothing about the quest or Rassul or Harry, and if she found the relic, she might spare them from the worst of it.

She closed her eyes, sucked in a deep breath, and exhaled by the teaspoonful. She must go. And her parents must know nothing about the quest.

"Are you all right?" Alex asked.

She opened her eyes. "Peachy."

Alex dragged his chair back to the window. The chair's legs scraped across the carpet. He picked up his attaché from its resting place on the floor by the desk.

"We should leave as soon as possible," he said.

"I have to be back by Sunday morning. I'm moving into Revenant House so I can start work Monday morning."

"You got the job?"

He stared at her with wide eyes, unblinking, his lips curving down at the corners.

"You don't have to look so shocked," she said. "I am qualified."

He strode to her and squatted beside her chair. The attaché he set on the floor at his feet. Grasping the chair's arm with one hand, he spun the seat so that she faced him. Her knees touched his chest. He clasped her hands in his. Their gazes intersected. A shiver raced down her spine, simultaneously hot and cold, and not entirely disagreeable. She'd felt the same sensation two days ago, in the woods seconds after their orb encounter, when Alex unconsciously touched her in a protective gesture.

It meant nothing. She was too sensitive, that was all. Ranting about her personal space.

Still, his hands felt warm and comforting.

"Listen," he said, "I don't want you to take the job."

"Excuse me?"

"I realize I have no right to ask, since we are essentially strangers, but I am asking. Stay away from Revenant House. It isn't safe."

"Why?"

"Call it a gut feeling, based on some information I found online." He opened the attaché, sliding out a thin stack of papers. "Do you know what 'revenant' means?"

"It's another word for ghost."

He offered her the papers. "It's a bit more complicated."

She took the pages. A heading on the first sheet read "Revenants: The Living Dead." The first paragraph explained how, in medieval times, many people believed corpses could become reanimated and rise from the grave to torment the living in a manner similar to the modern concept of zombies or vampires. Some tales mentioned the consuming of blood. Revenants were often thought to be wicked people condemned to walk the earth after death. The term revenant derived from a French word meaning to return. In modern times, revenant had come to mean a ghost, or literally one who returned. The term could also refer to someone who seemed to have come from another age, a living anachronism.

"Let me get this straight," she said. "You think Revenant House is haunted."

"I don't know. There's definitely something off about the place. Something… menacing."

"Let me see if I understand. Revenant House is too dangerous for me, but I'm perfectly safe going with you on a quest for a mysterious thingamabob that's also wanted by a murderer and his bosses."

He let go of her hands. Lowering his head, gaze on the floor, he said. After a moment, he lifted his head. "Give me the coordinates, please."

"Why?"

"You're right, I should never have asked you to take the risk with me. Give me the coordinates, then forget you ever saw them."

"Rassul will kill you."

"Let me worry about him."

He grabbed for the notepad. She nabbed it first and held it behind her back, between her body and the chair. She said, "Rassul will kill me if I don't find the relic. He specifically said I had to find it."

A scowl engraved lines across his forehead, down from the corners of his mouth, and outward from his eyes. His eyes seemed darker somehow. A muscle in his jaw twitched.

She folded her arms over her chest. "I'm going with you."

"Absolutely not."

"I'm going. And I'm taking the job."

In the hallway, concealed by the closed door, Freya whined.

The notepad clasped to her chest, Erin tromped to the door. Freya pawed at the wood. Erin flung the door open and stomped into the hallway.

Alex jumped to his feet. "Wait—"

"The dog needs to go out."

She shut the door behind herself.

What did Harry's coordinates mark? They might lead to whatever Rassul wanted. Whatever Harry possibly died protecting. She assumed if he'd died, then he perished because of whatever lay at the coordinates encoded in the petroglyph panel.

If he had, and if she and Alex deciphered the coordinates correctly, then they possessed the magic numbers capable of leading them to the relic. Whatever the hell it was.

Something worth dying—worth killing—for.

THE DOOR LATCH CLICKED INTO PLACE. WELL, AT LEAST SHE HADN'T SLAMMED the door. Alex stood there for a minute, transfixed by the door. His talent for saying the wrong thing succeeded again. Just once he'd like the talent to desert him so the right words could make it past his lips. Some men wove words into a magical tapestry that cast a spell over even the most hardhearted women. He was not one of those men. Neither was Erin hardhearted, though she did evince a peculiar attachment to the airspace surrounding her. *You're in my bubble*, she'd chastised him. So he'd backed off.

He didn't make a habit of getting so close, physically, to people. Harry tried to hug him once, in greeting, and he'd backed away swifter than a gazelle retreating from a lion. Why then did he keep invading Erin's bubble?

Never mind, he had more urgent matters to consider. If Erin would give him the coordinates, he'd lure Rassul away from here—away from her. But she thought he was trying to steal her discovery, or abandon her to Rassul, or…

Stop. He had no idea what she thought. Not quite true. He knew one thought of hers. She thought he was a fool, or worse, a criminal. One of Rassul's cronies. He hardly helped matters when first he wanted her to accompany him, then he changed his mind, ordering her both not to go and not to take the job at Revenant House. His brilliant strategy worked wonders, if he'd intended to alienate her. Dammit, what did he want from her?

He wanted her to go with him. Her brain worked differently than his, spawning thoughts that never would've occurred to him. Without her, he might fail to find the relic. A gut feeling told him as much. Harry must've agreed, or else why did he send Alex here? Harry's encoded message said "you two," Alex and Erin, could solve the mystery. They needed to work together.

Blood. Screams. Bodies strewn across the crevasse. The memories hit him hard, but faded as quickly as they'd come. He collapsed into Erin's chair, shut his eyes. He couldn't risk anyone else's life, not again. Yet he needed Erin— needed her help.

So he waffled. Add it to the list of his character flaws.

Christ, he should've stayed in Alaska where his worst problem had been how to keep from getting whacked in the head by icicles.

A fist clinched around his gut. Liar. Jerk. Schmuck.

His cell phone warbled. Slumping in the chair, he dug the phone out of his pocket and mumbled hello.

A feminine voice said, "Honey, you sound terrible."

"Thanks, mother."

"I'm not old enough to be your mother."

"Then you must be sexually harassing me, because only my mother calls me honey."

Katy laughed. The sound rang bright as notes on an antique piano. He tried to muster the energy to sit up, but his body had other ideas. Instead, he lodged his free arm behind his head for support.

He said, "You should replace me on this one."

"Nobody else is free." She paused. "Tell me what happened."

"I insulted her, invaded her personal space, bossed her around, and she left in a huff."

"Not the *TV Guide* blurb. The whole story."

His stomach growled. He glanced at his watch—12:15. Lunch time.

Katy's sigh hissed like static through the cell phone. She was waiting for his report.

He recited the morning's events. The fist around his gut tightened with each sentence he spoke. When his recital ended, she groaned.

"Oh sweetie," she said, "you've been spending too much time with Warner."

"I don't understand."

"You commanded Erin to stay put while you jet off to Arizona to locate something she's been charged with finding. To top it off, you used the zombie defense to order her not to take a job."

"Well, I—"

"And now you're mystified as to why she's mad. Hanging around with Warner has given you a mercenary complex. The ends justify the means and the meaner the means, the quicker the result. That about sum it up?"

He grumbled into the phone.

"When I met you," she said, "you were so sweet. So polite. "

Sweet? He thumped his fist on the chair arm. For pete's sake, sweet? He'd settle for polite, but "sweet" made him sound like a puppy. He whumped his fist on the chair's arm in a slow rhythm. Whump. Whump.

"Alex."

Whump. Whump. Whump.

"You know the stakes," she said. "Get it right this time."

Pow!

Alex bolted out of the chair. Spinning around, he thrust the chair aside to reach the window. Erin's father hunched thirty feet from the house holding a .22-caliber rifle, with the butt braced against his shoulder.

Pow! The shot struck a plastic milk jug balanced on a tree stump twenty feet in front of Mr. Turner. The jug bounced and toppled onto its side.

"Alex?" Her voice rang through the earpiece of the phone, which he still held to his ear.

Mr. Turner fired another shot. The milk jug rolled off onto the ground.

Alex turned around and slumped against the wall. "I'm here."

"We have no time for personal hang-ups. Forces are at work," she said, "forces beyond our conception."

"Forces? What the hell does that mean?"

"It means even our allies are worried."

Their allies didn't worry about anything. They lived a sheltered existence where the concerns of average humans rarely touched them. For their superiors to worry meant bad things were coming. Extremely bad things.

Things like blood. And death. And cries for mercy that went unanswered.

He gritted his teeth. "I don't want another Utah."

"It wasn't your fault, Alex. Get over it, move on, and get the job done."

She hung up. He shoved the phone into his pocket.

The glowing orb he and Erin witnessed. Flashes of light that seemed to make people and objects disappear. Forces at work.

Did Rassul constitute one of those forces? No, he served as a tool for greater powers.

Forces beyond our conception.

He wheeled Erin's chair to the desk and sat down. Harry's book—now Erin's book— lay on the bed. Erin had taken the notepad, with the decrypted text from Harry's notes. He grabbed the book off the bed. He could figure this out on his own. What happened in Utah must never happen again.

Never.

F REYA TROTTED TO THE END OF THE RETRACTABLE LEASH, TUGGING AGAINST
it. Erin muttered, "Hold on, will you?"

The dog stopped. Erin halted too. She grasped the leash handle in her right hand and the notepad in her left. Tucking the leash handle under her left arm, she opened the notepad to the page where she'd written the coordinates from the petroglyph panel.

The coordinates pointed to the Grand Canyon, specifically formations called the Isis Temple and the Cheops Pyramid. Maybe Victorian explorers hadn't named the landmarks out of an obsession with ancient Egypt. Maybe they named the formations because they found remains of ancient Egyptian culture there. She remembered reading an article on a website about Egyptian treasures supposedly discovered in the Grand Canyon. The article discussed a news story that appeared in the *Phoenix Gazette* on April 5, 1909. The story detailed how an expedition, headed by an expert from the Smithsonian, discovered an immense tomb in the Grand Canyon. The tomb contained ancient Egyptian relics, as well as artifacts in styles typical of other cultures around the world. The treasures were a multicultural mishmash. The find was unprecedented and virtually unknown in modern times, except for the occasional mention of it on a paranormal website.

According to the articles she'd read, the Smithsonian claimed to have no record of the archaeologist mentioned in the original news story, a man called S. A. Jordan.

Freya tugged at the leash. Erin strolled down the road after the dog. She let her gaze wander to the forest, where an overgrowth of ferns and weeds already concealed the ground. The first wildflowers, tiny blue blooms, hugged the ground along the road.

While her gaze wandered, her thoughts wandered as well. The original story about the Grand Canyon tomb quoted the man who'd discovered it. He claimed the tomb lay almost 1,500 feet down a sheer cliff. The deciphered coordinates led to a location near or on the Cheops Pyramid. Deciphering the petroglyphs might lead to the lost tomb. She'd never visited the Grand Canyon, but on the map she downloaded the Cheops Pyramid looked like a craggy mountain. The coordinates might lead to the 1909 tomb, or something else entirely. Someone could've planted the 1909 story to cover up a real tomb in the Grand Canyon. Insert a fake story, one that sounds rather silly and relies on unverifiable details, in order to paint an aura of the ridiculous around the very idea of an Egyptian tomb in the Grand Canyon.

The archaeological establishment needed no cover-ups to ridicule the idea of an Egyptian tomb in the Americas. They did a fine job of ridiculing such ideas without fake news stories.

She looked at her watch. 12:21. She'd better get back the house for lunch, before her mother hatched a grand plan to marry her off to Alex. Of course, Mom needed to convince Alex first.

Tugging Freya's leash, Erin turned around to head back home.

Fifty feet ahead, a figure rounded the curve. Erin hesitated, until she recognized Alex. He was walking up the road toward her. No, not walking. Jogging. Within thirty seconds, he reached her.

Hands on hips, she eyed him. "In the mood for a little exercise?"

Panting, he glared at her. "Where the hell have you been?"

"Out for a walk. Why are you yelling at me? If this is about me going with you—"

"What?" His angry squint melted away. "You've been gone for over an hour. We got worried, so I volunteered to look for you. Your folks wanted to call the police."

Over an hour? A chill washed over her. She could not have been gone for that long.

She shrugged. "Guess I lost track of time."

"Did you see any orbs?"

"No." At least she didn't remember seeing any. "Not today anyway."

"What do you mean?"

While they half walked, half trotted back to the house, she told him. Everything. From her UFO sighting the other night to the day Rassul attacked her and the glowing orb that healed her bruises. Alex said nothing. When they hurried into the house, he still said nothing.

Her parents sat on the sofa, perched on its edge, faces taut and ashen. Erin shut the front door. Her parents sprang onto their feet.

"Where have you been?" Mom asked. "We thought you were kidnapped or lying dead in a ditch."

Oh crap. She needed to tell them a story, anything except the truth. A believable story. Nothing came to her.

Alex rested a hand on her shoulder. In a casual tone, he said, "Erin thought she saw a Bigfoot and got so excited she took off after it. Completely lost track of time. Finally, she realized she was following a bear and came back."

"Bigfoot?" Dad said.

Erin shrugged, trying to look innocent. "Sorry."

She caught the amusement flashing across Alex's features when she said the S word. It vanished in an instant, however, replaced by his usual noncommittal demeanor. In that instant she'd glimpsed another, less serious aspect of the man. And oddly, it comforted her.

At her apology, her parents exchanged unreadable looks. They either were planning to blockade her in her bedroom for the rest of her life, slipping her food and drink under the door, or they bought the story. She'd never done anything like this before. The benefit of the doubt seemed in order, she thought.

"Okay," her mother said. "We're just glad you weren't hurt."

Her father nodded. Erin relaxed.

Alex murmured to her, "Can we talk? Alone."

She grunted agreement. To her parents, she said, "Alex and I have things to discuss. Privately."

"He told us about the excavation," Mom said.

Excavation? Alex spun tall tales for her parents' benefit. Without her permission. She couldn't decide whether to thank him or smack him.

Her stomach growled. She hadn't eaten lunch.

Motioning for Alex to go into the bedroom, Erin ducked into the kitchen to steal a yogurt from the refrigerator and a spoon from a drawer. A minute later, she shut the bedroom door behind herself. Alex had planted himself the wooden chair. As she plopped down into her chair, she tossed the notebook onto the desk, opened the yogurt container, and downed a spoonful of her lunch.

"While you were gone," he said, "I arranged everything. We leave at six AM tomorrow."

She froze with the spoon halfway in her mouth. "I can't take off."

"I cleared it with your parents."

"You did what?"

She dropped the spoon into the container. Yogurt splattered on her shirt. Alex handed her a tissue from a box on the desk. She wiped the yogurt off her shirt.

He opened his mouth to speak.

She squinted at him, twisting her mouth.

He paused, cleared his throat, then said, "I told them we were going on an excavation in New Mexico. Your mom said she'd already googled me, and I assume she told you what she found. Apparently my checkered past doesn't bother her."

"Nobody told me anything. Librarians know how to use the Internet too."

"It wasn't my intention to offend you."

"Never is, but somehow you pull it off anyway."

He grimaced. "Maybe you shouldn't go. It could be dangerous."

"We had this discussion already."

Studying his hands, he sat silently for a moment. When he raised his head to meet her gaze, he looked like a man about to sentence his best friend to death.

He stretched a hand out to her. "Please give me the coordinates."

"You can have them once we're in Arizona."

"Harry went after the petroglyph panel and didn't come back. You'd like to see his decomposing corpse?"

"He flew to Albuquerque."

"On his way somewhere else." He reached for the notebook. "I can't risk taking you along."

She snatched the notebook away from him, stuffing it under her left thigh.

He frowned.

She swallowed a heaping spoonful of yogurt.

"Fine," he said, throwing up his hands in resignation. "We'll go together."

She chucked the notebook at him.

He caught it in one hand. "I'll pick you up at five thirty."

Saturday, May 21

It should've been dark. When a person dragged herself out of bed at five AM, the sky ought to be dark, rather than lit by the glow of sunrise. Yet the sunrise greeted Erin as she crawled out from under her blanket, torn from her sleep by the hideous screeching of her alarm. Now, twenty minutes later, the glow had turned into full-blown daylight.

Erin zipped the duffel bag. Its sides swelled like a pregnant whale's belly. She might've overpacked. Nobody instructed her in how to pack for a trip to an unknown location, possibly a lost tomb, possibly a trap to kill her, possibly something else entirely. And she couldn't exactly ask her mother for advice, considering she lied about the reason for her trip. Lying came so easily to her, not a hesitation in her delivery. What kind of scum had she turned into?

Seated on the foot of the bed, Mom asked, "Where did you say you're going?"

"New Mexico. Albuquerque."

Her stomach flip-flopped. Harry flew to Albuquerque and promptly disappeared. Her situation was different. Alex arranged for a private jet to ferry them to Albuquerque, where someone he referred to as "a colleague" would meet them with a car. From there, she and Alex would drive to the Grand Canyon, sans colleague.

"Where's the dig?" Mom asked.

"South of Albuquerque." Erin felt her throat tighten a smidge. Okay, lying wasn't quite so easy. "It's remote, so cell phones won't work."

"I like Alex, but are you sure about this? Who else will be there?"

"We've been through this. Alex has a friend, an archaeologist who works for the park service. They squeezed me in at the last minute. There should be thirty other people at the dig. And, yes, I'm sure about it."

Liar.

Her mother nodded, apparently satisfied. Thank heavens. If she told any more fibs, she felt certain her body would burst into flames or lightning would strike her.

Erin hefted the bag off the bed by its handles. The weight sank in her hands. The muscles in her shoulders stretched taut. The 9mm pistol and box of ammo added to the bag's weight, but she must take those items with her. Alex said she could bring anything—guns, knives, whatever—on the plane with her because he'd "smoothed the way" for them. She didn't ask what he meant by smoothing the way. If he told her, she'd most likely wish she never inquired. Luckily, her mother came into the room after she tucked the gun inside the bag. What would she have said if her mother saw the gun?

Uhh…I have to take a sharpshooting test, Mom. It's a new federal requirement for volunteering at archaeological digs.

Yeah, right.

With both hands around the handles, she lugged the bag down the hallway into the kitchen. Dropping it on the floor, she snagged her denim jacket from the coat racks.

Her mother approached behind her. "Is Alex going to marry you?"

"I barely know him."

"You're going away with him."

"That's right, we're eloping."

Her mother shook her head, smiling.

Erin slipped on her jacket and picked up the duffel bag.

"Trust me," Erin said, "it's an archaeological excavation. Period."

Sort of true. It was an unsanctioned, illegal, highly dangerous archaeological excavation.

"He's a nice boy," Mom said. "You should marry him."

Boy. The term seemed inadequate to describe Alex.

A horn beeped out front.

Erin carted the duffel bag through the living room, out the front door, and across the yard. Alex's car idled outside the gate. On seeing her, Alex jumped out of the car to swing the gate open for her. As she sidled past, she thanked him. He nodded.

Without a word, he took the duffel bag from her. Shutting the gate, he trotted past her to open the passenger door for her. She climbed into the car. Alex shut the door, stowed her bag in the trunk, and jogged around to the driver's door.

Her father had joined her mother on the front steps. Erin rolled down the window. When Alex backed the car out of the driveway, she waved to her parents. Would she see them again, or would she become the next person to vanish without a trace?

From the front steps, her mother shouted, "Have a safe trip."

Tears stung the corners of her eyes. She blinked them back. She would see her family again when she and Alex returned from Arizona. *Think positive*, she admonished herself. Stop obsessing over the worst possible outcome.

The car accelerated down the road.

Erin rolled up the window. A safe trip. She repeated the words in her mind like a mantra or a prayer. Would Rassul follow them?

Find it now. Before we lose patience with you.

Images cascaded through her mind. A body slamming into her from behind. An arm wrapped around her neck. A fist slugging her in the side, ricocheting pain through her body.

"You okay?"

Alex's voice echoed from far away. The view beyond the windshield was replaced with a mental movie of the attack. Rassul could hurt her far worse than he had the other day. If they, his employers, ordered him to kill her, he would.

The car jerked to a stop. Alex touched her shoulder. Concern tightened his features, etching slender lines across his forehead.

"I'm fine," she said. "Absolutely fine."

She tried to smile. Even she knew the expression looked pathetic.

Alex drove down the road.

Someone watched. Someone teased her with slivers of truth. If they owned the technology to conjure glowing orbs, then surely they could find the relic on their own, without the help of a librarian.

Or not. Someone wanted her to find the relic. Someone.

She gazed out the window. *Them.*

Revenant House

THE CAT MEOWED. THE LADY WHO CALLED HERSELF DESHERET SHUT THE DOOR in the feline's face. In the hallway outside, the cat pawed at the door. Her black toes protruded from under the door into the office.

Desheret nudged the cat's toes with the tip of her boot. The feline batted at the boot.

"Stop tormenting Bastet."

At the sound of Samuel's voice, Desheret spun on her heels. She sauntered to the mahogany desk and draped herself over its edge, one hand flat on the desktop to brace herself. Samuel sat in his leather chair, straight and stiff as an obelisk. Unlike an obelisk, however, his face presented no text to explain its purpose and meaning. His hands he clasped on the desk.

Bending toward him, she caressed his hand. She knew her blouse drooped away from her bosom, revealing a hint of what lay beneath. She hoped for a reaction, of the man-woman variety. Instead, Samuel focused on her face, ignoring her suggestive pose. When she spoke, she kept her voice as soft and throaty as a cat's purr.

"Do you care more for your cat," she said, "than for me?"

Samuel frowned. "Bastet has more patience."

She yanked her hand away. Patience. She clenched her jaw. No woman evinced more patience than she.

He stroked her cheek with his fingertips. Placating her. Trying to, at least. She felt the warmth of his fingertips on her skin, felt the anger leaving her, felt...placated.

Curse him.

The cat pawed at the door, meowing.

Desheret launched herself off the desk, into the chair situated in front of it. The chair's legs clacked on the wood floor as her buttocks hit the seat.

"The Egyptians," she said, "sacrificed cats to the goddess Bastet."

"Only in the later period of their history, when repeated invasions weakened their will. They sought refuge in religion, sacrificing animals out of desperation."

She hrumphed.

Samuel smiled, the expression more smug than jovial. "The goddess Bastet was a protector of women. You should appreciate her."

"Women betray me. I wish no protection for them."

"What about yourself?"

A lock of hair tumbled over her face. She tossed her head to shake it away. A smirk tugged at her lips. She let it rise. "I have you to defend me, my love."

"You need no protection, least of all mine."

Yes, she defended herself quite well. She dealt with foes encountered on her trips home, as well as in this place, without assistance from Samuel. If she did request his help, he would tell her to "adapt or die in the Darwinian fashion." The first time he spoke those words to her, she inquired about their meaning. He replied that she ought to read more, in order to understand the world in which she lived. She clenched her jaw. Samuel repeated his Darwin statement too often. She wished once he would sweep in like the medieval knights she read of in books, and spare her the suffering.

Samuel observed her from across the desk. A veil of indifference shaded his features. Yet, behind the veil, an emotion flickered for an instant. She could not describe the emotion. If she felt it herself, through a preternatural sense, she still might struggle to identify the feeling. Her own emotions, she understood. Samuels remained an enigma.

Desheret sighed. "I'm tired of waiting."

"A bit longer. A few weeks at most, I promise."

"I want this to end. Before he discovers my betrayal."

Samuel cleared his throat. No emotion breached his facade.

She said, "You know what he'll do to me if he finds out."

"He won't find out."

"I will not go back there."

"You must."

She pouted at him.

The corner of his mouth twitched.

Desheret picked up the Eye of Horus pendant that dangled around her neck and let it swing on its chain. Lamplight bounced off the metal, spraying the walls with golden hues. Outside the windows, a white light sparkled, then dissolved into the shadows.

She dropped the pendant. "They wish me to oblige you."

He smiled. Another version of the facade, she knew.

Samuel pulled out a drawer. From inside it, he produced a drawstring bag sewn from metallic fabric. Loosening the drawstring, he tilted the bag until an *akhet* ball rolled out onto his palm.

Desheret got to her feet and approached the desk. He handed her the two-inch-diameter ball. She cradled it in her palm.

"Go home," he said, "and attempt to diffuse the situation. I'll join you shortly."

Her stomach twisted as if someone wrung water from it. She froze her expression before pain transmuted it.

Through the clear exterior of the *akhet* ball, she spied the fluid-like interior writhing inside the shell. The ball warmed her palm. The human mind expected solid metal to feel cool. Five years ago, the first time she held an *akhet* ball, she pitched it aside out of fear that a fire lived inside the ball. Since that day, she shed her pagan ways, with Samuel's help.

She tossed the ball. It twirled up into the air, six inches above her hand. There it hung suspended for a heartbeat. It plopped down into her palm. She curled her hand around the little ball. Its surface felt smooth as glass, yet soft as velvet. Nothing on earth duplicated the sensation of an *akhet* ball in the hand. Nothing on earth duplicated its function either.

Samuel strode around the desk to her. He grasped her shoulders in his hands. She gazed into his eyes, those pools of honey that possessed the power to sweeten her mood and soften her to his will, if she let him.

He squeezed her shoulders. Tension charged his slender body, arcing through his sinews, sparking in his eyes. Strands of silver weaved through his dark brown hair. The lines around his eyes became visible only when he smiled, laughed, or frowned. Lately, she witnessed the latter expression most often.

The inflection of his voice matched his eyes. He whispered, "One last time."

The twists in her gut slackened. She lifted her chin. "This time, do you mean it?"

Bending his head down, he brushed his lips against hers.

"Go," he said. "Once more."

She murmured agreement. Not because he ordered her to go, not because he persuaded her with his kiss, but because she knew she must. They told her as much.

He released her.

She pushed past him and flung the door open.

Bastet growled at her. The cat had lain against the door in the manner a person might if one wished to eavesdrop. Cats did not eavesdrop.

Or did they?

Desheret hopped over the cat.

One final excursion. Samuel would keep his word. If he failed too, he would learn the punishment for disappointing her once too often.

Houghton County Memorial Airport
Hancock

It smelled like a new car. Erin ambled down the center aisle of the Gulfstream G650 jet, past a long table on the right and a sofa on the left. Further ahead, pairs of seats were arranged around tables, two groups on each side, both the tables and the chairs affixed to the floor. Between each grouping sat a single seat with a table. In back, a doorway accessed the lavatory and luggage compartment. The galley, or kitchen, must lie up ahead, past the chairs and tables. Leather covered every seat. The tabletops shone like the surface of Lake Superior on a calm day.

When Alex told her he had a plane, she pictured a biplane from World War I. Oil dripping from the underside. Rust on the engines. A few holes in the fuselage.

Sitting at the first table-seat group, Alex slapped his attaché onto the table. He unzipped it and slid out a laptop computer.

Erin glanced around the spotless interior. "Is this plane new?"

"Six months old," he said. "A friend lent it to me indefinitely."

"Nice friend. Do we really need this monstrous airplane?"

"Probably not. My friend believes bigger is better—and state of the art is best."

Several magazines lay scattered across one of the sofas. Erin wandered in that direction. With the tip of her index finger, she pushed the magazines around to see their covers. The titles were in German. She recognized some of the titles from citations in books she'd read. They were archaeology journals.

"You speak German?" she asked.

"Barely." While his computer booted up, he swiveled his chair toward her. "Why do you ask?"

She held up one of the magazines.

"Oh," he said. "Those belong to my friend."

"Doesn't he miss his jet?"

"He has five identical planes."

German, wealthy, generous to his pals. Alex's friend sounded a little too perfect. How did the man amass enough money to buy a fleet of Gulfstream jets? Anyone this rich must own a trunk stuffed with shrunken heads taken as trophies from those he annihilated.

She'd watched too many documentaries on the History Channel about the emperors of Rome. The guy might've earned his fortune through hard work, intelligence, and good fortune. Since she'd yet to meet a billionaire, she ought to wait until she encountered one before condemning the whole class.

Erin sank down onto the sofa. Like sitting on a cloud. A leather cloud.

Her purse, hooked around her neck, sagged onto her lap. She twisted her torso to look out the window. Did they call airplane windows portholes? The sun burned above the eastern horizon, amid a field of puffy little clouds. Closer to the jet, an eagle soared across the sky.

Alex twirled his chair to face the table, turning his back to Erin. He typed on his computer's keyboard. Clickety-clickety-clack-clack-click.

She unzipped her purse and extricated a piece of paper, folded in quarters, from the mess inside her purse. Before leaving the house this morning, she tore out of her notepad the page containing their rough translation of the petroglyph panel. On its backside she'd scrawled her interpretation of the text, though she had yet to share it with Alex.

The Gulfstream's engines rumbled to life.

Erin searched for a seatbelt but found none. Glancing at the other seats, she realized none of them included a seatbelt.

"How do we buckle up?" she asked.

"Don't worry about it," Alex said.

The plane stirred. The scenery outside the windows shifted.

No, no, this was no good. She dropped her hands onto the sofa. The plane accelerated. Her heart pounded fast as a hummingbird's wings. Her lips tingled, and the sensation spread outward into her face. *Breathe.* She balled her hands into fists. In, out, in, out. Her breaths came in staccato bursts, despite her mantra. She shut her eyes. In, out. Slow. Easy. Breathe.

Alex's voice cut through the ringing in her ears. "Are you afraid of flying?"

Eyes shut, she hissed, "No, I'm meditating."

The jet lifted off the runway. She canted sideways. The cabin seemed to spin around her as the ringing in her ears drowned out the engine sounds. The paper in her right hand crinkled. She willed her fingers to relax, before her nails tore the sheet.

Up, up, up.

Her fingers defied her orders. Her nails sliced through the paper to dig into her palm. Her stomach lurched, her gorge rose high in her throat, and then…it settled. The jet leveled off.

The paper was ripped from her fist.

She parted her eyelids. Through her lashes, she saw Alex hunched over in front of her. Blackness licked at the edges of her vision. In his right hand, Alex clasped the top three-fourths of the crinkled sheet of paper. The lower fourth was clenched in her hand, crumpled between her fingers and her palm. At the top of the sheet that poked out above Alex's hand, large black lettering declared "predynastic Burial Reveals Presence of ETs in Ancient Egypt." She forgot about stuffing that in her purse too.

"Don't pass out on me," he said. "I haven't got any smelling salts."

"Who does?" She inhaled, slow and easy. "I'll be okay in a minute."

She took several long, deep breaths. The ringing subsided, the blackness receded, and her pulse normalized. Some intrepid adventurer she made.

Alex crumpled the paper in his fist. "You don't need this."

She grabbed at his hand. He hurled the balled paper down the center aisle. The ball bounced toward the galley. She expected to watch his face tense in anger. It didn't.

"What'd you do that for?" she asked.

"You want the whole story." He sighed. "It's not in the article."

"Why not? Was there a cover-up?"

"Be quiet and I'll tell you."

Questions bubbled inside her. She clamped her lips together to seal in the words. Her fist had loosened, she realized. The scrap of paper lay free on her palm. She tossed it onto the table at the far end of the sofa.

"Scoot over," Alex said.

"Why?"

He puckered his lips.

She scooted over onto the adjacent cushion, at the end of the sofa.

He flopped down beside her. His thigh bumped hers. She squished herself into the corner.

Linking his hands on his lap, he said, "Seven years ago I went to Egypt with some colleagues. We signed on with a foundation that had been granted a concession to dig in the Valley of the Kings. The previous year, a couple of tourists who wandered off from their tour group found some pottery sherds lying near an old rubble pile. The pottery was predynastic. I think you're familiar with that era."

"Yes."

The predynastic period extended from about 5300 BC to around 3000 BC, when the first known king ruled over a united Egypt. Debate persisted over when exactly the transition from predynastic to dynastic occurred, and who the first king was. Prior to unification, Egypt existed as two kingdoms—the Upper Kingdom in the south, and the Lower Kingdom in the north. Since the Nile ran south to north, the ancient Egyptians oriented their world to the river that gave them life, turning south into up instead of down, as most modern people viewed it. The predynastic Period consisted of several sub-periods named after the cultures they represented. The Badarian was the earliest period, followed by the Naqada, which was broken up into three segments. Before 3200 BC, most of the archaeological evidence came from Upper Egypt. After 3200 BC, the cultures spread northward.

Predynastic artifacts ranged from simple vessels with red rims, dating from the early predynastic, to more elaborate vessels decorated with proto-hieroglyphs, indicative of the late predynastic. Early on, burials consisted of plain pits. Later, multi-chambered crypts emerged.

"Everybody else," Alex said, "thought the pottery was trash. Somebody in ancient times, or perhaps in modern times, tossed out the sherds while they were traveling through the area. Our team took a different view. If our theory turned out to be correct, it would significantly alter our view of predynastic Egypt. We set out to prove predynastic people used the Valley as a cemetery too."

"And?"

"We found the rubble pile, and some pottery sherds. Remote sensing equipment showed a cavity behind the rubble pile. A rock slide must've covered up the entrance to a crevasse. We cleared the rubble pile and followed the crevasse to a hidden wadi—a little valley, sort of a box canyon."

"You found a burial there?"

"Yes, we found a burial. But it wasn't Egyptian." He sank deeper into the sofa. "It wasn't even human."

Valley of the Kings, Egypt
10 years ago

ALEX SHIMMIED SIDEWAYS INTO THE CREVASSE. HIS DENIM SHIRT SCRAPED BITS of limestone off the crevasse walls. The backpack he grasped in his left hand rubbed against the rock too. The space widened, and he faced forward. Three feet wide now, the crevasse wound a path deeper into the mountainside. Ahead, around a bend, voices murmured. He followed the voices.

The crevasse curved leftward. He ducked under a low-hanging outcrop. The voices sounded nearer. He could almost make out the words. As he trudged onward, the crevasse narrowed by a foot. He squeezed through the constriction to the other side, where the crevasse broadened to six feet wide.

Thwack. The sound of metal striking rock.

"Careful!" someone shouted.

Alex trotted around another bend and through a ten-foot-high archway of limestone, a natural feature of the crevasse. The archway served as the entrance to an elliptical wadi one hundred feet long by thirty feet wide. Sunlight filtered down between the wadi walls, half as bright by the time it reached the bottom. A hole six feet long by three feet wide gaped in the wadi's center. Dirt was piled on one side of the hole. Oil lanterns crouched in three-foot intervals around the hole's perimeter.

Four people crowded around the cavity. Alex walked toward them. His colleague from the University, Bill Emerson, and the expedition's leader, Viveka Sandstrom, knelt at either side of the hole. Michael Goode, their remote sensing expert, hunched at the nearest end of the grave, slanting forward to peer inside the hole. Various tools lay scattered around the hole—picks, spades, brushes. Backpacks stuffed with other items squatted fifteen feet away near the wadi wall. Alex dropped his pack at the pit's rim.

The fourth person, a man, stood separate from the others. He held a shovel upright with its tip balanced on the ground, his hands folded atop its handle.

The man was a digger. He'd joined them yesterday, replacing Salim, the digger who worked with them for the past month. Two nights ago, Salim drove into Luxor for supplies and no one had seen him since. Rassul showed up yesterday morning looking for work. Convenient. Alex disliked convenience when it followed a mystery.

Alex halted next to Michael Goode. He glanced at the digger. What was the guy's name?

Rassul.

Yesterday, Alex asked around in Luxor to see if any of his contacts knew Salim's whereabouts. None did. Today he'd driven to Salim's home in Qena. The man was not there. Salim's wife hadn't seen him since the day of his disappearance.

"No sign of Salim," Alex said.

No one spoke. No one looked at him.

He shuffled closer to the hole. The lantern light rippled over the lip and down into the pit's depths. At the bottom, about three feet down, the light shimmered on the white outline of a skeleton. Dirt clung to the bones, masking the skull, yet the shape was undeniable. A human skeleton.

A fragment of a reed mat poked out from under the dirt. Predynastic burials sometimes incorporated mats placed under the body. The people who buried the skeleton oriented the remains westward with the legs drawn up to the chest, another signpost of predynastic burials. Someone, presumably one of his colleagues, had draped a handkerchief over the skull.

"Why did you stop?" Alex asked. "We need to clear the skeleton."

He turned to Michael. Although the man stared into the hole, his eyes seemed unfocused, as if he were in a trance. His lips were parted. His arms hung slack, his thumbs hooked in his belt loops.

Alex shook Michael's shoulder. The man didn't respond. Alex waved his hand in front of Michael's face. Nothing.

At the far end of the grave, Bill and Viveka stared into the hole with the same expression, or lack of expression, evident on Michael's face. What in blazes was wrong with them? They should be jumping up and down, slapping each other on the back, grinning like idiots. They found their proof.

Alex looked at Rassul. The digger smirked.

"What happened?" Alex asked.

"Shock."

"Over what?"

Rassul shrugged.

Alex crouched beside Viveka. He snapped his fingers near her ear. No response. He clapped his hands inches from her ear. She blinked.

"Viveka?" he said.

She turned her face toward him and blinked again, in slow motion. The look of her eyes gave the same trans-like impression.

"Can you hear me?" Alex asked.

She spoke, but her words were slurred and her Swedish accent thickened. He thought she spoke English, though he couldn't say for certain. She studied him as if gazing at a semitransparent apparition that her brain struggled to comprehend.

After several seconds, she blinked quickly three times, glanced around, and at last met his gaze.

"Alex?" she said. "When did you get here?"

"A few minutes ago. What happened?"

Across the grave, Bill blinked and yawned. He rubbed his eyes.

At the foot of the grave, Michael moaned. He shook his head, rolled his shoulders, exhaled with a hiss reminiscent of air escaping a tire.

They were waking up. From what?

"Too bad," Bill said. "It looked so promising."

"There's always next season," Viveka said.

Alex leaped to his feet. He eyed each of his colleagues in turn. They looked normal, awake, alive.

"The grave," Alex said, "is predynastic. We found our proof."

Viveka shook her head. "Sorry, Alex, it's clearly a modern burial. No more than a few centuries old."

"Two hundred years," Rassul offered.

"Yes. Two hundred years."

Bill said, "I agree."

Michael muttered his assent.

Bill Emerson and Viveka Sandstrom had spent twenty years excavating predynastic sites. Five years earlier, they discovered a predynastic cemetery a mile from the temples at Abu Simbel. Nobody knew more about predynastic burials than Bill and Viveka. Alex surveyed the burial visually one more time, in case his original assessment was flawed. It wasn't. Even an undergraduate could've recognized the predynastic features.

Alex glanced at Rassul. The digger's smirk flattened, compressing his lips into a line. Rassul no longer held the shovel, which rested on the ground beside him. Both arms lowered at the man's sides, palms clenched, Rassul squinted at Alex.

"Out of respect for the dead," Viveka said, "we must rebury the skeleton."

She reached for the shovel, but Alex grabbed it first. He said, "You three look tired. We can backfill the grave in the morning."

The others mumbled agreement. They shuffled out of the crevasse one by one. That they accepted his suggestion without discussion bothered Alex. On any other day, Viveka would've formalized a plan for the next morning and directed someone to lay a tarp over the pit for overnight before she left the excavation site.

The others were gone. Rassul lingered beside the grave.

"Time to go," Alex said.

A breeze swirled through the wadi. Rassul stayed put. Alex waved a hand toward the exit.

"Leave," Rassul said.

"You first."

Rassul reached a hand behind his back.

Sand twirled up on the breeze, into Alex's eyes. He rubbed them. The wind seemed to swirl down above. Impossible. Wasn't it? Cliffs five hundred feet high surrounded the wadi. He bent his head back, to gaze up at the sliver of sky visible above the wadi. A few stars twinkled. Darkness blended into the remnants of sunset.

Wind blasted his face. The lanterns snuffed out.

Wait. The lanterns were battery operated. No amount of wind could snuff them out.

Alex tugged his mini flashlight out of his pocket. Switching it on, he swept the beam around the wadi. Rassul was wriggling into the exit. As the light hit his head, Rassul paused to glare at Alex.

"You should have left with the others," Rassul said. "Now the grave will become yours."

A warped smile split Rassul's face. He slithered deeper into the narrow part of the crevasse, making his way to the desert beyond. A gust of wind plummeted down into the wadi, churning around Alex. He checked the heavens. Clouds blotted out the western half of the sky. Thunder grumbled. Lightning flared within the clouds, brightening the whole sky, pulsing faster and faster with each burst. Soon the lightning flickered like machine-gun bursts. He sensed something wrong about the storm. It sprang up out of nowhere, yes, but his unease stemmed from more than the storm's sudden onset.

He froze. No thunder.

A chill washed over him. The silence...

Boom.

The explosion echoed into the crevasse from outside, across the desert. The ground trembled. Sand and bits of rock rained down from the cliffs above. Alex held his breath. The grave lay open before him, its contents vulnerable to the elements. When his colleagues regained their senses, they would realize the importance of the find. He must protect it.

Ours.

The word popped into his head like a thought. Not his, though. He stiffened. The thought was not his.

Boom.

The ground shook. His feet lost traction, and he threw his arms out to the sides for balance. Fist-size chunks of rock whumped onto the ground. Dirt and sand cascaded over him. He sneezed. The explosion had been much closer this time.

The grave. He ran toward it, bounding into the pit. His feet struck the ground on either side of the skeleton's torso. The lightning pulsated faster. Silence blanketed the wadi, heavy as a wet quilt.

No time to save everything. His backpack slumped at the pit's edge. He grabbed it, tore open the main zipper, and yanked out his camera.

The lightning pulsated. He yanked the handkerchief off the skull.

He gasped. My God, the head. The shape.

No time. He snapped a dozen photos of the skeleton in the space of ten seconds. Sweat dribbled down his temples, dripped off his nose, splattered on the ground. Done, he ripped the roll of film out of the camera and stuffed it in his pocket. Tossing the camera aside, he dropped onto his knees. The skull. It offered the most vital evidence, but it was partially embedded in the ground. With both hands he grasped the skull and tugged. It wouldn't budge. He clawed at the dirt until blood oozed from under his fingernails. The earth refused to relinquish the skull.

The sky grumbled.

He held still. Not thunder. The sound was mechanical.

Hurry. His thought this time, he hoped. Digging pliers out of his pack, he bent close to the skull. He seized a nearby rock and smashed it into the jaw. The mandible fell away from face. With the pliers he grasped a tooth and pulled. The tooth popped out.

Static electricity rippled over him. His scalp tingled.

Shoving the tooth in his pocket, he vaulted out of the pit.

The grumbling escalated into roaring.

He bolted for the wadi exit. Just as he squeezed through the narrow part, the wadi exploded in a blast of light.

Starbursts filled his vision. His ears rang. Pinned between two slabs of rock, he stopped. Ten feet above his head, the rock jutted out over the narrow part of the crevasse, blocking the sky. He couldn't see them, but they couldn't see him either.

Them. Who?

If he left the shelter of the crevasse, he would die. Lightning would strike him, he knew, though he couldn't explain how he knew. He felt it. They destroyed the grave, and he was next. How long could he hide here?

Until he felt certain they'd written him off as dead. He must stay that long, however many minutes or hours it took. He must not move until every cell in his body assured him it was safe.

His hair stood up, and his scalp tingled. He squeezed his eyes shut, clenching his jaw. *Here it comes.*

Lightning blew apart the wadi.

Present Day

Alex leaned his head back on the sofa. He closed his eyes, sighing. Erin poked his arm. "Hey, you didn't finish the story."

Without moving his head, he opened one eye to look at her. A smile crept across his face, though his lips stayed knit together for several seconds, until he said, "No. Not until you're on the edge of your seat."

"I am."

He patted the front edge of the sofa. "No, you're not."

She rolled her eyes at him.

His smile broke open, revealing white teeth.

He had a sense of humor after all. A kooky one, but a sense of humor nonetheless. Thank goodness. She couldn't spend all day with a humorless academic. Of course, he wasn't an academic anymore.

"Tell me what happened," she said. "Pretty please?"

The smile dissipated. He averted his gaze to the window across the aisle but his eyes seemed unfocused, as if he stared at a memory rather than the view outside the window.

"I stayed in the crevasse for an hour," he said. "Then I crawled out and made my way back to Luxor. My room had been ransacked, probably by Rassul. I have no idea what he thought he'd find."

"The grave was completely destroyed?"

He nodded. "The cliffs collapsed into the wadi."

"What about the tooth and photos?"

"My colleagues denied the incident ever happened. They claimed they were having dinner at a local restaurant at the time. I went to the press but, naturally, they turned the story into a joke and me into a laughingstock. No lab would touch the tooth. Nobody believed me." He sat up, turned toward her, and rested his left arm on the sofa back. "Until I met Harry."

His hand lay behind her right shoulder, his thumb touching her. He stared right at her, and she stared right back.

"I quit archaeology," he said, "and took a job teaching high school in Alaska. Two years ago, I came across a website called the Foundation for Amarna Research and Exploration. They investigated taboo subjects like contact between the ancient cultures of Egypt and the Americas. I submitted a paper to their journal, the one you printed out. Harry contacted me a few days later. He invited me to join his foundation, which I did immediately. That was only the beginning."

"How so?"

He leaned toward her, shrinking the distance between them. His face hovered inches from hers, his eyes close enough she noticed the darker streaks in his irises. He whispered, "Are you sure you want to know?"

She scrunched her eyebrows.

"Once I tell you," he said, "there's no going back. You're one of us. A crackpot, a fruitcake, an escapee from the asylum for the criminally deluded."

She crossed her arms over her chest. Lifting her chin, she said, "If you can handle it, so can I."

"I know you're capable of handling it, but do you want to?"

She opened her mouth to answer. He placed two fingers on her lips. She stopped, her pulse quickening.

He retracted his fingers. "Wait until after this expedition before you answer."

"Yes, master."

He pulled away from her, back to his previous position.

Erin grabbed her purse, dug out the paper containing the rough translation of the petroglyph panel, and unfolded it. After studying the literal translation, she'd decided a little creativity might help. Two and half hours later, she arrived at an interpretation that made sense and fit the literal meanings of the hieroglyphs.

> The serpent god-king of the Two Lands traveled on the water to this place to reside. The god-king's army subdued our king and his subjects. The serpent king became our king, causing the rage of the sun god. The fiery abomination smote all human beings to make known the sun's dominion. The people hid in the desert cliffs. Many died. The sun god returned to the sky. The dead god-king will be buried in the pyramid mountain, on the river at the doorway to the duat, and sealed there for eternity.

The next and final line comprised the coordinates they flew toward at this very moment. The *duat* referred to the underworld the sun god Ra traveled through each night before reemerging at sunrise.

"I figured out the hieroglyphs," she said.

"And?"

Propping his head up with one hand, he watched her with a blank expression. The paper collapsed at the horizontal fold. She snapped it upright and recited her translation.

"Hmm," he said.

"That's all you have to say?"

He shrugged. She blew a breath out through her nose.

"Well," he said, "maybe you aren't as smart as I thought."

"What's that supposed to mean?"

Alex chuckled. She frowned.

Grinning, he said, "I had you going for a minute."

A joke. He made a really dumb, annoying joke at her expense. A sense of humor might not be a plus after all.

"Relax," he said. "You made sense out of the senseless. I'm impressed."

Her cheeks flushed. She turned her face away from him. Impressed. When referring to her, most people used words like mystified, disgusted, or vexed. Maybe Alex was still teasing her.

"Um," he said, fidgeting in his seat, "one of those orbs tried to spook me last night."

"Did it work?"

He hrumphed. "I yelled at the incandescent bugger."

She whipped her head toward him. "You what?"

"I yelled at it."

"Let me get this straight. You tell me not to take the job at Revenant House because it's too dangerous, and you freak out when my mother signals UFOs with her spotlight. Meanwhile you're harassing glowing orbs."

"Yes."

She growled. He made a face at her, one that signified either irritation or amusement. She had trouble telling the difference with him. He saw nothing wrong with risking his own life while ordering her to hide in the basement, figuratively speaking.

Abandoning the argument, she said, "What do you think of the translation? Sounds to me like an Egyptian pharaoh emigrated to the American Southwest."

"Possibly. We'll know more once we get there."

"The part about the sun god's rage could describe a UFO."

"Can't rule out anything. Someone with an enormous amount of technology and power has a keen interest in this discovery."

"No kidding."

They sat in silence for a few minutes. She gazed out a window on the opposite side of the plane, watching clouds zip by.

"Once we get to the Grand Canyon," she said, "how will we get to the location the coordinates lead to? Will we hike there?"

"Not exactly."

"What does that mean?"

He hesitated. "You'll see."

Her stomach tightened as if a web of steel filaments encircled it.

Alex winked.

Albuquerque International Sunport
Albuquerque, New Mexico

THE FLIGHT TOOK JUST TWO AND A HALF HOURS. ERIN UNDERSTOOD WHY someone disgustingly rich would want a fleet of private jets. She'd put a Gulfstream jet on her Christmas list and send it to Alex's German friend, in case he was as generous as he was rich. Then again, her new employer might provide a private jet along with a new car.

Nah. She wasn't that lucky.

The plane rolled to a stop. Her duffel bag squatted on one of the seats across the aisle, next to the seat on which Alex's attaché and backpack sat, right where she stowed it before takeoff. She stood up, stretched, and ambled to the seat.

Alex sauntered down the aisle toward her. He had gone to visit with the pilots, something about giving them instructions for their stay in Albuquerque. Apparently they would wait for her and Alex no matter how long their expedition took. Wonder what it felt like to have people at your beck and call. She knew all too well what it felt like from the other side.

Just as she stretched a hand out for her duffel bag, Alex reached her. With his left hand, he snagged the bag's handles, hefting it off the seat.

"What's in here?" he asked. "The Rosetta Stone?"

"I didn't know what to pack. This is my first time playing Indiana Jones."

He switched the bag to his right hand. With his left, he grabbed his backpack and slung it over his shoulder. When he reached for the attaché, she snatched it first.

"I can carry this," she said.

One of the pilots, a mustached man in his fifties, emerged from the cockpit. He walked past them to the plane's door, opening the exit. They flew with a skeleton crew for security reasons. The fewer people on board, the fewer chances of anyone letting something slip.

Alex led her toward the exit. She passed the pilot on her way out the door.

The pilot said, "Enjoy your trip."

She almost laughed. Enjoy your trip? Maybe the pilot had no idea what they were doing here. She thanked him and followed Alex down the airstairs to the tarmac. A car was parked fifty feet away. Alex veered toward it, and she trailed after him. The car waiting for them, an old Cadillac, bore little round craters on its hood, roof, and trunk. Patches of darker blue paint splotched the original coat, a dusty blue color that was faded and chipped. The car must've gotten pelted by a few hailstorms, then repainted by someone whose skill stopped at the finger-painting level. The engine purred, but something inside it chirped like a sickly bird. A loose belt probably. A couple times before she'd heard a similar sound coming from her parents' Explorer and it turned out to be a belt. Whatever a belt was.

Taking the attaché from her, Alex stashed their bags in the Cadillac's trunk. A man with curly white hair and a stubbly white beard slouched behind the steering wheel of the car, his left arm on the window, his right palm resting on the gear shift lever between the driver's and passenger seats. She couldn't remember the last time she spotted a car with a stick shift, much less got into one. The man behind the wheel raised his right hand to aim it at her palm out, in a stationary wave. He wiggled his fingers and arched an eyebrow. She waved at him.

He winked.

Alex opened the front passenger door. He motioned for her to get in.

Inside the car, the white-haired rogue patted the passenger seat. "Come on, sweetie, I won't bite. Can't promise I won't smack one on ya though."

"Cut it out, Lou," Alex said. "You're scaring the librarian."

Erin planted her hands on her hips. "I'll take flirty old geezers over bossy archaeologists any day."

She hopped into the car. Her butt hit the seat with a thud. She unfurled the seatbelt and buckled it.

Alex shut the door. He climbed into the backseat.

The flirty old geezer offered his hand to her. "Lou Valentine at your service, milady."

She shook his hand. "Erin Turner."

"Oh yes, I know all about you."

When she tried to pull her hand away, he grasped it tighter, lifting it to his lips. He kissed the top of her hand, then let go.

Folding her hands on her lap, she glanced in the rearview mirror. Alex's reflection stared back at her, his expression pinched. He seemed to be studying the back of her head. Darned if she knew what he was thinking.

To Lou, she said, "What did you mean when you said you know all about me?"

He hummed a single note. "Not sure if I'm allowed to say. Your dossier may be top secret."

"Dossier?" She twisted around in her seat to look at Alex. "What's he talking about?"

Alex stared into her eyes. A hint of wrinkles fanned out from his narrowed eyes. His frown flattened out into a line. Exhaling, he widened his eyes out of the squint. His lips curved up at the corners a touch, into a near smile that brightened his face.

"We checked you out," he said. "We needed to know if we could trust you."

"What's the verdict?"

"I trust you."

"Nice to know."

He kept staring into her eyes. She felt a blush rising in her cheeks. She willed it to stop, but her body paid no attention. Dammit, she would *not* blush every time he looked at her.

If she couldn't stop it, she'd hide it.

Whirling toward the front of the car, she said, "The real question is can I trust you and your mysterious buddies."

"You have to decide that for yourself," Alex said.

Erin glanced at Lou. He was squinting into the rearview mirror.

"Sorry, kid," Lou said. "I'll keep my hands to myself from here on out. Didn't know she was your girl."

Erin stiffened. Through clenched teeth, she said, "I am not his girl."

"No offense intended." He glanced at her sideways. "You one of those modern women who'd rather be called a significant other?"

"I am not his significant anything."

"Sure, hon. I get it."

Lou nodded slowly, smirking in an endearing way only a flirty old geezer could achieve. She didn't really view him as an old geezer, though, despite referring to him as one earlier. He looked about sixty, with hazel eyes that sparkled like gemstones. His biceps bulged beneath the long-sleeved T-shirt he wore. Both the shirt and his jeans hugged his trim, muscular figure. His leather boots looked scuffed, and possibly of military origin. Either he shopped at the army surplus outlet, or he'd served.

She looked out the window. Lou shifted the car into gear, released the parking brake, and hit the gas pedal. The car lurched forward.

In the rearview mirror, she spotted Alex scrutinizing the back of her head. She ran a hand through her hair. Did she have dandruff?

Lou repositioned the rearview mirror. Though she could no longer see Alex in the mirror, she sensed him watching.

Mare's tail clouds fanned across the blue sky. Somewhere out there, other eyes observed. In daylight their craft remained invisible. She felt them watching too.

Watching. And waiting.

THEY AVOIDED THE FREEWAYS, STICKING TO THE SMALLER HIGHWAYS AND SIDE roads. First they drove south, but after an hour they turned westward toward Arizona. Alex stared out the windows mostly, while Lou regaled her with tales of his Navy days. From glancing at the speedometer occasionally, Erin calculated their speed averaged seventy. Twice she saw the needle spike up to eighty-five. Since they avoided the major roads to avoid detection, she expected Lou might drive slower to stay off the police radar. Half an hour into the trip she asked Lou about it.

"Complain to the kid, sugar," he said. "I'm followin' orders."

"What or—"

Alex interrupted, "We need to hurry."

She eyed him in the rearview mirror. "Why didn't we fly to a closer airport?"

"Misdirection. With any luck, the bad guys lost track of us."

"Don't we risk exposure by rushing?"

"We have to balance security and speed. It's a tightrope."

The bad guys pursuing them possessed technology far in advance of anything the average human villain could get his hands on, no matter how much money he had. Misdirection seemed a vain effort in the face of such power. She kept the thought to herself.

At 1:15 they rolled into the small town of Snowflake, Arizona, where Lou drove straight to a grocery store. Pulling up to a pay phone near the main entrance, Lou jumped out of the car and made a beeline for the phone. Once he'd extracted a wrinkled slip of paper from his pocket, he dialed the number he must've written on the slip. After a brief conversation, he returned to the car.

"All set," he said.

On the road again, they navigated a maze of side streets until they arrived at a small blue house. A dark green Jeep Wrangler occupied the driveway, so Lou parked on the street in front of the house. He and Alex both got out of the car this time. Erin swung her door open and planted her right foot on the ground. Alex stepped in front of the open door, blocking her path.

"Stay here," he said. "Please."

He was squinting, and the faint lines around his eyes had returned. Crescent shadows darkened the skin under his eyes. His shoulders sagged.

She said, "Okay."

He and Lou trudged up the driveway to the front door of the house. Lou rang the doorbell. What on earth were they up to? Guess she needed to join their secret society before they'd share their plans with her. The mention of a dossier hinted they knew an unnerving level of detail about her. And she knew squat about them.

Erin swung the car door shut and rolled down the window. An elderly man opened the door for Alex and Lou. The three men chatted for a moment, then the elderly gentleman gestured for Lou and Alex to come inside the house. He shut the door behind them.

Erin leaned her head back against the headrest, shutting her eyes. Her body ached. Her eyes burned. The shooshing of the wind lulled her mind until she felt herself drifting into the limen between sleep and waking. Her quest for sleep last night netted her brief periods of dozing, with genuine rest racing away from her like a balloon caught in the jet stream. Thoughts had ricocheted in her mind, colliding and merging with each other, thoughts of glowing orbs and mother ships and shadowy beings. Fear, excitement, and exasperation flowed through her in a never-ending loop. Now, in the daylight, her mind felt empty. Aside from the occasional burst of annoyance, she felt calm. Or numb. She had trouble distinguishing the two.

Rousing herself, she yawned and stretched. The door to the house swung open and Alex exited, followed by Lou, who twirled a set of keys in his right hand.

The men marched to the Cadillac. While Lou retrieved their bags from the trunk, Alex yanked her door open. He gestured for her to get out.

"What's up?" she asked.

He pointed at the Jeep. "A change of venue."

A light flashed in the blue sky. She saw it peripherally. Her heart thudded, and she glanced toward the flash. Nothing there. She blinked. Still nothing. Puffs of white skidded across the sky on an upper-level wind. She closed her eyes. *Get a grip.*

A hand grasped her arm. She opened her eyes.

Alex squeezed her arm gently. "You okay?"

"Fine."

She forced a smile. She hadn't lied. Other than suffering from a permanent case of the heebie-jeebies, and excluding the exquisite fatigue, she was fine.

Alex scrunched his lips. Releasing her arm, he ushered her toward the Jeep. Five minutes later, they rolled out onto the road and, ten minutes after that, they flew down a two-lane highway at eighty-two miles per hour, with Snowflake vanishing into the distance in the rearview mirror. Lou found an oldies station on the radio.

The desert rushed past the window in a brown blur. She let her eyelids flutter shut. The music on the radio faded into the background. Her mind floated away into the darkness behind her eyelids.

Blackness. An orb glowed mottled white overhead. She pushed through a barrier, feeling tiny needles brush against her skin. Something crunched under her feet. She looked down. In the pale light she recognized the shapes scattered over the ground as pine needles. She blinked. The scene around her came into focus. She stood barefoot, dressed in her nightie, within a forest of pine trees. The orb hovering overhead was the moon. The air felt dry and chilly. Words echoed in her mind, thoughts but not her own.

Find the relic. Only you, satseshat, possess the key.

She wanted to ask a question. Her own thoughts were hazy, though, and so slippery she couldn't hold onto them.

Find it or die.

The orb flew at her face.

She woke with a jerk. Breathing hard, she struggled to make sense out of the scene around her. Dashboard. Steering wheel. Glass. Brown blur.

Alex leaned forward between the seats. Lines creased his forehead.

"Bad dream?" he asked.

She said nothing, hypnotized by the brown blur whizzing past her window.

He was staring at her. Again. Either she had food stuck between her teeth or she looked god-awful.

"It's nothing, I'm fine," she said. When he didn't look away, she added, "If I had a bible I'd swear on it. I am truly and completely fine."

She flashed a tight smile. Patting her arm, he leaned back into his own seat.

Lou murmured, "Looks significant to me."

Erin focused on the brown blur outside the window. They were bouncing down a gravel two-track. Dust plumed up behind the car. Up ahead, perhaps a quarter mile away, a house squatted in the desert near a second, indistinguishable shape. Maybe it was an outbuilding. As the car rolled down the road, ever closer to the mystery object, the blob separated out into constituent parts she recognized. A helicopter. Tan with a dark blue stripe across the side.

"My private helipad," Lou said.

"Great." She glanced over her shoulder at Alex. "This is how we're getting into the Canyon?"

"Yes."

Lou parked in front of the little house, more of a shack actually. Inside a fenced-in yard, two German shepherds barked and wagged their tails. She studied the helicopter. Tiny compared to the Gulfstream jet, the helicopter featured large windows on the sides and front. She imagined flying over the Grand Canyon, with four thousand feet of nothing below her. A lump congealed in her stomach, rock hard and cold.

Shutting off the engine, Lou flung his door open and bounded out onto the desert floor. Alex disembarked too. Out the corner of her eye, she watched him lean over to peer at her through the window. She traced the helicopter's stripe with her gaze.

The chopper plummeting. The canyon floor rushing up. Pow! Incinerated in a ball of fire.

No, first the impact would crush her. Bones shattered. Bleeding to death. If she were lucky, she might die on impact.

Alex knocked on the window. She jumped. Rolling down the window, she tilted her head to look at him.

"It's safe," he said.

"Uh-huh."

"Are you getting out of the car?"

She bit the inside of her lower lip.

"You can stay here," he said.

Erin shoved the door open, forcing Alex to scuttle backward. If he thought hiring a helicopter to take them to the canyon would convince her stay to behind, he'd better think again. She was going. She might be utterly insane, and she might die in a fiery crash, but she would go.

She hopped out of the car, slamming the door shut. Lou had already trotted to the helicopter. The lump in her gut swelled. Her throat tightened. A wave of dizziness broke over her. She clenched her fists until it passed. Alex reached for her arm, but she waved him away.

Suck it up, she commanded herself. She straightened her posture, crossed her fingers, and marched toward the helicopter—and whatever awaited them in the canyon, whether priceless treasures or faded rock art.

Or death.

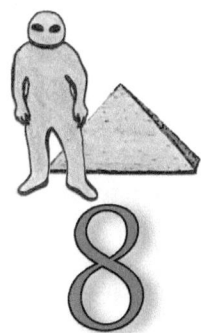

8

Cheops Pyramid
Grand Canyon

Lou LEANED AGAINST THE OUTSIDE OF THE HELICOPTER, HIS BACK AGAINST the rear door. The helicopter squatted atop the relatively flat plateau they'd landed on, two hundred feet from the edge. The plateau lay on the west side of Cheops Pyramid, a craggy mountain on the north rim of the Grand Canyon.

Erin glimpsed bits and pieces of the scenery during the flight, in the moments when she managed to peel her eyelids apart. One peek out the windows, though, induced a tornado of dizziness and nausea that made her squeeze her eyes shut again and grab onto the nearest object. Her fingers ached from clutching her own thighs. They must sport fingertip-size bruises. Her jaw ached too. She must've gritted her teeth.

Minutes earlier, they flew over the Colorado River, with its opaque green waters reminiscent of the turquoise the ancient Egyptians used in jewelry, and rapids spewing white foam downriver. Now they stood atop a plateau that, on its eastern side, sloped up into Cheops Pyramid. Tan and reddish soil intermingled across the plateau and up to the reddish summit towering over 1,000 feet above their heads.

The sun burned in a blue sky, without a cloud anywhere in sight. The temperature hovered around fifty degrees, with a faint breeze tickling Erin's face. She zipped up her windbreaker, which she'd dug out of her duffel bag, along with a wide-brimmed canvas hat, right after they landed. Alex crouched a couple yards in front of her fiddling with the straps on his backpack. Lou stood six feet to her left, as she faced north.

After another thirty seconds of fussing with the straps, Alex rose and hoisted the pack onto his shoulders. He wore a two-way radio clipped to his belt, the twin of the radio secured to Lou's waistband. In his left hand, Alex held an electronic device a little shorter than his hand and half the width of his palm. He tilted the device toward her.

"GPS unit," he said. "I've entered the coordinates you deciphered."

She leaned forward to see the device better. It featured a full-color touch screen populated by six icons arranged in two columns, above a battery indicator bookended by two arrow icons pointing left and right, respectively.

Straightening, she asked, "Are you finally ready?"

"Yes."

He tapped the touch screen on the GPS unit several times. Pointing northeast, he said, "That way. About a third of a mile."

A third of a mile. Good thing she wore hiking boots. She cinched up the tie-down strap on her hat.

Alex strode across the plateau in the direction he'd indicated. She trudged after him. They ascended a steep grade toward a meandering line of shadows about halfway up the slope. After a few minutes, Erin's thighs ached. A crick formed in her low back. Walking in the nice flat woods failed to prepare her for mountain climbing. Despite the cool temperatures, sweat rolled off her forehead and down her temples. Her breaths came in gasps.

Alex stopped. He flopped onto his butt on the ground. Sweat trickled out from underneath his baseball cap, running down his temples and cheek. She collapsed onto the dirt a few feet from him. Lying back against the slope, she struggled to calm her breathing.

From his backpack Alex retrieved a canteen. He took a couple swigs from it then passed it to her. She gulped the cool water. At the bottom of the slope, far away across the plateau, the helicopter looked like a toy. She couldn't make out Lou.

Five minutes later they resumed their trek. Up, up, up they went. The meandering line of shadows drew closer and closer, until she discerned the true shape concealed behind the shade. The shadows masked the underside of an overhang that drew a jagged line across the mountainside. As they mounted the last thirty feet, she gauged the overhang at eight or ten feet high and at least four hundred feet long. Alex halted at the overhang's periphery. It projected out six feet from the mountainside.

"This is it," Alex said.

Erin scanned the back wall of the space under the overhang. She saw rock. Lots and lots of rock. Nothing jumped out at her as relevant to the petroglyph panel.

Alex dropped his backpack on the ground. He unzipped its main pocket, extricating a flashlight from the interior. He clicked the power button and swept the beam up and down the rock wall. The light skimmed across blank rock.

"How accurate is your GPS thingamajig?" she asked.

"It should get us to within thirty feet of the target."

"Okay, you go left and I'll go right. Look for anything out of the ordinary."

Saluting her, he spun on his heels to amble away from her. She turned in the opposite direction. In wide, deliberate steps she explored the overhang for more than thirty feet from the spot where she split from Alex. Rocks. Dirt. She discovered nothing of importance. Ten minutes later she met Alex back at their starting point. Shoulders slumped, he frowned at the touch screen of his GPS unit.

She gazed out across the canyon separating Cheops Pyramid from another mountain, dubbed Isis Temple, the big sister of this peak. Isis Temple adjoined Haunted Canyon, and Phantom Canyon carved through the landscape east of Cheops Pyramid. To the west of Cheops Pyramid lay the Tower of Set, named after the ancient Egyptian god of chaos. Why did eighteenth-century explorers choose mystical and ancient names for the features surrounding Cheops Pyramid? Isis was a beloved goddess in ancient Egypt and later in Greece and Rome. The other names, though, carried spooky or downright evil connotations. Did something about this mountain, or this area, give explorers the heebie-jeebies?

She glanced down the length of the overhang. The petroglyph panel mentioned a pyramid mountain, a description fit by Cheops Pyramid, but the text also described the vicinity of the mountain. What had it said? The king will be buried in the pyramid mountain on…what?

"Hey," she said, poking Alex's arm, "do you have my translation of the petroglyph panel?"

"Mm-hm."

She poked him harder. When he finally looked at her, she asked, "May I have it please?"

He retrieved it from his pack, offering it to her. She unfolded the sheet and skipped down to the second to last line of her translation.

The dead god-king will be buried in the pyramid mountain, on the river at the doorway to the Duat, and sealed there for eternity.

The river. She glanced over her shoulder toward the Grand Canyon, where the Colorado River snaked a path, though she couldn't see the river from here. She stood on a pyramid-shaped mountain adjacent to a major river. The phrase "doorway to the *Duat*" might signify a feature found on Cheops Pyramid or on a nearby mountain, or in one of the canyons. She swept her gaze out across Trinity Canyon to the peak of Isis Temple, a mountain to the northwest. Isis and Cheops were both Greek versions of names for the goddess Aset and the pharaoh Khufu, respectively.

The book. In *A Spiritualist History of Ancient Egypt*, Gilbert Covington used the Greek versions of ancient Egyptian names Amenophis instead of Amenhotep, Cheops instead of Khufu. She stood on the slope of Cheops Pyramid, overlooking Isis Temple. So what? Harry chose the book, and unknown people inscribed the petroglyph panel.

"Where did Harry get the book he sent me?" she asked.

"He didn't," Alex said. "I bought it in a used bookstore and gave it to him."

"Did you read the book?"

He shook his head.

"Did Harry read it?"

"I'm not sure. I never asked."

The book seemed like a dead end, for the moment. Even if Harry sent her the book as a clue, what did the cryptic coot expect her to glean from it? The text dealt with death and the afterlife, specifically how spirits interacted with the living, and what the Egyptians believed about such matters. The Egyptians harbored many beliefs about death and the afterlife, including the idea that the deceased returned as spirits, walking among the living during the daytime, and that the spirits needed their bodies in order to live on after death. For this reason, the Egyptians preserved their dead, interring them in cemeteries and tombs. The Valley of the Kings served as a burial ground for the pharaohs. Tombs carved deep into the mountainsides riddled the Valley. Great, more information that helped her not one bit. She already knew the petroglyph panel most likely referenced a tomb. Come on, come on, she could do this. *Think.*

Over the centuries, sand covered up the entrances to the tombs in the Valley of the Kings. The same thing might've happened here.

Death and the afterlife. Spirits. According to Egyptian mythology, each night the Aten—the disk-like face of the sun—sank into the western horizon between two mountains. The shape of the horizon flanked by twin mountains formed the hieroglyph *akhet*, meaning horizon. The *akhet* also served as the gateway to the *Duat*, the underworld of Egyptian mythology, into which spirits journeyed each night. Many Egyptologists thought the pharaoh Akhenaten selected the site for his new capital city, Akhetaten, because the nearby mountains resembled the *akhet*, a vital symbol in his new religion of Aten worship. Another pharaoh, one who traveled far from his homeland, might choose a location for his tomb based on similar ideas, perhaps as a means of staying connected to his roots.

"You have an idea," Alex said.

"Maybe."

Striding out from under the overhang, she stopped ten feet away and turned to look back. The overhang drooped down in places. She shuffled backward. Nothing grabbed her attention. Backing up farther, she swiveled her head left to right, up and down, waiting for a shape to pop out at her.

"There!"

She thrust a finger into the air, aimed at a spot a dozen feet to the left of Alex. He trotted out from under the overhang, halting next to her.

"What are we looking at?" he asked.

Erin raised her other hand. With her index fingers, she pointed at two low spots on the overhang. Between them, the rock arched upward.

"Imagine it inverted," she said. "It would look like the *akhet* symbol."

He tilted his head, squinted, and frowned.

"Can't you see it?" she asked.

"I suppose. So what?"

"The entrance must be under the *akhet*."

He opened his mouth, stopping short of speaking. *Entrance to what*, he wanted to ask. She practically heard the words bouncing around in his head. Until they found the entrance, she couldn't answer the question.

Alex sighed. "You can tell me later how you reached your conclusion. Right now let's find out if you're right."

They walked side by side back to the overhang. The *akhet* shape embraced fifteen feet of the overhang's length. Erin dropped onto her knees. She thrust her fingers into the dirt and felt around. For what, she wasn't sure.

"Wait," Alex said.

He unzipped the main pocket of his backpack, reached inside, and pulled out a folding shovel about a foot long. The handle was folded over onto the blade. Alex opened up the shovel to its full length, about eighteen inches.

Waving her out of the way, he bent into a half crouch. With the shovel grasped in one hand, he crab-walked the length of the overhang under the *akhet* shape in one-foot increments. After each step, he tapped the shovel into the dirt four or five times, drawing a dotted line perpendicular to himself. A few minutes into his search he arrived at the center of the *akhet* shape. He plunged the shovel into the dirt. Meeting no resistance, he swung the shovel to his left and plunged it in once more.

Thunk.

His shovel had hit a solid obstacle. Rushing to him, Erin dropped onto her knees at his right side. Alex explored the dirt with the shovel's tip. When he found an edge, he traced its length with the shovel's tip until he hit a corner, then he traced the other edges in the same manner. He drew a perfect square in the dirt, recessed about seven inches. The object was a stone slab four feet square and three inches thick. A layer of dirt and pebbles several inches thick concealed the stone slab. Alex scraped the dirt off the slab with the shovel's edge, using it like a knife. Once he removed the bulk of the dirt, he bent forward to wipe the rest off with the sleeve of his jacket. The slab's face was smooth and blank.

Alex slid his fingers down the slab's edge. His fingertips sank into the earth.

"I feel a gap," he said. "A seam."

He lifted. A grimace contorted his features but the slab didn't budge.

Erin moved to the opposite side of the slab from Alex. Sliding her fingers under the slab's edge, she felt the seam too. She looked at Alex. He nodded. They both lifted. She gasped as pain sliced up her arms into her shoulders and up her neck. The slab stayed put.

Alex said, "We need leverage."

He jumped to his feet, jogged to his backpack, nabbed one of the straps, and carted the pack over to the slab. He pulled a crowbar out of the pack.

"Find a big rock," he said, "to wedge under the slab."

He jammed one end of the crowbar under the slab's edge.

Erin glanced at the surrounding landscape. About fifteen feet away down the slope, she spotted a large rock. Leaping to her feet, she ran down the slope to the rock. It was as big around as her head and four or five inches thick. With both hands, she hefted the rock off the ground and hugged it to her belly. The weight of it slowed her down as she scrambled up the slope. By the time she got back to Alex, her arms ached and she was panting. Collapsing onto her knees in front of the slab, she dropped the rock.

Alex had raised the slab a few inches. The gap revealed a stone lip a couple inches thick, with a void inside it. She slid the rock toward the gap. It wouldn't fit. Alex leaned on the crowbar. His face contorted. The slab jerked upward. She shoved the rock under one corner.

The crowbar slipped from Alex's hands. The other corner whumped down into the dirt. Alex grabbed the crowbar, thrusting it under the fallen corner.

"When I lift this," he said, "you shift the rock into the middle."

"Okay."

He pried the corner out of its slot. She jostled the rock into the middle of the lip. Alex lowered the slab. Balanced on the rock, the slab rested at an angle with its other end on the chasm's lip.

"Now what?" she asked.

Panting, Alex mopped sweat from his brow. He flopped onto his butt on the ground. "I don't know. This was the extent of my plan."

A breeze tickled her cheeks. She looked down the mountain toward the helicopter, then scanned the tops of the neighboring mountains. An airliner's contrail raced across the blue sky.

Alex rolled forward to kneel before the slab. Hands on his thighs, he frowned at the darkness visible under the slab.

She said, "Maybe we could—"

He slapped both hands on the slab's raised end and pushed. The slab flipped up. For a heartbeat it teetered on the opposite lip.

Then it fell.

The slab skidded backward off the lip. It twisted sideways, tumbling forward into the abyss. Ka-whump. The slab had landed at the bottom of the shaft.

Alex settled a hand on the lip at either side of the opening. He bent forward to stare into the darkness below. Sweat dripped off his nose.

Erin patted his shoulder. "Congratulations, you did it."

"I guess we won't be sealing it up when we're done."

"Apparently not. I thought archaeologists were cautious and meticulous."

"We don't have time for cautious and meticulous."

"Right." She peeked over the edge. "Do you have a flashlight?"

He rooted in his backpack and pulled out a lantern flashlight. Switching the light on, he aimed it into the hole.

The ground was about thirty feet beneath them. The stone slab rested flat on the bottom, a little off-center from the hole. Alex swept the flashlight in a circle. The entrance lay at the end of a tunnel or passage that extended eastward under the overhang, into the mountain. Directly under the entrance, the passage dead-ended flush with the hole's lip. As the flashlight's beam struck the wall under her, Erin noticed indentations in the rock face.

"Footholds," Alex said.

The Anasazi built dwellings high on the sides of steep cliffs. They accessed the dwellings via removable ladders or footholds and handholds carved into the cliffs. They must've been nimble folk, the rock climbers of their day. Erin gripped the hole's rim, her fingers curling over the edge. It was a long drop. If she fell, she might whack her head on the slab.

Alex folded the shovel and stuffed it into his backpack along with the flashlight. He hoisted the pack onto his back.

The radio on his belt bleeped. Alex twitched.

Lou's voice emanated from the radio. "Whoops, sat on the radio. Ignore me, kids."

The radio bleeped again, signaling the end of Lou's transmission. Alex sighed. Gazing into the hole, he said, "I'll go first."

Erin scuttled backward on her knees to give him room. He knelt in front of her, swung his left leg over the edge, and hesitated. He jiggled his leg as if searching for a foothold. Finding it, he swung his other leg over the edge while grasping the lip in both hands. His torso and head ducked below the lip. Soon he retracted his fingers too.

She crawled nearer. As she leaned forward, she caught sight of him ten feet below. The darkness enveloped him until only the top of his head and his hands were visible. In a moment, they disappeared. The scritching and grunting sounds told her he hadn't fallen. How could he navigate the footholds in the dark? She couldn't do it. Or wouldn't do it. Jeez, she needed to grow a spine.

The noises stopped. The lantern flashlight clicked on at the bottom of the shaft. The light revealed Alex's silhouette at its periphery and illuminated the wall beneath her.

"Your turn," Alex shouted.

"Maybe I should stay here. As lookout."

"Lou is our lookout." He patted the wall with his free hand. "Come on, you can do it. The first foothold is about three feet below the opening."

Her stomach twisted. Her mouth felt dry. *Just do it.*

She swung her right leg over the edge into the chasm. With the toe of her boot, she explored the wall, feeling for the first foothold. Her boot hit an indentation. She pressed her toe into it, testing her weight. The foothold supported her. She grasped the rim of the opening in both hands and swung her left leg over the edge. Her left foot swung through the air.

"A little to the right," Alex said. "And down about a foot."

She lowered her left foot, swinging it to the right. Her toe locked into the foothold.

Alex aimed the flashlight just below her chin. "The handholds are kitty-corner to the footholds."

Guided by the flashlight's beam, she located the handholds, grasped one with her right hand and then her left, and lowered herself down to the next foothold. She repeated the process a couple dozen times. Though each step brought her closer to the floor, she avoided looking down any farther than the next foothold. The flashlight's beam brightened, Alex's voice grew louder, and she sensed the space below shrinking. But each time she considered glancing down, her jaw snapped shut, shooting pains through her skull. She winced, forced her jaw to relax, and concentrated on reaching the next foothold.

"You're doing great," Alex said. "Ten feet to go."

She peeled her right foot out of the foothold. Eyeballing the next target, she dropped her right foot toward it.

Alex's radio bleeped.

Erin jumped. Her foot jerked right, plunging into empty air. Her whole right side sank downward. Her right hand popped out of the handhold.

Plop. An object hit the floor. The flashlight's beam sliced straight up into the air.

Her right foot swayed in the air. Her left hand slipped halfway out of the handhold. She flailed her right hand toward the indentation as she braced the sole of her boot on the wall. Her fingers grazed the handhold's edge and she tried to close her fingers over it.

Her right foot slipped off the wall. She sailed backward and down.

Alex caught her.

She lay cradled in his arms with her butt sagging between them, her feet sticking straight up with the backs of her knees slightly above his right arm. Her heart pounded against her ribs. Her ears rang. Her breath came in gasps that echoed off the shaft walls. For a few seconds, she thought she was still falling, despite the solidity of Alex's arms under her and his body pressed against her right side.

He lifted his left arm, drawing her face closer to his. He squinted at her. "Erin? Are you hurt?"

She shook her head, still incapable of speaking. His eyes captured her gaze and she stared into the blue rings of his irises, which encircled the dark pools of his dilated pupils. The flashlight sat a half dozen feet away, aimed up the shaft. They stood in the half-light at the beam's perimeter.

He deepened to squint. "Erin?"

She blinked slowly. "I'm not hurt."

"Good." He dropped her feet onto the floor, setting her upright. Her knees buckled. He grasped her forearms and told her, "Breathe."

She sucked in a breath.

"Easy," he said.

She exhaled more gently and took a few deep breaths at the same pace. Her ears stopped ringing as her heartbeat slowed and her breathing calm. She looked up at Alex. He kept his hands wrapped around her forearms, his body heat leaching through her shirt onto her skin.

She swallowed. "Thank you."

"You're welcome."

He let go and stepped away from her to retrieve the flashlight.

She had swooned. Sheesh, what was she, a Victorian socialite?

Flashlight in hand, Alex strode past her into the tunnel. She hustled after him.

Clearing her throat, she asked, "How did you climb down the shaft in the dark?"

"Practice."

"You do this a lot?"

"Yes."

"Why? What are you searching dark shafts for?"

"Answers."

So much for conversation.

The tunnel was fifteen feet wide by seven feet tall, stretching deep into the mountain farther than the flashlight's beam could reach. The walls were blank, the floor solid rock like the walls and ceiling. With every breath, a dusty smell filled her nostrils. The air felt dry. They walked ten feet, then twenty, thirty, forty. At the edge of the flashlight's beam, where its light dissolved into the darkness, she caught sight of an indistinct shape. While they marched onward, a wall came into view, the dead end of the tunnel. There, a six-foot-high niche carved into the solid rock housed a statue.

Alex halted a few feet from the niche. Erin stopped beside him, taking in the statue. It depicted the god Osiris, the ancient Egyptian deity associated with death and rebirth. The statue showed him in a common form, wrapped as a mummy with arms crossed in front of his chest, one hand holding a crook and the other a flail. In ancient Egypt the crook and flail represented kingship. Archaeologists found a similar statue in a maze-like tomb in the Valley of the Kings believed to be the tomb for the sons of the pharaoh Ramses II. Egyptian tombs featured walls covered in hieroglyphic texts and paintings of gods, pharaohs, animals, and scenes from the afterlife alongside portrayals of daily life among the living. This tunnel, despite housing an Osiris statue, lacked any wall or decorations.

Erin glanced left and right. The tunnel extended in both directions.

"Which way?" she asked.

Alex pivoted left. "Here."

"Any particular reason?"

"No."

He started down the left-hand corridor. With no flashlight of her own, she shadowed him in the twilight wake of his flashlight. She jogged to catch up and walk beside him. As in the main corridor, the walls here were blank yet smooth. About a hundred feet in, the corridor dead-ended. The wall here was rough and lumpy, as if the workers who built this place gave up in the middle of the project, collected their gear, and fled.

Whirling on his heels, Alex headed back the way they'd come. At the intersection he continued straight across into the other corridor. Erin trotted to keep pace with him. His longer legs carried him much further than hers did at the same speed. The flashlight's beam bobbed as he moved, mimicking the motion of a boat. Nausea swelled inside her. She sucked in a deep breath, releasing it gradually, and focused on the floor. The motion sickness abated.

Alex halted. She paused, lifting her gaze from the floor. He swung the flashlight left. The beam dove through a doorway. The doorway opened into a chamber with walls as bare as the corridor's. Alex crept toward the doorway and bent forward to peek inside. Straightening, he strode into the chamber. Erin faced the doorway.

A light flashed to her left. She glanced down the corridor toward the T intersection. Darkness. The backwash of the flashlight's beam bled out into the corridor, where it dissipated into the blackness around her. She canted her head to listen but heard no sounds issuing from the main corridor. She must've imagined the flash.

Into the chamber she went.

Alex had set the flashlight on the floor, aimed at the ceiling. The chamber was twenty feet square, with a barrel ceiling fifteen feet high at its apex. The ceiling and walls appeared smooth, prepared for whatever decorations the artisans intended to carve into them. Alex hunched near the chamber's far side, hands on his hips, staring at the wall. She approached beside him. From his coat pocket, he pulled out a pen-size flashlight, which he switched on and directed at the wall, holding the light at chest height. His chest height. Her collarbone height. The light revealed lines etched into the rock.

The lines resembled the start of a hieroglyphic inscription, carved in sunken relief. The inscription was rough, the hieroglyphs incomplete and jagged. She recognized the sign for hetep, meaning offering. Tomb inscriptions for pharaohs often began with the phrase *hetep di nesu*, meaning "an offering the king gives." The *hetep* glyph had other uses and other meanings too.

"Is this a royal inscription?" she asked.

"Possibly."

"If this place was meant as a tomb, it looks like they never finished it."

"Evidently."

She folded her arms over her chest, turning to glare at him. He stretched a hand out to the unfinished inscription. With his index finger, he traced the rough outlines of the glyphs. His gaze seemed intent on some sight beyond the wall or perhaps within his own mind. She waved her hand in front of his face.

He blinked. Rotating his head, he met her gaze.

She said, "You awake in there?"

"Yes."

She huffed a breath out her nose. "Have you lost the ability to speak more than one-syllable sentences?"

"No." He wrinkled his brow. "Why?"

"Never mind." Shaking her head, she gestured at the inscription. "Could this have anything to do with the pharaoh Akhenaten?"

"That's a huge leap. Why do you suspect Akhenaten?"

"You make it sound like a police investigation. I don't suspect Akhenaten, I simply wondered if this place might link to him. After all, the *akhet* symbol, a favorite of Akhenaten's, led us here."

"True."

Twirling left, Erin wandered the chamber's perimeter. Here and there tools littered the floor, ancient tools by the looks of them. Along one wall, she discovered a pile of hammerstones, rocks shaped by human hands for the purpose of pounding on other rocks. Ancient peoples the world over used tools like these, and some primitive tribes used them even today. She picked up an oval hammerstone with a groove around its middle. The groove indicated where an ancient person wound a rope around the rock to strap it onto a stick. The rope eventually wore down a groove in the rock. Some hammerstones in the pile were broken in half, most likely for use as crushers, but others were vaguely triangular in shape. Similar tools from Africa dated back millions of years. The ancient copper miners of Michigan used similar tools.

While she strolled a bit further, she noticed a long, thin object with a greenish tinge to it lying under a hammerstone. Kicking the stone aside, she plucked up the object. It felt like metal. The object looked almost arrow shaped.

"Alex," she said, "come and look at this."

He trotted to her. In his left hand he cupped an object she couldn't quite see. Leaning over her shoulder, he studied the object in her hand.

"Interesting," he said. "It looks like a predynastic copper razor."

"Predynastic as in Egypt?"

"Precisely."

Glancing at his left hand, she asked, "What have you got?"

He raised his hand, palm up, and unfurled his fingers. A crescent-shaped object curved across the width of his palm. Each end of the crescent bent up, giving it the outline of an ancient Egyptian boat, and its copper had developed the green patina also evident on the razor. Crescent objects identical to the one in Alex's hand turned up in Michigan's Copper Country, left there by the ancient miners. No one knew the purpose of the crescent objects. This one sported an abstract design, a series of jagged lines, etched onto its surface.

Alex reclaimed his backpack and flashlight from where he'd set them on the floor under the unfinished inscription. He plucked the predynastic razor from her hand, tucking it inside his backpack along with the crescent-shaped object. From a nearby pile, he snagged a small, grooved hammerstone and a split hammerstone. He stowed both objects in his backpack, zipping it shut.

"Let's check for other chambers," he said.

After hefting his pack onto his shoulders, he led her through the doorway and left down the corridor. She stayed beside him as they traveled deeper into the mountain, past yard after yard of blank walls. They must've covered a hundred feet before Alex stopped. His flashlight shined through a doorway, fifteen feet ahead, identical to the entrance for the previous chamber. From her angle, she saw a slice of the room inside the doorway, where more piles of hammerstones littered the floor along with other objects she couldn't identify from this distance.

Alex walked into the chamber.

A growling noise, faint and low pitched, emanated from the opposite direction down the corridor. Erin tilted her head in that direction, listening. The noise was gone. Maybe it never existed.

She shuffled into the chamber.

The floor was dirt, flush with the rock floor of the corridor outside. Alex knelt in the left rear corner of the chamber. He held the flashlight in his right hand, aimed into the corner. She trotted across the room to crouch beside him. In front of them, a human corpse lay prone on the floor.

Her mouth went dry. She had never before witnessed a dead body, or any kind of human remains, except on television or in magazines. Judging by the haircut and the clothes that still draped the body, the individual was male. The head was bent to one side with the left cheek flat on the floor. The skin, brown and leathery, stretched taut over the bones and peeled back from the teeth. The eyelids were closed, sunken where the eyeballs rotted away. Dark hair clung to the scalp. The corpse was mummified, most likely by natural means.

The mummy's left arm was bent toward the head, as if reaching for something, the hand flat on the ground with fingers dug into the earthen floor. The right arm rested parallel to the body with the hand palm up on the floor, fingers clenched around a small piece of parchment. The legs sprawled straight out with the feet, clad in leather boots, stretched out to the right of Alex's feet.

The most striking aspect of the mummy was not, however, his pose or the desiccated nature of his remains. No, the thing that raised goosebumps on her arms and prickled the hairs at the nape of her neck was the object protruding from the mummy's back. Wedged hilt deep, centered between the shoulder blades, was a knife.

Alex had begun an inspection of the mummy's head. Erin explored the area around the knife, which was lodged between two vertebrae. A dark stain on the mummy's shirt spread outward from the knife wound. Blood, she realized, the stain was dried blood.

Erin pointed at the knife. "I can tell you why he croaked."

He paused to glance at her. "What?"

"Glad you're paying attention. I know how this guy died." She tapped the blade's hilt. "Somebody stabbed him."

"Interesting."

Alex grasped the mummy's right wrist. With his other hand, he tugged lightly on the parchment until he'd freed it from the mummy's grasp. Turning over the parchment, he raised it so Erin could see it too. Words handwritten in black ink scrawled across the page.

August 15, 1858

To whomsoever happens upon my mortal remains— Tell my brother Broderick he was right. Nothing but evil can come from allying oneself with those who serve the darkness that masquerades as the light.

Ridley Covington

"Creepy," she said. "Wonder what it means."

Alex shrugged. He tucked the scrap of parchment into his coat pocket and rose, taking the flashlight with him.

In the backwash of the light, she stared at the mummy's eye sockets, empty and sheathed by leathery skin, where once eyes glimmered with life. What color had the irises been? When he smiled, had dimples puckered at the corners of his mouth? She knew nothing about him, yet she felt certain Ridley Covington deserved a better resting place than this dark, unfinished tomb.

Covington. She recognized the name.

Alex shuffled backward a few feet. He panned the flashlight left and right.

Of course she knew the name Covington. The book Harry sent her, *A Spiritualist History of Ancient Egypt*, was written by Gilbert Covington. Was he related to the man whose mortal remains lay before her? To brush it off as a coincidence strained the meaning of the word.

Erin stood. While Alex swept the flashlight beam around the chamber, she made a mental inventory of the objects scattered throughout the space. To the left of the mummy she noted a knapsack and canteen. Further back, in the corner, a single hammerstone sat alone. The room housed nothing else, no treasures, no evidence of what transpired here, either in ancient times or in the nineteenth century when Ridley Covington died in this chamber.

Erin glanced over her shoulder at Ridley's mummy. He lived long enough to write a cryptic note, yet he looked as if he simply collapsed in the corner, unable or unwilling to move, until the blood drained from his body. Given the size of the catacombs, he must've survived for quite awhile.

Or did he? Marching back to the body, she dropped onto her knees beside Ridley, on his left, where his arm twisted up toward his head. His fingernails were embedded in the dirt, pushing his fingers up into a tent-like pose, but his palm was flattened against the floor. Did he reach out in agony, or struggle to grasp something?

Alex stooped opposite her, on Ripley's right. He met her gaze, his expression dour. "No secret exit in here."

"Don't give up just yet."

Erin took hold of Ridley's left hand and lifted. The hand remained stuck to the floor, virtually nailed down by his fingernails and the stiffness of his mummified limbs. Releasing his hand, she eased a fingertip under Ridley's palm. She felt weird messing around with a human body, especially one whose name she knew. Knowing the name made the dried-out corpse seem more human and, in an odd way, more alive. If Ridley suddenly opened his eyes and demanded to know what the blazes these strangers were doing to him, the act would not have surprised her. It would've scared her, but not really surprised her. Granted, that made no sense.

Focus. She slid her finger farther under Ridley's palm. Her fingertip met an object that felt like metal. It was trapped beneath Ridley's palm. He must've tried to close his fist around the thing but was too weak to complete the motion. She snagged the object's end with her index finger and eased it out from under Ridley's hand, straightening as she withdrew her finger. She took the object between her thumb and index finger. It was a blackened key, probably fashioned from iron. The key measured about four inches long. Its top end curled into an inch-diameter loop filled in with ornate scrollwork. The key's body was thin and cylindrical, with a serrated metal tongue sticking out from one side of the tip.

Across the mummy from her, Alex crouched with his head bent close to Ripley's, intent on the hair. Maybe he was hunting for mummified lice.

She waggled the key. "Look what I found."

Alex eyed the key. He said nothing, his expression blank. Finally, he said, "What's it for?"

"Nothing in this room. Unless he swallowed a lockbox."

She tucked the key inside her pants pocket.

Alex jerked his head toward the doorway. Squinting, he pursed his lips.

Erin got to her feet. "What should we do now?"

Alex jumped to his feet and ran to the doorway. He tilted his head as if listening. She walked up behind him and listened too, but heard nothing.

"What is it?" she asked.

"Sh."

At last she heard it. Rumbling. Faint. Coming from the direction of the main corridor. She planted a hand on the doorway to brace herself while she leaned past Alex, ducking her head into the corridor.

Boom.

The walls and floor trembled. The vibrations ricocheted up her legs and through the arm she braced herself with, bleeding into the rest of her body. In the wake of the boom, the rumbling resounded louder. Closer. Though she tried to breathe, her lungs felt frozen. Her heart pounded.

Boom. Tremors rippled through the rock around them.

"What the hell's that?" she asked. "Thunder?"

"Not quite. We should leave. Fast."

Alex took two steps into the corridor. Erin rushed after him, grabbing his arm to stop him. He grasped her hand and pulled her down the corridor with him. Another boom shook the tunnels. They were headed right for the source of the explosions.

She yanked him to a halt.

He gaped at her. "We are leaving. Right this second."

"Running toward the scary noise? Great plan."

"We have no choice." He slashed the flashlight beam down the corridor, lighting its dead end. "There's no way out besides the way we came in."

Holding fast to her hand, he took off down the corridor at a fast trot. She sprinted to keep up with him. Every ten or fifteen seconds another boom reverberated through the tunnels, and with each concussion the tremors intensified, impeding their pace. Boom, she swerved left. Boom, she stumbled to the right. The rumbling drowned out their footfalls. Even the thudding of her heart, the rushing of the blood behind her eardrums, got lost in the din. At the T intersection they veered left toward the entrance.

Alex froze. She collided with his back.

Up ahead, a shaft of twilight shined down from the entrance thirty feet above.

A bright flash blinded her. Thunder exploded. The walls shook. Clods of dirt and rock rained down through the entrance. Erin lost her balance, stumbling into Alex.

Silence followed.

Alex's radio bleeped. They both jumped.

A second later, Lou's voice rasped through the radio. "Kid, you there? Are you reading me?"

The radio bleeped again, signaling the end of the transmission.

"Yes," Alex said, "we hear you."

"Your fan club is here. And they ain't happy."

"I gathered that. We're coming out."

"Bad idea."

"We're com—"

"Stay there." The urgency in Lou's voice spiked a shiver through Erin. Lou added, "Forces beyond our conception, kid. Beyond our conception."

Alex stiffened.

Erin looked up at his face. "What does he mean?"

Alex spoke into the radio. "I understand."

She opened her mouth to speak. Before she could utter a syllable, Alex clasped her shoulders. He bent his knees to scrunch down until their eyes were level.

"Stay here," he said. "Please."

He stared into her eyes, tightening his grip a smidgen. She nodded.

Lightning glanced through the gloom. Pow!

The earth convulsed. Erin wobbled and flung her arms out for balance. Alex's tone had matched Lou's—sharp, definitive, yet with a hint of well-concealed panic. If Alex and Lou were scared...

Shit.

Alex sprinted for the entrance.

THE WALLS QUIVERED AROUND ALEX AS HE CLIMBED UP THE CRUDE LADDER formed by the foothold-handhold pairs. By the time he reached the halfway point, the tremors subsided. The thunderclaps and the earth's rumblings faded into a deep silence suited for a tomb. At the shaft's apex, he stopped to peek over the rim. The mountain hunkered in a false twilight. The lightning had stopped. He couldn't see the helicopter. The hush outside felt as profound as the silence in the farthest reaches of the catacombs within the mountain.

With both hands planted on the rim, he climbed up a few more rungs until his torso cleared the opening, with his hips braced against it. No breeze. No rain. The world seemed frozen, as if time had screeched to a halt.

A chill coursed through his veins.

Lightning sparked in the clouds, across the canyon beyond the Tower of Set, a couple miles away. He waited for the thunder, counting the seconds in his head. One Mississippi, two Mississippi, three Mississippi. The humidity enveloped him like a giant, sweaty hand. If a fist caged him, the hand belonged to them, the hidden enemy who seemed to have no name.

He stopped counting at twenty Mississippi.

A bolt of lightning zigzagged across the base of the clouds. Another bolt slashed across the cloud base in the opposite direction. Another bolt, then another, and another. No thunder, no sound whatsoever, breached the silence. Maybe he'd gone deaf.

From below, Erin's voice echoed up to him. "What are you doing?"

Lightning danced across the cloud base in bursts of three to four bolts. He glanced down the shaft. Erin, positioned a dozen feet from the wall, stared up at him. In the backwash of the flashlight, she resembled a ghost.

"Back away," he shouted.

She didn't move. He opened his mouth then clamped it shut. She wouldn't move. No point in wasting breaths to yell at her.

The lightning pulsed in fusillades of machine-gun intensity with no more than a half second between the salvos. A sound approached from the west. Wind? An airplane? He shut his eyes to listen. The whirring sounded mechanical, though unlike any machine he could imagine. As the lightning intensified, with the pause between salvos shrinking, the whirring grew louder. Within ten seconds, the lightning coruscated nonstop.

A thick bolt exploded from the cloud base, slamming into the canyon floor. The earth shivered. God almighty. The words echoed in Alex's brain as he hugged the shaft rim. His left foot bounced off the foothold. He found the slot, jamming his toe into it. The shaking dwindled.

The hairs on his head stiffened and his scalp tingled. He recognized those signs. They meant the lightning was striking too damn close. He ducked down into the shaft, grabbed the nearest handholds, and clambered down the ladder. The clouds kept firing their machine-gun volleys of lightning.

Boom.

Closer. That one must've hit the mountainside.

Erin aimed the flashlight up at him, blinding him for a second. She shouted, "Get your butt down here."

"I'm trying."

His heart jackhammered against his ribs. Cold sweat trickled down his temples. He climbed as fast as he dared, skipping every other rung. The hairs all over his body jumped to attention. Fifteen feet to go. He felt the tingling of electricity in the air. *Oh shit.*

Screw it. He leaped off the ladder.

His right foot struck the floor, his left grazed the slab. He stumbled, regained his footing, tripped again, and staggered into Erin. She slapped a hand on his chest.

Bam!

The earth convulsed.

The rumbling of the earth around him drowned out all other sounds. Dirt rained down through the shaft opening. Fist-size lumps of rock and dirt plummeted to the bottom. Behind the rumbling he heard another sound, like the cracking of the ice.

He seized Erin's arm and dragged her down the corridor.

Ow! " Erin tried to wrench her arm free but Alex's grip was too strong. He hauled her toward the T intersection. Twice she tripped, and twice he hoisted her onto her feet with barely a hiccup in his step. "Slow down, would you?"

Whump.

Dust billowed down the corridor.

What the hell?

The dust cloud thinned as it reached them, swirling around their bodies. The dust infiltrated her nose and throat. She coughed once, twice. The third coughed segued into a fit of hacking. Her throat burned, her stomach muscles ached, her eyes watered. Rivulets of tears streamed down her cheeks, etching muddy streaks on her face. Through the dust, out the corner of her eye, she saw Alex coughing. Her own hacking drowned out everything else until, after what felt like ten minutes but probably was one or two, her coughing fit ended.

A dust cloud settled onto the ground. A skin of grime coated her. Alex looked equally dirty, with his hair tinted a lighter shade of brown thanks to the dust. Bending over, she brushed the dirt out of her hair with her hands. When she straightened, she shook her whole body. Dust plumed off her.

Alex scowled in the direction of the entrance. "We are dead."

"Thanks for the pep talk."

"It's true." He rubbed his eyes. "A section of the overhang collapsed onto the entrance. We are trapped, hence we are dead."

Hence? She must mark this moment in her memory. For the first time in her life, she heard someone use the word hence in conversation.

"Hold on," she said. "Let's make sure before you start digging our graves."

Erin tromped down the corridor. She hopped over rocks and clods of dirt that had fallen through the opening into the corridor. A larger pile of debris heaped smack under the shaft's opening. Halting there, she looked up at the entrance.

No opening. No sky. Nothing but dirt.

Alex shuffled up behind her, his shoulders sagging, his scowl deepening. He waved a hand at where the opening had once been. "I was right. We're dead."

"The fact you were right about being trapped doesn't mean we're doomed."

The thunder no longer grumbled. Either the storm moved on or so much earth entombed them that the sheer weight of it blocked outside sounds. They *were* trapped. How long might the air in the tomb last? How many minutes until they suffocated?

There she went, letting Alex's pessimism infect her.

She faced him. "We have to look for another way out."

"There's no—"

She slapped her hand over his mouth. "Say one more word about dying and I will slug you."

His eyes widened. The toughness of her tone surprised her too. Maybe her body did possess one tough bone, and one might sprout more.

Alex huffed a breath out his nose, blasting air over her hand.

She pressed her hand harder against his mouth. "I mean it. "

They stared at each other for a moment. Then she said, "No more doomsday talk. Right?"

He nodded. She pulled her hand away. He executed an about face and stalked down the corridor toward the T intersection. She sprinted after him. Maybe the miners dug an emergency exit, hidden somewhere in the tomb. She'd grab onto any thread of hope, no matter how frayed. At the intersection, Alex jogged left. Erin hesitated at the junction. She closed her eyes and sent out a silent prayer for divine assistance. It couldn't hurt.

A chill wriggled down her spine. She peeled her eyelids apart, turned her head right, and...

She knew where to look for a secret exit.

The light from Alex's flashlight grew brighter. He was coming back. In a few seconds he trudged up to her.

"This way," she said, pointing down the right-hand corridor.

"Why?" he asked.

"Shut up and follow me."

She scampered down the corridor with Alex keeping pace beside her. She yanked the flashlight out of his hand and arced it back and forth across the corridor. The beam dove through the entrance to the chamber where Ridley Covington rested in peace, of a sort. Erin swerved toward the doorway.

"Where are you going?" Alex demanded. "That's a dead end."

"Trust me."

"Why?"

She sighed through her nose. It came out like a growl. He fell silent, his lips pursed as if restraining another question.

Erin surged through the doorway. A dozen feet inside the chamber, she halted. What now?

Alex bumped into her. He cleared his throat. In a voice devoid of emotion, probably on purpose, he asked, "May I ask what your plan is?"

Good question, she almost said. She had no plan. A voice inside, however, whispered for her to trust her instincts—and her instincts told her the solution to their predicament awaited them here, in this chamber.

"The plan," she said, "is to find a hidden exit. Help me look for it."

"What makes you think there is one?"

"Shut up and help me."

He squared his shoulders. Together, they searched the chamber, prodding the floor with their boots in case the dirt concealed a trapdoor, pounding on the walls in hopes of hearing a hollow answer indicating a void behind the stone. They found nothing.

Erin shuffled toward Ridley's mummy. Hands on hips, Alex watched her. The corners of his mouth curved up in a smirk.

Kneeling beside the mummy, she frowned at Alex. "What?"

"Imminent death makes you bossy."

She clenched her teeth and fisted her hands.

He threw up his hands in the universally acknowledged gesture of submission. "Sorry, I meant possible imminent death. No need for violence."

Her fingernails dug into her palms. She relaxed her hands. Despite her earlier threat, she hadn't thought about slugging him. Why did she clench her fists? Oh, maybe because she raced into this chamber overcome by the belief a hunch would lead her to a secret exit from the tomb. Yet this room contained no exit.

Or did it? If an exit existed, why didn't poor old Ridley get out of the tomb? Someone murdered him, as evidenced by the knife in his back. Maybe he never got the chance to escape. Too weak to flee, he may have collapsed in the corner, dying right where his mummy lay.

Alex squatted opposite her beside the mummy. "What are you thinking?"

"A really dumb idea, no doubt." She considered Ridley's face. "Let's move the mummy to see what's underneath."

Alex crinkled his forehead.

"It's a hunch," she said.

He shoved his right hand under the mummy's legs, slid his right hand under the back, and lifted. Erin hopped out of the way.

"I'll be damned," Alex said.

He set the mummy down two feet to the right of its original position, on the spot where Erin crouched a moment earlier. Under where Ridley's head had lain, revealed in the ambient glow from the flashlight, a four-inch metal ring jutted out from the dirt.

Alex grasped the ring and pulled. Nothing budged.

Erin waddled closer. "Too much dirt on top of it?"

Alex closed both fists around the ring. He pulled hard, his face contorting. The dirt shifted and cracked. The first crack stretched two feet wide parallel to the wall. As the lid raised, two more cracks of the same length split open along the sides. A hinge creaked.

Letting out a low cry, Alex released the handle. The lid had opened away from the wall at a forty-five-degree angle, its hinge perpendicular to the wall. The cavity exposed by the lid was black. The flashlight's glow penetrated only a few feet into the chasm. A faint musty smell wafted out of the hole.

The dirt sloughed off the lid in clumps. Erin touched the lid. Flakes of rust molted off on her fingers. The metal hinge was bolted into the solid rock lid, with the stone blanketed in a quarter inch of dirt.

A light glanced in her face. She winced. Alex's camera beeped. Cradling the camera in one hand, he gazed down into the hole. Sparks danced in her vision, the aftermath of Alex's attempt to photograph the lid and the hole.

"Thanks for blinding me," she said.

"Hand me the flashlight."

She obliged. He shined the beam into the hole.

His cheek grazed her forehead as they both leaned over to peer into the hole. Beneath them, a stone corridor extended away from the wall into darkness. The passage below paralleled the one that led to the chamber in which they crouched.

"Where do you think it goes?" she asked.

"Someplace dark." He frowned. "Doesn't seem like an exit."

"Unless there's a door at the other end."

Boom.

The mountain gyrated around them. She stumbled into Alex. He clasped an arm around her waist, keeping them both upright despite the bone-vibrating concussions. A cloud of dust and debris blew through the doorway into the chamber. Erin coughed and shut her eyes against the grit.

The quaking of the earth subsided, while the trembling of her hands worsened. Christ, wasn't sealing them inside an underground labyrinth enough?

"They're back," Alex said.

"Great." She cringed at the crack in her voice. "They must know there's another way out."

"Or they want to be damn certain we're dead."

Another explosion rocked the mountain. The corridor outside the doorway collapsed, shooting a wall of dirt and debris into the chamber.

Alex gripped her tighter against him. She buried her face in his shirt, feeling the debris pummeled them. Alex flinched. The falling debris sounded like rain, but pricked her skin like a cascade of tiny needles. She held her breath, clutching Alex's shirt in her fists, until the melee settled into an eerie silence.

Cautiously, she lifted her head to look at Alex. He was covered with dust and tiny bits of dirt and rock. Their gazes intersected. Neither of them needed to ask the question. Simultaneously, they said, "I'm okay."

Backing away from him, she took in her own appearance. Coated with dirt and debris, just like him. Alex swiped the arm of his shirt across his face, removing some of the dust and smearing the rest.

Boom!

The concussion rattled her eardrums painfully. It seemed to have come from directly overhead. Whump. In the far corner, a chunk of the ceiling struck the floor.

Alex's face blanched. A chill washed over her too. The last explosion had been too close.

Without a word, Alex shoved her toward the hole. "Jump."

She jumped. Her feet met the floor ten feet below with a force that sliced pain up her legs and threw her off balance for a second. She flailed for a handhold, found none, and stumbled forward until she found her footing again. Shadows closed in around her, kept at bay only by the pale light filtering down through the hole. The shadows writhed like apparitions of serpents. She hugged herself as she turned toward the hole.

Alex's backpack sailed down through the hole. It landed with a thud.

She scuttled forward just enough to nab the backpack.

He called down to her, "Catch."

Glancing up, she watched him toss the flashlight into the hole. She caught it and retreated a half dozen steps. Alex leaped into the hole. He hit the floor flat on his soles, with knees bent and arms flung out for balance. No staggering. No wince of pain. He strode down the tunnel. In one swift motion as he breezed past her, with one hand he snagged the backpack's strap, plucking the pack from her arms and slinging it over his shoulder, and with the other hand he snagged the flashlight. She trotted after him.

Another detonation rocked the mountain.

Alex seized her arm and hauled her forward as he sped up into a fast jog, and then a full-on gallop. She heard debris slam through the hole but she didn't dare look back. She didn't want to know if the tunnel was caving in behind them. The quaking made her stumble. Alex let go of her arm and hooked his right arm around her waist, propelling her forward alongside him. The vibrations from the mountain's quaking lessened, replaced by the thudding of her heart against her rib cage. Although her innate sense of direction scored a D, her sense of distance scored an F. She had no idea how far they ran before the passage jogged right, rising at a gentle grade. The passage looked identical to the ones upstairs, except for the upward slope.

Alex slowed to a jog. Though he loosened his grip, he kept his arm around her waist. The sensation of his muscular arm against her body, and his hand curled protectively over her hip, comforted her. She felt a little less endangered—but only a little.

No breeze penetrated this corridor. The air smelled funny. She couldn't explain why or describe the odor. Maybe she suffered from an olfactory hallucination triggered by sheer terror. While they ventured further into the passage, the walls transitioned from smooth to roughly hewn, as if the workers ran out of time to finish off the walls. The floor's slope deepened. Something about this network of subterranean passages struck her as off. She could accept Akhenaten sailing to America, perhaps to escape a backlash against his theological doctrine. Archaeological evidence suggested Egyptians continued worshiping the old gods in spite of the pharaoh's Aten-only doctrine and, after his death, Egyptians destroyed images of Akhenaten. His own son, Tutankhaten, changed his name to Tutankhamen in deference to the old pantheon, in which Amen-Ra served as chief god. The change heralded the official return of the old gods. If Akhenaten didn't die after all, but fled to the Americas, he would've wanted a tomb for himself. Why then did the workmen construct an emergency exit?

Alex clutched the flashlight in his left hand, his arm dangling at his side, the light rocking up and down as he moved. She spotted a black lump on the floor, on the left side of the passage. Alex trotted past the lump. She shook free of his arm and halted beside the object. It looked like...hair. She touched it. Her fingers slid between the strands.

"Hang on," she said. "Have a look at this."

Alex knelt alongside her. She grasped a handful of the hair and lifted. The black hair was woven together into a shoulder-length wig with short, blunt bangs. A reddish brown substance stained the hair near the wig's crown. Underneath where the wig had lain sat a fist-size rock tarnished with an identical stain.

"Blood," Alex said.

The rock was oval, with a groove around its equator. Tracing the groove with her fingertip, she said, "A hammerstone. Someone bashed their head on it."

"Or someone else did the bashing for them."

"Another murder?"

Alex shrugged.

Ridley's mummy. A blood-stained wig. Only in the movies did ancient Egyptian tombs have curses attached to them.

Alex rose. "We have to go. Before our friends finish the job they started."

She swallowed, hard. This place felt cursed.

He nudged her with his boot. She dropped the wig, hopped up, and followed Alex up the sloping passage. Ten minutes later, they reached the passage's end, a flat wall with notches carved into it identical to the footholds and handholds in the entrance shaft. These notches also led up a shaft. Crumpled on the floor at the base of the pseudo-ladder rested a mummy.

The beam of the flashlight highlighted the body, its flesh desiccated and preserved by the natural conditions within the tomb. A white tunic with long sleeves robed the body down to mid-calf. Leather boots sheathed the feet. A gold band encircled the neck. The mouth hung open, but the eyes were shut. The mummy's legs were bent with the calves almost parallel to the thighs. The torso sat erect, its back against the wall, the right arm draped across the waist. The left arm rested on the floor. Both the skin above the arm, at the shoulder joint, and an area on the chest appeared blackened. A spot on the left side of the head also looked singed.

Crouching beside the body, Alex probed the blackened area on the head with his finger.

Erin asked, "What do you think happened to this guy? If it's a guy."

"The gender is unclear. These blackened areas look like burns—serious ones."

"Fatal wounds?"

He pointed at the head wound. "Since this one seems to have penetrated the skull, I'd say so."

Questions ricocheted through her mind. What on earth happened in this place? When did it happen? Did both Ridley and this individual meet the same fate?

Alex leaned forward to stare into the mummy's mouth. He reached in, grasped a tooth between his thumb and forefinger, and jiggled. The tooth didn't move. He selected another and tried again. This time the tooth wiggled. He worked the tooth side to side, back and forth, until it popped free. He tucked the tooth in his pants pocket.

"A souvenir?" Erin asked.

Rising, he said, "A sample for testing."

She almost asked what he wanted to test the tooth for—then the reason dawned on her, bright as an exploding star. A tooth provided material for DNA testing as well as radiocarbon dating. They might learn how long ago the person died, and what part of the world he called home. If he came from this world.

While Alex photographed the mummy, Erin visually examined the area around it. No scorch marks blackened the floor or the wall. However the departed got burned, no collateral damage resulted.

The camera's flash pulsed. The light glinted off an object on the floor near the wall, to the right of the mummy. She squatted beside the body and picked up the object. A brooch. Composed of golden-colored metal dusted with a green patina, the brooch was engraved with a pattern of swirls and lines. The pattern reminded her of Celtic designs.

Alex sighed. He hunched beside her with his head tilted back, studying the shaft overhead. His flashlight still pointed down at the mummy.

"Well," he said, "I suppose I ought to climb up there."

Erin tucked the brooch in her pocket and hopped to her feet. She grabbed his hand, lifting it to point the flashlight straight up into the shaft. The ceiling, barely visible at the tail end of the beam, must've soared twenty feet above their heads. A faint rectangular outline suggested a slab plugged the top of the shaft, like the slab that sealed the main entrance. Unseating the slab from outside required a huge effort. How could they open this slab from inside, while clinging to the footholds and handholds?

Alex cleared his throat. "May I have my hand back?"

Her right hand was cupped over his left hand, which gripped the flashlight. She'd forgotten to let go. Oops.

Erin yanked her hand away. "Sorry."

"That's my line." A smirk curved his mouth for an instant, then vanished. "You should hold the flashlight. I have quite a climb ahead of me."

He handed her the flashlight. She peeked up the shaft. No ledge at the top. Nothing to provide support as he struggled to wrest the slab off the opening.

"What's your plan?" she asked.

Alex tucked the toe of his right boot into a foothold two feet above the floor. Slipping his fingers into handholds, he pushed up off the floor. He caught a foothold with his left toe and climbed two more rungs before pausing to glance over his shoulder at her.

"My plan," he said, "is to make it up as I go along and pray I don't break my neck."

"Brilliant. And if you die, what am I supposed to do?"

"Now who's pessimistic?"

He reached for the next handhold. She watched him ascend the shaft, with each step an exercise in caution and precision. If the shaft was an emergency exit, why did the workers seal it with the slab? Why did a tomb need an emergency exit?

The labyrinth might not be a tomb. It might've served as a subterranean fortress. The Hittites, a mysterious people who 3,000 years ago lived in the region today known as Turkey, built underground fortresses furnished with stone disks they rolled across the doorways to keep out invaders. The people who built this system of tunnels and chambers may have used it as a fortress, like the Hittite tunnels. Harry's petroglyph panel talked about a battle, a massacre really. The panel also mentioned how the survivors hid in desert cliffs. Later, inside a mountain tomb, they buried their king, who hailed from across the sea. The labyrinth could be either a tomb or a secret place where the people hid from their enemy.

A secret exit screamed fortress. A tomb needed no emergency escape route. If she assumed the shaft was an emergency exit, then sealing it with a slab made no sense. Criminy, why must ancient riddles be so enigmatic?

She set the flashlight on the ground, aimed up the shaft. Alex grunted. The sound echoed down the shaft. She asked, "Everything okay up there?"

From halfway up the shaft, he grumbled a syllable that resembled a terse "yes."

Erin walked to the left-hand wall. She skimmed her hands over its surface feeling for…something. When she didn't find it, she moved to the wall that where the tunnel dead-ended and groped its surface across the entire width and up as high as she could reach. If a civilization with advanced technology built this fortress, or whatever the labyrinth was, they certainly could've included a latch for the emergency exit. But an advanced civilization wouldn't use hammerstones to hack out the tunnels. Aargh. She'd get a migraine if she thought about it anymore. Contradictions plagued ancient history, whether the mainstream version or the true story. The primitive coexisted with the advanced. The enlightened accompanied the barbaric. Come to think of it, things hadn't changed much in the past few thousand years.

The ancients left plenty of clues, but few answers. The Great Pyramid at Giza evidenced sophisticated construction methods—joints so tight a piece of paper wouldn't fit between them and 200-ton granite blocks lifted hundreds of feet above the ground. The entire structure, which stood more than 450 feet high with a base covering thirteen acres, was aligned to true north with a margin of error measured at one-twentieth of a degree. Yet archaeologists expected everyone to believe the ancient Egyptians used nothing more sophisticated than copper chisels and plumb bobs to build the pyramids.

Egyptian workers might've used primitive tools to finish off the tombs in the Valley of the Kings and the temples dotting the banks of the Nile. They might've found such tools easier to work with for crafting the inscriptions on the walls. After all, modern painters used the same kind of brushes artists had used for centuries. But if the rulers of the ancient world could call upon advanced technology, then they wouldn't waste time forcing workers to chisel out blocks of stone one by one using hammerstones and soft copper chisels. This line of reasoning led Erin to grope the walls. A latch or other mechanism to release the slab covering the exit might hide under the surface of the tunnel walls.

The dead-end wall hid nothing. She switched to the right-hand wall. Three feet from the joint where the wall met the dead end, four feet above the ground, she felt a groove. Tracing her finger down it, she drew a rectangle on the wall about three inches wide by five inches tall. The surface within the rectangle felt different than the surrounding wall. She scratched at the rectangular area with her fingernail. Bits of dirt flaked off onto the floor.

She fished out of her pocket the key she'd found under Ridley's hand. With its wide oval end, she scraped off the dirt encrusted on the rectangular patch of the wall. Within a couple minutes she cleared the patch of its dirt covering. With the smaller end of the key, she dug the dirt out of the groove surrounding the patch.

"Ah!"

Alex's shout reverberated down the shaft. He unreeled a string of curses whose echoes merged into a cacophony of verbal angst.

Erin glanced up at him. She bit her lip. He kept his feet balanced in the footholds while clinging to one handhold with his left fingers. With his right hand, he pounded on the slab that blocked the shaft's apex.

"Be careful," she hollered.

His left foot slipped. His torso twisted. He flailed his right hand in the air.

Her heart thudded. What on earth possessed him to try such a stupid stunt? If he fell—

Alex swung his right hand toward the wall and grasped a handhold. He stepped his left foot into one of the notches in the wall.

She asked, "Are you hurt?"

He leaned his forehead on the wall. "No."

Thank heavens. She looked at the rectangular patch on the wall to her right. The patch seemed metallic. "I have an idea. Don't move."

"I can't hang here forever."

"Gimme a few seconds."

She stuffed the key in her pocket. With the fingers of both hands, she took hold of the rectangle's edges and pulled. The panel sprang out in her hands, exposing a small cavity that housed a metal lever. She pulled the lever.

Pow!

The walls and floor shuddered. At the top of the shaft, where the slab sat previously, a rectangle of blue sky glowed. Alex clung to the rim of the opening, his body dangling beneath it.

She gaped up at him. Soon he'd lose his grip and fall. Her heart pounded. She couldn't move. She should do something. What?

A mini movie played in her mind. Alex plummeting twenty feet down the shaft. A sickening thud. Blood everywhere.

She squeezed her eyes shut for a heartbeat. When she opened them, she saw Alex pulling himself over the rim, out through the opening, onto the ground outside. First his torso, weighted down by his backpack, disappeared through the hole. His hips crossed the threshold next, followed by his legs. His feet slid over last. Half a minute later he poked his head into the hole.

In a cheerful tone, he said, "Your turn."

She shook her head. How could someone who nearly died several times today sound so chipper?

"Come on," he said.

Erin chewed the inside of her lip. The shaft was deep, the handholds and footholds narrow. She pictured herself falling, heard her scream, felt her spine cracking as she hit the floor.

Alex thrust his right arm through the opening. He stretched out his fingers as if offering her a hand. If she had elastic arms she could grab his hand for him to pull her up the shaft. She was stuck with normal flesh-and-bone limbs. Bones had an annoying tendency to break when smacked into solid rock.

She couldn't stay in the tomb. Not that she wanted to hang out here any longer.

Get a grip, she urged herself. The tang of fear trickled over her tongue. She marched to the ladder, stepped her right foot into a foothold at knee height, grasped one of the handholds, and pushed her body up off the floor. Rung by rung she climbed the shaft. Time seemed to slow in direct proportion to the acceleration of her heartbeat. By the time she reached the top of the shaft, her entire body ached.

Alex proffered his hands to her. She clutched his left hand, then his right. Her toes slipped off the rungs. She let out a yelp reminiscent of a squeaky toy being squeezed. He heaved her up through the opening. She flopped onto her butt in the dirt, her arms around Alex's neck, his hands clasped behind her back, both arms cinched around her waist.

He let go and jumped to his feet. Taking her hands, he helped her to her feet. Unclipping the radio from his belt, he pressed the button to talk. "Lou, are you there?"

No response. Alex repeated his call. Static crackled on the radio. Lou's voice boomed through the noise. "I'm here, kid. For a minute there, I thought you two were goners."

"We found an alternate route to the surface."

"Where are you?"

"On top of Cheops Pyramid."

"Be there in a jiff."

The sky was clear, the sun low to the horizon. A breeze tickled Erin's face as she and Alex waited in silence for their ride to arrive. Five minutes later they heard the whoomp-whoomp-whoomp of helicopter rotors approaching from the northwest. Seconds later they spotted the chopper swooping down over the peak of Isis Temple toward them.

They had escaped. This time.

Revenant House
Sunday, May 22

A DOOR SLAMMED DOWNSTAIRS. RASSUL WAS HOME. UPSTAIRS, WESSICK stood in the open doorway to the artifact room. The manor was his home, not Rassul's, yet the brigand acted as if he owned the property and everything on it. No one owned Revenant House. Tenants lived within these walls at the manor's discretion.

Footfalls pounded up the stairs, eliciting creaks and squeaks from the old wood. Wessick surveyed the artifact room one last time, shut and locked the door, and walked to the main passage. He arrived at the staircase as Rassul cleared the top step. Wessick, locking his gaze on Rassul's, rested his left hand on the post at the top of the stairs. The digger squinted at him.

"I told you," Wessick said, "never to go upstairs without my express permission."

"My orders come from a higher source."

"What is it you want?"

"I am to see the artifact room."

Wessick tightened his fist around the orb-shaped newel atop the post.

Rassul leaned toward him. Three inches shorter than Wessick, the digger had to tilt his head backward to sneer up at the older man.

"The key," Rassul said. "Give it to me now."

"Why?"

"They believe you have ignored their requests."

Wessick almost laughed. They never requested. They commanded, like gods issuing orders from the peak of Mount Olympus.

Rassul tapped a finger on Wessick's chest. "You have not destroyed the artifacts."

"I will destroy them when the time comes. We can learn from them in the meantime."

"The choice is not yours."

Wessick ground his teeth. The vibrations rattled his skull. He narrowed his eyes.

Rassul blinked. The digger backed away two steps.

"They give you until tomorrow," Rassul said. "Then you show me or I break the door."

Through clenched teeth, Wessick hissed, "Fine."

With Rassul two paces behind him, Wessick stomped down the stairs. At the bottom of the staircase, he turned left, toward the library and drawing room. At the drawing room door, he brought out his keys, selected the correct one, and unlocked the door. Rassul peered around his shoulder. When Wessick shoved the door inward, Rassul pushed past him to enter the room first. Wessick fisted his hand around the keys, his nails digging into his palm. He had lost control. But not for long.

He seized the back of Rassul's shirt, yanked him backward, and threw him against the doorjamb. The back of Rassul's head smacked into the wood. Rassul grunted. Wessick jammed his left arm under the man's chin, pinning him to the jamb.

"You obey me," Wessick said. "Do you understand?"

Rassul croaked, "Yes."

Wessick released him. Rassul scampered into the drawing room. The man was a tool, nothing more. Although an Oxford education may have given Rassul academic knowledge, and perhaps a rudimentary understanding of politics, the man lacked cunning. Brutality was a poor substitute. Sometimes, however, Wessick saw the value in it.

At the desk, Rassul halted. Head bowed, he clasped his hands behind his back.

Wessick seated himself in the chair behind the desk. Leaning back, he interlaced his fingers over his belly. A grandfather clock in the corner ticked out the seconds. He took a long breath, held it for five seconds, then exhaled.

Rassul hunched in front of the desk, his mouth twisted into a frown.

Wessick said, "I'm waiting for your report."

Hissing a breath out his nose, Rassul stared at Wessick.

"Your report," Wessick said. "Now."

"They traveled to the Canyon, as you said. I lost them when they entered the mountain, so I do not know what they found."

"And the test results?"

"She is the *satseshat*."

Wessick rocked his chair backward. The tests confirmed what he suspected, and what his employers must already know, though they declined to share the information with him. Erin Turner was the *satseshat*. She knew nothing of the destiny laid out for her. He must ease her into the realization, or she might rush to the wrong conclusion. If he lost her, he lost everything.

They needed her too—for the moment. She was safe until he revealed the truth to her.

Rassul cleared his throat. "I must return. To find them."

In this instance, by "them" Rassul meant Erin Turner and Alex MacKay. Wessick removed an *akhet* ball from the drawer and passed it to Rassul. The digger left, shutting the door behind himself. His footsteps clapped down the passage, toward the front door.

In two days Erin would move into Revenant House. His plan would commence. Provided Erin went along with the plan, whether unwittingly or with suspicion, in a few weeks he could accomplish the feat he had struggled for three decades to finish. Countless others failed or died in the quest. When he first learned of Erin Turner, he suspected she might be the one they waited for, the only being capable of solving the mystery. With a little persistence, and a little subtlety, he could guide her to the solution. If she fought him…

He must use whatever means the task required, for he must find the relic before they did. More than his own fate relied on the mission's success. The fate of all history, of every living thing that ever lived or would ever live, rested on the shoulders of one woman. Irrelevancies distracted Erin Turner from the path she must take, the path destiny selected for her. He must eliminate the distractions.

Wessick parted his lips, about to call for Rassul. No. He closed his mouth. This task demanded care and subtlety, therefore he must handle it himself. He must separate Erin Turner from any distractions, beginning with the most irritating and dangerous diversion of all.

Alex MacKay.

Arizona

THE PHONE RANG. SEATED ON THE EDGE OF THE BED, HALFWAY DOWN ITS LENGTH, Erin stretched her arm out to grab the phone. It rang a second time before she snatched it from its cradle.

She mumbled, "Hello."

"Are you dressed?" Alex asked.

The bedside clock read 6:20. She examined her jeans and baby-blue T-shirt, the same clothes she'd worn yesterday. Dirt streaked her pants and her shirt bore a ketchup stain from last night's hamburger. Too exhausted to drive back to Albuquerque, they ate a quick meal at a roadside diner about a hundred miles from the Canyon before checking into the first motel they passed. The last thing she remembered clearly was yanking the bedspread off the bed and collapsing onto the mattress. She vaguely recalled taking off her boots. She fell asleep wearing her clothes. Dreams haunted her sleep, though the memory of them faded after she woke up ten minutes ago, leaving behind a residue of mental discomfort.

"Well?" Alex said.

Erin yawned. "Yeah, I'm dressed. Why?"

Click. He had hung up.

Someone knocked on the door connecting her room to the one next door, where Alex and Lou had slept. Erin peeled her butt off the bed, shuffling to the door. The person on the other side knocked again. She unlocked and opened the door.

Alex stood straight and tall, with one hand resting on the doorjamb, the other raised in a fist, about to knock for a third time.

"May I come in?" he asked.

She motioned for him to enter. He walked past her to the table by the window, next to the bed, where he pulled out a chair and plopped onto it. Erin slouched onto the bed, facing him. He settled his right arm on the table to drum his fingers on the surface.

"Why did you call first?" she asked.

"In case you were…indisposed."

Whatever he meant, she wasn't awake enough to understand.

Alex traced his gaze up and down her body. He arched an eyebrow. "Did you sleep in your clothes?"

Straightening, she tried to brush the dirt off her pants. Alex wore blue jeans with a crease ironed into them, a short-sleeve dress shirt, and leather boots polished until they glistened in the sunlight that filtered through the window blinds. His hair looked clean, and a tad damp. He took a shower? She felt like a kidnap victim dumped off in a ditch and rescued after three days of wandering the desert, whereas he looked ready for a television interview. If Lou walked through the connecting door wearing a tuxedo, she just might throw herself out the window.

Since the room was on the ground floor, she would accomplish nothing more than getting herself dirtier. If that was possible.

A lock of frizzy hair fell over her eyes. She blew it out of the way.

Alex lowered his arched eyebrow. "Are you all right?"

"Don't you get tired of asking me?" She waved her hand at his clothes. "You're dressed up. Hot date tonight?"

A hint of a blush spread across his cheeks. He fidgeted in the chair. "My clothes were filthy, so I changed."

"Did you look at the brooch I found yesterday?"

He nodded. "Looks Celtic. Made from bronze, but the green discoloration isn't a patina. It's bronze disease, a type of corrosion caused by exposure to moisture."

When "I didn't see any water in the tomb. Or whatever the place was."

"Even a brief exposure to water or humidity can start the process. Maybe the brooch's owner dropped it in the Colorado River on his way to the tunnels, or spilled his drink on it. Or it's possible the brooch got rained on at some point before it ended up down there."

She thought about what they'd seen in the tunnels yesterday. A Victorian explorer, mummified, clutching an enigmatic note. An unfinished inscription, written in Egyptian hieroglyphs, that might've mentioned a king. A rock overhang resembling the *akhet* symbol. Hammerstones and copper tools alongside a predynastic object. An Egyptian wig stained with blood. A Celtic corpse. A secret, exploding exit. Add in a petroglyph panel composed of Egyptian hieroglyphs, apparently written by someone with a poor knowledge of the language, and the mystery deepened further.

What did the clues mean? The 1909 newspaper article about a tomb supposedly found in the Grand Canyon described a similar hodgepodge of artifacts found by S. A. Jordan of the Smithsonian Institution. Mainstream archaeologists pointed to the mixture of cultures as evidence of the find's inauthenticity. Since no one could locate any mention of an S. A. Jordan in the Smithsonian's records, skeptics easily dismissed the 1909 article as a hoax. The article's author must've exaggerated. The network of underground passages, along with the artifacts and human remains housed there, suggested the story may have begun with a genuine discovery.

After she related her thoughts to Alex, he said, "Hmm."

"Makes sense, doesn't it?"

"I suppose. We need more information before settling on a theory."

"Of course."

Take a risk and have an opinion, she wanted to say. But she understood why he shied from endorsing her harebrained ideas. Ten years ago he gambled his career on a claim about an alien skeleton, and he lost the bet. The experience made him skittish. She would let it go.

For now.

Alex leaned forward. Palms flat on his thighs, he drooped his head.

The lock of hair fell over her face again. She tucked it behind her ear.

Alex tilted his eyes up to look at her. "I want to apologize for my behavior yesterday."

"What behavior?"

"I said we were going to die. I was rude and self-indulgent."

She held back a chuckle. "And I was bossy. What say we call it even?"

"Agreed." He sat up straight. "What inspired you to look for a hidden exit in the tunnels?"

I had a feeling and, well, it felt sort of like fate. Sure, she could say that, if she wanted to sound like a total whackjob. Alex might believe her. When an orb checked them out in the woods, he said he'd seen strange phenomena before. Glowing orbs, instructions provided by fate. Same thing, right?

Alex said, "I won't laugh. You can tell me."

She looked at him in the same instant he looked at her. Their gazes met. Her stomach fluttered.

"I can't explain it," she said. "I—I had a feeling. A gut instinct or fate or dumb luck. Whatever you want to call it."

He studied her with a thoughtful expression. "You remind me of someone, the head of our organization. She gets hunches and takes off running, literally."

"Is that good or bad?"

"She's always right." Alex pushed up out of the chair. "Someone wants you to find this relic. I guess we'd better comply."

"Do I have time to shower first?"

"Yes." He walked halfway to the connecting door. "This quest of ours will only get more dangerous, you know. It's not too late to back out."

"I can handle it."

He strode through the door and shut it behind him.

Maybe she should back out. She was a librarian, not an adventurer. No, like she told Alex, she could handle it. Although she had no clue what "it" might entail, she could no more back out of the challenge than she could chop off her own head.

Actually, she did have a clue what the quest entailed. Not much of one, but a clue nevertheless. Lou mentioned "forces beyond our conception," right after he warned them to stay put in the tunnels during the freakish storm that besieged the Canyon. The storm that buried them in the tunnels.

Storm. The word seemed inappropriate somehow, or at least inaccurate. No rain fell. The clouds formed out of nothing to shoot bolts of pure electricity at them. She remembered what Lou said when he picked them up after the fireworks ended.

"Whopper of a storm."

To which she said, "I think nature is conspiring against us."

He chuckled. "Ain't nature doing the conspiring, sweetie."

She hadn't bothered asking who he thought was conspiring against them. Forces beyond our conception, he would probably say. Then he and Alex would trade a look she couldn't decipher. Questioning them, about anything, usually confused her more.

In spite of the mysteries, in spite of the danger, she needed to see the quest through to its conclusion. Wherever the clues might lead them, she must go. She was in this.

Till the end.

Revenant House

COTTON-BALL CLOUDS DOTTED THE BLUE SKY. ERIN YAWNED AND GAZED OUT the library window toward the driveway, where her father and Alex leaned against the back of the Ford Explorer, chatting. The day had been a long one, starting with a cross-country journey by private jet and ending here at Revenant House a few hours ago. Twenty minutes ago they finished lugging her boxes into the manor, up the staircase, and to her room. Her mother was in the bathroom, most likely admiring the spiffy fixtures.

Erin twirled the keys Anna Newman gave her, three of them on a metal ring. A plastic luggage tag dangled from the ring too. Newman handwrote Erin's name in capital letters on the slip of paper inside the luggage tag. Currently, Newman was in the dining room tidying up the paperwork Erin signed earlier—an employment contract, and an agreement stating she wouldn't destroy the house while she lived here. The agreement also explained which parts of the house she could enter and which were off limits. The drawing room, the cellar, the attic, and several rooms on the second floor fell under the off-limits category. Although the rooms in question were locked, her employer wanted a promise in writing that she would keep out of those places. Samuel N. Wessick, whoever he was, suffered from a serious case of paranoia. He made Erin feel downright trusting.

High heels clacked in the hallway.

Erin turned in time to see Newman cross the threshold into the library. The door hung open, its bronze knob an inch from the bookshelves behind it.

Newman halted three steps inside the room. "Unless you have any final questions, I'll be off."

"I'm good."

"Remember, absolutely no visitors during working hours, 8:30 AM to 5 PM. And overnight guests must be cleared with me first."

"Guess I better cancel the pajama party."

Newman stared at her with an impassive expression.

"I'm joking," Erin said. "I understand the rules and I'll behave like a perfect lady."

With a curt nod, Newman left. The ticking of her high heels dwindled. The front door clapped shut.

Through the window, Erin watched Newman get into her car and drive off. Near the Explorer, Alex and her father were laughing. She couldn't decide how she felt about Alex bonding with her parents. She knew he kept things from her. At the same time, he shared with her stories about his past, about events he must've preferred to seal up in the deepest recesses of his memory. She shared nothing with him.

Leaning against the windowsill, she studied the keys in her hand. Two were silver, one gold colored. Newman didn't give her a key to the library door, because the library remained unlocked at all times. The silver keys opened the manor's exterior doors and her new car, a Cadillac Escalade. The luxury SUV dwarfed her parents' Explorer. Its black exterior and darkened rear windows lent the SUV the aura of a monster, the kind children believed lurked under their beds. She knew the thought was silly. It was a car, nothing else. A perk of her new job.

Still, she felt a little like a condemned soul waiting to board a ferry to the underworld, with the Escalade as the ferry.

The gold-colored key opened the door to her bedroom. Alex said the key was bronze. On the handle end of the key, scrollwork formed a cross inside a circle.

A Celtic cross, she suggested, and Alex agreed. Except for the scrollwork at the top, the key resembled the one she found tucked under the buttocks of Ridley Covington. Ridley's key featured three spirals crammed inside a circle. Similar spirals showed up in the artwork of many ancient cultures, from the Egyptians to the ancient Britons to the Anasazi of the American Southwest. The key to her new bedroom sported an ancient symbol too. The wood carving above the library door depicted ancient Egyptian motifs. The house's very name evoked the supernatural. Whoever built the house must've been obsessed with history and the occult.

Did the builder share a connection with Ridley Covington? Or Gilbert Covington, the author of Harry's book? The more she searched for answers, the more questions she uncovered.

The front door banged. She heard voices in the hallway. Alex and her parents.

A car horn beeped. Erin glanced up to see Chloe's VW Beetle roaring up the driveway. The car swerved to a stop inches from the Escalade's bumper. Gravel spewed up from the VW's rear tires. Dust obscured the windshield. Chloe flung the door open, hopped out, and slammed the door shut. The little car rocked. Spotting Erin, Chloe waved. Erin returned the gesture, then pointed toward the front door. Chloe trotted in that direction.

Erin stuffed the keys in her pocket. Answers would have to wait.

An hour later Erin waved goodbye to her parents from the porch as they drove off down the driveway. Alex and Chloe lingered inside. She hoped they weren't poking into places they shouldn't. Getting fired before officially starting the job might look bad on her resume.

Erin wandered into the house. She found Chloe at the foot of the staircase, gawking at the woodwork. Erin tapped her friend on the shoulder.

Chloe grinned. "This house is awesome."

"Don't let Newman hear you call it a house." Erin slipped into her best imitation of the British woman's accent. "Revenant House is a manor. Never mind that its very name identifies it as a house."

Chloe rolled her eyes.

"Have you seen Alex?" Erin asked.

"The cutie-pie's in the kitchen. Cleaning up." Chloe's grin tightened into a smirk. "He's trying to impress you."

"Not likely."

Alex cooked dinner for the group, some Italian dish involving pasta and white sauce. The kitchen was, as Newman promised, fully stocked. By "fully" Newman apparently meant stuffed with enough produce, beverages, and canned and dry goods to satisfy the appetite of a major metropolis. The beverages included juice, milk, and bottled water. When Erin asked what was wrong with the tap water, Newman tilted her nose up and said, "Nothing. The bottled water is a courtesy."

So much for female bonding.

Metallic bangs echoed from the kitchen.

Chloe's cell phone chirped. She dug it out of her jeans pocket, flipping it open to check the caller ID. "It's my sweetie."

Answering the call, Chloe sashayed down the east passage toward the library. She stopped halfway there.

Erin marched down the west passage, veered right into the north passage, and walked into the kitchen. Alex was holding a stainless-steel pot in both hands. Lips scrunched, he glanced around the kitchen.

"Problem?" Erin asked.

"I seem to have forgotten which cupboard this belongs in."

Erin pointed at a cupboard directly in front of him, at floor level. He returned the pot to the cupboard and faced her. A marble-topped island hunkered in the center of the kitchen. Alex stood across the island from her, with the double sink behind him.

"Thanks for dinner," she said. "It's time to talk about your organization."

He leaned back against the counter, bowing his head.

Erin approached the island. She leaned her hips against it, laid her hand atop it, and linked her fingers. Her gaze she focused on Alex. He focused on the floor.

"You told me to wait," she said, "until after the Grand Canyon expedition, then make up my mind. Well, I've decided. I want to join your little secret society."

He raised his head to look at her. "It's not a secret society. We operate several websites and publish two journals."

"What journals?"

"Fringe publications, some would say. Harry ran the *Journal of the Foundation for Amarna Research and Exploration*, and our leader manages *True Origins*, a journal she founded about alternative history and the paranormal."

"Who do you work for?"

"No one. I work with a number of people."

Erin unhooked her fingers and drummed them on the counter. "You called someone your leader. A woman, by your choice of pronouns."

"An honorary designation."

She expelled a breath out her nose. "What is your boss's real name, the one on her birth certificate?"

"I need permission before I can tell you."

She slapped her palm on the counter. Alex winced.

Her hand throbbed. She hoped the gesture made a similar impression on his brain. She wanted to join his group. She needed to join his group. They seemed to know things she didn't and have assets she lacked. Money, equipment, cushy private jets. Finding the relic might take less time if she could exploit the assets of a powerful organization like Alex's. Yet if his superiors refused to trust her with their names, how could she trust them with her life?

A few days ago, her worst problem was unemployment. Today she lived and worked in a somewhat spooky manor on a tiny peninsula the locals couldn't find and fought to join a shadowy organization that, for all she knew, was run by omnipotent aliens bent on galactic domination.

No. Alex wasn't the galactic domination type. Besides, if he worked for omnipotent aliens, she wouldn't have needed to draw him a map so he could find Revenant House. Despite following her here once before, without her permission, he'd asked her for directions.

Erin froze. *Even locals can't find this place.* She backed away from the counter. How did Chloe know where to find her?

Alex said, "I think—"

Erin bolted out the kitchen door.

She sprinted down the north passage, to the intersection with the west passage. Chloe's voice echoed down the passage from the vestibule. Erin trip-stopped. The pitch of Chloe's voice was lower than usual, her tone sharp.

"I am not," Chloe said. "And if I were it'd be none of your business."

It's my sweetie, Chloe announced when her cell phone rang. She must be talking to Greg. Arguing with him. Until the other day outside the cafe, Erin thought they never argued.

She tiptoed halfway down the fifteen-foot-long passage. Chloe's voice got louder.

"No," Chloe said, "I won't marry you. I will not be a slave to another man. Especially you."

Chloe's use of "another" suggested she once tied herself to a man, and the relationship went sour. Erin wondered how much she really knew about her friend. They talked about work, the job search, hobbies.

No. They talked about Erin's hobbies, Erin's job search. Chloe mentioned sending out resumes once or twice but, in general, evaded any questions about herself. Why?

Great. Now she questioned her one and only friend. Chloe might simply dislike talking about herself. Erin disliked it too. She shared as little information as possible with Chloe, not out of conscious effort, but purely as a habit. In the movies, women gabbed to their friends about the minutest details of their lives. In real life, at least in Erin's life, friendships didn't work that way. Most people wanted to yak at her, rather than to her. They rarely wanted to hear about her life. Chloe did, for unfathomable reasons.

She was wrong. Chloe wasn't her only friend. She had Alex—sort of.

Chloe's shoes slapped on the floor, as if she'd stomped her feet. "I will not discuss this anymore."

Snap. She must've flipped her phone shut.

Erin moseyed toward the vestibule, hoping she looked nonchalant. Chloe stepped out into the passage in front of her. The girl's face was red, her eyes narrowed.

"Everything all right?" Erin asked.

The angst vanished from Chloe's face in a heartbeat. She flashed a smile.

"Oh fine," Chloe said. "My sweetie can't live without me, that's all."

Erin bit the inside of her cheek. Although she wanted to ask a question, she felt like a heel for even considering it. But she must ask.

"How did you find Revenant House?" Erin asked. "I didn't give you directions. I had no idea you were coming out today."

"Don't ya love online maps?" Chloe wiggled her fingers as if typing on a keyboard. "Plunk in the address and out pops a map with directions."

"I don't remember giving you the address."

"Oh, I typed in Revenant House and poof! There it was."

Chloe's answer sounded reasonable. She ought to accept it.

Of course she accepted it. No reason to doubt it.

The doubt niggled at her brain anyway.

Alex stared at the space where Erin stood until a moment ago. When she took off, he listened to her footsteps clap in the corridor, the sound diminishing with each step. He knew she was fed up with his cageyness, and he expected her to yell at him, but fleeing the room seemed excessive. It was also out of character for her. Something else must've upset her. He had no idea what.

His cell phone warbled. Leaning against the counter, shoulders slumped, he pulled the phone out of his hip pocket and answered the call with a muttered hello. His gaze he kept trained on the doorway. When Erin came back, he'd tell her—

"Greetings, old friend."

Alex jerked upright. He grasped the phone tighter. "What do you want, Rassul?"

"I have e-mailed you a set of coordinates. Harry is waiting for you there."

"Is he alive?"

"That is for you to discover."

"How do I know," Alex said, "this isn't a trap?"

Rassul sniggered. "You don't."

The bastard hung up.

Harry is waiting for you there. Alex bolted out of the kitchen and down the passageway. He veered around the corner into the main corridor. His right foot slipped. He stumbled, found his footing, and ran past Erin and Chloe, through the front door, and down the steps to his car. Inside the car, he slammed the door shut and started the engine. Yanking the gear shift lever into drive, he rammed his foot on the gas pedal. The car shot forward, speeding down the driveway with gravel spraying up behind it. He swerved the car out of the driveway onto the road. The rear end fishtailed. He regained control inches from diving into the ditch alongside the road.

His pulse thundered in his ears. Jesus, he should slow down. No, if Rassul had Harry then he must get there. He gripped the steering wheel with one hand and with his other hand he punched buttons on the phone to retrieve his e-mail and get the coordinates Rassul sent.

How do I know this isn't a trap?

You don't.

Alex jammed his foot on the brake. The car shimmied and jerked to a stop. This wouldn't do. By running off like a stampeding wildebeest, he stepped neatly into the role Rassul wrote for him. He must calm down. Think. Plan.

Plugging Rassul's coordinates into a simple map program would give him the location and directions for getting there. He needed more. On his laptop, he'd installed software that overlaid satellite imagery onto road maps. Once he got the lay of the land, he could rewrite his role in Rassul's depraved play. He twisted around to reach behind his seat, pulling his computer bag onto his lap. Let act one, scene one commence—with a few rewrites.

Hold on, Harry.

Erin gaped at the front door, which Alex had left hanging open. A breeze wafted through the doorway, tickling her face. A moment earlier, Alex rocketed out of the north passage, flying past her without a word or a glance on his way out the front door.

Erin called after him, "Hey, where are you going?"

Chloe bulged her eyes. She rounded her lips in a silent "oh."

Erin bent her knee, about to take the first step to run after him. Why? She wasn't his servant. Let him storm out of the house with no explanation. He probably left because she asked him uncomfortable questions he had no answers for, or at least no answers he deigned to share with her.

Erin shuffled to the door, swinging it shut. Later she could grill him about his behavior. And he would likely grill her too. She left the kitchen rather suddenly herself. From the glimpse she got as he raced past her, his face was red and his lips were tight. Despite the careless speed of his departure, he held his arms straight at his side with his hands fisted. Okay, he'd been disturbed. She wouldn't be mad at him. This time.

"Do I get the grand tour?" Chloe asked.

"Huh?"

"A tour." Chloe waved a hand in Erin's face. "Of the house?"

Erin shook off thoughts of Alex and said, "Yeah, sure. A tour it is."

They started in the library and made their way westward, then up the north passage to the back staircase. Along the way, they peeked into every unlocked room, even the old waiting room that served as a closet. Upstairs they tromped, to the second floor, where they found the first door locked.

Chloe jiggled the knob. A grin crept across her face. "Can you pick a lock?"

"Sure, Burglary 101 is a required course in library school."

Chloe twisted her grin into an exaggerated pout.

Erin shepherded her down the passage, past another locked room, beyond the open doorway of a spare bedroom, into the main passage. Chloe showed no interest in the other spare bedrooms, or the gigantic walk-in closet between them, or the locked bedroom at the east end of the hall. They toured Erin's suite, across the hall from the locked bedroom. The door from the hallway led into a little rectangular room, about five feet wide by ten feet long, that opened onto a bathroom on the left and the main bedroom on the right. She had her own walk-in closet and a whirlpool tub in the bathroom. Centered against the rear wall sat a four-poster bed, its canopy of pale yellow fabric tied back at the corners. An antique dressing table, made of walnut, was pushed up to the east wall, to the right of the window. No clothes hung in the closet yet, though her boxes squatted there. The closet was almost as big as her bedroom at home.

Erin escorted Chloe back to the stairs. She hopped down the first step.

Chloe bit her lip. "Um, I need to use the bathroom."

"Go ahead." Erin pointed to the first door past the stairs, on the right. "It's there."

"I'll meet you downstairs."

Erin shrugged. She started down the stairs. At the first landing, she paused to look up, and saw Chloe padding toward the bathroom door. Erin clomped down the rest of the stairs into the vestibule. Several minutes later, Chloe trotted downstairs. After they exchanged goodbyes, coupled with promises to keep in touch, Chloe left. Erin watched her zoom down the driveway, the VW kicking up a dust storm in its wake, until the woods swallowed the car and the dust. Erin shut the door.

She wrapped her arms around herself. She was alone. In the belly of a ghost house.

Abbaye Peninsula

THE SUN HAD SUNK BELOW THE HORIZON, TAKING WITH IT THE DAYTIME breeze. Stillness reigned. The only sound was the shooshing of waves on a beach to the west. Alex crouched in the woods fifty feet from the cliff. After parking his car half a mile down the road, he hiked through the densest part of the woods toward the spot represented by Rassul's coordinates, a remote section of woods alongside what seemed to be the sole road leading into this tiny peninsula. The drive here took over an hour, with his route leading him south, then east, then north again. Or northeast. He got a little turned around. A few minutes ago, he risked pushing the button on his watch to illuminate its face. His hand, cupped over his watch, should've minimized the risk. The time had been 9:10.

The trees, visible at silhouettes, hulked around him like demons stalking a lost soul. That scenario cast Rassul as the archdemon, who waited somewhere up ahead, prepared to summon forth his unholy army.

Alex felt the Glock in his hand, its metal warmed by his skin. Demons, bah. Rassul was nothing more than a slimy little worm who burrowed into other people's lives. No, not a worm. A dung beetle. Rolling a ball of excrement across the ground.

The ancient Egyptians worshiped the dung beetle as one of their most sacred symbols, the scarab. Okay then, back to a slimy little worm.

Alex spotted something through the trees. A faint glow. Still squatting, he shifted to the left for a better view. His jacket crinkled. The dark brown suede-like material of the jacket covered his pale blue shirt, which would've glowed in the moonlight, revealing his position. The jacket's crinkling might do the same, but less quickly. If he'd had time to go back to the motel, he could've changed into something more appropriate for nighttime reconnaissance.

Forget it. He'd had no time. At least the jacket, zipped up all the way, concealed his shirt. Dirt smeared on his loafers dulled their shine. Dirt also masked his face. Black cloth gloves disguised his hands. His watch was digital, hence no ticking. He'd done everything possible to deter Rassul from spotting him.

Leaning left a little more, this time without crinkling, he got a better angle on the glow hovering in the woods up ahead of him. Not an orb. Not a flashlight. The glow resembled a reflection. Moonlight bouncing off of...what?

The wide boughs of a pine tree blocked his view. He lowered onto all fours and crept between two aspen trees toward the pine. He'd done nothing like this in eight months. His instincts might be rusty, his memory of the techniques faded. *Dammit, MacKay, concentrate.*

He ducked around the pine tree, and froze. The glow was most definitely a reflection. The moonlight glimmered off the windshield of a dark-colored vehicle. The car, a four-door sedan, was parked twenty feet ahead of him in a small clearing. The moonlight reflected off glass but also cast an eerie glow on the figure slumped behind the steering wheel.

His pulse quickened. Harry.

Without moving his head, Alex surveyed the woods around him. Nothing gave away Rassul's position, although the man must be close. Alex shut his eyes and listened. A breeze rustled the aspen leaves high above him, eliciting a sound like rain falling. The breeze died for half a minute. Still, he heard nothing. Rassul was nearby, he felt it. What would he do, crouch here until sunrise?

Screw it. He crawled toward the vehicle. When he was alongside the driver's door, he rose onto his knees and peeked through the window. The figure in the driver's seat was pale, stiff, and expressionless. It also lacked any hair on its body and a bright yellow complexion. It was a crash test dummy, dressed in camouflage pants and shirt. Where in blazes did Rassul get a crash test dummy?

Never mind. He crawled around the back of vehicle. It sported a Utah license plate. The number looked familiar. Though he couldn't say for certain, he had a feeling this was Harry's car.

Alex's cell phone rang. He yanked it out and punched the button to pick up the call. Before he could speak, Rassul said, "I see you have found my gift."

The worm's voice rasped through the phone in a throaty whisper. Alex sprang to his feet. "It's not my birthday."

"Have you realized the best part?"

Turning in a circle, scanning the woods, Alex said, "I'm not playing this game."

"I'm afraid the game is already over, old friend. And you are nowhere near the playing field."

"What do you mean?"

Click.

Alex said, "Rassul?"

Silence. The worm had hung up.

If this wasn't the playing field, then where was Rassul? He must be here. The worm said *I see you have found my gift*. Rassul could see Alex, and know when he found the gift, only from somewhere nearby.

Maybe not.

Alex yanked the driver's door open. From his coat pocket, he brought out a pen-size flashlight. Flicking the light on, he rifled the pockets of the dummy's pants and shirt and inspected its head for a camera, but found none. Next he searched the dashboard and glove compartment then—with his body half inside the car, leaning over the dummy, his palms flat on the passenger seat—he hesitated. An odd feeling tickled his spine. Slowly, he turned his head to the right, rotating his shoulder to look backward and up. His gaze passed over the light fixture attached to the inside of the roof. The tickle on his spine intensified. He withdrew the knife from his back pocket as he flipped over to sit on the dummy's lap. With the knife, he pried the cover off the light texture. A dark ball dropped out of the cavity behind the cover. He caught it with his free hand.

The ball was a quarter inch in diameter, smooth, shiny, and pure black. He rolled it between his thumb and forefinger. The ball's surface felt soft and slightly warm. He scratched it with a fingernail, but his nail left no marks on the object. Was this a camera? The logical side of his brain said no, yet his instincts told him yes. He'd seen far stranger things.

Tucking the ball in his pocket, he searched the rest of the car. No traditional cameras were hidden on the inside or outside of the vehicle. Rassul might've hidden a camera on one of the trees.

Forget the camera. He wasn't about to search the entire woods.

You are nowhere near the playing field.

What did Rassul mean by those words? If the playing field didn't surround the car, if Rassul meant his trick with the dummy as a distraction, then where in hell was Rassul right now?

His cell phone bleeped. Extricating himself from the vehicle, he plucked the phone from the ground where he'd dropped it upon entering the car. Someone had sent him a photo. He opened the image. It showed Erin Turner standing by a bed. He recognized the bed. He'd seen it up close a few hours ago, when he carried Erin's boxes into the house. Rassul must've taken the photo from outside, as if floating near the second-story window. The timestamp dated the image to five minutes ago.

A bolt of ice-cold lightning shot through him.

Revenant House

SILENCE. LIKE A LIVING THING, IT ROAMED THE HALLS OF THE MANOR. ERIN rubbed her arms. The chill she felt originated inside, rather than outside, her body. She felt weird. She half expected a reanimated mummy to spring out of a closet to attack her, which meant she ought to stop watching 1930s horror movies. In the movies, big old houses always harbored dark secrets.

She would get used to living in a big old manor. Eventually.

In her bedroom, she unpacked her boxes. Her clothes filled half of one wall in the closet. After changing into her pajamas and completing her nightly routine in the bathroom, she stood in front of the outer bedroom door, in the little rectangular room. Should she close the outer door? No one else was in the house, and the outside doors were locked. Closing the bedroom door seemed silly.

She padded to the door and closed her hand around the knob.

Clink-clink-clink.

The sound echoed in the passage, from the direction of the stairway. Erin's scalp tingled as the hairs stiffened. She held still, her hand fisted around the knob.

Clink-clink.

Closer. She sucked in a breath, released the knob, and stepped into the passageway.

From ten feet away, to her right, a cat examined her. The feline sat on its haunches, its green eyes fixed on her. The cat was black, with faint brown stripes on its long body and oversized ears compared to its head. A tiny metal charm, so small she couldn't identify its shape, dangled from a black collar around the cat's neck. The clinking must've been the charm.

"Hi, kitty," she said.

The cat trotted down the passage to the head of the stairs, where it paused to look back at her. The cat was female, based on its lack of visible genitalia. Erin took two steps down the hall. The cat bounded downstairs. Erin started to follow but stopped. Newman mentioned a cat lived in the house, though Erin assumed she meant the cat lived there when the manor's owner visited, traveling with Mr. Wessick. Obviously not.

Erin returned to her bedroom. She left the outer door ajar, leaving enough of a gap to admit the cat if the feline so desired. A little company, even the four-legged variety, might evict the chill residing on her spine.

At the bed, Erin peeled back the patchwork quilt and cotton blanket. She slid halfway under the silky sheets—were they actually silk, she wondered—before a question stopped her. Who fed the cat?

Newman said nothing about feeding the cat. The woman mentioned the cat once, in passing. Although Newman didn't seem like the type to forget anything as important as feeding an animal, she ought to check. Beside the bed, a modern telephone perched atop an antique end table. She snatched up the handset. On its digital face, the cordless handset displayed, among other things, the current time of 10:45.

Sure, she could call a virtual stranger at 10:45 to ask about the cat's feeding schedule. If she wanted to get fired. Newman might not mind, but why risk it? The cat looked well fed, and therefore able to wait until morning.

She set the phone in its cradle. A few minutes later she was snuggled under the sheets, in the dark, in the quiet. Out in the passage, something creaked. The house settling, nothing more. She raised her head, twisting to glance out the window. The trees blocked any view of the sky. She rested her head on the pillow, shut her eyes, and tried to relax.

It didn't work.

ALEX HUDDLED BEHIND A CEDAR TREE. HE PICKED UP A BRANCH TO PEEK through the space beneath it at the darkened house sixty feet away. Inside Revenant House, Erin must be sleeping. If Rassul lurked nearby, he wouldn't be asleep. He would be waiting for Alex.

What if Rassul waited inside the house? He might sneak into Erin's bedroom to steal an earring or a hairbrush or some other item, to prove beyond doubt he could access her private quarters whenever he wished. While she remained unaware of his presence. Vulnerable. In danger.

Alex clenched his jaw. He must find Rassul.

His cell phone warbled.

He jumped. Should've left the blasted thing in the car. He must be the most incompetent spy in history. His mentor would cringe if he learned Alex brought his cell phone along on a reconnaissance mission. *Stop it.* He made a mistake, forgot the phone was in his pocket. This would be his last mistake.

The phone rang a second time. He brought out the phone and was about to shut it off when he noticed the caller ID. Unknown number, it said. He should turn off the phone. That odd feeling niggled at him again. He answered the call.

"Rassul," Alex said into the phone.

The worm said nothing for a second or two. Then he sniggered. "You reached the playing field at last. But, as usual, you fail to recognize the true nature of the game."

"No games. Tell me what you want."

"I intend to, but not over the phone. Walk behind the house, to the cellar door. It will be open. Go inside."

Rassul disconnected the call.

So much for stealth. Alex tucked the phone in his pocket and strode out of the trees toward the house. Around the back, he found the cellar's entrance. The wooden door hung open. Alex pulled the Glock out of its shoulder holster. The cellar was dark. He stepped into the doorway.

Light blinded him.

Someone had switched on the overhead fluorescent lights. Alex blinked. His eyes began to adjust, and he saw rows of wine racks. Down the first aisle, directly ahead of him, hunched Rassul.

Alex kept the Glock aimed at the floor, both arms slack at his sides. Rassul stood thirty feet away. Let the worm think Alex wouldn't shoot him. If Rassul so much as twitched, he'd swing the Glock up and pull the trigger.

Rassul didn't twitch. Instead, he smirked.

"Let me guess," Alex said, "you're about to warn me to keep out of your way or you'll hurt Erin. Then you'll inform me that you have access to the entire house and can sneak into her bedroom while she's sleeping to kill her. Does that about cover it?"

"You think you are clever."

"No, I think I've heard your spiel before."

"Ah, but you are only partially correct." Rassul fisted his hands, then slowly unfurled his fingers. "They want you to help the Turner woman, yes. When I tell you to stop, however, you stop. You leave immediately, giving whatever explanation you wish. Disobey, and she will suffer."

"Precisely what am I supposed to help her do?"

"Find the relic, of course."

"What is this relic?"

"That," Rassul said, "you must discover for yourself. They command you to do so."

"They." Alex leveled the gun at Rassul. "I'm fed up with hearing about your enigmatic friends and their goddamn relic. Give me something more informative than the hot air blowing out of your mouth."

"You have no choice."

Alex stomped toward Rassul. The man didn't flinch. Alex jammed the Glock's muzzle into the soft underside of Rassul's chin. The man chuckled, but grimaced as his Adam's apple rubbed against the gun.

"Kill me," he said, "and another takes my place. They command a vast army of servants."

Alex squinted at the rotten little troll in front of him. He cared nothing about why Rassul served his shadowy masters. "They" might be a fabrication anyway, designed to distract Alex in the same manner as the charade with the crash test dummy. Both tricks worked.

No more.

Bending his head close to Rassul's, Alex said, "Who are they?"

Light glinted in Rassul's right hand. Alex leaped backward at the instant Rassul swung the knife up at the spot where Alex's chest had been a split second earlier.

Alex aimed the gun at Rassul and fired.

The troll ducked sideways, dove past Alex, and shot out the door.

Alex bolted after him. Rassul veered around the end of the house. Alex skidded around the corner, tripped in a depression, and hit the ground on his knees. Pain stunned him. He flung his hands out, catching himself before his face smacked into the ground. A dark figure raced into the woods ahead of him. Alex bounded up.

Pop!

In the woods, light exploded. For a moment, Alex stood mesmerized. The light, pure white, shimmered like water. The rays lapped around the trees, through the branches, across the ground. Alex blinked. Rassul went that way and if he didn't hurry the troll might escape. Alex ran toward the light.

The glow steadied and faded, darkening into an amber glow. He pushed through a stand of fir trees into a small clearing.

He froze. Rassul stood fifteen Feet away, his back to Alex. The man faced what looked like a huge, circular window—except it was attached to nothing, no house, no vehicle, no structure at all. The window, about ten feet in diameter, hovered a few inches above the ground. Alex saw no frame for the window, no defined edges. Within its circumference, the vista of the dark woods was replaced. The window looked out on a city street lit by amber streetlamps, the light of which cascaded out into the woods.

Rassul glanced back over his shoulder. He twisted his lips into a malevolent smile.

Alex couldn't move.

Rassul stepped through the window onto the city sidewalk. The window contracted, slowly at first, then progressively faster until it zipped into nothingness.

Alex gaped at the woods where the window had hovered. Tiptoeing forward, turning on his flashlight, he explored the vicinity. Rassul's boots left faint imprints in the newly sprouted grass. Alex saw nothing else, no sign of the glowing portal.

In the clearing's center, Alex halted. He tilted his head back, surveying the sky. A chill tingled along the back of his neck. He might've been looking for answers in the wrong place. To find the answers he sought, perhaps he should change his frame of reference.

By looking up.

THROUGH THE WINDOW, WESSICK WATCHED ALEX MACKAY TROT OUT OF THE woods behind the house. MacKay skulked across the lawn toward the trees on the opposite side. Wessick ducked behind the curtain as MacKay passed within thirty feet of the window. Though the room was dark, he preferred not to risk being seen.

MacKay disappeared into the woods, no doubt returning to his car. What had Rassul done? Wessick ordered him to lure MacKay into the cellar, not the woods. He must deal with the digger later. If Rassul obeyed the rest of Wessick's orders, then he'd warned MacKay that he must help Erin only until instructed otherwise. Against his better judgment, Wessick followed the plan his superiors laid out for him, a scheme devised by a virtual child.

Rustling issued from deeper inside the room. Desheret said, "May we turn the lights on now?"

He sidled toward the desk. Moonlight filtering through the window glistened on the metal base of his desk lamp. He touched the base, felt his way up to the pull chain, and yanked it. Light sprayed across the room.

Seated on the sofa, legs stretched across its length, Desheret watched him with half-closed eyes. "Has your guard dog frightened him away?"

"Temporarily." Wessick crossed behind the desk and sank into the chair. Planting an elbow on each arm of the chair, he linked his hands over his abdomen. "He will be back, I've no doubt."

"Just as we planned."

"As you planned. I'm no longer comfortable with it." He tapped his thumb tips together in a silent drumbeat. "We need Erin to concentrate. MacKay is a distraction. I can't understand why you think she needs him."

"Alex will help her, which helps you. Besides, their mutual interest in each other provides an added incentive for her to find the relic before our adversaries happen upon it." She smiled. "Alex is quite attractive."

"Which is a distraction."

Desheret shook her head. "You truly don't have a romantic bone in your body, do you?"

He dropped his hands onto the chair's arms. Desheret thought life should follow the formula of a Gothic romance novel. Erin Turner was not Jane Eyre, however, a fact Desheret seemed unwilling to accept. What could he expect from Desheret, a girl barely old enough to have graduated from college? Desheret, of course, never attended school at any level. Her knowledge, and apparent wisdom, stemmed from life experience. In her brief time on earth, she experienced more than many people knew in their entire lifetimes.

Confronted with her youthful face, he often forgot that she was no innocent. He knew no more about Desheret than the tidbits of information she doled out to him. Her birth name remained a mystery, for she'd adopted countless aliases. He knew two of her pseudonyms, but she preferred the nickname Desheret. With each change of name, her appearance transformed as well. Today, she'd removed her black wig to reveal her natural hair color. Her clothing was modern and casual. She looked younger, less worldly. Which Desheret was genuine? She guarded that secret most of all.

Yes, she kept things from him. Yet he kept an equal number of secrets from her. Perhaps they deserved each other.

Wessick sighed. "I'll give your plan a bit longer to work—but only a bit."

Desheret slid off the sofa into a kneeling position on the floor, facing him. She bowed her head. Stifling a giggle, she said, "Yes, my lord."

"Enough." Wessick leaped to his feet, gesturing for her to rise. When she did, he said, "It's time to return to your second life. The first can do without you for the time being."

Her expression darkened. "I despise him. He is beneath me."

"Soon you'll be able to end the charade, but not yet. No one forced you to consort with a weakling, it was your choice."

"Yes, you wished me to hide in this house, confined to one room." She met his gaze head-on. "A separate room from yours, naturally. Do I frighten you, Samuel?"

He felt a frown tugging at his lips but restrained it. Realizing he was tightening his hands into fists, he relaxed them. Desheret, focused on his face, hadn't noticed the movement. The child was an expert at goading him, though she remained ignorant of her power, for he masked his reactions well.

Retrieving an *akhet* ball from a desk drawer, he tossed it to her. She caught it in one hand.

With a bland tone, he asked, "Can you leave without waking Erin?"

Lifting her chin, she puckered her lips into a slight pout. "Certainly."

She flounced toward the door. Halfway there, she paused to glance back at him. "I wonder if you care what happens to any of us."

"Emotion is a luxury I choose not to indulge in."

Desheret swept out of the room, shutting the door behind her with the barest click. Without sitting down, he grabbed the mouse and brought up the security camera software on his computer. The hidden cameras allowed him to monitor every room in the house, save Erin's bedroom and the bathrooms. He had no desire to invade her privacy. Neither she, Desheret, nor Rassul knew about the cameras. Security required secrecy.

He switched to the feed from the camera in the cellar. Desheret was shutting the door, having just entered the cellar. A light flared, blinding the camera for a moment. When the image cleared, Desheret was gone.

Her final words replayed in his mind, her tone of voice when she suggested he didn't care about anyone. He knew better than to trust her fits of emotion, especially the ones dressed as solemn sincerity. On the occasions when he paused to reflect on his circumstances, he often wondered about Desheret. He entrusted her with vital tasks, each one capable of destroying the entire endeavor—not to mention destroying him. Her demeanor switched from fiery to frigid with disturbing swiftness.

Right now, Rassul posed more of a problem than Desheret. The digger disobeyed Wessick's orders yet again by leading MacKay into the woods. Since Rassul hadn't reappeared, he must assume the man left through the woods as well, another act of disobedience.

Dealing with Rassul could wait. A more important task demanded his attention.

From a small drawer on the right-hand side of his desk, he retrieved a small book. A network of thin cracks webbed across the leather cover. Flipping open the book, he grazed his fingers over the handwritten text on the first page. He felt a tightening in his chest, a spasm in his gut. He felt...

He slammed the book shut. Complete the task. Nothing else mattered.

Cradling the book in his right hand, he exited the drawing room. In the passageway, he hesitated. A grandfather clock in the drawing room ticked, the sound barely audible. Nothing else breached the silence.

He walked into the library.

10

E RIN LINGERED OUTSIDE THE LIBRARY DOOR, MESMERIZED BY THE WOOD carving above it. In the carving, the sun beamed down on two Egyptian figures who raised their hands in worship. Each beam of light terminated in a tiny hand.

During the Amarna Period, the era when Akhenaten ruled Egypt, the artwork depicted the sun in the same manner—with the disc of the sun, called the Aten, stretching its hand-rays down to the pharaoh and his family as if the sunbeams might caress them. The practice of personifying natural elements seemed to date back as far as humanity itself. And who knew how far back the human race went.

She remembered reading about evidence human beings had existed for millions of years or more, far outside the 200,000 years or so granted by evolutionary theories. Human bones turned up in deposits from the Tertiary Period, and fossilized footprints showed up in rock from the Cretaceous. The Tertiary dated back 1.8 to 65 million years ago. The Cretaceous dated back 66 to 145 million years. Human beings weren't supposed to exist that far back in prehistory, therefore mainstream scientists dismissed such anomalously ancient discoveries as hoaxes or misidentifications.

The wood carving above the library door imitated ancient Egyptian art. Archaeologists accepted the existence of ancient Egyptians because, according to mainstream dating techniques, the ancient civilization of Egypt fell within tolerable boundaries for human existence. Since archaeologists, rather than the evidence itself, defined those boundaries, the conventional story remained intact no matter what. Oh, archaeologists might make slight corrections to their timelines, but nothing too drastic. A century here or there didn't upset the balance.

Erin walked into the library, to the desk in front of the window. The mahogany desk chair, which looked antique, was upholstered with fuzzy red fabric. Buttons sewn into the high back dimpled the fabric. The chair seemed more like living room furniture than an office chair. She lowered her butt onto the seat, feeling the springs under the cushion bounce a little. Nice. If she could figure out a way to shelve books without leaving the chair, she'd be set.

Chink-chink-chink.

The chinking of the cat's collar drew nearer. A black, furry face peeked around the edge of the doorjamb at Erin.

"Hey, kitty," she said.

The cat scampered away, her little bell jingling faster than before.

Erin sighed and leaned back in the chair. Someday she would make friends with the cat, though clearly not today.

A computer occupied the right side of the desk, with its keyboard and mouse tucked away on a shelf-like drawer under the desktop, while a cordless phone resided on the left side of the desktop. She snatched up the phone's handset. Newman demonstrated how to use the phone, and the numbers programmed into it, including Newman's cell number. Erin punched the buttons to dial Newman's number. The woman picked up on the second ring. "Yes, Ms. Turner."

"I was wondering, am I supposed to feed the cat?"

"No, the groundskeeper takes care of Bastet."

"Groundskeeper?"

"You're unlikely to see him. He keeps to himself, and he feeds Bastet in the cellar."

Groundskeeper. The word sent a shiver down her spine. Silly. She had no reason to fear a gardener who dabbled in cat husbandry.

"I'm late for a meeting," Newman said. "Feel free to call me anytime if more questions arise."

Newman disconnected with a faint click. Erin wanted to ask about the groundskeeper—what his name was, what hours he worked, what exactly his duties were.

Did he have a key to the house.

She plunked the phone back in its cradle. The groundskeeper must have a key, to the cellar anyway. The sole door leading to the cellar was outside, around the back of the house. No one could get into the house from the cellar, assuming the groundskeeper had a key to the cellar but not to the main house.

The creaking she heard last night. It sounded like a person walking down the corridor.

The shiver tickled her spine again. She redialed Newman's number, getting the woman's voicemail, and left a message asking Newman to call her.

How did the cat get in the cellar for the groundskeeper to feed her? Erin saw no pet doors in the house. Only two doors led outside and both were locked.

Stabbing the buttons on the phone with her index finger, she called to leave another message for Newman, this time asking the woman to call back as soon as she received the message. Brilliant. She was harassing her employers on her very first day, in her very first hour, on the job.

Erin grasped the front edge of the desk, pulling her chair forward. Its metal casters whirred as they slid across the plastic mat that protected the wood floor under the desk. She wriggled her butt to angle the chair toward the computer. Her cell phone, clipped to her waistband, dug into her side. Repositioning herself, she set the cordless mouse and keyboard on her lap. A pale green folder lay on the desk, smack in the center. Erin opened the folder. Inside, she found a detailed job description and a list of tasks for her to undertake. The list was numbered and prioritized with the most urgent items at the top. The first item directed her to "inventory and catalog library holdings."

Erin scanned the room. Each wall, except for the one behind the desk, held eight shelves. Divide the length of each wall by the average thickness of a book and...

She had no idea how many books the library held. Hundreds, at least. Many of the books were skinny. A few were thick, possibly encyclopedias or dictionaries. Inventorying and cataloging the collection would take awhile. Call it job security.

Logging onto the computer with the username and password Newman provided, she discovered someone had already installed spiffy software designed for creating and maintaining an electronic catalog of books and other materials. The software was much, much fancier than what she'd used at the Shadow Bay Public Library.

For the next two hours, Erin wandered the length and breadth of the library, perusing the books lined up on the shelves to get an overview of the topics covered in the collection. Samuel Wessick's interests ranged from architecture to ancient history, and from mythology to biographies of obscure people. A ten-foot-wide section of the shelves housed books dedicated to the history, culture, and mythology of ancient Egypt. Wessick owned more books about Egypt than any other topic. His fascination with the subject might explain the wood carving above the library door, except the carving looked as old as the house itself. Unless Samuel Wessick was over 150 years old, he hadn't commissioned the carving above the door. He might've inherited the Egypt books along with the house, making the original Egyptophile his ancestor.

Alex had given her a printout of information he dug up online related to Revenant House. Although she remembered reading the part about the meaning of the word revenant—it referred to a zombie, a ghost, or a person who seemed out of his time—she forgot to read the rest of the papers. What did she do with them? No need to search. She was a librarian, after all. She knew how to find information.

Back at the desk, she opened the web browser on the computer and navigated to a search engine. She searched for the exact phrase "Revenant House." The search engine returned three links. The first took her to a post on an architectural blog. The post listed the top five most unusual historic houses in Michigan, ranking Revenant House as number three. The blogger, someone called T. R. Young, wrote a grand total of two sentences about Revenant House:

```
This mysterious home is unavailable for public viewing, and
it can't be seen from the road. I heard about it from the
late Ignatius Underwood, who used to be the groundskeeper
there.
```

The post included a small, grainy black-and-white photo of the manor. The caption said simply, "Photo by Ignatius Underwood, circa 1952." The second and third links in the search results took her to other blogs that re-posted the entry from the first site. Back on the first blog, she hunted the site for contact information for T. R. Young. Finding an e-mail address, she composed a quick missive asking him if he knew anything more about Revenant House. She told the blogger she worked at the house and had become curious about its history, which wasn't a lie, though the statement omitted much. Then she hit the send button, and the message disappeared into cyberspace.

Next, she searched for Samuel N. Wessick. The results led her to vague, congratulatory articles on business sites that mentioned Wessick's company, SNW Inc., and its expansion across the globe. The company specialized in robotics for military and civilian applications, whatever that meant. None of the articles included a photo of Wessick. One referred to the man as reclusive. Big surprise.

Her eyes burned. She'd been staring at the computer screen without blinking. The computer's clock told her she'd browsed the Internet for forty-five minutes. Great, on her first day of work she wasted nearly an hour on cyber snooping, because she'd let Alex's paranoia infect her too. So what if her employer was a bit mysterious. Samuel Wessick gave her a well-paying job, trusting her to perform her duties without supervision. Alex planted a seed, and she let its vines choke her brain. Time for some pruning.

She grabbed a notepad from the drawer and a pen from the desktop. She spent the next two hours inventorying the books on one wall of the library, both counting the books and jotting down title and author information for each one. None dated to later than 1965. She recognized a handful of the authors, but most were obscure. Virtually all the books were first editions. Some included handwritten notes in the margins, but whether the authors or readers scribbled the notes, she couldn't tell. The collection must've been worth a fortune.

In the Egypt section, her progress slowed. She couldn't stop herself from skimming through each book, pausing at each illustration, scrutinizing the handwritten notes. In the Egypt books, the notes all seemed to have been written by the same hand. A man, she guessed from the tight, angular shape of the letters. She pulled out a thick tome called *A History of Egyptian Mythology, Beginning in the Predynastic Era and Continuing through the New Kingdom.* Through the gap left by the book, she spotted another book lying face down behind the row, lengthwise to the upright books. She slid out two more books, setting them on the desk along with the mythology book. Returning to the bookshelf, she grasped the spine of the book that had been hidden behind the others and eased it out into the open. The leather cover had no title printed on it. Instead, the cover featured an Egyptian hieroglyph, the *akhet* symbol, embossed in gold.

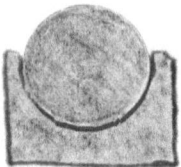

Sitting down at the desk, she laid the book flat on the desktop and carefully opened it. The text was handwritten. The first page said, "Notes on an Extraordinary Discovery, or, Evidence of Transoceanic Contact among Ancient Cultures and of Otherworld Influences." Below the title, the author had written his name. Ridley Hyde-Peters.

The book's author was the man whose mummified remains she and Alex discovered inside the tunnels in the Grand Canyon. So Ridley did have a connection to the manor. Since she refused to believe his book showed up here by coincidence, that left two possibilities. Either Ridley Hyde-Peters had lived in or visited the manor, or someone placed the book here for her to find.

She flipped to the next page. Text written in Ridley's modest cursive spelled out "Part 1" followed by the phrase "Derivation of a Hypothesis." She turned the page. Here began the body of the manuscript:

Chapter 1

I must begin with a question. Of the ancient world, are the truths we cherish the truths we know in certitude? If any man responds with an immediate affirmative, then I must query once more. How shall we demonstrate the indisputable nature of these truths?

I assert that we cannot, for the past is gone, vanished into the ether. Time has bequeathed to us written chronicles fraught with inaccuracies, inconsistencies, propaganda, and barefaced lies. Yet our beloved truths depend upon these flawed histories. I have whiled away innumerable hours contemplating the available histories in the vain hope of gleaning authentic truth from their words. Disheartened by the quest, I abandoned it. I soon realized the truth lay elsewhere – namely, in the physical remains of extinct civilisations. Thenceforth, I embarked on a global mission to

The page ended mid sentence. She flipped to the next page. Blank. She ran her finger down the inside of the spine, between the pages. The edge felt ragged. Someone had ripped a page out of the book.

She fanned through the remainder of the book, but the pages were blank. Back at the bookshelves, she searched the area where she discovered Ridley's book. Although her fingers acquired a good coating of dust, she located no missing pages or secret clues that might help her reconstitute Ridley's book. Since he apparently filled just two pages, the single missing page seemed unlikely to contain the solution to even one of the mysteries of the universe. On the second page, Ridley probably expounded on his views of history and its inherent flaws. She agreed with his assessment. But what had his "global mission" involved?

A search of the internet yielded nothing. The life of Ridley Hyde-Peters left no posthumous footprints in the digital sands. His book was never officially published, as far as she could determine, and no information about him appeared on any website—not even a genealogy site. The man was a ghost. A revenant?

Maybe Alex's buddies could uncover more about Ridley. She plucked the cell phone from her waistband and dialed Alex's number. Voicemail. After leaving a message asking him to call her, she returned the cell phone to her waistband. She grabbed her notes about the library's collection. Back to work.

Outside, an engine growled to life.

The grumbling sounded like a lawnmower. Erin spun her chair around, raising her butt off the seat to see out the window. No lawnmower in front of the house. No cars other than the gigantic SUV provided for her. The groundskeeper must've parked out back, but she heard no vehicles approach the house.

Erin leaped out of the chair. It smacked backward into the bookshelves under the window. She sprinted out of the library and down the passageway, past the vestibule and stairs, veering right into the north passage. The rubber soles of her shoes slapped on the wood floor as she dashed past the kitchen to the end of the passage. There, a door on the right led outside. She unlocked the door, slowly twisted the knob, and eased the door outward a few inches. Peeking through the opening, she surveyed the open area behind the house. The lawn stretched 150 feet away from the house, right up to the edge of a cliff. Newman said the cliff was eighty feet high, a sheer drop down to Lake Superior. Although Erin spied nothing in the portion of the lawn she visible to her, the house blocked most of her view.

A breeze chilled her cheeks. Clouds blocked the sun. Her blouse was long-sleeved but thin, admitting every wisp of wind. She already felt goosebumps popping up on her arms. *Just do it.*

She thrust the door wide open and trotted down the steps onto the lawn. The east and west wings of the house stuck out into the lawn so that, though she was outside now, the house still surrounded her on three sides. She marched out into the open lawn. A gust of wind buffeted her. Scanning the lawn, she saw no one. The engine noise seemed to come from around the west end of the house. She turned in that direction. The sound grumbled closer. Her teeth chattered. Rubbing her arms, she took a step.

The lawnmower burst out from behind the house into the backyard. The groundskeeper sat straight as a flagpole in the seat of the riding lawnmower. He—she assumed it was a man—wore a long-sleeved canvas jacket, black gloves, and a brimmed hat fitted with a mosquito net that covered his entire head and neck. The dark color of the netting obscured his face.

She waved. No response.

The woods hemmed in the house, about twenty feet away on the east side, and fifty feet on the west. The groundskeeper drove his mower along the west tree line toward the cliff. About thirty feet from the cliff's edge, he steered the mower left onto a trail that led westward into the woods. Soon, the groundskeeper and his mower putted out of sight, and the engine's grumbling faded.

Erin started to follow, then halted.

She would make a great impression today—pestering Newman with silly questions, wasting time on the Internet, and finally stalking the groundskeeper. Alex thought Revenant House was creepy. So what? As of today, she lived and worked here, whether Dr. Alex MacKay approved of her choice or not. She needed to embrace reality, and shed her paranoia blanket, if she wanted to keep his job.

Trotting back into the house, she shut and locked the door. The barrier locked out the cold wind, but a chill lingered deep inside her. She rubbed her arms until the goosebumps went away.

The chill remained.

THE GATES TO REVENANT HOUSE WERE CLOSED. ALEX SCRUTINIZED THE GATES through binoculars for another ten seconds. The pitted windshield blurred his view somewhat, a fact he could not overcome unless he got out of the car. He saw no point in getting out, given that no vehicles had come or gone through the gates since six o'clock this morning, when he began his vigil.

He'd spent the night propped up against a pine tree, alternately dozing and spying on Erin through the same binoculars he used this morning. Not spying. Guarding. Someone ought to make certain Rassul stayed the hell away from her. This morning he relocated to the car, and his vigil began anew. With less bugs and no itchy pine needles. God, he hoped Michigan didn't have poisonous insects. He hadn't been entirely certain the weeds he slept next to weren't poison ivy.

Setting the binoculars on the passenger seat, he rubbed his eyes. What precisely did he hope to accomplish here? He didn't know. Six hours ago, he'd parked in this spot about three hundred feet from the gates, a dozen yards past a bend in the road, where the branches of a large pine tree concealed his car. The space between the two bottommost branches afforded him a view of the gates to Revenant House.

The first time he traveled down this road, when he followed Erin to her job interview, he noticed a security camera perched atop one of the gate posts. The camera must've recorded his arrival early this morning. The person who monitored the camera—Rassul or his employer—knew Alex had driven past the gates without returning in the opposite direction. He no longer cared if they knew he was here. In fact, he wanted them to know.

I'm watching you too.

Fifteen minutes ago, Erin had called him. He instinctively reached for the phone then stopped, letting his voicemail take the call. Erin wanted answers, deserved answers, yet every time he considered telling her anything—much less everything—one of two things happened. Either his vocal cords froze, or idiotic words tumbled out of his mouth until Erin gave him a look of such profound annoyance that at last he was able to shut off the flow. If he held onto any shred of sense, he'd keep away from Erin and guard her from a distance, as he did now. Then again, his tendency to confuse and annoy Erin encouraged her to dive deeper into the mystery, into danger. If he told her the truth, she might change her mind.

And he might grow a pair of wings.

His phone rang. He snatched it off the dashboard and glanced at its display. Erin was calling him, again. He hovered his thumb over the button that would connect the call.

Blood. Screams. A hand, pale and lifeless, yet still seeming to reach out for him. A rock wall exploding.

The phone rang a third time. Alex tucked the phone in his jacket pocket. Erin would not become another victim of his recklessness. Harry must be the last.

Until last night, Alex had kindled the hope that Harry might turn up alive and unharmed. Hope's flame, though weak, burned nonetheless—until the moment he heard Rassul's voice growling through his cell phone. Despite Rassul's stunt with the crash test dummy, today Alex assumed Harry was dead. He lacked any evidence to prove it, but he felt certain it was true. Why did Harry travel to Michigan? The clues in the book Harry sent Erin pointed to the Grand Canyon, not to the northernmost reaches of Michigan. If Harry collected more information, beyond what the petroglyph panel contained, why did he omit that information from the clues he gave Erin? Harry's encrypted notes drew them to Arizona. Harry might've found additional evidence after he mailed the book.

Alex slammed the bottom of his fist into the steering wheel. Dammit, no one except Harry knew what the hell Harry was thinking. Alex knew Harry about as well as he knew his mailman. In spite of working with Harry off and on for the past eighteen months, Alex knew virtually nothing about the man. He liked, even admired, Harry. Yet he couldn't answer the most basic questions about the man. Had he been married, did he have children, where did he grow up, what music did he like. Although Harry and Alex shared a quest, they had shared little else.

His cell phone rang. He extricated it from his pocket, glancing at the display, then punched the connect button and grumbled hello.

"Somebody's grumpy today," Katy said.

"I left you a message four hours ago."

"I know." A child's voice giggled in the background. "I was busy. What is it?"

"Erin. I need to tell her everything. Is that acceptable?"

"Honey, you don't need permission. We gave you carte blanche to do whatever you think is right."

He cleared his throat. "My last decision of this nature didn't turn out so well."

"No one blames you for what happened."

He clenched the phone tighter. His jaw muscle twitched. He felt the pressure of his teeth clamped together. No one blamed him. Wonderful. Although the logical part of his brain recognized that he wasn't at fault, he couldn't shake the feeling he should've known. He might feel better if he knew with whom, or what, the blame lay.

"I need help," he said.

Katy sighed. The sound conveyed sympathy, not exasperation. When she spoke, her voice was soft and almost motherly. "I know this is your first assignment since Utah—"

"This has nothing to do with Utah. Rassul knows I'm here. I've decided to take advantage of that fact, but I need backup. Someone they won't recognize, someone who's not on their radar."

"Everybody's busy."

"There must be someone you can reassign."

"You can ask Rick," she said, "but I'm sure he'll say no. We don't get directly involved anymore, unless the situation is exceptional. Help has to come from other members of the organization. You knew the deal when you signed on."

Yes, he had known. With the organization's resources stretched so thin these days, finding help often proved difficult.

"What about Lou?" Alex asked.

"He's been reassigned. The entire organization has been mobilized to chase every lead, no matter how flimsy. Something's coming, something incredibly bad, and everybody has to scramble to prepare."

"If we can prepare."

"This is no time for pessimism. You of all people understand the dangers we're facing."

He gazed down the road, at the gates. "I know."

She made a sympathetic noise. "Relax, honey. I'll figure something out. In the meantime, talk to Erin. It'll make you feel better."

"I doubt it," he said. "Everything I say aggravates her."

A figure shifted in the trees. He jerked upright, squinting at the movement.

"Gotta go," he said, and hung up.

Tossing the phone onto the dashboard, he eased the driver's door open. The figure in the woods, whether man or beast, paid no attention to the click of the door latch.

Alex climbed out of the car in near silence. As he crossed the gravel road in front of the car, on his way toward the roadside ditch, he walked in the manner his mentor taught him. Toes down first, rolling down to the heel, a method designed to reduce noise. He bridged the ditch with one step, settling his feet down on a bare patch on the opposite bank. There, he dropped into a crouch, listening and observing.

About forty feet away, a figure darted side to side while skulking ever farther from Alex. The figure was human, and looked to be a man. Trees and other natural obstacles forced the man to duck left, then right, then left again to find a clear path. The stranger wore a white T-shirt with some kind of emblem on the front. He might as well have strapped a flashing light on top of his head. The white shirt gave away his position equally as well.

Alex visually inspected the rest of the woods. He looked through, rather than at, the vegetation, searching for any other figures lurking there. After several minutes, he decided no one else accompanied the white-shirted stranger.

Crunch. Snap. The stranger crushed leaves and twigs under his shoes, clearly oblivious to the racket he created. The would-be prowler made Alex feel like a man-tracking pro. Forget stealth. This idiot wouldn't hear an elephant stampeding up behind him.

Sliding a hand under his jacket, Alex touched the butt of the Glock. Satisfied, he retracted his hand and jogged into the woods toward the stranger. He hopped over leafy patches and twigs and ducked around bigger obstacles. Twenty feet from the stranger, Alex halted to conduct another visual search of the area. Still no one around but the bumbling prowler. No one Alex could see, anyway. *Trust yourself.* The thought smarted like a slap to the face. He resisted the urge to survey the woods again. He hadn't missed anything. No one else was around, unless they were invisible.

A possibility he perhaps shouldn't dismiss, given the nature of the enemy. Not that he, or anyone else, truly understood their nature. However, since he could do nothing about invisible stalkers, he may as well ignore the possibility.

"Ah!"

The fool in the white shirt tripped on something, possibly a rock or a hole, triggering the cry. The man flailed forward half a step and flopped onto the ground face first. The ground muted his grunt.

Alex ran toward the stranger. As the man pushed up onto his hands and knees, Alex seized his right arm and yanked him onto his feet. The stranger yelped. Alex spun him around and thrust him backward, pinning his back against a tree. The stranger's mouth dropped open. Alex whipped out the Glock. He jammed the muzzle against the man's temple, slapping his free hand onto the stranger's chest.

"Who are you?" Alex said.

"W-what?"

Alex nudged the man's temple with his gun. Enunciating each word carefully, he said, "Who are you?"

"I'm, uh, Greg."

"Greg who?"

"Virtanen." Greg swallowed hard. "Look, man, if this is your land, I'll go, I swear. No hard feelings, huh?"

Alex guessed Greg was in his mid twenties, and a couple inches shorter than himself. The boy's hair was scraggly, though not long, as if he needed a haircut. A fresh cut sliced across his left cheek. His face and hands were dirty. Green and brown smudges stained his T-shirt which, Alex now saw, bore not an emblem but a series of bright-colored stripes and dots. Greg's lower lip trembled. Alex started to lower the Glock, then froze. Evil often masqueraded as innocence.

He returned the muzzle to Greg's temple and asked, "What are you doing out here?"

"Looking for my girlfriend."

"She's missing?"

Greg glanced around, as if hoping a savior might arrive to rescue him. After a few seconds, he gave up and faced Alex, but avoided eye contact.

"No," Greg said, "not missing. Not the way you mean it, or the way I think you mean it."

The boy bit his lower lip and sniffled. His hands, stiff at his sides, quivered.

Aw hell. Alex lowered the gun, aiming the muzzle at the ground. He dropped his hand from Greg's chest as well. The boy seemed as dangerous as a kitten stuck in a drainpipe.

"My girl," Greg said. "She's inside, I know it."

Greg pointed through the woods. There, between two maple trees, a sliver of a building was visible. A sliver of Revenant House. The only one inside Revenant House was Erin.

Alex's jaw ached. He forced his clenched muscles to relax. "Your girlfriend is Erin Turner?"

"Erin's her friend. But Chloe—that's my girl—I know she's in there too."

Chloe. The redhead who giggled a little too much and pushed a little too hard to get personal information out of strangers. She tossed her hair too, a habit that made Alex wince.

Alex holstered the Glock. "Why do you care if she visits Erin?"

"It's a cover. She's in there with him, I know it."

"Who?"

"The creep she's been seeing behind my back. Don't know his name."

"Erin works at Revenant House," Alex said. "Chloe had never been there before yesterday."

Greg straightened and squared his jaw, though his hand still trembled. "Erin's helping them sneak around, letting them use the house for their…get-togethers."

Alex suppressed a laugh. Get-togethers? Greg made it sound like Chloe and her mystery man belonged to a knitting club. He also claimed Erin abetted the faithless couple. Alex couldn't believe she would provide an alibi for Chloe's trysts, much less sit downstairs cataloging books while they fooled around upstairs. Greg must be confused.

"Did you see Chloe go into the house?" Alex asked.

Greg scrunched his shoulders, shoving his hands in his pants pockets. "No."

"What makes you think she's inside?"

Greg shrugged one shoulder.

"Get out of here," Alex said. "Your girlfriend is not at Revenant House, trust me."

"But—"

"Go."

Greg trotted off through the woods, away from Revenant House, back toward the road. Alex watched until the boy disappeared from view, then he trudged back to his car. Greg was shuffling down the gravel road, kicking up tiny dust clouds on his way back toward the gates of Revenant House. Alex kept an eye on Greg until he scuffled past the gates and on down the road to a red Volkswagen parked within sight of the entrance. Chloe's car, Alex realized. While he waited for Greg to clamber into the Volkswagen, Alex stared at the gates. No sign anyone detected Greg's clumsy attempt at surveillance. They might've spotted him and simply chosen not to react.

Perhaps no one was monitoring the cameras today. According to Erin, she was alone in the house—or so she thought, because Ms. Newman told her so. Yet Rassul was in the house last night, or at the very least in the cellar.

Greg drove down the road. Alex squeezed back into his own car. He retrieved a can of pop from the cooler on the backseat. Sipping the drink, he let his thoughts wander back to Harry. Rassul would withhold the secret of Harry's fate for as long as possible, using the knowledge as a tool to manipulate and control the situation. Harry must be dead. Alex gritted his teeth. He stared down the road, zeroing in on the gates to Revenant House. Was this place connected to Harry's death? He needed to know, because Erin was inside the house right now, and he felt certain she was not alone. Although Rassul was a nasty bugger, he followed orders handed down to him by someone far worse. Hovering nearby, unseen and unknown, Rassul's master waited.

For what? Until Alex could answer the question, and probably after that as well, Erin was in danger. Knowledge didn't always confer power. It did, however, offer sanctuary. Erin needed all the protection knowledge could offer her, which required full disclosure from him.

Alex grabbed his cell phone and dialed Erin's number. No one else would die on his watch. No one.

ERIN RAISED THE PHONE TO HER EAR AND GOT HALFWAY THROUGH THE WORD hello before Alex interrupted. "We need to talk. It's urgent."

His voice sounded different. Deeper, stronger. Sexier. Her stomach fluttered. When she spoke, her voice fluttered a bit too. "With you it's always life or death, isn't it?"

Her attempt at sarcasm instead sounded whiny. *Get a grip.* Mentally slapping herself, she straightened in the chair. Grip gotten.

She hoped.

Alex said, "I'll tell you everything you want to know."

"Everything?"

"Yes." He lowered his voice to a near whisper. "But not at Revenant House."

"You still think it's haunted by zombies."

"No, I think it's riddled with bugs."

She glanced at the floor, half expecting to see flesh-eating insects swarming toward her feet. Nothing there, naturally. She said, "Termites?"

"Electronic surveillance equipment. Bugs."

"Oh." She couldn't keep the relief from coloring her voice. "Where should we meet then?"

"The Shadow Bay Inn, room one-twelve."

A lump formed in her throat. "At your m—"

"Don't say it. Bugs, remember?"

"Uh-huh."

"This isn't a proposition, Erin. Bring your gun if it makes you feel better."

She said nothing. Her brain had stopped functioning when he spoke the words Shadow Bay Inn. The motel sat on the edge of town, right along the main highway. She wasn't worried Alex would murder or molest her. So what was her problem? The guy apologized for the slightest transgressions. Heck, he apologized for apologizing too much.

Alex said, "We've been alone in a motel room before."

"I know." She flashed back to that morning in an Arizona motel, when Alex called first to ask permission to knock on her door. "It's fine, we can meet there. I have to work until five, but I can come right after."

"I said it's urgent."

"And I said that's the soonest I can come."

He let out a heavy sigh.

She let her silence speak for itself.

"Fine," he said, sounding peeved. "I'll be waiting."

He hung up.

She spent the remainder of the morning devising a scheme for cataloging the library collection. After lunch, she settled into the chair behind her desk, intending to dive back into the job. The memory of Ridley's book, and its missing page, kept returning to her. What global mission had he undertaken? What happened to the missing page? How did he wind up in an unknown tunnel in Arizona, mummified and forgotten?

Work, she reminded herself. They paid her to work, not muse about the mysteries of the world.

Ridley's remains. The tunnels. The other mummy, possibly Celtic in origin. The key she found under Ridley's hand. His book, found here in Revenant House.

The key.

If Ridley's unfinished book ended up in this house, then maybe his key opened a door in this house. The key to her bedroom was bronze, though, not iron like Ridley's key. She was assuming every door in the house had a bronze key, an assumption that may or may not prove true. One way to find out.

Work now, explore later.

No. Her employer was connected to Ridley, and therefore to whatever insanity she'd been sucked into against her will. Although she couldn't prove it, she knew it with a gut-level conviction that defied reason. She rose from the chair. Reason flew out the window the moment she accepted this job. Total, eye-popping insanity ruled her life these days. Might as well go with it.

And if they fired her, oh well. She'd expose her employer's true motives, whatever the blazes they were up to, whether she worked here or not. Time to teach them a lesson.

Don't mess with a librarian.

HALF AN HOUR LATER, SHE'D TRIED RIDLEY'S KEY IN EVERY INTERIOR AND exterior door of the manor. The key fit none of them. Wessick or a previous owner might've changed the locks at some point. Of course, the key might open something other than a door. Countless objects required keys to open them. Chests, desk drawers, cabinets. Most of the manor's rooms were locked. She searched anyway, nosing into every accessible corner, checking behind every piece of artwork. Nothing. If Ridley's key unlocked something inside the manor, the object must lie inside one of the locked rooms.

With her search foiled, she trudged back to the library. At the doorway, she hesitated. She glanced over her shoulder at the closed and locked door to the drawing room. A shiver sidled up her spine. Newman described the drawing room as "Mr. Wessick's private sanctuary." If anyone fit the house's name, it was Samuel Wessick. He shared the traits of a ghost—unseen, mysterious. At times she swore she felt a presence around her, as if the walls had become infused with a remnant of a consciousness, perhaps Wessick's, or perhaps someone else's. Logically, she knew the idea was ridiculous. In the new, bizarre version of reality she found herself in, however, anything seemed possible. Absolutely anything.

She crossed the corridor in three steps to stand face to face with the drawing room door. Closing her hand around the knob, she turned it. Locked, of course. Duh. She tried to peek through the space between the door and the jamb, but the fit was too snug. Not even a sliver of light penetrated the gap. She dropped onto her belly on the floor and tried peeking under the door. She couldn't see much. Carpeting. The legs of some furniture, what looked like a few tables and a sofa.

Bugs, remember?

The memory of Alex's words chilled her blood. In slow motion, she pushed onto hands and knees and sat back on her heels with her palms flat on her thighs. She felt eyes watching her. Invisible, electronic eyes. And somewhere, human eyes locked on a computer monitor or TV screen.

Erin hopped to her feet. Let them watch. When she spun around, the wood carving above the library door caught her eye. The two figures worshiping the sun wore the traditional linen kilts seen in many Egyptian tomb paintings. The figures also wore objects on their chests. She lifted onto her tiptoes to get a few inches closer to the carving. The objects on their chests resembled pectorals, a type of breastplate the ancient Egyptians had worn. Most pectorals were elaborate and bejeweled rather than functional. These pectorals bore some kind of symbols, possibly writing, on them. She ducked into the library, grabbed the ladder meant for accessing the upper bookshelves, and dragged it into the passageway. Positioning the ladder under the carving, she climbed up the steps until the two carved figures were at eye level for her. The pectorals each bore the same symbol, she now saw. The symbol consisted of three interlocked spirals identical to the scrollwork on Ridley's key.

What on earth did it mean? The answers could lie behind one of the closed doors, like the drawing room door. If she broke down the door, somehow, she just might attract the attention of Samuel Wessick and encourage him to come out of the shadows. So far, she'd inspired one man to emerge from the shadows—Rassul, whose motives for attacking her remained a mystery. Alex called Rassul a "little worm." To her, the term sounded a bit too innocuous. Rassul jumped her, bruising her entire body, until a glowing orb he healed her. She couldn't decide which disturbed her more, Rassul or the orb. Rassul, definitely. The orb helped her.

What would Wessick do if she provoked him? With a choice between Rassul and Wessick, she'd take her chances with the man who offered her a high-paying job rather than the scumbag who assaulted her. She didn't want to think about Rassul anymore. Events might seem clearer after she talked to Alex later. She hoped he'd have a plan. Almost anything would be better than her current tactic of stumbling around in the dark while an unseen enemy, equipped with night vision, observed.

For now, she had one option. Get back to work.

Shadow Bay Inn

Erin raised her fist to knock on the door. Her mouth felt dry. Her stomach grumbled. Why hadn't she eaten before leaving the manor? She'd noticed a vending machine adjacent to the motel office. Alex could wait two minutes while she grabbed a bag of chips or a candy bar.

Hunger was an excuse. She was procrastinating. For pity's sake, Alex was not a maniac. *Knock on the damn door and get it over with.*

She knocked on the damn door.

A few seconds later, the door swung inward. Alex stood at an angle in the opening, half lit by the sunlight from outside and half shaded by the dimmer light behind him. His off-white shirt looked freshly pressed, as did his blue jeans. His leather belt was shiny, his suede boots as clean as if he brought them home from the store today. He had a knack for making her feel dingy and mousy, even when her clothes were clean and wrinkle free.

Alex swung the door wide, stepping aside and motioning for her to enter. A slight smile curved his lips.

Perfect order. That was the quality he unknowingly flaunted.

Alex arched his eyebrows. "Is something wrong?"

Realizing she'd been staring at him, she shook her head and shuffled across the threshold. Alex shut the door. The brightness of the outdoors was snuffed out, replaced by the yellowish glow of a lamp on the bedside table. In front of the window, two chairs flanked a larger table. Erin seated herself in the closest chair, dropping her purse on the floor beside it. Her handgun, concealed inside the purse, thunked on the floor. Alex glanced at her purse but said nothing. He sat on the flower-print bedspread with his hands clasped on his lap and his spine erect, refocusing his gaze on her.

She crossed her ankles. "You said you'd tell me everything."

"Yes, I did."

His expression was unreadable. The slight smile had evaporated. When she met his gaze, he sighed.

"Some of what I'm about to tell you," he said, "will sound impossible. You may wonder if I'm insane. I need you to listen with an open mind. Can you do that?"

She leaned back in the chair, linking her hands on her lap. "You've read my blog. What do you think?"

He smiled.

Her stomach fluttered. Maybe she'd developed a strange gastrointestinal disorder.

Alex's expression grew solemn. "Let me start at the beginning. I met Harry eighteen months ago, after he contacted me via e-mail. He'd come across an old article about the fiasco in the Valley of the Kings and my insistence that we'd uncovered alien remains. Harry invited me to attend an expedition with his group, the Foundation for Amarna Research and Exploration. It wasn't much, we excavated what Harry hoped might turn out to be an Egyptian burial in East Texas."

"And was it?"

"No. The anonymous person who e-mailed Harry the tip about the burial was either confused, delusional, or lying. Hoaxes are a problem in this line of work."

"I can imagine."

"The expedition served as my initiation into Harry's group. But his foundation was affiliated with a larger group that provided the bulk of Harry's funding. After the Texas expedition, he introduced me to the people who run the larger organization, the Human Origins Project. That's how I met Katy and Rick Bergren."

"Which one's your leader?" she asked. "Excuse me, honorary leader."

"Katy. She cofounded the Human Origins Project with Rick's father, Charlie, who's semi-retired now, leaving Katy and Rick in charge of the project. We have approximately a hundred members around the world whose backgrounds range from professional scientists to dedicated amateurs."

"What exactly does this project do?"

Alex stared into her eyes. "We investigate the true origins of human beings and any ancillary phenomena that may shed light on the main question. If human beings didn't evolve from apelike ancestors—a hypothesis we have evidence to support—then where did we come from?"

Ancillary phenomena. She restrained a smirk. Next he'd reach for his attaché and pull out an alphabetized, cross-referenced list of such phenomena. "You mean like glowing orbs and stolen artifacts?"

"Among other things."

She tapped the nail of her index finger on the chair's arm, waiting for him to elaborate. When he didn't, she said, "What sort of other things?"

He averted his gaze to the window. Clearing his throat, he said, "Cryptozoology, ufology, weather manipulation, out-of-place artifacts—"

"Cryptozoology? You mean Bigfoot and the Loch Ness monster?"

"Along with other creatures science says can't exist."

Cryptozoological creatures? That Alex and his cohorts investigated UFOs and Bigfoot, along with archaeological mysteries, shouldn't surprise her. Yet it did. Deep down, she expected him to act like a typical scientist, denying the existence of anything outside the boundaries of mainstream science and accepted history. Why she felt that way, she couldn't explain. Maybe she got used to people thinking she was crazy, even people who professed an interest in unexplained phenomena. Connecting any two phenomena, like Bigfoot and UFOs, drew the ire of countless researchers from both the Bigfoot and the UFO fields. Neither camp wanted the other crossing into their territory, and neither side wanted to admit to the truly strange nature of both phenomena. Oh, and for heaven's sake never use the word paranormal in the same sentence as either Bigfoot or UFO. Doing so might instigate a riot.

The word paranormal simply referred to anything that was not scientifically accepted, something that existed outside the realm of normal experience. Try discussing the real definition of paranormal with one of the I-investigate-the-paranormal-but-I'm-not-a-paranormal-researcher folks, and you'd pine for a wrestling match with an alligator. Of course, not all Bigfoot and UFO researchers were rabid anti-paranormalists. Erin had run into enough of the anti-paranormal variety, though—from comments seared onto her blog and e-mails fired into her inbox—that she may have grown a bit sensitive. After all, if connecting two phenomena earned you the crazy designation, connecting multiple phenomena was the equivalent of sewing a straitjacket around yourself.

Alex was different. She knew that. When a glowing orb confronted them in the woods, he treated the incident matter-of-factly. When she told him about her intuition, and offered fate as an explanation of it, he believed her. Not once did he roll his eyes or snort with derision. After the glowing orb incident, he mentioned he'd seen strange phenomena before. In his work for the Human Origins Project?

Besides cryptozoological creatures and UFOs, Alex cited out-of-place artifacts and weather manipulation. She recognized both terms. Out-of-place artifacts referred to objects unearthed in a context where mainstream archaeology said they didn't belong, such as an Egyptian amulet dug up in Arkansas or a human skull found in 50-million-year-old rock.

Although out-of-place artifacts certainly might shed light on the real story of human history, weather manipulation seemed unrelated. For years people had speculated about the possibility of humans controlling the weather, to prevent disasters or as a new type of warfare. Nikola Tesla reportedly experimented with weather manipulation. The biggest conspiracy theory related to weather manipulation, however, centered on a facility in Alaska known as the High Frequency Active Auroral Research Program, or HAARP. According to mainstream scientists, the facility existed solely to enable scientists to study the ionosphere, the region of the Earth's atmosphere that begins fifty miles above the surface. Scientists at the HAARP facility beamed high-frequency radio waves into the ionosphere, then studied the effects the radio waves had on the ionosphere. Conspiracy theorists said HAARP was more than a research facility. They suggested the HAARP facility also affected the weather, perhaps to alter the course of a hurricane or generate severe weather, either on purpose or by accident.

Erin occasionally wrote about weather manipulation on her blog. She couldn't help wondering why it seemed like every crippling snowstorm hit the big cities on the East Coast but left unharmed the less populated areas across the Upper Midwest. Massive hurricanes made a beeline for the American coast, only to veer off at the last second. And then she had her personal experiences to consider.

Three days ago in the Grand Canyon, lightning from a freak thunderstorm sealed her and Alex in the tunnels. Three days ago. It felt like weeks had elapsed between those moments in the tunnels and the present. The storm erupted out of nowhere. One minute the sky was clear and blue. An instant later, thunderclouds blossomed to fire lightning bolts down at the tunnels where she and Alex hid. With eerie precision, the bolts had edged nearer and nearer until they struck the exact right spots, caving in the entrance and, moments later, the tunnels themselves. Thinking back to the incident, she felt goosebumps prickle her arms. If a storm could acquire the ability to think, then the storm in the Canyon that day had wanted them dead.

Or the intelligence guiding the storm wanted them dead.

Glowing orbs watched them. Storms attacked them. Either she'd lost all capacity for reasoned thought, or something very, very bad was targeting her and Alex.

"Have I lost you?" Alex said.

She blinked and looked at him. "Huh?"

"You went away for a minute. I thought you might've decided I'm hopelessly insane."

"Actually, I was more worried you might think I'm bonkers."

He eyed her without expression. After a couple seconds, he smiled. His eyes seemed brighter, their intense blue irises sparkling. With his usual serious expression, he was attractive. Smiling, he was gorgeous.

She fidgeted in her chair. The air felt warmer all of a sudden.

"I don't think you're bonkers," he said. His mouth twitched with amusement as he pronounced the last word. Maybe he'd never uttered the word bonkers before. He continued, "In fact, you may be the smartest person I've ever met. Harry clearly thought so. He believed you and I could sort out this mystery together, which means he thought I couldn't do it alone."

She opened her mouth to disagree. He raised a hand to silence her.

"That's not low self-esteem talking," he said. "You have a unique way of looking at things. Take, for instance, the way you found the hidden escape route in the Grand Canyon tunnels. I doubt I would've thought to look under the mummy for an opening. Then you figured out how to open the sealed exit by pushing a concealed button in the wall. It's more than intuition, it's almost…extrasensory."

She snorted. "I'm not psychic."

"Are you positive?"

"Yes." The word came out as more of a hiss than she intended. She sucked in a deep breath and exhaled slowly. "Trust me, I don't have ESP. If I did, I would've won the lottery a long time ago."

"At the very least, you have extraordinary insight."

She looked away, tucking her hands under her thighs. Her fingers suddenly felt cold. "Right now, I'd rather talk about what you and your pals think paranormal phenomena have to do with human origins. And what kind of evidence you have for your theory about humans not evolving from apelike ancestors."

"This may take awhile."

"It's what I came here for."

He nodded.

She waited for him to speak. Her pulse accelerated. The coldness in her hands evaporated under the searing pressure of her heartbeat. She was about to learn everything she wanted to know, or at least everything Alex knew. Since he seemed to need prodding to get started, she might as well demand an explanation for the one thing she most wanted explained.

"Tell me," she said, "about these forces beyond our conception."

Revenant House

THE DOOR TO THE DRAWING ROOM WAS CLOSED. DESHERET JIGGLED THE KNOB. It was locked, of course. Samuel allowed her into the room only in his presence. He demanded her trust in all matters, yet he refused to reciprocate. Every man in her life showed her the same disrespect. They treated her like a troublesome child, except when they needed her assistance. As for the others—the great masters who ruled all beneath them—they regarded her as akin to an animal trained to do their bidding.

Samuel concealed his every secret within the walls of the drawing room. She wanted to know, needed to know, not for her masters but for herself. For too long she had served others, catering to their whims, aiding them in achieving their goals while never gaining what she desired.

Her cell phone rang, playing a cheerful melody as its ring tone. She dug the phone out of her tiny purse and glanced at the phone's display. Recognizing the name on the caller ID, she switched off the phone and tucked it back into her purse. No longer would this animal leap whenever someone beckoned her.

She strolled upstairs, turning right at the landing and right again at the north passage, finally halting in front of the door at the end of the passageway. She tried the knob. Locked. Curse him, and his paranoia. This door safeguarded more of Samuel's secrets. Rassul had spoken of this room, though he omitted details of its contents, saying merely that the masters were displeased with Samuel because of what he kept inside the room. Samuel wished to protect his secrets from everyone, even his sacred Erin Turner.

Desheret's lip curled involuntarily. Erin. Samuel spoke of the woman as if she possessed the power to cure all ills, unite people throughout the world, and usher in a new world of peace and prosperity for everyone. Perhaps she exaggerated his sentiments a bit. Yet he had stated, without equivocation or qualification, that Erin would find the relic and end the masters' quest forever. Only then would Desheret be free. As much as she despised Erin Turner, and Samuel's fondness for her, Desheret longed for liberation. If Erin failed to find the relic, then Desheret would have no further use for the woman. She had struggled for too long, battling nature and other women and time itself, to let slip through her fingers the two things she desired most.

A light flashed to her left. She swiveled her head in that direction. An orb floated at chest height, fifteen feet away. Its white ring encircled its mottled blue interior. Desheret fisted her hands at her sides until her nails dug into her palms. They could not read her mind, not here, not at this time. Yet the orb appeared at the precise moment when she considered betraying them. Coincidence, surely.

The orb shimmered. Its mottled interior swirled as if alive. Perhaps the orb had appeared for another reason.

She unfurled one hand to grasp the door knob.

The orb surged toward her. It stopped a few feet from her face. She felt the kiss of static electricity on her skin. These tactics would not frighten her. She knew, though, the tactics that followed would frighten her. And worse.

She withdrew her hand. The orb backed away.

They wished her not to know what lay beyond this door. For the present, she would let them win. Soon, however, she would know all of Samuel's secrets—and all of theirs. She would snatch the power from their hands, the way they snatched it from hers countless times before.

Desheret faced the orb. Behind its brilliant glow, at the other end of the passage, a familiar figure waited. The orb raced toward him, ducking past his right shoulder to disappear around the corner. Samuel strode down the passageway to her. Neither his facial expression nor his body language betrayed his emotions, though she felt certain she knew what he felt as their gazes locked. He was infuriated, by more than her blatant attempt to access his room.

She donned her sweetest expression, complete with a smile. "Samuel, darling, there you are. I've been searching for you."

"You've been searching," he said, "but not for me."

He moved between her and the door, still facing her. His mouth was set in a firm line. "What is it?" she asked.

She tinged her voice with an appropriate level of concern and confusion. He leaned toward her and bent his head to peer down at her. She looked directly into his eyes. His body was tensed, his eyes narrowed enough that wrinkles webbed out from the corners. An icy thrill washed over her. He could not know her plans and yet, staring into his eyes, she felt he did know. He perceived her thoughts.

Nonsense.

When he spoke, his voice was husky and soft. "This room is off limits to your curiosity. "

"If you confide in me, perhaps I can help. I know they're displeased with you."

His nostrils flared. "Go back where you belong…darling."

Neither his body language nor his expression changed, but his voice had grown fierce. She sensed the anger simmering inside him, despite his effort to contain it. Others might be fooled. She was not deceived, nor was she afraid. More frightening men than Samuel had wielded their anger at her. If she could stand tall before those men, then Samuel certainly would not intimidate her. But let him believe he had.

She tiptoed backward, quivering her lower lip. "Please, don't make me go. I'll behave exactly as you wish."

"Yes, you will." He thrust out his right arm to stab his index finger in the air, motioning down the passageway. "Leave."

With a bow of her head, she complied. As she turned left at the corridor to head for the stairs, she glanced back at Samuel. He was unlocking the door. She paused and leaned forward. If she found the right angle, she might see into the room when he opened the door.

He looked in her direction. As his gaze targeted hers, he held still with his hand cupped over the door knob. Neither of them moved.

Bastet's collar jingled from down the stairs, the sound growing louder. Peripherally, Desheret saw the cat reach the top of the stairs.

Samuel waved a hand at her in a dismissive gesture, the way he might shoo the cat. Desheret pursed her lips, glaring at him. He opened the door, blocking it with his body, and slipped inside the room. She tilted sideways and craned her neck. She could almost see inside.

He slammed the door shut.

Rage boiled over inside her, hot as molten metal. Her cheeks blazed with it. Her thoughts roiled from its heat. She felt her fists tighten until the tension vibrated up her arms and into her shoulders. She would enter the room. Soon, she would pass through every door that currently barred her way. Very soon.

From the top of the stairs, Bastet observed her. The cat growled softly.

Desheret hissed at the cat.

Bastet scurried down the stairs, her collar jingling. When the sound faded into silence, Desheret trotted downstairs too, through the passageways to the back door, and outside. She followed a path into the woods. The two-track path, worn down by the riding lawnmower, petered out fifty yards into the woods. At the dead end, she located her favorite trail, a narrow path carved out by deer. The deer trail took her south, parallel to Revenant House, though she couldn't see the manor from here. After a several minutes of brisk walking, she spied an area of sunlight up ahead that indicated a break in the trees.

She marched into the small clearing. Her vehicle awaited her in the clearing's center. No one else knew of this clearing. She used it on those occasions when she needed to reach Revenant House but lacked the preferred means of transportation. Samuel rarely provided her with an *akhet* ball when she was performing her more local duties, which meant she must find her own method of transport.

Inside the car, she turned the key in the ignition. The engine sputtered, then purred. Automobiles were vile things, tiny boxes of death that appealed to her slightly more than a sarcophagus, mainly because automobiles at least had windows. Once, she'd witnessed an automobile accident. Watching the two vehicles collide, their metal crunching and collapsing, she felt the bile rising in her throat. Though her homeland may have lacked the modern conveniences that she enjoyed, after spending time here she understood why some people of this land eschewed technology.

At home she was a slave, to men and their whims. Samuel wished her to live in the same manner here. Yet he and Rassul would, separately and unwittingly, aid her in her own quest to achieve her twin goals. First, freedom. Second…

Vengeance.

11

Shadow Bay Inn

THE CLOCK READ 5:40. ERIN HAD ARRIVED TWENTY MINUTES AGO. ALEX perched on the edge of the bed, avoiding Erin's gaze and trying to work out a way of explaining the unexplainable in such a way that the unbelievable would sound believable. He drummed his fingers on his thighs. Although he heard no sound from his drumming fingers, he felt the rhythm on his skin. Thumpety-thump. Thumpety-thump. A headache sprouted behind his eyes. If he persisted in thinking this much, he'd wind up with a migraine. Besides, Erin already believed in the paranormal. He shouldn't worry about convincing her. But he did. What he needed to tell her sounded, even to his ears, like utter balderdash.

He looked at Erin. A curlicue of hair had fallen over her forehead. It touched her eyebrow, leading his gaze across her brow bone to the bridge of her nose, and down to the perfectly round bulb of her nose. He found himself studying her mouth next, thanks to the sheen of barely noticeable pink lipstick that accentuated the curves of her lips.

Erin brushed the hair from her forehead.

Alex focused on the floor. His fingers drummed thumpety-thump, thumpety-thump.

"It's not working," Erin said.

"What?"

"If you're trying to communicate with me telepathically," she said, "it's not working."

"I'm sorry." Seeing her lips part, probably to chastise him for his apology, he raised a hand to stop her. "Don't shoot, it was a reflex."

Erin clamped her jaw shut and glanced at her purse. She must've brought her weapon after all. He remembered the 9mm well, having stared into its barrel the first time they'd met.

She said, "Forces beyond our conception. Explain."

"I can't." When she gripped the arms of her chair and exhaled loudly, he said, "We're not sure what it means. I need to tell you the whole story."

Seven years ago, Katy and Rick Bergren stumbled upon a tribe of hairy hominids, the creatures commonly known as Bigfoot or Sasquatch, living in a network of caves and tunnels deep in the northern woods of Michigan's Lower Peninsula. DNA testing had identified the hairy hominids as the true descendents of *Homo erectus* and *Homo heidelbergensis*, long-extinct species that mainstream scientists labeled the ancestors of modern humans. The tests performed on behalf of the Human Origins Project, however, disproved the accepted story of human origins. Humans were not the direct descendents of the ancient hominids. At best, we were remote cousins, perhaps a little closer to each other than humans and chimpanzees. Few credentialed scientists publicly supported the findings, since to do so jeopardized their careers, though privately a small but growing circle of academics recognized the validity and importance of the work conducted by the Human Origins Project.

Harry was among that group, and eighteen months ago, he recruited Alex. After proving his worthiness on the Texas dig, Alex found himself diving headfirst into a swamp of forbidden knowledge and forgotten history. The hairy hominids in Michigan and elsewhere around the world existed as discrete tribes, each living in its own network of caves and underground tunnels. Their subterranean homes were artificial, created by a mysterious race of humans who called themselves the Planners. No one, not even the Planners themselves, knew how long their race had existed. For thousands of years, at the minimum, the Planners had possessed and utilized technology far in advance of anything developed by the rest of humanity, technology that overshadowed even the stunning advances of the late twentieth and early twenty-first centuries AD. The Planners lived and traveled in craft best described as spaceships, although they'd stopped traveling into space longer ago than any of them could remember. For reasons no one fully understood, the Planners despised the rest of humanity, whom they called Low Ones, but treated the hairy hominids as sacred, referring to them as the Revered Ones.

About 12,000 years ago, a volcanic eruption threatened the entire planet. Confronted with the impending cataclysm, the Planners decided to build underground fortresses for the hairy hominids in order to protect the creatures. With the Revered Ones sheltered from the devastation, the Planners fled their home in the region today known as Egypt, taking their ships to the bottoms of the oceans, their version of a fallout shelter.

The rest of humanity, they left to die.

Despite sequestering themselves from the majority of the human race ever since, the Planners ventured out on occasion to interfere with the lives and technological development of their long-lost brethren. The Planners had bequeathed their hieroglyphic language to the hairy hominids, as well as to the Low Ones, inspiring both groups to worship them as gods.

Alex explained all of this to Erin.

She rested her left elbow on the table, propping her head up with her hand. "Are you saying you and your buddies still haven't figured out how long human beings have been around?"

"We have a minimum date."

"Twelve thousand years."

He shook his head. "Approximately half a billion years."

Erin lifted her head and blinked. "Half a what?"

"Half a billion years. A member of our group once found a human skeleton, or the fossilized remains of one, in the Burgess Shale. It's a rock formation in—"

"British Columbia. The fossils date back to the Cambrian Period, over five hundred million years ago."

"Correct."

"What happened to this skeleton?"

"It was destroyed by agents of the Planners. Other, unsubstantiated evidence suggests humans have existed for more than a billion years."

Erin propped her head on her hand again, her index finger touching her forehead. She closed her eyes.

The story sounded ludicrous. He knew it. He'd hoped Erin's predilection for flouting the mainstream late lead her to accept the story. Either he'd overloaded her with bizarre information or his luck had just run out.

Erin opened her eyes. "The Plotters are bad guys then."

"What?"

"They destroyed your skeleton. The Plotters."

"The Planners. And it wasn't my skeleton." He paused. "Not all of the Planners are bad. In fact, they've become our allies."

"Maybe they can find this damn relic."

"I'm afraid not. The Planners have gone into hiding again."

"Why?"

Why indeed. The Planners offered excuses in the weeks leading up to their departure, yet none of the reasons given seemed adequate to explain their behavior. Over the millennia, the planners had erased most of their own historical records in their zeal to prevent the Low Ones from learning too much about them. The Bergrens helped them recover some of their lost history by locating the Book of Thoth, a tome mainstream Egyptologists thought contained medical and scientific information. The Book turned out to contain a history of the Planners, albeit a history so cryptic that neither the Planners nor a single historian or archaeologist who joined the Human Origins Project could decipher the Book in its entirety. Katy Bergren managed to translate a small portion of it. The rest remained locked inside riddles and metaphors, accompanied by peculiar images that seemed to bear no relationship to the text.

One might expect the Planners to be grateful for the help in recovering a small piece of their history. Some of them were grateful. For a long time, the Planners had suffered under the rule of dictators bent on squashing the Low Ones. During the quest for the Book of Thoth, the Bergrens helped rid the Planners of the last dictator, a man called Setesh. They thought he was the last anyway. Over the past six years, however, supporters of Setesh repeatedly tried to regain power among the Planners. The unrest explained why the Planners gradually pulled back from their relationship with the Human Origins Project. But it failed to explain why the Planners went into hiding eight months ago.

Something had terrified them.

Alex was present the last time a Planner spoke to a member of the Human Origins Project. A few days after leaving Utah, Alex met with Katy and Rick at their home to discuss the incident that occurred there. Incident. It had been a catastrophe—a deadly one. Katy and Rick wanted to discuss the event in person, perhaps hoping a face-to-face encounter would affect Alex more than a telephone conversation. It hadn't. Their efforts to assuage his guilt failed. Only time could accomplish that feat.

Toward the end of their meeting, however, a knock at the back door surprised them all. Katy opened the door to find the Planner known as Aset standing outside. Aset wore a grave expression, her posture straight and stiff, her voice flat. She announced the Planners were leaving, and offered excuses about internal dissension. The memory of her final words, spoken an instant before she disappeared in a flash of light, unsettled Alex even now.

"Beware," she'd said. "The Ancient Ones have returned. No living thing is safe from them. Forces beyond your conception are at work here."

The Planners had mentioned the Ancient Ones only once, when pressed for an explanation of why they no longer traveled outside of Earth, despite owning the technology to do so. Their answer had been simple, if ambiguous: *The Ancient Ones forbid it.*

Thereafter, the Planners refused to discuss the matter. Any mention of their mysterious enemy prompted a conspicuous silence, accompanied by panicked glances, from any Planners within earshot. Throughout the entire recorded history of mankind, the Planners exerted awesome power over the rest of the human race, power derived from technology so advanced that it often seemed like sorcery. For the Planners to fear another race, the other beings must possess technology beyond even that of the Planners. Technology of unimaginable power.

Forces beyond conception.

ONCE ALEX TOLD ERIN ABOUT THE ANCIENT ONES, SHE SAT STILL AND SILENT for several minutes. The Ancient Ones. Were they the unseen puppet masters controlling Rassul? Did they push her to find the relic?

Alex had told her everything he knew. She believed him. The rush of information, coupled with its terrifying implications, left her with a cold knot in her gut. How on earth could she and Alex unearth a relic that eluded beings as powerful as the Ancient Ones? If they brandished power beyond conception, no one could expect two lowly humans to find it.

Two humans. Her and Alex. At some point during the conversation, she switched from viewing herself as alone to becoming part of a team. Alex's team.

"When do your friends get here?" she asked.

"They don't. We're in this alone."

The lonely feeling came back. She clasped her hands, trying to warm her fingertips against a chill that originated inside her.

Alex rushed forward to kneel in front of her. One hand he settled on her right knee, and the other he wrapped around her clasped hands. His warmth seeped through her skin, into her flesh. It washed through her in a wave that made her heart thump, just once.

"Don't worry," he murmured. "I won't let anything happen to you."

She wanted to ask how exactly he thought he could protect her from "forces beyond conception." But then his thumb began to massage her hand in a slow twirling motion. She couldn't look away from his eyes, those blue jewels sparkling in the dim, slightly golden light.

He squeezed her knee.

Her cheeks flushed. She averted her gaze.

"You have my word," he said. "We will get through this. Together."

He intended to comfort her. Instead, the tone of his voice and the feel of his skin on hers caused the opposite effect. She considered yanking her hands away from his, but she couldn't move. No. It wasn't that she couldn't budge, but that she didn't want to move.

When he promised to keep her safe, she believed him. As impossible as the promise was, she knew he meant it.

Alex released her hands and stood. "I have something to show you."

He dragged his briefcase out from under the bed, flopped it onto the mattress, and popped it open. He gathered loose papers from inside the briefcase and carried them to the table beside Erin. A number of the sheets looked like photographs printed out from a computer.

First, Alex laid the photographs on the table one by one, his motions precise and careful. Next, he laid down sheets of paper with typed text on them, one sheet next to each photograph. Thirteen photographs, with their accompanying text, covered the tabletop. Erin inspected the array of images and text. The photographs showed artifacts that appeared ancient. She recognized some as Egyptian, Mayan, and Celtic. Others looked familiar, though she couldn't quite place the cultures responsible for creating them.

"What do you see?" Alex asked.

"A bunch of old stuff."

"Obviously. What else?"

She selected the ancient Egyptian artifact, a necklace inlaid with lapis lazuli and carnelian. The sheet next to the photograph outlined the salient facts about the artifact in a bulleted list. The necklace had been stolen from a museum in Berlin six months ago. Alex mentioned before that Rassul stole thirteen artifacts from museums and private collections around the world. The information on the sheet also stated the necklace originally turned up during an excavation in England, buried in a stratum dating back to approximately 4000 BC. Alex had printed the photograph from the museum's website, a fact she ascertained from the URL printed in the page's header. The photo's caption described the artifact as an Egyptian necklace brought to Britain during the Roman occupation, circa 150 AD.

She stabbed a finger on the photo. "What makes you think this dates to 4000 BC?"

"A member of our group, an archaeologist, helped excavate the site where the necklace was found. He told us the necklace was impossibly ancient, to use his exact words, and that it dated to circa 4000 BC. The archaeologist in charge of the excavation insisted a flood must've washed the necklace into older strata and that it could not possibly be older than 150 AD. His explanation became the official story."

Erin perused the other papers. The Mayan artifact was a stone slab jam-packed with carvings of glyphs, humans, and animals. Back in the 1800s, tomb robbers in Egypt discovered the object inside the crypt of an official who lived during the Eighteenth Dynasty, circa 1352 BC. According to Alex's bullet points, similar Mayan artifacts were dated to the eighth century AD. Mainstream archaeologists declared, of course, that no Mayan artifacts belonged in Egypt and therefore the discovery was a hoax. Skimming the other pages, she learned every artifact shown had been unearthed in a location or dated to a period where it didn't belong, or both.

"They're out-of-place artifacts," she said. "Each of them was found outside of its accepted context."

"Precisely. What else do you see?" When she didn't respond, he said, "I was hoping for a little of your special insight."

Oh great. First, Rassul ordered her to find an artifact of undetermined nature. Now, Alex expected her to burst out with amazing insights into the artifacts he'd shown her. Pure luck led her to discover the secret exit under Ripley's mummy.

She was flattered Alex thought so much of her, but for crying out loud, she was no clairvoyant.

Alex leaned close without touching her. His mouth hovered so close to her ear that she felt his breath whisper across her earlobe.

"Stop thinking," he said. "Look at the photos. Let your mind go blank and just look at them."

She glanced at each photo in turn, trying not to think. Alex's breath tickled her earlobe and the skin tingled in response.

Slapping a hand on his chest, she shoved him back. "Give me some space, okay?"

He backed away two paces and sat on the bed.

She let her gaze wander over the photos. *My God.*

Alex sprang off the bed and to her side. He asked, "What is it?"

She looked at him sideways.

"You thought of something," he said. "I can tell from the look on your face."

She had thought of something. But the idea was so outlandish she couldn't bring herself to consciously accept it, much less say it aloud. She definitely needed more time to consider it before she would tell Alex.

"I'm not sure," she said. "I need to think about it more. Can I take these photos with me?"

"Yes."

She checked her watch. It was nearly seven o'clock. "I should go."

"I'm coming with you."

"No, you're not."

She swept the papers together into a stack. Grasping the papers in one hand, she snagged her purse off the floor. As she reached for the doorknob, Alex grasped her forearm.

"You shouldn't be alone in that house," he said.

She glared at him over her shoulder. He held onto her arm, his grip firm but not tight. She scrunched her face, as if angry, hoping to deter him. It didn't work.

He said, "I will not let you go back there alone."

"I'm not supposed to have overnight guests. And they'll know you're there. Remember the bugs?"

"They won't admit they know I'm there. Confronting you about it would force them to disclose the fact they've been spying on you."

He had a point. The thought of sleeping in the same house as Alex bothered her, for reasons she couldn't articulate and, if she could put it into words, she certainly would not tell him. She felt weird enough standing this close to him, with his hand wrapped around her arm. She ought to feel threatened, she thought, yet she didn't. Alex wouldn't hurt her. Of that, she was certain. As for everything else, she couldn't be certain of any of it.

"I don't have access to the other bedrooms," she said. "There won't be anywhere for you to sleep."

"I have no intention of sleeping."

For a second she thought he meant— no, of course he meant that he planned on staying awake all night to guard her.

She could think of no other argument, except for the I'm-a-strong-woman-who-doesn't-need-a-man's-protection line which, at this moment, she felt incapable of delivering with any conviction. Everything Alex told her about the Planners and the Ancient Ones, coupled with the other things she'd learned of late, infected her with a severe case of the creeps. The weirdness of Alex sleeping over bothered her less than the weirdness of her new home. Plus, spending another night alone inside Revenant House, trying to sleep and failing, appealed to her less than the prospect of getting fired because she neglected to get Newman's approval for an overnight guest.

"Fine," she said. "You can come."

Swinging the door open, she led him out to her car.

In the car, Alex said little. As she turned the car onto Revenant Point Road, Erin decided the time had come to ask a few questions.

"Tell me," she said, "why do you care so much what happens to me? We barely know each other."

"I care about other people. It's called compassion."

"Uh-huh. I get the feeling it's a little more than that."

He stiffened. Despite concentrating on the road ahead, she sensed his whole body go rigid.

"What's really driving you?" she asked. "Why are you obsessed with saving me from Rassul?"

"I…" He slumped his shoulders, resting an arm on the window ledge and staring out at the woods that whizzed past on the right side of the road. "Six people died because of me. I won't let it happen again."

She wanted to ask more questions. When she glanced at him, however, his dark expression froze the words in her throat.

After several seconds of silence, he said, "Eight months ago, I led an expedition into eastern Utah, to a canyon along the Green River. Harry had been combing the archives of a local library when he found a diary written by a Mormon settler. The diary talked about a strange crypt hidden inside the canyon, and the writer gave vague but usable directions to the crypt. I took seven volunteers from the Human Origins Project into the canyon."

He pinched the bridge of his nose between his thumb and forefinger. Shutting his eyes, he let out a long sigh. He dropped his hand onto the window ledge.

"On our way to the canyon," he said, "one of the team members, Frank Delancy, got sick with what later turned out to be food poisoning. The others wanted to go back, but I told them to keep going and I'd catch up with them later. I helped Frank hike back to where we'd parked the cars and drove him to the nearest hospital. By the time I returned to the canyon, it was dark. Our GPS units had a buddy tracking feature that lets you see where the connected units are. That's how I found them."

He fell silent. She waited a couple seconds, then said, "And?"

His voice became flat, almost a monotone. "They'd found the crypt."

Utah
8 months ago

WHITE LIGHT BATHED THE RED WALLS OF THE LITTLE CANYON IN A PALLOR. At the canyon's narrowest end, a two-tiered waterfall fifteen feet high spilled into a shallow pool. Alex entered at the opposite end, where the canyon's walls spread twenty feet apart. On either side, the canyon soared eight hundred feet overhead, seeming to touch the stars that glittered above.

The white light poured from three spotlights mounted on tripods. The bubble of false daylight glowed at the base of the canyon's left-hand wall, a dozen yards from the waterfall's pool. Climbing ropes dangled from the sheer face of the canyon wall. Four people loitered on the canyon floor immediately below the ropes, their faces upturned, intent on the spot high up the cliff. Reaching his colleagues, Alex halted and followed their gazes up the rock face. About a hundred feet up, the ropes disappeared into a dark oval. A cavity in the cliff. A pale face poked out of the cavity.

"It's here." A voice crackled over their two-way radios. "Just like the Mormon dude said."

The voice belonged to Dale Jacobs, a college kid with more enthusiasm than common sense and a knack for rock climbing. Alex heard Dale's words, but the meaning failed to register. They'd found it? He glanced at the four people standing in front of him. Sarah Miller, a computer engineer in her forties, stood closest to him. Clustered on her other side were Neal Quinn, a retired engineer; his brother Ken, a civil servant; and Steve Peterson, a man Alex's age who'd abandoned a career in the hotel industry to join the project, volunteering for any manual labor tasks, other than rock climbing.

"Where's Ian?" Alex asked.

Sarah jerked. She turned her gaze on Alex, eyes wide. "You snuck up on me. Ian's with Dale."

Alex bent his head back to squint up at the pale form of Dale's head, surrounded by the blackness of the cavity. Another face appeared briefly beside Dale's, then retreated. Ian Wallace, who'd traveled from Scotland to take part in the expedition, was a few years older than Dale. The young men shared a reckless enthusiasm for any activity that involved the possibility of serious injury or death.

The radios crackled. Dale said, "I'm sending you a gift."

The group below watched as Dale lowered a rope to them. The object tied to the rope's end swayed during its slow descent down the cliff. When the package came within arm's reach, Alex nabbed it and untied the parcel, which Dale had swaddled in a handkerchief. Alex unwrapped the item.

It was a *shabti*, an Egyptian figurine made of glazed, fired clay. The glaze gave it a translucent blue shimmer. *Shabti* were placed in tombs, designed as servants who would perform menial labor in lieu of the deceased. For a *shabti* to wind up in Utah meant either a hoaxer scaled this cliff with the sole purpose of planting a fake artifact in the cavern, or an Egyptian had visited the canyon. A local might also have visited Egypt, returning with a souvenir.

Dale's voice echoed down to them. "There's more where that came from."

An odd feeling washed over Alex, and he looked up at the sky. No stars. Clouds must've rolled in with remarkable swiftness. Lightning skittered across the cloud base. He counted the seconds until the thunderclap, but none came. The gushing of the waterfall might drown out thunder. The thought did nothing to ease the tension growing inside him.

Lightning exploded, blinding him for a few seconds. The ground shivered in the wake of the explosion. Dirt and small rock fragments rained down around them.

Sarah grabbed a hand-held spotlight and trained its beam on the cavity opening. Dale was gone. Sarah screamed his name.

Dale poked his head out. His voice came through the radios. "We're fine. Must be a wicked storm coming, huh?"

Lightning chased back and forth across the cloud base. The bolts contained within the clouds seemed to writhe and twirl in an unearthly dance.

Cold certainty gripped Alex. They had to get out of here.

Alex plucked the radio from belt. Keeping his voice calm, he spoke into the radio. "You guys should get back down here. It's not safe to be up there in a storm."

A blinding bolt lanced across the clouds.

The spotlights winked out. Static sputtered and popped through the radios.

The cloud-to-cloud lightning vanished. Darkness swallowed them. Alex's heart raced. Sweat trickled down his temples onto his neck. His fingers ached. He uncurled them from around the radio. They should run, but with no light to guide them, they could never navigate through the canyon and back to safety.

They must try.

He pushed the radios button and said, "Get down here now."

Lightning slashed down from the clouds, impaling the cliff mere feet above the cavity. The canyon wall exploded.

Sarah screamed.

Light twirled and writhed in the clouds, creating an eerie glow that filtered down to the canyon floor.

From where the cavity had been, a mass of debris plummeted toward them. "Run!"

His own voice sounded distant to him. The others gaped at the mass hurtling down toward them, as if transfixed. Alex seized Sarah's arm, hauling her away from the cliff. Steve stumbled backward.

Too late Neal and Ken spun around to run. The debris pummeled them into the ground. Their bodies disappeared under the mound as a cloud of dust erupted from the canyon floor.

Alex tripped, landed on his butt. Sarah careened into him, fell to her knees, and scrambled on all fours toward the debris mound.

Alex flailed to grab her arm. "No!"

She shook free of him and kept going.

Another bolt slammed into the canyon wall. Boulder-size chunks of the cliff broke free, tumbling downward.

Darkness enveloped the canyon. A mass thudded into the ground. Sarah shrieked.

The spotlights flickered on.

Alex pushed onto his knees, surveying the scene before him. A cry caught in his throat. His stomach heaved.

Sarah's hand stretched out from under a pile of debris. Blood dribbled down her wrist into her upturned palm, where it dripped onto the ground. Neal lay three yards from her, his legs twisted at an agonizing angle, his hair wet with blood, eyes wide and lifeless.

Alex fought back a wretch. His mind reeled with half-formed thoughts. They were dead. All of them. If he'd insisted they stick together, his six friends would still be alive. If he'd only—

A whirring started up in the clouds. The noise was mechanical, low, and drawing closer.

His heart thudded. Dear God, what now?

He ran for the canyon's exit.

Present Day

Alex lapsed into silence. Erin steered the car around a curve. He looked pale and shaky, as if he'd been transported back to the time and place he described. She asked, "All of them died?"

"Yes. Frank should've been safe, since he was in the hospital."

"But he wasn't."

"No." He straightened in his seat. "The next night, when I visited Frank at the hospital, I walked into his room and found Rassul there. He knocked me down and ran out before I could stop him."

Although she had a sick feeling she knew the answer, she asked anyway. "What was Rassul doing?"

"Holding a pillow over Frank's face. Rassul murdered him."

"None of it was your fault."

He snorted. "I should never have left them alone. They were my responsibility and I—"

His voice broke off. She glanced at him. His face was contorted in anger or pain or both. She wanted to touch him, to comfort him, but she needed to keep her attention on the road and her hands on the wheel. Besides, she had a feeling he wouldn't want comfort.

He let out a ragged sigh. "I abandoned those people. I left Frank alone where Rassul could find him. I might as well have blown their heads off myself." His voice turned rough. "I will not make the same mistake this time."

The hell with what he wanted. She slammed on the brakes, and the car skidded to a stop. They both jerked forward into their seatbelts. Dust swirled around the vehicle. She twisted sideways to face him. Grasping his face in both her hands, she tilted his head toward her. His look of anguish melted, replaced by widened eyes and an uplifted brow.

She leaned close to him, her gaze locked on his. "What happened wasn't your fault."

"I realize that now," he said, the roughness smoothing out of his voice. "But I also realize the mistakes I made. I won't make them again. I won't lose you."

"No one's losing anybody." She pulled him closer until their noses touched. "You said we'd get through this together. So dump the guilt and work with me, because I don't want to lose you either."

They stared into each other's eyes for so long that her back started to ache from the strain of holding the unnatural pose. Finally, he curved his mouth into a sly smile and said, "Either kiss me or let me go."

His voice, now soft and deep, set off the familiar blush in her cheeks. Dammit.

"Well?" he said.

She dropped her hands and leaned back. "Will you be okay from here on out? Or do I have to worry about you sliding into guilt mode again?"

"No more guilt."

He sounded different. He looked different. Confident. Determined.

"Good," she said.

She pressed her foot down on the accelerator, a bit too forcefully. The car wrenched forward. She took a breath to calm herself and steered the car down the dirt road, depressing the accelerator with more delicacy this time. Out the corner of her eye, she spotted Alex smirking at her.

Well, it was better than an anguished expression.

She heard his cell phone ring. Scuffling noises ensued. She glanced at him without moving her head and caught him fumbling with his cell phone.

Returning her attention to the road ahead, she heard beeping noises as he punched keys on his phone.

"Stop," Alex said.

She braked hard, flinging them into their seatbelts. "What?"

"I'm getting off here." He dug something out of his backpack, which lay on the backseat, then thrust him his door open and bounded out. Bending down to smirk at her, he said, "Take it easy with the brakes, will you?"

He shut the door before she could respond. He cupped a black box in one hand. She watched him traipse into the woods, out of sight.

What in tarnation was he up to? She gave up trying to figure him out. Let him stumble around in the woods, in the dark, alone. If he got himself killed, she'd cast a spell to resurrect him just so she could murder him herself for acting like a fool.

Releasing the brake, she drove down the road.

The headlights cast a semicircle of light on the road and the forest on either side. As trees ducked into and out of the headlights, they seemed to grow and shrink. Pushing the illusion out of her mind, she concentrated on the road.

A figure darted out of the trees into the road.

The figure halted directly in front of her car. She jammed her foot on the brake pedal. Gravel sprayed up, popping against the car's body and undercarriage. A grunt burst from her lips as her torso was thrust forward into the seatbelt. It dug into her breasts and belly. The car fishtailed, then jerked to a stop.

The figure in the road turned to face her. Rassul raised a hand as if in greeting.

Jesus. What did this psycho want from her? She peeled the seatbelt from her chest and released it, letting it rest loosely over her torso. Her hands clenched the steering wheel in a death grip. Exhaling, she pried her fingers free.

Rassul stood an arm's length from her car's bumper. The corner of his mouth scrunched into a half smirk.

The difference between Rassul's smirk and Alex's was incalculable. Alex managed to make a smirk look cute. Rassul transformed the expression into a glimpse of hell.

Erin confronted Rassul's gaze with her own, and shuddered. She started to release the brake. The engine sputtered and died. The headlights stayed on.

Rassul gestured for her to get out of the car.

Yeah right. Her purse lay on the floor beside her right foot. Cautiously, she bent forward and slipped a hand into her purse, felt the gun, and closed her hand around its grip. As she settled back against the seat, she brought the gun with her. With her thumb, she clicked off the safety.

Rassul gestured again, more insistently. The headlights went dark.

She pressed the door lock button. The simultaneous chunk of all four doors locking broke the silence.

Chunk. The doors unlocked.

What the hell? She hit the lock button again.

The locks popped back up. A white glow appeared overhead, shining a cone of light down around Rassul and the car.

Erin leaned forward, her chest pressed against the steering wheel, and looked up. A glowing orb floated maybe ten feet above Rassul's head.

Get the hell out of here.

Even she didn't have to tell herself twice. She flung the door open, leaped out, and ran straight past Rassul down the road toward what she hoped would be sanctuary at Revenant House. Why did Alex have to take off into the freaking woods? She needed backup. She needed him.

Footfalls crunched behind her. She dared to look back and saw Rassul galloping after her. Cold fear sluiced through her. If he caught up with her—

The gun. She grasped it in her hand, for God's sake.

Erin spun around, hopped to a stop, and leveled the gun at the psycho barreling toward her.

The orb kept pace with him above his head.

She fired.

The orb dove down in front of Rassul. The bullet punctured a hole in its mottled interior.

Erin waited for Rassul to collapse. He froze mid step but stayed on his feet.

The orb's interior roiled and shimmered. The hole closed in on itself. The orb floated up to reclaim its original position in the air above Rassul.

The man smirked at her. His chest, where the bullet should have entered, was untouched. The orb had swallowed her bullet.

Rassul stalked toward her. Her muscles refused to move. Her voice refused to function. She stared dumbly at him as he grasped her shoulders and yanked her close to him. Her nose grazed his. His black eyes drilled into hers like a laser beam.

He spoke in a whisper that rippled ice through her entire body. "You waste time. MacKay is not your objective, the relic is. We grow weary of your distraction. Concentrate."

He growled the last word, like a rabid dog.

She jammed the gun into his belly. "Let go of me or I'll blast a hole in your gut."

Rassul chuckled.

She pulled the trigger. Nothing happened. Oh crap.

He shoved her backward. She tumbled to the ground.

The orb flew into the woods. Rassul chased after it.

Her entire body was shaking now. She felt cold, weak.

Rassul was getting away.

She leaped up, stuffed the gun inside her waistband, and took off after Rassul.

The orb's light guided her through the woods. She saw it bobbing up and down, back and forth, no more than fifty feet ahead of her. A little closer, a shadow weaved back and forth in the orb's wake. Rassul. She ran after the shadow. The orb's glow offered some illumination, but still trees seemed to materialize out of nowhere to block her path. She ducked left, then right, then vaulted over a fallen trunk. Though adrenaline chased away the weakness at first, the longer she ran, the more it seeped back into her flesh. An icy quivering that tugged at her. An unspoken plea to stop.

She couldn't.

Behind her, something crashed through the brush.

She dared not look back. Pinpointing Rassul's silhouette, she pushed her muscles harder. The gap between them narrowed inch by inch.

Footfalls crashed and breaths gasped behind her. *Don't look.*

Rassul's shadow got bigger. She was getting closer.

The orb exploded. The brilliance blinded her, and she staggered into something. The sapling snapped back in her face. She stifled a cry.

The orb's light flooded the woods. Wincing at the brightness, she tried to see what lay behind it. In a matter of seconds, her eyes adjusted enough that she recognized the ring of white light that hung suspended mere feet above the forest floor. She struggled to make out the shapes inside the ring—smaller lights, amber colored, lit a sidewalk. Rassul stood before the portal.

Footfalls thudded behind her, closer.

She ran toward Rassul. As her legs pumped, hurtling her forward, she suddenly realized the portal was a bubble, not a ring. The bulk of its three-dimensional shape bulged out behind the view seen within the ring. The white light composed a bubble with its inside scooped out, replaced by the cityscape.

Rassul ducked through the portal.

Erin raced through after him.

She tripped and froze. Darkness closed in on her from every direction except straight ahead, where amber lights studded the gloom in the distance. A clopping sound echoed nearby. Raucous voices overlapped each other. Straight ahead, Rassul fled toward the lights.

She lifted her foot chase after him.

Hands seized her shoulders, yanking her backward.

White light. The amber-studded scene directly in front of her, the woods all around. The portal telescoped shut.

The hands still clasped her shoulders, holding her tight against a body. She wrenched free and whirled to face her attacker.

Alex stared at her, eyes wide, face ashen. He breathed hard, his chest heaving with each inhalation. Sweat dribbled down his forehead and face.

Her voice malfunctioned. The woods whirled around her as her knees buckled.

Alex caught her. Darkness licked at the edges of her vision. Cradled in his arms, she managed to say "thanks" a second before she passed out.

HER EYELIDS FLUTTERED OPEN BEFORE SHE WAS FULLY AWAKE. ERIN BLINKED several times, struggling to resolve the scene around her. She lay on a bed, head propped on a pillow, arms at her sides. She was in her bedroom at Revenant House. The lamp on the bedside table cast a yellowish glow. A breeze wafted through the open window.

"You're awake."

Erin started at the sound of Alex's voice. She glanced to her left. He sat in a high backed, upholstered chair in the corner beside the bed. His left arm was draped along the length of the chair's arm. His right elbow rested on the other arm of the chair, with his arm bent upward so that his curled fingers supported his chin. He watched her with a placid expression.

She sat up and scooted backwards until she could lean against the headboard, with a pillow between her backside and the wood. "How long was I out?"

He checked his watch. "Twenty minutes."

"You didn't take me to a hospital."

"No. You seemed all right—uninjured, I mean." He rose from the chair and walked around the end of the bed to the side where she sat. As he perched on the edge of the mattress, he said, "I assumed it was shock."

He sat beside her knees with his hand resting on the quilt a few inches from her fingertips. Shock. Yes, that word described what she'd felt after she stepped through Rassul's portal. The abrupt change in surroundings had struck her with the force of a tidal wave. Her brain seemed incapable of sorting out the sensory input that assailed her. One moment she stood in the woods. The next, she skidded to a halt in another world.

Was it another world?

Alex picked up a glass from the bedside table and offered it to her. She hadn't noticed the glass before. She hadn't noticed much of anything. Her brain needed until a few seconds ago to reach full awareness. Now, she realized the glass held water. Accepting the proffered drink, she sipped the cool water.

Then she noticed her sock-clothed feet. Alex must've removed her boots. She touched her hair, feeling the strands that hung loose over her shoulder. He removed her hair tie too. A quick glance down assured her he had removed nothing else.

"Better?" he asked.

She nodded and took another sip of water. As the liquid slid over her tongue and down her throat, she thought back to the moments immediately after she fired her gun at Rassul, only to have the glowing orb swallow the bullet. Her muscles had refused to obey her commands. Despite wanting to fire again, or at least run, she couldn't move. She could do nothing but watch as Rassul stalked toward her. When he grabbed her, she pulled the trigger again but the gun malfunctioned. After that, she'd been overcome by a weakness and dizziness that incapacitated her for what felt like ten minutes but had probably been one or two. Shock seemed a logical explanation for her condition.

Logic was illusory at times, though, especially when it was used to explain away the inexplicable. Sure, shock might explain her weakened condition, but how could anyone logically explain the bullet-eating orb or the portal to another place?

She still felt a bit fuzzy.

Alex slid his hand closer to hers, his fingers almost touching hers. She felt the old urge to shrink away from his touch, but she didn't.

"I think the orb affected me," she said.

"It's entirely possible." He looked into her eyes. "I've seen my colleagues and friends behave as if they were mesmerized, either just before or just after a strange occurrence."

"But in those cases it was a freaky lightning storm."

"You don't think the lightning and the orbs are connected?"

She hadn't thought about it. Too much else distracted her—like, oh, fleeing from a collapsing tunnel or launching herself into a space-time portal. Both the orbs and the lightning masqueraded as natural phenomena, until they tried to kill you. Debunkers often dismissed glowing orbs as nothing but ball lightning, an explanation which hardly solve the mystery. Scientists did not yet understand ball lightning, and it exhibited behavior that seemed unnatural, such as the ability to move against gravity and the wind. Scientists called the mysterious lights ball lightning. Laymen, especially those interested in UFOs, refer to them as orbs. Both terms referred, in her mind, to the same phenomenon.

Why then shouldn't orbs and lightning, particularly the sort of lightning that tried to kill people apparently on purpose, originate from the same source? It made a frightening kind of sense. The storm in the Grand Canyon blew up out of nowhere to rain freakishly powerful bolts of lightning on their heads.

Worry lines had etched paths across Alex's forehead. His middle finger twitched, brushing against the side of her hand. He must think she was lost in an orb-induced catatonia. Well, she was sitting here not speaking or moving.

She smiled a little. "I suppose they must be connected."

He lifted his hand to her face, settling his fingertips on her cheek. "You still look a little pale. When did you last eat?"

Good question. She tried to remember. "Lunch."

"I'll make you a sandwich."

He hopped off the bed, bounded out of the room, and disappeared into the hallway. She sat there for a moment feeling a bit dazed. First they were talking about glowing orbs, then all of a sudden he wanted to feed her. Exactly how god-awful did she look?

Pushing up off the bed, she wandered into the bathroom to look at herself in the mirror. Her cheeks were a bit paler than usual, ditto for her lips. Okay, she looked less than spectacular. It was hardly a new look for her. She'd looked and felt much worse after Rassul attacked her the first time, when he left her lying in a ditch with bruises blooming all over her body. Alex hadn't seen her then, however.

An orb had healed those bruises.

Why heal her then, only to aid Rassul in his attack on her tonight? Christ. Just when she thought she understood the orbs' intentions, she remembered she didn't.

Unless the orb that healed her originated from a different source than the ones that surrounded Rassul and kept tabs on her and Alex.

She felt a headache stabbing at the backs of her eyes. Her neck ached too. She pushed aside thoughts of orbs and scuffled downstairs to the kitchen.

There, she found Alex slicing a sandwich into diagonal quarters. Picking up the plate on which the sandwich sat, along with a glass of dark liquid, he walked toward the doorway. As he passed her, he snagged her forearm in a gentle grasp and urged her to follow him. They went to the end of the hallway, where it dead-ended at the west passage, and entered the room to the left of the dining room. Erin had glanced into this room when Newman gave her a tour of the house the day before, but she'd been too busy to spend much time here. It was a living room or den—the proper term eluded her at the moment—filled with a sofa, a coffee table, a leather recliner with an ottoman, two upholstered wooden chairs, and a state-of-the-art home theater system complete with an enormous flat-screen TV.

Alex urged her to the sofa. "Sit."

She was too tired to argue, so she sat. He handed her the plate and the glass. The dark liquid inside the glass was, she now realized, pop. As he settled his rump on the coffee table, she sipped the pop.

"Root beer?" she said.

"In case you're suffering from hypoglycemia." He gestured at the plate. "Eat."

Low blood sugar might explain some of her symptoms, including the fainting. He worried about her blood sugar? She took a bite of the sandwich and ate it, then consumed the remainder faster than she'd intended. She hadn't realized how hungry she was. Gulping down a mouthful of pop, she set the plate on the coffee table. She said, "I think I should tell you a few things."

For the next five minutes, she told him about the strange things that happened to her lately. Her UFO sighting at the beach. The first time Rassul attacked her, leaving her with many bruises and a puncture mark on her arm. The orb that healed her injuries. During her entire speech, Alex's gaze never wavered from hers. When she finished, he took her hands in his. His hands felt warm, highlighting the chill in her own fingers.

"What the hell is happening?" she asked.

"I'm not sure."

Another thought occurred to her. "Why did you run off into the woods?"

"I had to meet some Bigfoot."

She stared at him. Bigfoot? He said it so matter-of-factly that for a moment she assumed she'd misheard him. Yes, she believed Bigfoot existed. She believed a lot of things existed. But his statement made absolutely no sense to her.

Apparently, her expression gave away her confusion. He said, "The Planners aren't our only allies. I told you about the tribes of Bigfoot that live in numerous places around the world. Well, one of those tribes lives in the woods near here. Katy got a message to them, and they've agreed to help us."

She felt her mouth drop open. Before any bugs could fly in, she said, "Help how?"

"By keeping an eye on the woods and what's happening around Revenant House. So you and I can concentrate on finding the relic."

She clamped her jaw shut. The relic. She had expended all her mental energies on trying to figure out what the relic was and where it might be. Why? Because "they" told her to do it, via their minion Rassul.

"My car went dead," she told Alex. "How did you get it running again?"

"I didn't. I found it idling in the road."

She shook her head. "I guess the orb affected my car too. And my gun."

"Your gun?"

She told him about her two failed attempts to shoot Rassul, and how her gun had refused to work the second time.

"It misfired," Alex said. "The orb might've caused it. I'm more interested in how the orb absorbed a bullet."

"Really? I'm more interested in the goddamn relic that people keep threatening to kill me over."

He averted his gaze to the floor between his feet. His hands still cradled hers, investing her with a warmth that, bit by bit, erased the chill from her own flesh.

She did care about the relic, though not because Rassul warned to find it or die. If a virtually omnipotent enemy wanted the relic, then it must be powerful and dangerous. She must find it before her enemies did.

But not on their timetable. Not by following their rules. Not by reacting to what they told her, what they showed her, and what they wanted her to know.

It was time to take the initiative.

"May I see the photos of the stolen artifacts again?" she asked.

"Of course."

He released her hands and trotted out of the room. The warmth of his skin lingered on hers. She clasped her hands in hopes of prolonging the sensation. His footsteps clapped on the wood flooring of the passageway, the sound diminishing and then increasing as he returned to the room.

Kneeling beside her, he dropped his attaché onto the floor between them. From inside the bag, he brought out the stack of papers she'd seen in his motel room.

The doorbell chimed.

Alex thrust the papers at her. "Here. Look them over while I go greet our guest."

"You're expecting someone?"

He smiled, patted her thigh, and left the room. She started to get up to follow him, then dropped back onto the sofa. If a Bigfoot had rung the doorbell, maybe she should stay here. Believing in Bigfoot and shaking hands with one were different things. She wasn't quite ready for the latter. She felt stupid for considering that a Bigfoot might have rung the doorbell, but was she supposed to think? Alex told her a tribe of Bigfoot was lurking in the woods around Revenant House, helping guard the place. He told her the Bigfoot worshiped a race of people called the Planners. How could she say it was impossible for a big hairy creature to ring the doorbell?

Waiting here seemed prudent.

Erin fanned the artifact photos out across the coffee table. Alex had reclaimed the photos as soon as they'd gotten into her car, when she dumped the stack of photos onto the floor behind her seat. Ever the neat freak, Alex gathered them up, stacked them evenly, and tucked the sheets into his attaché.

Jeez, now he had her thinking of the briefcase as an "attaché."

The photos spread out before her showed, as she'd already determined, out-of-place artifacts. They had turned up in locations far from where they belonged, or in a time where they didn't belong, or both. If they were out of place only in terms of geographic location, then she could dismiss it as another example of archaeologists and historians refusing to admit that far-flung ancient cultures had been in contact with each other. All but two of the artifacts shown in the photos, however, belonged to the other categories of out-of-place artifacts. They were out of sync with the time periods when their source cultures existed. The Mayan stone, for instance, turned up inside an Egyptian tomb dating to the fourteenth century BC, yet mainstream history said such an artifact could date to no earlier than the eighth century AD.

Archaeologist could be wrong about the dates they assigned to ancient cultures. Even so, some things seemed certain. The ancient Egyptian culture certainly seemed to predate the Olmec culture of Mesoamerica, which in turn seemed to predate the Anasazi culture of the American Southwest. She picked up two of the photos. The first showed an Olmec figurine that had been found in a predynastic Egyptian burial. Problem was, archaeologists said the Olmec culture began just under 4,000 years ago but the burial had been dated to a segment of the Predynastic Period known as the Badarian, which ended about 6,000 years ago. The second photo showed an item identified as a split-twig figurine of the kind found in the Grand Canyon and attributed to a culture known as the Late Archaic. This artifact turned up clutched in the hand of a bog mummy dug up in Denmark. Archaeologists used the radiocarbon method to date the mummy to approximately 7000 BC, the early Neolithic era in Europe. Archaeologists said the split-twig figurines of the Grand Canyon dated to no earlier than 4,000 years ago, or 2000 BC. Either archaeologists were thousands of years off on their dating of these cultures, and the radiocarbon method was flawed, or something else was going on here.

If she assumed the relative dating of cultures was correct—meaning that ancient Egypt, for instance, came before the Olmec, even if archaeologists got the exact dates wrong—then the artifacts still posed a problem. An Olmec figurine did not belong in a predynastic Egyptian burial, because the cultures were separated not only by thousands of miles, but by 2,000 years. The Late Archaic culture of the Grand Canyon and the Neolithic culture of Denmark, like the Olmec and Egypt, were separated by thousands of miles and thousands of years.

The split twig figurine looked vaguely like a deer, complete with antlers. The artisan responsible for the figurine constructed it out of willow twigs, according to Alex's notes. The willow tree was sacred in ancient Egypt, which perhaps explained why someone chose to inter the figurine with a human being. Reverence for the willow tree failed to explain how the figurine wound up stranded in time and place.

The Olmec figurine was stranger. Fashioned from greenstone, it looked relatively human in shape, except for the head. The long, narrow head squatted atop sloping shoulders and jutted forward in a posture reminiscent of a very old, very feeble man. The posture of the robust body, however, hinted at strength. The elongated, bulbous crown of the head looked almost cone shaped. She held the photo closer. The head of the Olmec figurine reminded her of ancient Egyptian sculptures from the Amarna Period, the time of Akhenaten's rule. Those sculptures, along with other artwork, depicted members of the royal family as having elongated heads similar to the greenstone figurine shown in the photograph. The mummy of Akhenaten's son, Tutankhamen, preserved the boy's elongated skull, and a mummy found in Tomb 55 in the Valley of the Kings had a similar skull shape. The skulls discovered around the world, particularly in South America, evidenced a similar elongation. Some of the South American skulls were so stretched that it boggled the mind how a person could live with a head shaped that way.

Archaeologists dismissed the misshapen skulls as simply a result of skull binding. If so, it seemed utterly bizarre that throughout history people around the world chose to deform their children in such a manner. Since no one knew why ancient people might do it, religion became the scapegoat. No one knew what religion, if any, many of the ancient peoples subscribed to, but that didn't stop archaeologists from blaming religious beliefs for the perverse practice of squeezing children's heads into bizarre shapes.

What might have triggered the practice? If skull binding was the cause, then the people performing rituals must've been mimicking something. The skull binding itself boggled the mind, but to think disparate peoples around the world developed the exact same ritual independently exceeded all reason. In Erin's mind, only two reasons for the elongated skulls made sense. Either the skull binding ritual was an attempt to mimic an entity or race of entities known to peoples worldwide, or the individuals with the elongated skulls were not human. The former possibility might lead to a similar conclusion as the latter, since the entity or entities who inspired the worldwide epidemic of skull binding could be nonhuman themselves.

The idea was strange, but not unique. Alternative researchers had theorized about the phenomenon of the elongated skulls for years, reaching similar conclusions. At this moment, she was no closer to proving either variation of the theory then were the countless researchers who posted their thoughts online and wrote articles about it for new age publications.

She returned her attention to the artifact photos. The thought that struck for the first time she examined the pictures, in Alex's motel room, came back to her now. These were not simply out-of-place artifacts. They were out-of-time artifacts. Earlier this evening, she hadn't dared let the thought fully form in her brain, because she knew where it would lead. The subsequent thought, the one she'd blocked from her mind, suddenly felt inevitable. She must think it—and then she must speak it, to tell Alex of her revelation. Not that she had a clue what it meant.

Voices rumbled in the passageway, too distant for her to make out the words. Glancing up, she resisted the urge to sneak to the doorway and eavesdrop. Alex would introduce her to his friend when he decided the time was right. She had to trust his judgment, if only because she had no one else to trust.

She focused on the pictures again. Out-of-time artifacts. She felt herself rolling down a mental hill, faster and faster, tumbling toward a destination she could no longer avoid. One explanation seemed adequate to account for the facts Alex provided about the artifacts. Cultures separated by more than miles, but by time itself, had met in the distant past. But how? The answer was clear.

Time travel.

12

ONCE SHE ADMITTED THE WORDS INTO HER THOUGHTS, ERIN FELT MUCH better. Freer to explore the full ramifications of everything she'd experienced lately. Ideas clicked into place in her brain. Either she'd gone irretrievably insane, or at last she had figured it all out.

Her brief trip through Rassul's portal replayed in her mind. In the light of her revelation, the disjointed images that assailed her senses when she stepped through the portal abruptly became clear. She closed her eyes, cleared her thoughts, and immersed herself in the memory.

She jumped through the portal after Rassul. Darkness surrounded her on all sides, except straight ahead. She stood in an alley, with windowless walls on either side of her. The portal blocked her view of what lay behind, but up ahead, she gazed out at a street scene. The amber lights that studded the darkness were gas streetlamps and gas lights within the building across the street, which glowed through windows. The clomping noise resolved into the sharp clop-clop-clop of horses' hooves on the paved street.

Opening her eyes, Erin leaned back against the sofa. Rassul fled not merely into another place, but into another time. A time when gas lamps lit the streets and people's homes, and horse-drawn carriages and wagons served as transportation. No cities like the one the portal dumped her into existed in this part of Michigan, either in the present or in the past. Yes, at last she understood. Her enemies, Rassul and his masters, wielded an immensely powerful convergence of weapons—the ability to travel through both space and time.

And now she understood what "forces beyond conception" meant. The enemy they faced possessed the technology to travel through time at will, to traverse both outer space and earthbound distances in a heartbeat, and to manipulate the weather for their own purposes. The storm that collapsed the tunnels in the Grand Canyon labyrinth, as well as those Alex encountered in the Valley of the Kings and Utah, were manufactured as the truest embodiments of the term weapons of mass destruction.

No wonder ancient peoples around the world, throughout history, sought shelter inside the earth. Around 1,000 years ago, the Anasazi built dwellings high up on steep cliffs, fortresses tucked into natural alcoves, accessible solely by climbing ropes or treacherous handhold-foothold ladders identical to the ones she and Alex braved to enter the Grand Canyon labyrinth. In the Paleolithic era, tens of thousands of years ago, Europeans crawled deep into barely accessible caves to paint masterpieces of stone-age art. But they also hid in the caves, at least for short periods, as suggested by fossilized footprints that showed child-size tracks as well as adult-size imprints. Erin had for some time thought people must've spent lengthy periods inside the caves, since creating the sophisticated cave paintings would take time.

Over 3,000 years ago in a region of today known as Cappadocia, in modern Turkey, a people called the Hittites built an underground fortress to hide from their enemies. Archaeologists assumed the Hittites were hiding from the Sea Peoples, a mysterious race about whom little was known. The Egyptians fought the Sea Peoples too, but no one knew who they were or where they came from, or whether the Hittites at Cappadocia built their subterranean fortress to ward off the Sea Peoples. The underground chambers featured huge stone disks that could be rolled in front of the doorways to block passage from the outside. Evidence suggested the Hittites stored food in their underground hideout, as if they intended—or were required—to spend long periods sequestered down there.

About a thousand years later, the people of ancient India carved temples out of a 250-foot cliff, high up the sheer face. Temples could also provide a hiding place during emergencies. All these cliff-side and subterranean structures seemed like an attempt to hide from something, from an enemy capable of penetrating a regular fortress. Surrounding yourself with hundreds of feet of solid rock offered far greater protection than even a stone roof could provide. If they wanted to fend off a human enemy with technology equal to, or perhaps slightly better than, their own, then these ancient folks didn't need to scale steep cliffs or burrow underground to build their fortresses. They could've erected their forts at the base of a cliff. She saw but one damn good reason to go to such lengths in search of security.

They were hiding from the sky.

ALEX SAUNTERED THROUGH THE DOORWAY. ERIN LIFTED HER GAZE TO WATCH as another man succeeded Alex into the room. The newcomer was of average height, a few inches shorter than Alex. His bald head glistened in the light from the floor lamp. He wore pants and a long-sleeved T-shirt both decorated in camouflage patterns and held a knit cap, also camouflage, in one hand. In his other hand he gripped a palm-size object, silver in color and disk shaped with curved edges. Gloves concealed his hands. Along his arms and across his chest, muscles bulged through the skin-tight fabric of his shirt. He looked around fifty, though few wrinkles lined his face. His expression was stoic, unreadable. Catching sight of Erin, he smiled faintly, for half a second. The intensity of his gaze sent a shiver down her spine. She wasn't afraid of him. Instead, the shiver stemmed from the magnetism of this stranger, who exuded the contained energy of a panther stalking its prey.

Lifting the silver object, the stranger waved it about like a magic wand. A pale blue light within the object's casing zipped back and forth across the top edge. The stranger stepped further into the room as he waved the object some more. The light sped up to a frantic pace, then ceased moving. The man tapped the object's face. The blue light turned green.

The stranger tucked the device in his pocket and looked at her again. She skimmed her gaze over his muscular chest and arms, returning to his face after a good long perusal.

Alex cleared his throat. She tore her gaze from the stranger to eye Alex. He was frowning, with his brow knit tightly over the bridge of his nose.

"What?" she asked.

He gave her a funny look she couldn't decipher, then waved a hand at the stranger. "He was disabling any electronic surveillance devices in this room."

"Who is he?"

"Warner."

"Doesn't he have a first name?"

Warner strode to the sofa and, bending at the waist, grasped her hand like a knight greeting his lady. He planted a light kiss on the back of her hand. "Errando Warner."

She assumed that was his name, and not a seductive phrase in another language. His tone was sultry, in a macho sort of way. He held onto her hand even after uttering his two-word introduction.

Alex hissed a sigh. Erin glanced at him sideways. Mouth squashed into a line, he shot a squinty-eyed look at Warner. The older man glanced at Alex, turning only his eyes, then locked his eyes on Erin. His expression remained unreadable, though she swore amusement sparkled in his dark eyes.

Warner set her hand on her knee and rose, backing away from her a few steps.

Alex relaxed his expression yet he stayed vigilantly aware of the other man via sideways glances. Another revelation blossomed in Erin's mind, but she pushed it aside for the moment. She asked, "Don't you think the bad guys will notice you've disabled their bug thingies?"

Warner's lips twisted into a partial smirk. "Let them. Your employer clearly wants to remain anonymous, and to confront you about our visit or the disabling of the bugs would force him to reveal himself."

It made an odd sort of sense, so she moved on to her next question. "What's the plan?"

Alex answered. "Warner is here to monitor the house from the outside while you and I try to sort out the intellectual part of the puzzle."

"I already did that, at least partially." He blinked as though he hadn't understood her words. She said, "I'll explain later." She gestured at Warner. "What's he going to do? I thought your big, hairy friends were guarding us."

"The creatures are intelligent and powerful, but they lack training. Warner's going to guide them."

She arched her eyebrows at Warner. "Commander of the Bigfoot army, eh?"

"Precisely," Warner said. "I will marshal them into a covert unit like none you have ever seen."

He spoke with a slight accent, she realized. Warner was a German name. He must be Alex's mysterious friend, the German gazillionaire who lent them his private jet. Thinking back on his words, she admitted, "I've never seen a covert unit."

"And you will not see this one," Warner said. "That's the meaning of covert."

"But you said it'll be a covert unit the likes of which I've never seen."

"A figure of speech." To Alex, Warner said, "I like this one. She is much cleverer than the girl you almost—"

"I get it," Alex said, "you like her. Can we move on?"

Erin eyed Alex with a newfound interest. The girl he'd almost what? Asked out on a date? Gotten killed? She wanted to ask Warner, but she got the impression doing so would aggravate Alex. Maybe she could wheedle it out of him later.

"Before Warner heads outside," Alex said, "we're going to sweep the entire house for bugs."

"Okay." Although Warner didn't seem in need of help, what with his spiffy doohickey and all, Alex probably wanted to get away from her before she asked him about the girl he'd almost. "I'll wait here, I guess."

Alex nodded. He ushered Warner out the door. As the German ducked through it into the hallway, he glanced back at her, his face stoic. He winked and left the room.

After a reasonable wait to let the men wander out of sight, Erin headed out into the hallway. Angling right, she trod down the passage and into the library. The ladder for accessing the upper shelves stood along the left wall. She dragged it across the library to the doorway, then paused to peek into the passageway. Alex and Warner were climbing the stairs to the second floor. She positioned the ladder directly under the wood carving and climbed its rungs until her face was level with the Egyptian figures in the wood carving above the door. When she'd performed this inspection earlier today, the design on the pectorals worn by the Egyptian figures caught her attention. The design involved three interlocking spirals, like the symbol on Ridley's key. Fishing the key out of her pocket, she held it up beside one of the Egyptian figures. Yes, the symbols were identical.

She swept her gaze over the rays that stretched downward from the sun, which hung high over the figures' heads. Each ray terminated in a hand reaching out to the figures. One ray, like the others, ended in a hand—but the hand clasped an *ankh*, the cross-like symbol for life. Erin climbed higher on the ladder until the *ankh*-wielding hand was at eye level. Every *ankh* consisted of a vertical bar topped by a crossbar, with a loop above that.

The vertical bar of this *ankh* looked strange, though. She leaned closer. A slender slot was carved into the vertical bar. The hand holding the *ankh* pointed straight down at the area between the feet of the two figures. There, a series of hieroglyphs spelled out a word she recognized. It was one of the most important words in ancient Egypt—*maat*. The meaning of the word varied according to context, and it could even refer to the goddess Maat. Here, the word stood alone, devoid of context. She couldn't be certain what the creator of this carving intended for the word to mean. Often, however, the word *maat* was translated as truth.

Harry used the word truth as the key to his Vigenère cipher.

Might he have seen this carving? If so, surely he would've told her about it in his encoded message or in the text file on the memory card he'd hidden in the spine of his book. The appearance of the word truth in Harry's cipher and this carving could be a coincidence. A very creepy coincidence.

She looked at slot in the *ankh*, then down at the key in her hand. The key might fit into the slot. Ridley was connected to Revenant House. His unfinished book showed up in the library and his key bore a symbol identical to the ones in the wood carving above the library door.

What the heck. She raised the key to the slot in the *ankh*, took a deep breath, and pushed.

The key slid into the slot. She turned the key left. It didn't move. She turned the key right. A lock chunked. The entire wood panel tilted outward at an angle. While the top edge stayed fastened to the wall, the other three edges hung free. The bottom edge stuck out half an inch.

Grasping the bottom edge, she lifted. The panel swung up with a sharp creak that echoed down the passage. She winced and glanced toward the stairs. When neither Alex nor Warner came rushing down the staircase, she returned her attention to the wall. The panel had flipped up to reveal a cavity as tall and wide as the wood panel and about a foot deep. Now she could see the brass hinges that kept the top edge attached to the wall. Inside the cavity lay two objects—a rolled-up paper two feet long and an envelope. She collected the two items and descended the ladder. Just as she hopped off the last step onto the floor, Alex and Warner came down the staircase. They walked briskly to her.

Both men looked at the items in her hand, the cavity in the wall, then her face. Alex said, "What did we miss?"

"Not much," she said. "I found Ridley Covington's secret compartment, that's all."

She marched into the library, gesturing for the men to follow. They reconvened at the desk, with Erin standing behind it and the men facing her on the other side. She set the rolled-up paper on the desktop and examined the envelope. The flap was unsealed, so she flipped it up to reveal the interior. The envelope protected a single sheet of paper, unfolded. Sliding out the sheet, she realized it was the missing page from Ridley's book. His elegant cursive writing filled the page.

"What is it?" Alex asked.

She raised her hand in a silencing gesture as she skimmed the text. The opening line ended the sentence begun on the first page, which she'd read upon discovering Ridley's book hidden in the bookshelves. The first page described Ridley's quest uncover the truth about human history and what he called "evidence of transoceanic contact among ancient cultures and of otherworld influences." After exhausting all available histories, he decided the answers must lie in the physical remains of ancient cultures. "Thenceforth, I embarked on a global mission to..." the final line of the first page began. Now she at last knew the conclusion of that statement. It read, "Thenceforth, I embarked on a global mission to seek out those remains in the hopes that doing so would grant me the evidence I require."

The rest of the page listed the locations he'd visited around the world. Egypt, Peru, Japan, the Middle East. He seemed to have traveled the length and breadth of the Americas too. The last two paragraphs stopped her.

In Egypt I met an American who introduced himself as Mallory J. Harriman from the Utah Territory. He shared my interest in otherworld influences upon the ancient world and whilst we partook of the local ale, I found myself confiding in this stranger the details of my quest. Mallory gravely inquired what my goal might be in undertaking such an endeavour. I replied that truth was my sole object. A haunted expression overcame his features and Mallory warned me to abandon my quest before the truth, in his words, "bites you on the arse." I replied, "Vincit omnia veritas," to which he laughed most heartily, though with a note of despair. He departed soon thereafter, leaving me to ponder his reaction. I continue to believe what I said to him, and the motto spurs me onward.

VINCIT OMNIA VERITAS.

Erin read the phrase aloud. "What does that mean?"

As one, Alex and Warner said, "The truth conquers all."

"Well, it certainly conquered Ridley." The vision of his mummy lying prone on the ground flashed in her mind. Harry's discovery of the petroglyph panel led them to Ridley's final resting place. Ridley mentioned meeting an American named Mallory Harriman. She wondered aloud, "Could he be related to Harry?"

Alex and Warner stared at her.

She recounted for them how she discovered the items hidden behind the wood carving, then she read aloud the relevant paragraph from Ridley's book. "Harry used *veritas* as a clue to help me figure out the key to his Vigenère cipher. The key was truth. And the Egyptian version of the word truth pointed me to the keyhole in the carving. Is it a coincidence that Ridley and a man named Harriman had a conversation all about truth and its consequences?"

Alex said, "I don't believe in coincidences anymore. Besides, the Harriman clan lived in New England during Ridley's time, not the Utah Territory."

He fidgeted, eyes focused on the floor. She knew by now that meant he wanted to say something. She said, "What is it?"

He stilled and looked straight at her. "Do you remember I said Harry hates his first name? He prefers the nickname Harry, which is derived from his last name." Alex cleared his throat. "His full name is Mallory J. Harriman."

The breath froze in her chest. "Harry traveled back in time."

Alex shook his head. "That's impossible."

"Oh, I forgot to tell you what else I realized." She explained about her revelation concerning the stolen artifacts and time travel. "If the artifacts could travel through time, then why not people too? It would be a hell of a coincidence for Ridley to have met a different Mallory J. Harriman who also lived in Utah."

Warner nodded slowly as the corners of his mouth curved upward a smidgen. He aimed a sly smile at Erin and said, "Of course."

"Harry left us a clue," she said. "He told Ridley his full name and that he was from Utah so that when we found the missing page from Ridley's book, we'd figure out the man Ridley met was actually our Harry. He's giving us a clue about what happened to him."

Alex shuffled backward, collapsed into the padded wooden chair that faced the desk, and stared straight ahead without expression. The color had drained from his face. He treated Bigfoot and glowing orbs like everyday occurrences, hardly worthy of noting, but the notion that time travel might be possible left him blanched. Everyone had their limits, she supposed, even a guy who specialized in the bizarre and the seemingly impossible.

"I thought Harry was dead," Alex said.

His voice was flat, almost a monotone. Erin rushed to him. She kneeled in front of him and clasped his hands in her own, feeling a chill in his skin that she recognized, having felt it in her own flesh not twenty minutes ago. Slouched in the chair, he stared past her at nothing, or at least nothing that she could see. Inner demons were invisible to everyone else.

"He's not dead," she told him. "Harry sent a message so you would know. His death isn't your fault because he *isn't dead*."

"But Rassul said—"

"Rassul is a lying son of a bitch."

She tightened her hands around his. For a moment they sat there in silence. She shut her eyes for a second, and when she opened them again she noticed the color returning to his cheeks. His hands felt warmer too. His gaze, formerly glazed, now cleared and zeroed in on her own. His lips curved up at the corners just a touch. In a soft voice, he said, "You're right, Rassul is a liar."

He shifted his hands to sandwich hers between his palms. Heat flushed through her, all the way to her face. She felt the blush rising in her cheeks. Yet, strangely, she didn't want to move.

Alex sat up. "Have you looked at the other item yet?"

He nodded toward the desk, where the rolled-up sheet lay. Erin went to the desk and picked up the roll. A skinny strip of fabric, knotted tightly, fastened the roll. A daub of wax sealed the knot. She picked at the wax-covered knot with her fingernails but it refused to come loose. Next she tried sliding the binding down the roll's length to remove it but the wax, dribbled onto the fabric in a sloppy manner, had also oozed onto the paper beneath. The wax glued the fabric in place.

Beside her now, Alex grazed his fingertips over the paper. He murmured, "Papyrus."

Great, it really helped her to know the paper was made from strips of reed glued together. The knowledge didn't help her loosen the seal. She picked at the wax, scraping off tiny slivers without making much of a dent.

In one quick motion, Warner reached into his pocket and whipped out a knife. He flipped the blade open, handing the knife to her hilt first. She took the blade. Sliding it under the fabric adjacent to the wax daub, she snapped the binding. Then she gently sliced through the wax at the paper's edge. The papyrus stayed rolled in a tight cylinder.

Alex brushed her hands away from the roll. "Clear the desk. We'll need room."

Warner helped her remove the items from the desktop, save for the computer. They deposited the items on the floor beside the desk, except for the page from Ridley's book, which she kept in her hand. Alex laid the roll on the desktop. Flattening the free edge, he unwound the papyrus inch by inch until it lay spread out across the desk. The papyrus measured about three feet wide by two feet high. The colors splashed across the papyrus—mainly reds, blues, and greens—seemed as bright as the day they'd been painted onto the sheet. The left-hand side contained horizontal registers of hieroglyphic text, while a complex series of interconnected images filled the remainder of the papyrus's width. Sacred symbols and representations of gods and goddesses formed a border around the edge of the entire papyrus.

The images adjacent to the hieroglyphic text appeared to form a cohesive whole. A squiggly blue line traced a path across the center of the compound image. Green strips with uneven edges bordered the blue squiggle and, further out from the green, brownish blobs edged with black lines were drawn at irregular intervals. A smattering of other shapes and squiggles appeared here and there in the image.

As part of the top border of the papyrus, the goddess Nut stretched her elongated body across the page, centered over the image of the blue squiggle and brown blobs. Nut represented the sky. Her presence above the image might suggest the colored blobs and squiggles represented geographic features.

"It's a map," she said.

"I know," Alex said. He was running his fingers along the registers of hieroglyphs. "This text is real Egyptian, not the kindergarten version we've seen before on the petroglyph panel."

"What does it say?"

"The text talks about the *duat*, the Egyptian underworld that the sun descended into at dusk and emerged out of at dawn. I've never heard anything like this." He paused as if considering the text. "It says the Aten sent his double, the god Ra, to escort the pharaoh through the *akhet* and beyond the *duat*, to a place of darkness where the pharaoh was reborn as a son of the Aten. The king returned, and ruled Egypt with cruelty and disregard for the old gods, forcing everyone to worship his father the Aten, whom he had come to resemble."

Alex frowned at the text. Erin laid a hand on his forearm. "What else does it say?"

"More things that make no sense." He planted both hands on the desk to lean over the map. "It says the river runs into and out of the *duat*, then back into it before emerging in the excellent lake. The pharaoh was buried in a tomb near the lake. First buried in the land between the river, in the pyramid mountain at the doorway to the *duat*, he now rests for eternity in the land at the river's end."

"The land between the river, singular?"

He shot a sideways glance at her. "Yes. But land cannot be between a river."

"If it's an island it can."

Alex let out a heavy sigh, his frown deepening. "The petroglyph panel said a king was buried in the Grand Canyon. This text seems to refer to the same pharaoh, called the serpent god-king of the Two Lands."

"Actually," Erin said, leaning her hip against the desk, "it said the king *would* be buried there. Sounds like they intended to bury him there but changed their minds before the tomb was finished."

"And according to this text, he was buried at the river's end, in the land of the excellent lake."

She tried to imagine what the text might mean, since Alex seemed baffled. If the text's author were trying to describe a place or event far beyond the everyday experience of the average Egyptian, he might've struggled to find the right words to explain it. The language of ancient Egypt might lack the proper words.

Beside her, Alex mumbled. She asked, "What?"

With a flourish of his index finger, he indicated a section of the hieroglyphic text. "This is very strange. It talks about the Brothers of the Aten which, as far as I can tell, was a secret society charged with protecting the interests of the Aten."

"How can the sun have interests?"

"I don't think they're referring to the sun." He straightened. "The text repeatedly refers to the Aten in the plural. It says they hide behind the sun, unwilling to taint themselves by coming down to earth. They rely on the Brothers of the Aten to exact their will."

Erin felt her stomach churn. Her jaw tightened. "Are you saying the Aten were people?"

"No," he said. "I'm saying they were living beings not of this earth."

ERIN FELL SILENT, HER EXPRESSION IMPENETRABLE. ALEX WATCHED HER AND waited. He heard Warner amble up next to him on the opposite side, though he kept his focus on Erin. He didn't think the news would stun her. Apparently, it did.

Finally, she said, "That's a big leap, don't you think? Maybe they were human beings with advanced technology, like your friends the Planners."

Yes, that was the response he expected. He hadn't read to her the most disturbing passage yet. She needed to hear the rest before she would accept his conclusion. Once she heard the omitted passage, he felt certain she would agree with him.

"Listen to this," he said. Then he located the passage he'd left out before and, tracing the line with his fingertip to keep his place, he translated it aloud. "They are not Egyptians. They are more than gods. Their will commands the sky to open up and rain fire upon us. Their anger causes the earth to tremble. Only the dead are safe from them. Beware the Aten, the ancient ones who seem to give light but bring only darkness and death."

Erin cocked her head. A half-suppressed smile lit her face, glittering in her eyes.

"You think this is funny?" he asked.

"No," she said. "But I think I understand now."

Alex glanced at Warner. The barest hint of a smile teased at his lips. He stood ramrod straight, hands clasped behind his back, eyes focused on Erin. Warner's expression conveyed appreciation. His mentor liked Erin. She seemed to like Warner too. Alex gritted his teeth. He couldn't compete with a billionaire who kissed women's hands.

"Tell me about the Aten," Erin said. "The Egyptian mythology surrounding it."

The Aten was, essentially, the disk of the sun seen in the sky. Originally known as Ra-Harakhti, the name given to the rising sun, the Aten served as a minor deity for most of Egyptian history. In 1350 BC, however, the pharaoh Amenhotep III died and his son, Amenhotep IV, succeeded him to the throne. After three years as king, the younger Amenhotep decided, for reasons no archaeologist or historian truly understood, to overhaul the Egyptian religion. Gone were the old beloved gods like Ra and Amun. Amenhotep IV replaced them with the sun-disk, declaring the newly elevated deity the one and only god he would allow his subjects to worship. Ra-Harakhti became the Aten, the ruler of the horizon, and acquired a new epithet that roughly translated as the living one who awakens in the horizon, who is known as the light of the sun-disk.

He explained the mythology to Erin. She scrunched her mouth, something he'd seen her do whenever she was deep in thought, and particularly when a piece of information confused her. Though the expression lent her face an air of annoyance, he'd come to realize it meant nothing of the sort. The look meant she was about to ask an important question that would most likely lead to a revolution.

Her lips un-scrunched and she said, "So the Aten was the face of the sun."

"No," he said, "the sun-disk was the vehicle that allowed the Aten's light to reach the earth. The Aten was the light itself. The sun was no longer seen as the source of life-giving light, but as a kind of conduit for the light that came from the Aten."

Erin raised her left hand. Her fingers held the page from Ridley's journal. She looked at the page, then at him. She said, "In the note we found with Ridley's body, he mentioned the darkness that masquerades as the light."

Here it comes. He felt her revelation building like an electrical charge between them. He had no idea what she might've figured out.

"The hieroglyphic text you translated," she said, pointing at the papyrus, "said the Aten hide behind the sun. And what did it call them? The ancient ones who…"

"Seem to give light but bring only death," he said.

"I bet Ridley was talking about the Aten." She smiled at him. "I think you're right, they are living beings not of this earth. They're aliens. And they can control the weather."

For awhile now, he'd thought the Ancient Ones mentioned by the Planners must've been behind the destruction of the predynastic burial in the Valley of the Kings and the deaths of his colleagues in Utah. The storm in the Grand Canyon that nearly buried him and Erin was clearly connected to the Ancient Ones as well. But today he'd learned a new name for the mysterious enemy that wielded forces beyond conception.

The Aten.

Might he have made the connection on his own? Perhaps. He wondered, though. No one could have made the connection without access to the papyrus and the missing page from Ridley's journal, both of which the Victorian explorer hid inside a secret compartment. He doubted whether, given the same clues Erin puzzled out, he could've found Ridley's hideaway. His thought process tended toward the linear, whereas hers careened like a pinball, gathering information with each bounce.

Erin tapped her fingernails on the desktop. "The hieroglyphic text mentions how the Aten's power can make the sky open up and rain fire. That sounds a lot like the storm that tried to bury us alive in the Grand Canyon."

"I know," he said.

"Well, when you didn't say anything, I figured you were working out a polite way to say the idea of weather manipulation was ridiculous."

"On the contrary, I was thinking about how right you are."

Warner cleared his throat. To Erin, he said, "This conversation is beyond my expertise. I will leave it to you, *meine Kinder.* I must attend to our covert army."

Alex asked, "You have your phone?"

Warner nodded. "I'll text you with any developments."

With that, Warner strode out the door. His footsteps clapped down the corridor, diminishing into silence. Alex never heard the front door open and close. Warner would've slipped into stealth mode before leaving the house.

Erin looked out the window. "What, he's just going out into the woods by himself to commune with Bigfoot? Doesn't he need backup or something?"

Alex smiled. "Warner is his own backup."

"He's tough, huh?"

He swore he caught a glimmer of appreciation on her face as she peeked out the window again, probably hoping to catch a glimpse of the German god.

Alex clenched his teeth. "Would you rather be out there with him?"

Erin chuckled. The sound was light, melodic, charming. Yet it made every muscle in his body tense up because she must be thinking about Warner.

She chuckled again. "Why would I want to be tromping around in the woods in the dead of night, surrounded by hairy monsters, when I can be inside a nice cozy house?"

"A cozy house riddled with bugs."

"You turned those off." She tapped his arm. "Hey, what's the matter with you? We just figured out some important stuff and you look like your best buddy just stole your girlfriend."

He jerked his head to look at her. "Why would you say that?"

"Because you look angry and hurt."

"No," he said, turning toward her. "The part about my best buddy stealing my girlfriend. Of all the things you could've said, why that?"

She shrugged. "It just popped into my head."

Could she have known what he was thinking? Was it that obvious? He wanted to say more on the subject, but she beat him to it.

"We need to do a little exploring," she said. "Can you pick a lock?"

"Um…no."

Her mouth twisted into a half frown. She flapped the page in her hand as she tapped the toe of her boot on the wood floor. He wished he could pick a lock. Warner laid claim to that skill, of course.

Wonderful. He was jealous of the man who taught him everything he knew about covert tactics—not that he held a candle to Warner in that arena. Despite Alex's lack of experience and relative clumsiness, Warner gave freely of both his time and his expertise. Alex liked, even admired, the man. They'd spent a lot of time together in the field. Maybe if Warner had gone with him to Utah, events would've turned out differently.

No. Even Warner wasn't tough enough to fight the Aten. No one was.

Erin stopped flapping the page. Her partial frown morphed into a triumphant smile.

"You found something," Alex said.

Holding the page between her thumb and forefinger, she flipped it around for him to see it. Writing was scrawled on the back of the page. He squinted at the words, but she held the page too far away for him to decipher the writing. As if she read his thoughts, Erin stretched her arm out to hold the page closer to him. The words came into focus.

He read it aloud. "All doors shall open for the one who commands the spinning path."

Erin bounced on her tiptoes. She slapped the page down onto the desktop.

"I give up," he said. "What does the riddle mean?"

"We don't need to pick any locks." From her pocket, she withdrew Ridley's key and raised it in front of his face. Three interlocking spirals formed one end of the key. "See the spirals?"

"Yes."

"That's a spinning path if ever I saw one."

"I suppose. So what?"

"All doors shall open for the one who commands the spinning path, meaning the one who has this key." When he didn't respond, she lowered her hand and screwed up her face in frustration. "It's a skeleton key. You know, a key that opens any door."

"Oh."

"Ridley left clues hidden in a secret compartment in this house," she said, "which suggests this was his home. Plus, Ridley's key is similar to the one that opens my bedroom door, another hint that this was Ridley's house. The skeleton key must open all the doors inside Revenant House."

"You really think they haven't changed the locks in 160 years?"

"From what Newman told me," Erin said, "I think Samuel Wessick is obsessed with historical accuracy, keeping the house the way it would've been back in olden days. I bet the locks haven't been changed."

Her logic was solid and he had a suspicion her hunch would prove right. Her hunches usually did. She deciphered every riddle, figured out every clue, and linked it all together into a chain of evidence.

He looked down at the map. If only the text explained how to fight the Aten.

"Well," Erin said, "I'm going to try the key anyway."

Her voice was quiet, the self-assured tone absent. The irritation had left her features, replaced by a solemn expression. She turned to leave. He clutched her wrist to stop her. She froze, turning her head to look at him.

He slid his hand past her wrist to clasp her hand. "You're brilliant. I just wanted you to know that."

A smile flickered across her face, then faded. She pulled her hand free and walked out the door.

THE SKELETON KEY OPENED EVERY DOOR ON THE FIRST FLOOR. THE KEY ALSO opened the doors on the second floor, or at least the ones she tried so far. One door remained.

The door at the end of the north passage, near the back stairs.

Erin halted facing the door. Alex had trailed her on her quest to explore the forbidden rooms. So far, she'd found nothing of note. Samuel Wessick's study looked like, well, a study. Alex suggested they should rifle through the desk drawers and, in his words, "poke into every nook and cranny" until they uncovered something worthwhile. Erin wanted to wait until after they explored the other rooms. Then, if they found nothing, they could search Wessick's study. She didn't want to waste time there if another room housed bigger and better secrets. Reluctantly, Alex agreed.

Back in the library, he'd called her brilliant. The words sent a delicious shiver through her. Never before had another person called her brilliant. If anyone else said it, she probably would've dismissed it as empty flattery and assumed the other person wanted a favor from her. Alex didn't want favors. He wanted…

"Are you going to do it or not?" Alex asked.

"Huh?"

He stood a couple feet away, sideways to her. Glancing at the door, he said, "The key. What are you waiting for?"

Heat bloomed in her cheeks. While she got lost in her memory of the moment in the library, he'd waited for her to try the key.

She inserted the key into the lock and rotated it. The lock disengaged with a click. Removing the key, she twisted the door knob and pushed inward.

The door swung open before her. She stepped into the doorway. The room was dark, the air inside a little warmer than the rest of the house. She felt along the inside of the wall next to the door, found a light switch, and flicked it. Light cascaded down from bulbs set into the ceiling. The room lacked windows. The only furniture was a long table pushed up against the back wall. She spied objects lying on the table at equidistant intervals.

Moving closer to the table, she surveyed the objects. "I'll be damned."

Alex approached beside her. "These look like the stolen artifacts."

"Yes, they do." Spotting the split-twig figurine, she picked it up. "Why is Samuel Wessick collecting these artifacts?"

"I don't know. But this tells us one thing for certain. Rassul works for Wessick."

"I'd already guessed as much."

He snatched the split-twig figurine from her hand, tossed it onto the table. Grasping her shoulders, he spun her toward him and pulled her close. Their bodies almost touched.

She tilted her head up to gaze at him. The expression contorting his features seemed, on the surface, like anger. She knew better. He was scared, for her.

"I'll be fine," she said.

"If Rassul works for Wessick, then Wessick probably works for the Aten. Your new employer is in league with forces beyond our conception."

She was sick of hearing that phrase. After experiencing the Aten's power first-hand, she no longer considered their technology beyond conception. She might not understand it yet, but she knew she could, given enough information. One day she would have the requisite knowledge.

"It's not safe for you here," Alex said. His voice roughened as he added, "Please leave with me. Now."

She shook her head. "If anyplace holds the answers we need, it's here. I have to stay."

His eyes still held the power to mesmerize her. This time, though, she fought it. Although she understood why he wanted her to leave, and his reasoning was sound, she meant what she said. The answers awaited her here. Revenant House held the key.

"Please," he said.

She took his face in her hands. "If Wessick wanted to hurt me, he would've done it already. Both he and the Aten need me to find the relic for them, though I'm not sure why. If I'm going to figure out any of this, I need to stay here. And I need your help. Are you with me?"

"You know I am. But—"

"Good. Now let's go search Wessick's study."

Erin dropped her hands, pushing away from him. He drew her tight against him and kissed her.

Then he let go, turned, and marched out the artifact room. Outside the door, he paused to glance back at her. She stood where he'd left her, unmoving, thoughts spinning in her head, eyes locked on the spot where he'd been a moment earlier.

"Coming?" he asked.

As if reviving from a trance, she blinked slowly then shook her head as that might clear the muddle in her mind. He'd kissed her. On the lips. Firmly.

"Aren't we searching the study?"

His voice jerked her out of the reverie. She nodded, and headed out after him. Just as they reached the stairs, he said, "You live in a house that's riddled with bugs. You work for a man whose motives we don't understand but that I'm pretty sure aren't good. Doesn't any of it bother you?"

"Not really. Not anymore."

His description of her circumstances should've alarmed her. It didn't. She felt oddly at peace with her situation—in danger, for sure, but at peace. They figured out a big piece of the puzzle. And somehow, she knew this quest belonged to her. No longer did she feel like an outsider horning in on Alex's mission, or like an unworthy person accidentally thrust into this mess. She belonged here. Though she couldn't say why or how or what it meant, she knew she must see this quest through to its completion. No one would scare her off. Not Rassul. Not the Aten. No one.

She led Alex down the stairs to Wessick's study.

THEY FOUND NOTHING OF INTEREST IN WESSICK'S STUDY. SHELVES ON ONE WALL held knickknacks, antique wine glasses and the like. A wood cabinet held office supplies, including boxes of pens and paper for the laser printer mounted on a cart beside the desk. The desk itself was huge and crafted from mahogany like the desk in the library. Its drawers were locked, and the skeleton key didn't work for them.

Erin stood in front of the desk, hands on hips. They'd searched everything, even the cushions of the sofa. Alex suggested prying open the desk drawers with a knife or similar device. If they forced open the drawers, their snooping would become obvious. She wanted their efforts to stay clandestine, for the moment. The disabling of the surveillance devices might look like a simple equipment malfunction. Prying open the drawers could in no way be construed as an accident. With no other options available to them, they gave up on the drawers.

Which left them with squat.

Alex flopped onto the sofa. He gazed at the desk with his jaw tense, his eyes narrowed. He really, really wanted to break into the drawers. She knew it because she felt the same way. But for the time being, she preferred to maintain the appearance of a good employee. Though her work record was far from stellar, she'd always tried to be a good employee. *Tried.* She never quite fit in, however, no matter how hard she tried to squeeze herself into the box the world expected her to fit inside.

Maybe she'd fit in better with Alex's buddies, the Planners. If they sequestered themselves from the rest of humanity, then they likely fit into so-called normal society no better than she did. Of course, with their advanced technology they could smite anyone who mistreated them.

Advanced technology.

She dropped onto the sofa beside Alex. "What was that doohickey Warner used to shut off the electronic bugs?"

Alex arched an eyebrow. "Doohickey?"

"You know, the thingamabob with the flashing lights."

"Oh, that." He slouched down to lean his head against the sofa's back. "It's a neat little device the Planners gave us."

Aha. She twisted sideways toward him. "If the Planners gave you one device, won't they give you another? Say, one that opens locked drawers without leaving a trace."

He sighed. "No. They don't want to share their technology with us. One of their leaders gave us a couple of devices, but the gift didn't go over well among the other Planners. It added fuel to the fire of their internal conflicts." He rubbed his eyes. "And anyway, now that they've gone into hiding we can't ask them for anything else."

Darn. She forgot about that. Well, if she couldn't find out what the drawers contained, she could at least do something.

Erin jumped to her feet. "I'm going back to the library to study that map some more."

She got to the library door before Alex rushed after her, and it took him until she got to the desk before he caught up with her. The map lay where they'd left it, spread out across the desktop. The hieroglyphic text on the left-hand side filled three-fourths of the papyrus's height. She tapped her finger on the text. "Did you read me everything this says?"

He shook his head. "I gave you the highlights."

"Tell me the rest. Please."

He skimmed his finger over the text line by line. His lips worked as if he silently read the text to himself. Halfway down the stack of registers, he paused. "It talks about how the Egyptians made offerings to the Aten in an attempt to appease the sun-gods. They offered bread, wine, et cetera, but the gods were still displeased with them."

"Why?"

"Because the pharaoh was gone. He abandoned his people and even the Aten didn't know where he'd gone. It seems that one day the pharaoh entered the sanctuary as usual, but when he emerged he was agitated. That night, he vanished—along with his favorite wife, their children, a great many of their possessions, several servants, and a dozen soldiers."

"They couldn't have just disappeared."

Bent over the desk, he frowned at the text. "It says there was no evidence the party had left the palace. They simply vanished." He scanned several more registers. "The Aten were very angry. They threatened to destroy the whole city if the pharaoh wasn't found. The vizier pleaded with them—not directly, but apparently through the priests at the temple. The Aten relented, and soon they too abandoned Egypt. Before they left, though, they gave a message to the high priest."

Alex fell silent, his finger poised over the last register of hieroglyphic text. His brow furrowed.

Erin poked his arm. "What was the message?"

He pursed his lips, then relaxed them. "It says the object from another time, which the pharaoh has taken, must be found. But it can only be found by she whose identity is hidden, the daughter of Seshat, the daughter of Thoth, the incarnation of another time."

"Object from another time?" Erin said. "Sounds like a relic to me."

"Possibly."

"What do you think the rest of it means?"

"I don't know. Thoth was associated with the moon. He was the god of knowledge and science, and also the keeper of the gods' records. He gave the hieroglyphic language to the Egyptians. Seshat was Thoth's consort and shared many traits in common with him. She was revered as the goddess of writing, mathematics, and related disciplines. In her duties as keeper of historical records, she was known as the Mistress of the House of Books."

"She was a librarian."

He tilted his head to smirk at her. "I suppose."

"Cool." She bit her lip, thinking back to his translation of the text. "Hidden could also mean unknown, as in she whose identity is unknown. An unidentified woman."

"The god Amun was sometimes referred to as *amun renef,* he whose identity is hidden. The name Amun means hidden one. The name of his consort, Amaunet, also means hidden one. But I've never seen an Egyptian text refer to a woman as *amun renet,* she whose identity is hidden." He raised a hand before Erin could protest. "Or an unidentified woman. Either way, it's a unique epithet."

"What about the rest of it? The other epithets, I mean."

"Daughter of Thoth and Daughter of Seshat," he said, "could be honorary titles. The pharaoh was often referred to as the Son of Ra. I've never heard these particular titles, though."

She probably knew less about Egyptian mythology than he did. If he couldn't figure out what the epithets meant, what chance did she have?

He thought she had some sort of special insight. She was unconvinced, but maybe...

Still focused on the papyrus, he said, "The last epithet makes even less sense. The pharaoh was sometimes called His Incarnation or, when someone addressed the king directly, Your Incarnation. It was similar to calling a king Your Majesty. To call a person the incarnation of another time, though, is another unique epithet. And a bizarre one." He pushed away from the desk. "I have no idea what it means."

Neither did she. The term "object from another time" matched the common definition of a relic. But how could someone be the incarnation of another time? Maybe a ghost could qualify for that title.

Ghost. A shiver coursed through the depths of her being. A revenant.

When Alex asked her not to take the job at Revenant House, he presented her with a stack of papers, printouts of information he found online. One printout talked about revenants. Although the term originally referred to people who came back from the dead, the word revenant was derived from a French word meaning, literally, to return. The term could also refer to someone who seemed to come from another age, a living anachronism.

The incarnation of another time.

A time traveler?

When she said Seshat was a librarian, she'd only been half kidding. Seshat guarded the historical records of the gods and answered to the title of Mistress of the House of Books. Seshat's consort Thoth was also associated with divine records and books—namely, the Book of Thoth.

"Didn't you say," she asked, "that your friends found the Book of Thoth?"

Alex nodded. "It was mostly gobbledygook."

She suppressed a chuckle. "Gobbledygook? And you think it's funny when I say doohickey."

"Gobbledygook is a technical term for utter nonsense," he said matter-of-factly. She assumed he was joking but she must've looked confused, because he added, "I don't know what else to call it. As I said before, no one has been able to fully decipher the text. The Book seems to contain historical information couched in riddles and metaphors and accompanied by bizarre images. The text itself is composed of hieroglyphs, but most of the images don't look Egyptian at all."

Thoth was associated with books. Seshat was associated with books. Both could qualify as librarians. It seemed odd then that she—Erin Turner, the unemployed librarian—should wind up embroiled in a quest somehow related to the librarian gods of ancient Egypt. If the unidentified woman whom the Aten saw as the only person capable of finding the relic for them was the daughter of Thoth and Seshat, even in an honorary capacity, she might be a librarian too. The text also referred to the unnamed librarian as the incarnation of another time. No, it couldn't be.

Well, maybe.

A time-traveling librarian?

How did she, Erin Turner, fit into all this? Maybe the Aten chose her at random from all the librarians in the world, in the hopes any old librarian might be able to find the relic for them.

She explained her thoughts to Alex. A series of emotions flickered across his face, though each vanished before she could identify it. He settled on slight amusement and said, "Do you have a secret life as a time traveler that I don't know about?"

"I'm not that interesting."

"I disagree."

The memory of his kiss raced through her mind, triggering a cascade of sensory memories. She pushed those thoughts aside and asked, "Do you think this *amun renet* person really exists?"

He shrugged. "What matters is that the Aten seem to think so. It's possible they believe you are the *amun renet*."

"They're mistaken."

She felt obligated to say it. However, a voice whispered to her from deep in her core, the voice of the memory all but forgotten in the rush of events that transpired over the past few days since their trip to Arizona. On the drive to the Canyon, she'd fallen asleep and dreamed of an orb that spoke to her in her mind. Now that telepathic voice whispered to her once more, as a memory.

Find the relic. Only you, satseshat, possess the key.

A curse escaped her lips.

At the time, the word *satseshat* meant nothing to her. She needed to be certain, though. Alex was watching her with concern. She felt shaky, and her face must look pale. Her hands were trembling, she realized with dismay.

Alex took her hands in his.

"I think—" Her voice broke off as her mind flailed for the right words. She felt as if she'd lost control of her own mind and body. Her voice quavered as she said, "Does *satseshat* mean Daughter of Seshat?"

"Yes. But I think you know that."

The orb in her dream called her the Daughter of Seshat. She, like the goddess, was a librarian. She might've dismissed the coincidence if not for the fact that she had never heard the term *satseshat* before the dream. Now it turned up on an ancient papyrus. Both the Aten and Samuel Wessick must have a damn good reason for thinking she could find the relic. Why else would they bother with her?

She sucked in a breath, squared her shoulders, and looked Alex straight in the eye as she said, "I think you're right. They believe I am the *amun renet*."

He grasped her hands tighter. Neither of them spoke for a long moment. Finally, she voiced the question she felt certain he was thinking too.

"What the hell does it mean?"

13

A TREE BRANCH TICKED AGAINST THE WINDOWPANE. A WIND HAD KICKED up outside. Erin stared out the window into the darkness, staring through her own reflection on the glass. She felt as transparent as her reflection, as if everyone looked through her to see what they wanted to see beyond the glass, and no one really saw her. Erin Turner. The nobody librarian.

The sound of Alex's breathing pulled her attention back into the room. His hands still cradled hers. She looked down at his fingers, then up to his face. He saw her. He didn't try to redraw her reflection into an image that suited his own purposes. The Aten did that. Samuel Wessick did that. They were the bad guys. Alex was the good guy. And a very, very good one at that.

"It might mean nothing," he said. "The Aten think you're the *amun renet*. But they are evil aliens bent on…well, I'm not sure what, but whatever it is can't be good."

She couldn't stop the closed-mouth smile that stretched her lips taught. He seemed as confused as she felt, which oddly comforted her. She was not in this alone.

If the Aten thought she was their *amun renet*, then they were terribly confused themselves. Although she might qualify as the honorary daughter of librarian gods, she in no way qualified as the incarnation of another time. Sure, she felt out of place in this world much of the time. But she knew for a fact she had never time traveled, except for maybe that one time when she followed Rassul through his funky portal. But that trip lasted seconds. Perhaps the phrase "incarnation of another time" meant something different.

The idea of time travel fit in with the stolen artifacts, which she had decided were out of time as well as out of place. Why had the Aten, probably via Wessick, ordered Rassul to steal the artifacts? Modern-day archaeologists and historians dismissed the artifacts as forgeries or concocted far-fetched stories to explain how they wound up in contexts where they did not belong. A flood washed it into an older layer of dirt, for instance. The scientific establishment refused to consider the idea of time travel. Heck, they wouldn't even consider the idea of transatlantic contact between cultures.

Not everyone followed their lead, though. People like Alex and his buddies at the Human Origins Project sought out anomalous evidence. Rassul's masters might wish to keep that evidence from such open-minded, and determined, people. The artifacts Wessick kept in the room upstairs provided evidence that time travel might not only be possible but might have happened already, albeit in the distant past. If the Aten wielded the power of time travel, then they might not want lowly human beings to find out about it. Steal the artifacts, cover up the time travel. Problem solved.

But why did Wessick keep the artifacts in this house, where she could find them? It was possible he knew Ridley kept a skeleton key that opened all the doors in the house. He had no way of knowing, however, that she and Alex would stumble upon Ridley's mortal remains in the Grand Canyon and find the key tucked under his desiccated hand.

Thank you, Ridley. Where ever he was now, she hoped he heard her.

She yawned. A torrent of weariness swept over her.

"It's late," Alex said. "You should get some rest."

She nodded, unable to think of an argument against his suggestion. Just the thought of sleep made her eyelids want to flutter shut. After a good night's sleep, she'd feel more able to battle an evil conspiracy.

He let go of her hands. "I have to get my suitcase out of the car."

Planting a quick kiss on her cheek, he left the room. She shuffled into the hallway, turning off the libraries overhead light as she passed the switch, and watched Alex until he disappeared around the corner into the foyer. A few seconds later, the front door thumped shut.

The door to Wessick's study hung open. Inside the room, the desk lamp burned. She wandered through the door, past the sofa to Wessick's desk, and shut off the lamp. Shadows swelled around her, penetrated only by the indirect light from the hallway, which petered out halfway across the room. She turned to leave.

A flash of light stopped her. It had come from outside.

She spun toward the bay window. A few seconds passed with no repeat of the flash. She had seen it, she was certain. As she tiptoed to the window, she squinted out at the darkness. Clouds masked the stars. While she waited for her eyes to adjust to the dark, she listened for any sound. What could she hope to hear through the glass?

A shape darted across the lawn. A humanoid shape. But huge. One of Warner's soldiers?

God, she hoped so.

Her life had really taken a bizarre turn when she prayed to see Bigfoot scampering across the lawn. Hairy monsters seemed preferable to Rassul or his masters. She didn't even know what the Aten looked like. Maybe she didn't want to know. She had no idea what Wessick looked like either.

A hand grabbed her shoulder.

She yelped and jabbed her elbow backward at her attacker.

He stumbled backward, away from her jab, and said, "What's wrong with you? It's me."

She strained to make out Alex's face in the ambient light. He took a tentative step toward her. Her eyes finely adjusted to the lower light levels, she recognized his features—and the irritated expression that pinched them.

"Sorry," she said. "But you shouldn't have snuck up on me."

"Point taken." He positioned himself alongside her, and set a black object on the windowsill. "What are we looking at?"

She pointed at the object. "What's that? You took it into the woods with you earlier."

"Night vision binoculars. They let me see in the dark."

"I know what night vision is." She gestured at the window. "I saw something out there. A flash of light, and then a silhouette running across the lawn."

He raised the night vision binoculars to his eyes. The device had two eyepieces connected to what looked like a small telescope with wings on either side. He said, "I don't see anything."

She snatched the binoculars from him and held them to her eyes. The lawn lit up in shades of green. She made out the trees on either side of the lawn, the blankness where the earth plummeted at the cliff's edge, but no humanoid figures. Keeping the binoculars raised, she said, "I saw something. It wasn't my imagination."

"Whatever it was, it's gone."

She glanced at him sideways. He looked like more of a shadow now, with her natural night vision hampered by the brightness of the view the binoculars gave her. She returned her attention to the binoculars.

A figure darted out of the trees near the cliff's edge.

Her heart skipped. There it was. She followed the figure trotted across the lawn. Halfway across, the figure halted. The person, or whatever, was too far away for her to make out much detail. The figure raised an arm. A familiar shape protruded from the hand.

"He's got a gun," she said.

Alex toward the binoculars from her hands. He looked through them.

She stared out the window, her vision still hindered from using the binoculars. Even with the handicap, however, she could discern the silhouette at the cliff's edge.

Pow.

The gunshot exploded with a bright flash. The sound was loud even inside the manor.

Red lights flared on inside the woods at either side of the lawn. They hovered in pairs scattered throughout the woods.

Alex muttered a wordless curse. He dropped the binoculars on the window-sill and bolted out of the room. Grabbing the binoculars, she ran after him. He raced to the end of the hallway, then veered right into the north passage. At its end, he yanked open the back door. She reached him then, and seized his shirt sleeve as he crossed the threshold. He hesitated.

"Where are you going?" she asked.

"It's Rassul, it has to be." He shook off her hand. "Stay here. I want to question the slimy snake."

He took off. She started to follow, but then stopped. As much as she did not want Alex to confront Rassul alone, she wanted to confront Rassul without her gun even less. Did Alex have a weapon of any kind? If he did, he kept it hidden. One of them should be armed.

Spinning around, she dashed down the passageways and upstairs to her bedroom. There, she found her purse slumped on the night table where Alex must've dumped it when he carried her to the bed. She fumbled with the zipper, finally got it open, and pulled out the handgun. She popped out the clip to make sure it still had bullets. Fully loaded. Slamming the clip back into place, she chambered a round and then she downstairs and out the back door.

She skidded to a halt. The intruder was gone, and so was Alex.

The night air chilled her bare arms. She held the gun in her right hand, the night vision binoculars in her left. No way would she drop either one to rub her arms for warmth. She wanted to call out to Alex, but that might be about the dumbest thing she could possibly do. She stood a few feet from the house, inside the section of lawn between the two wings of the house. The spot where she saw the figure at the cliff's edge lay directly ahead of her. The red lights in the woods had vanished.

Staying close to the north wing, she tiptoed to the corner. No sounds. No discernible movement on the lawn or in the woods. She lifted the binoculars to her eyes and scanned her surroundings. Dark shapes moved within the trees. They seemed inordinately tall and stocky. Bigfoot?

"Gah!"

The exclamation echoed from the woods on the left side. Her pulse pounded behind her eardrums. She couldn't tell for sure, but it had sounded like Alex.

She dashed toward the woods.

ALEX CRACKED OPEN HIS EYELIDS. THE MOON HAD EMERGED FROM BEHIND the clouds, its glow infiltrating the woods. Through his eyelashes, he surveyed the area around him. It was a small open area between the trees, populated with mossy ground cover. He sat against a tree with his legs stretched out before him.

Ropes bound his ankles and wrists. Another rope, cinched around his chest, fastened him to the tree. A folded handkerchief tied around his head served as a gag. He opened his eyes further. His attacker was nowhere in sight.

His jacket, shoulder holster, and Glock 9mm were gone too.

Someone had hit him from behind. He remembered that much. After he ran out of the house, he'd gotten within a dozen feet of the figure Erin spotted. It was a man, he felt certain. The intruder wore dark clothes that, combined with his dark complexion and black hair, made him difficult to track in the woods. Then all of a sudden, the man ducked behind a thick tree. Somehow the bastard got behind Alex and smacked him with a blunt object. The back of his head still throbbed. He wondered how long he had been out. He hoped Erin had stayed inside, but he rather doubted it.

A flash of movement caught his eye. He squinted into the gloom of the woods. A light glinted. It looked like a reflection on glass.

The night vision binoculars.

Though he couldn't say for certain, he had a sinking feeling in his gut that the glint of light came from the binoculars—and that the binoculars were in Erin's hands.

A figure stepped out from behind the tree alongside Alex. The man crouched beside him, reached behind his head, and removed the gag. The moonglow revealed his captor's face, and Alex sighed. He said, "What do you want, Rassul?"

The man whipped a knife out of a holster on his belt. Scuttling forward, he brandished the knife in Alex's face.

"Quiet," Rassul said in a raspy whisper. "Our guest has not yet arrived."

A cold, hard lump congealed in Alex's gut. Erin. "You won't hurt her. Your masters need her."

"Yes, but they do not need you." Rassul grazed the blade across Alex's throat. "The time has come. You will leave her, alive or dead. The choice is not yours, however, but mine." Rassul chuckled, the sound anything but jolly. "I have made my choice. And I wish for the woman to bear witness to your departure."

Anger flared in Alex, hot and sharp. He swung his knees up to smack Rassul, but the digger leaped sideways. Alex wriggled against the ropes. They held fast. Rassul hopped to his feet.

"Go ahead," Rassul said. "Struggle all you like. It will do no good."

Alex noticed a semiautomatic handgun tucked into Rassul's waistband. He asked, "What were you shooting at?"

Rassul ignored the question. He waved the knife at Alex. "I cannot promise your death will be quick. You have much to atone for."

"I'm not a thief or murderer. You fit that description."

Thump. The sound emanated from the woods behind Rassul. The digger ducked into a crouch again. He held the knife at his side, the tip pointing down. Head tilted, the digger seemed to be listening.

Alex clenched his jaw. If Erin was out there, he needed to distract Rassul so the lunatic wouldn't spot her. He said, "I think you—"

Rassul scampered away, out of sight behind the tree.

Dammit.

Through the night vision binoculars, Erin watched as Rassul scuttled off into the woods. Although both his and Alex's had lips moved, their words were inaudible. Alex sat bound to a tree perhaps thirty feet away. She needed to get closer. Much closer.

But she'd lost sight of Rassul. The psycho might be anywhere. When it became obvious Rassul wanted to kill Alex, she tossed the rock into the trees opposite her. Neither man seemed to notice the projectile as it sailed above their heads, though the thump as it hit the ground drew their attention. Rassul probably went to investigate the sound. She should have a clear path to Alex.

Pretty soon Rassul would figure out her ploy. Then he'd be back. She guessed she had a couple minutes at best.

With one eye, she peeked through the night vision binoculars. No sign of Rassul. Time to go.

In a half crouch, she crept through the sheltering brush as fast as she dared, taking care not to rustle the weeds and grass or get stuck on a bramble. Once out of the brush, she kept low and quickened her pace. At the edge of the open area, she paused behind a pair of trees. Using one eye again, since she'd realized the technique preserved her natural night vision in the other eye, she checked her surroundings through the binoculars. Still no sign of Rassul. Her gut tightened. Despite the warning from her body, she charged into the open area.

When Alex saw her, his eyes widened. He shook his head violently.

She dropped lower and hurried toward him. At his feet, she stopped to untie the rope binding his ankles.

In a hoarse whisper, he said, "Get out of here."

She sidled closer to him. Leaning behind the tree, she untied the rope around his chest.

He grabbed her wrist and yanked her out from behind the tree. His hands were still bound. Even in the wan light, she saw the anger contorting his features. Anger and fear.

Through clenched teeth, he said, "Rassul is here."

"I know."

She reached for the rope around his wrists.

A figure leaped out of the brush.

Erin choked back a yelp. Rassul landed inches from her on her right side. Before she could react, he grabbed her around the waist and hurled her across the clearing. She hit the ground flat on her butt, right leg splayed out in front of her. Her left foot caught on a tree root, twisting her knee. She grimaced at the pain that shot through her leg. She started to keel over backward, but thrust her hands out to stop the tumble.

Rassul was kneeling beside Alex. He held a gun to Alex's temple.

"Move," Rassul said, "and he dies."

Erin eased her back leg into an outstretched position. Her knee throbbed. She had worse problems. She hadn't even heard Rassul sneaking up on her. As a commando, she failed miserably.

Her gun. She visually searched the clearing. The night vision binoculars lay near Alex's feet. The gun was about ten feet in front of her, slightly to the right.

"Ah-ah," Rassul chided. "I can kill him before you reach it."

Erin pushed onto her knees. Pain seared her left knee anew. Wincing, she clambered to her feet.

Rassul jabbed the gun into Alex's temple. He said, "Come no further."

Erin raised her hands in submission. "What do you want?"

"To teach you." He urged Alex to stand up and they both rose. "You are *satseshat, amun renet, hem kyrek.*"

Her ancient Egyptian wasn't fluent, but she knew *satseshat* meant Daughter of Seshat and *amun renet* meant she whose identity is hidden. The last part must translate as incarnation of another time.

She made a face at Rassul. "Tell me something I don't already know."

Surprise flickered on his face for an instant, barely perceptible. "If you know what you are, then you know what you must do. For them."

"If you kill Alex," she said, taking one step closer to him, "then I have no reason to do anything for the Aten."

He sneered at her. "Your mother and father might disagree."

It felt as if her blood turned to ice and her muscles frosted over. The cold penetrated her every cell, leeching out her pores. An army of goosebumps rose up all over her body. Her mother and father.

Rassul sniggered. "This is the lesson I came to teach you." He curled a finger around the gun's trigger. "First, you will watch this one die. Then, if you don't follow their commands, others will die one by one."

Others. He meant her parents. Maybe Chloe too. He would kill anyone connected to her, she knew, from her loved ones all the way down to the mailman. And he would start with Alex.

No. She would not watch him die. She would not let Rassul kill one more person.

She clenched her hands into fists. *Do something.*

The gun was too far away.

"You have only begun to know your true purpose," Rassul said. "They chose you, and they alone decide your ultimate fate. You cannot escape it—or them."

"Screw what they want."

A shriek reverberated through the woods. It sounded inhuman, like a cross between a woman's scream and a lion's roar.

Rassul jerked. The gun swerved away from Alex's temple. Rassul gaped wide-eyed at the shadows between the trees.

Alex jammed his elbow into Rassul's gut. The man doubled over. Alex raised his arms high and slammed his elbow down onto Rassul's neck. The digger stumbled forward, fell to his knees.

Erin ran for her gun. She snatched it up and bolted for Alex.

Rassul rolled onto his back. He leveled his gun at Alex.

Just as Alex dove sideways, Erin skidded to a halt. She swung her gun toward Rassul and fired.

The bullet struck his leg. Rassul bellowed. Alex hit the ground on his side and leaped to his feet. Rassul jerked his gun toward Alex.

Erin and Rassul fired simultaneously.

Alex tumbled sideways. Rassul lay motionless as if frozen, with his gun raised, for two long seconds.

Then, as a dark stain bloomed on his chest, he crumpled.

Erin ran to Alex.

He lay on his side behind the tree where Rassul had held him hostage. Knees bent, eyes closed, he growled softly. A dark streak drew a line across his left forearm.

Her heart pounded and her hands trembled as she struggled to untie the bindings from his wrists. As she tore the rope free, he opened his eyes.

"Oh thank God," she said, relief constricting her voice. "I thought you were dying."

He pushed up to a sitting position. "I'm not dying. But it hurt like hell when I hit that rock."

She glanced over his shoulder to where he'd lain on the ground. A large rock, partially embedded in the dirt, occupied the spot where his shoulder had landed.

Fingering the bloody streak on his arm, she said, "He shot you."

"Flesh wound. What about you?"

"I twisted my knee, but I'll survive." She hesitated. "What was that scream?"

He smiled. "One of Warner's covert operatives."

"Bigfoot?"

Alex got to his feet. Offering her his hands, he helped her stand. Though her knee throbbed something awful, she managed to walk with only a slight limp. They came around the tree into the open area. She sucked in a breath as she caught sight of Rassul's body. She had never killed anyone before. She couldn't muster any guilt, however, for the evil man who lay dead a half dozen feet from her. She couldn't muster much of anything other than relief she and Alex both survived coupled with a weariness that intensified with each passing second.

Alex wrapped an arm around her shoulders. He squeezed gently. "Thanks for saving my life."

"You're not mad I didn't stay put like you said to?"

"No. If you'd listened to me, I'd be dead."

Keeping his arm around her shoulders, he led her around the tree and away from Rassul's body. They stopped just behind the tree. He pulled her tight against him, and she rested her head on his chest. He slid his other arm around her, linking his hands behind her back. She let her eyelids flutter shut.

A swishing noise broke through the haze of her weariness.

She jerked her head up. The sound originated from the woods over Alex's shoulder. She locked her gaze on that area. The swishing grew louder.

Alex tensed. He released her and whirled toward the swishing noise, blocking her with his body.

A figure stepped out of the woods. The newcomer clicked on a flashlight, which he aimed it at his face.

Erin slumped her shoulders. "Warner. You scared me half to death."

"I apologize," Warner said.

He held a package tucked under one arm. As he aimed the flashlight at the ground, he tossed the package to Alex, who caught it in one hand. Alex unrolled the package. It was his leather jacket, wrapped around a handgun and a leather shoulder holster. She recognized the latter items despite her lack of expertise in things that went boom.

Alex stepped aside and she moved forward. Warner tossed the flashlight to Alex, then cradled his right arm with his left. Alex shined the flashlight at Warner's arm, trailing the beam up to his shoulder. There, a dark spot stained his shirt.

"You're hurt," Erin said.

"It's not serious," Warner said. "But it slowed me down, which is why I arrived too late to help. Fortunately, my soldiers rendered assistance."

"The scream. They did that to distract Rassul?" When Warner nodded, she asked, "Why didn't they do something more constructive, like pummel him?"

"Orbs blocked their path. Several creatures were badly burned. So they improvised."

Smart, she thought. She had no idea Bigfoot were so crafty.

Warner glanced over his shoulder in the direction of Rassul's body. "The creatures will clean up the mess. They know how to dispose of a body so that no one will find it."

Of course they did. She yawned.

Alex slipped an arm around her shoulders. "Time for bed."

The weariness weighed on her like a heavy coat. She didn't argue as Alex and Warner led her back toward the house. When they got to the edge of the woods near the north wing of the house, Warner excused himself.

"I must rejoin the creatures," he said. "One enemy may be dead, but the rest lie in wait. We must be ready for them."

With that, he slipped back into the woods. This time he made no sound whatsoever. She watched his silhouette until it melted into the night.

Alex took her hand and escorted her into the house. While she changed into her nightie in the bathroom, he dragged a big chair into the hallway, positioning it beside the doorway to her bedroom. It was the same chair he dragged into her bedroom earlier to sit by her bed and wait for her to rouse after she passed out. The incident with Rassul and the portal felt like years ago. The day when Rassul attacked her, leaving her bruised and dazed, felt even longer ago. Yet only a week had passed.

Before climbing into bed, she said goodnight to Alex. He sat in the chair, his jacket draped over the back, his gun tucked in the holster strapped to his shoulder. In one hand he grasped a can of pop, the caffeinated variety.

"Do you want a pillow?" she asked.

"I won't be sleeping." He took her hand, squeezed, and dropped it. "Get some rest. This isn't over yet."

She thought about arguing that he needed rest too. He would never agree to sleep, however, not after the day's events. She knew he was right about the battle not being over yet. The Aten still expected her to find the relic for them. Starting first thing in the morning, she must search for more clues about what the relic might be and where the pharaoh might've hidden it. She felt pretty sure the pharaoh referred to in the papyrus text was Akhenaten. No other pharaoh had worshiped the Aten with the zealotry Akhenaten displayed.

Alex slapped her thigh. "Go to bed."

She bent to kiss his cheek, then retreated into the bedroom. As she pulled the sheets over her, she heard a familiar tinkling. Bastet, her feline housemate, trotted into the room and toward the bed. The cat sprang onto the bed, landing with a little thud that bounced the mattress and jingled the bell on her collar. Bastet curled up beside Erin.

At least the cat didn't want to kill her.

She wriggled onto her side so that the cat lay against her belly. The moment she settled her head on the pillow, sleep overtook her.

No dreams haunted her sleep. No sounds disturbed her. At shortly after eight in the morning, she awakened to the pale glow of sunlight streaming through the window, muted by the trees outside. The cat still slept beside her. As she shifted the feline so she could slide out of bed, the cat started to purr. She stroked Bastet's head, then dropped her feet onto the floor. She stretched and yawned. The weariness was gone. The fear had left her too. She worried about her loved ones, but she knew what she must do now. Find the relic. Complete the quest.

Destroy the Aten.

She hadn't quite figured out yet how to accomplish any of those goals. Details would come later. Together, she and Alex had figured out a good deal of the puzzle. The rest would fall into place too, given time and hard work and maybe a bit of luck.

Yawning again, she stood and faced the window.

An orb stared back at her.

She blinked. No, it wasn't a dream. The orb hovered outside the window, its bluish-white interior swirling, its outer ring burning bright white. The orbs no longer induced a stomach-twisting fear in her. She knew they wouldn't hurt her, because their masters needed her. Were the orbs sentient, or were they merely machines?

One day she would know the answer. Not today.

The orb surged closer. It passed through the window glass as if no barrier existed.

Erin held her ground as the orb stopped a few feet from her face, at eye level. Words entered her mind, not as a voice speaking to her, but as thoughts injected from outside.

The time is now.

14

E RIN FOUND HER GREAT PROTECTOR SLUMPED IN HIS CHAIR, SNORING SOFTLY. The tinkling of the Bastet's collar, as the cat trotted out of the bedroom and down the hall, woke Alex. He looked up at Erin with half-closed, bleary eyes.

"What time is it?" he asked.

"Good morning to you too."

He yawned, rubbed his neck. "Morning."

"It's eight-thirty," she said, crossing her arms over her chest. "What happened to 'I won't be sleeping'?"

"I shirked my duties. You have every right to throw me in the dungeon."

"There's no dungeon. As far as I know."

"With this place, you never can tell."

Twenty minutes later, they perched on padded wooden stools in the kitchen, on either side of the marble-topped island. Erin sat with her back to the doorway, while Alex faced her from the sink side. He'd insisted on making breakfast, which turned out to mean pancakes with strawberries and maple syrup. Samuel Wessick might work for evil aliens, but he sure knew how to stock a kitchen. Or maybe Newman took care of the household. Puzzling out the secrets of Revenant House and its master, as well as its master's masters, might take a good long time. She also needed to sort out why the Aten seemed to sometimes help her and sometimes try to kill her.

What else did she have to do? So long as they kept paying her, she could afford to keep hunting for answers. This morning, though, she needed to discuss a few things with Alex.

She swallowed a bite of pancake, swigged a mouthful of milk to wash it down, and looked at Alex. He was swirling a square of pancake in the syrup on his plate, oblivious of her. She cleared her throat.

He glanced up.

She rested her elbows on the counter, linked her hands under her chin, and gazed at him. "So Warner mentioned a girl you almost…"

Frowning, he dropped his fork.

For several seconds she waited for him to speak. He chewed the inside of his lip instead.

She wrapped her fingernails on the countertop. "Who did you almost do what to?"

"Damn Warner." He leveled his gaze at her. "I almost married a girl named Helen. We got engaged a few weeks before the Valley of the Kings fiasco. My insistence we found an alien skeleton quickly made me a laughingstock, and rumors floated around that I had a drug problem. Helen decided it was easier to believe the rumors than to stand by me. She demanded I recant my statements and admit to my drug habit. When I refused, she broke off the engagement."

"I'm sorry."

"I'm not." Without breaking eye contact, he picked up his fork and took a bite. "Not anymore."

She thought of a few choice words for dear Helen, but refrained from voicing them. Alex almost got married. His fiancée's reaction to his newfound interest in weird things probably explained some of his behavior. He didn't want to tell Erin too much at one time because he thought she might decide he was nuts. After reading her blog, he must've suspected she wouldn't. But rationality often flew out the window when human emotions got involved. Especially men's emotions.

He cocked an eyebrow at her. "Have you ever been married or engaged?"

She stifled a laugh. "No. As soon as I open my mouth, most men cringe and back away slowly."

"I guess we have something in common. Everyone thinks we're crazy."

He went back to slicing off perfect little squares of pancake, swirling them in syrup, and plopping them into his mouth one at a time. His love of perfect order once irritated her, but today she found herself admiring him as he performed his pancake ritual. He wasn't obsessive, just neat. If he tried to slice her pancakes into perfect squares, then she might get annoyed.

"I saw an orb this morning," she said. "It told me the time is now. What do you think that means?"

His head jerked up. "You saw an orb? Why didn't you wake me?"

"It happened right before I came out of the bedroom."

"Oh." He froze with a forkful of pancake inches from his mouth. "The orb spoke to you?"

"Sort of. I think it was telepathy, not the voice of God or anything. What do you think it meant by the time is now?"

He set down his fork, dabbed his mouth with a napkin. "The other night, Rassul told me I should help you—but only until he told me to stop. Then I'd have to leave or he'd hurt you. He wouldn't kill you, but he could've…"

"I get the picture. He attacked me once, remember?"

"Yes." Alex slid off his stool and trod around the island to her. "Then last night he told me the time is now, meaning the time for me to leave you."

"Maybe you should leave."

"Rassul's dead."

"Another thug will take his place."

Alex scowled at the floor. He sighed and slumped against the counter.

She jumped off her stool and moved closer to him. When he didn't look up, she hooked her finger under his chin and forced him to lift his head. He met her gaze but stayed silent.

"They think they have the power," she said, "and I used to believe it too. Now I realize I have the power."

"Really."

"Yep. I am their satsa-whatsit, after all."

"*Satseshat.*" He almost smiled. "And you know how to pronounce it."

"My point is, when people refer to you to by a long string of honorary titles, it means you're the one with the power." She laid a hand on his chest. "They need me. We can use that."

"I suppose." He pursed his lips. "If you have the power, then why do I have to leave?"

"We should play along, for the time being. Let them think they've succeeded in isolating me."

Although he said nothing, she knew he wanted to tell her no way. The tension on his face, and in his voice, betrayed his feelings. She wanted him to stay as much as he didn't want to go. Yet, for the moment, they needed to convince the Aten they'd won this round.

She held the power. She believed that. Soon she and Alex would find the relic. Unlock its secrets. Destroy the Aten.

For now, though, Alex must leave. Convincing him of that might take some work.

"I'm not leaving," he said.

Had he read her mind? When orbs communicated with her telepathically, she couldn't help wondering what else was possible.

"You have to go," she said. "Not forever. Just for awhile."

He stared down at her for ten seconds, maybe more. At last, he said, "All right. I'll stay away from you, but I am not leaving the area."

"Agreed." She flashed back to last night, and Rassul's threat about her parents. "I know some people who have a room available. And I'm sure you can get it cheap."

"What's wrong with the motel?"

"It'll get expensive long term. Besides, I'd rather you stay with my parents."

"Have you asked them how they feel about this?"

"I'm sure they'll agree. They like you." She swallowed against the tightness in her throat. "I need you to look out for them. In case the Aten sent another Rassul to—"

Alex wrapped his arms around her and pulled her close. She laid her cheek on his chest. He kissed the top of her head and said, "I'll stay with them. But they're smart people. Won't they wonder what's going on?"

"I have to tell them everything." She shut her eyes. "I thought keeping them in the dark would keep them safe. I was wrong."

Neither of them moved. She heard his heart thump-thumping inside his chest, his breath whispering through his lungs. Standing there, with his arms snug around her, she felt warm and protected from the dark forces converging on her. Alex would watch out for her parents. She could talk to Chloe, maybe convince the girl to take an extended vacation somewhere far away.

She opened her eyes but didn't move. "Can't your organization help us protect my parents and my friend Chloe?"

"Possibly. We are stretched pretty thin, though. I doubt we can afford to protect all of your friends."

"Chloe is my only friend."

"Don't I count?"

"No." She looked up at him. "You're not a friend, you're…something else."

He smirked. "You're something else too."

She pushed away from him. They needed to take care of a few things before he left. Before his departure last night, Warner gave them his fancy thingamajig for disabling the electronic surveillance devices. Alex took possession of the thingamajig.

"Can you turn the bugs back on?" she asked.

He made a face. "Why would I want to do that?"

"We need to play along, remember?"

His lips worked as if he contemplated questioning her plan but realized he couldn't talk her out of it.

"You said I have uncanny insight," she reminded him. "And that I'm always right."

"Actually, I said you remind me of someone who acts rashly based on hunches and is always right."

She folded her arms over her chest. "Which by extrapolation would mean that I'm always right."

He sighed, scrunched his lips, drummed his fingers on the countertop.

She fought back a smile.

With a note of resignation in his voice, he said, "Fine, we'll do it your way."

She let the self-satisfied smile stretch her lips tight.

Another battle won.

AFTER DOING THE DISHES, WHICH ENTAILED STACKING THEM IN THE DISH-washer and pressing the right buttons, she and Alex headed into the library. He made a detour upstairs to retrieve his bags. From his suitcase he extracted his digital camera and the doohickey that disabled the bugs.

In the library, they huddled at the desk with the papyrus map spread out before them.

"I want to take this," Alex said. "Do some tests, see if we can glean any additional information from it."

"But I want to study it."

He held up the camera. "That's why I brought this."

For the next few minutes he snapped at least a dozen photos of the papyrus, including images of the entire sheet as well as close-ups of specific areas. Alex previewed the images on the little screen on the back of his camera. Apparently satisfied, he turned off the camera and popped out the memory card.

As he offered the card to her, he said, "I noticed your work computer here has slots for memory cards. You can plug this in directly to study the papyrus whenever you want."

She took the card. "Thanks."

Next he handed her the bug-disabling thingy. He showed her how to operate it, and she jotted down notes on a small pad, because she felt certain she'd never remember the details without writing them down. Her notes made sense to her, though she doubted anyone else—like, say, bad guys—would understand them.

Done with his instruction, Alex leaned over her shoulder to peer down at her notes. "Is that English?"

"Yes." She poked his forehead. "Is this nosiness?"

He backed away. "I suppose I should leave now."

"Yeah."

Her throat tightened. Tears stung her eyes. She blinked them away, focusing on the pad in her hand.

He took the pad, dropped it on the desk, and pulled her into his arms. She hugged him fiercely.

After a moment, they separated. He rolled up the papyrus, grasping it in one hand. She trailed behind him as he gathered his bags, then offered to carry his attaché when it became obvious he couldn't carry all his bags and the papyrus. After he'd loaded everything into the trunk of his car, they retreated to the base of the front steps. He faced the house, and she faced him.

He took her hands. "Not forever, remember?"

She nodded.

He pulled her close and kissed her. Their first kiss had been quick and surprising. This one lingered, banishing all thoughts from her mind. When he pulled away, she could only stare at him and wait for her faculties to return.

With a sleight-of-hand trick worthy of a magician, he slipped a piece of paper into her right hand, then he said, "Au revoir."

"Is that French for 'to hell with the Aten'?"

He flashed her a sly, sexy smile that made her stomach flutter. "Something like that."

With a swift about-face, he turned and strode around the car to the driver's door. As he swung the door open, he paused to flash her another smile, this one more subdued. She responded in kind, though she didn't feel much like smiling. *Suck it up*, she told herself, *don't wimp out now.* Her battle with the Aten was far from over.

She would see Alex again. Soon.

He climbed into the car and shut the door. The engine roared to life a second later. Too soon thereafter, the car rolled off down the driveway. She watched until the last glimpse of the vehicle disappeared behind the trees. Suddenly recalling the scrap of paper he'd slipped into her hand, she unfolded it and read the message printed on the paper, in Alex's handwriting. The note said, "If you need me, send a text message—but do it Harry's way, with all your *potestas*." She could figure out what the Latin-sounding word meant later, Alex must intend for her to encode her text messages with a Vigenère cipher, "Harry's way," using the English translation of *potestas* just as Harry used the English translation of *veritas*, truth.

Tucking the note in her pocket, she marched back inside the house and straight up to the artifact room. She unlocked the door using Ridley's key, swung it open, and—

The artifacts were gone. The display table stood empty.

The evidence of time travel had been erased.

She could do nothing about that, and other matters needed her attention now. Back to the library she marched. She remembered seeing a Latin dictionary in the collection, so she took a few minutes to locate the book. Fanning through the pages to the V section, she hunted down the entry for *potestas*. The word meant power.

I have the power.

Seated at the desk, she popped the memory card from Alex's camera into one of the slots on the computer. She browsed the images until she found a close-up of the map.

"Okay, Ridley," she said, "let's see what else your map can tell us."

She panned across the image, examining every line and splotch. Until yesterday, she'd fumbled in the dark without so much as a birthday candle to light her way. As she scrutinized the image on the computer screen, a realization struck her. Deciphering the papyrus might take awhile, but she knew that in the end the map would give up all its secrets to her—and so would the Aten.

The quest began now.

About the Author

L ISA A. SHIEL RESEARCHES AND WRITES ABOUT EVERYTHING STRANGE, FROM Bigfoot and UFOs to alternative history and science. She has been interviewed for big-city newspapers, national magazines, drive-time talk radio shows, and TV news. Lisa has a master's degree in library science and was previously president of the Upper Peninsula Publishers & Authors Association. As a fiction writer, Lisa pens both full-length novels and short stories that blend her unique theories about human history and the paranormal into tales of high adventure. Her nonfiction books include *Forbidden Bigfoot*, *Backyard Bigfoot*, *Forgotten Tales of Michigan's Upper Peninsula*, and *The Evolution Conspiracy*.

www.LisaShiel.com

Continue the adventure!

with more books in

THE HUMAN ORIGINS SERIES

by

LISA A. SHIEL

BOOK 1

THE HUNT FOR BIGFOOT

Katy and Rick tumble into a double-edged mystery—a hidden Bigfoot society protected by an ancient race and a mysterious billionaire willing to kill to preserve the legend. Can they unravel an enigma half a billion years in the weaving?

BOOK 2

LORD OF THE DEAD

Continues Katy and Rick's quest for the truth about human origins and explores the debate between Egyptologists and New Age enthusiasts over the enigmatic Book of Thoth. This time, the fate of the human race itself is at stake.

BACKSTORIES, VOL. 1

BIGFOOT BEGINNINGS

Before they went on *The Hunt for Bigfoot*…Before they met the *Lord of the Dead*…Charlie, Rick, and Katy have never seen a Bigfoot. Yet soon each of them will, separately, experience something inexplicable in the woods, something that makes them question their worldview, something that sets them on the path to their destiny.

available from
your local bookstore, Amazon.com, BarnesAndNoble.com
or
www.JacobsvilleBooks.com